DISCARD

S0-ABR-164

SHE'S NOT SORRY

SHE'S NOT SORRY

MARY KUBICA

THORNDIKE PRESS
A part of Gale, a Cengage Company

Copyright © 2024 by Mary Kyrychenko.
Thorndike Press, a part of Gale, a Cengage Company.

ALL RIGHTS RESERVED
This is a work of fiction. Names, characters, places, and incidents are either the product of the author's imagination or are used fictitiously. Any resemblance to actual persons, living or dead, businesses, companies, events, or locales is entirely coincidental.
Thorndike Press® Large Print High Octane.
The text of this Large Print edition is unabridged.
Other aspects of the book may vary from the original edition.
Set in 16 pt. Plantin.

LIBRARY OF CONGRESS CIP DATA ON FILE.
CATALOGUING IN PUBLICATION FOR THIS BOOK
IS AVAILABLE FROM THE LIBRARY OF CONGRESS.

ISBN-13: 979-8-88579-684-2 (hardcover alk. paper)

Published in 2024 by arrangement with Harlequin Enterprises ULC.

Printed in the United States of America
1 2 3 4 5 6 7 28 27 26 25 24

For my family and friends

PROLOGUE

My phone starts to ring as I open the door to walk into the store. It's buried in the depths of my bag and is difficult to find. I shove aside a wallet and a cosmetic bag, knowing the search is likely futile. I will never get to it in time.

My fingers make contact on the third or fourth ring. I fish it out of the bag, but as soon as I do, the phone goes quiet. I'm too late. A missed call notification from Sienna appears on the screen. I'm taken aback. I physically stop in the open doorway and stare down at her number on the display. Doubt and confusion fill my thoughts because it's just after ten o'clock in the morning and Sienna is at school, or rather, she should be. Sienna texts from school sometimes, sneaking her phone when the teacher isn't paying attention — Can I hang out with Gianna today? I lost my water bottle. Did u buy tampons? My stupid calculator won't work. — but she doesn't call. My mind goes in a million different directions thinking how, if she was sick, the nurse would call and, if she got in trouble at school for something, then the dean would call. Sienna wouldn't ever be the one to call.

I don't have a chance to call her back. Almost immediately the phone in my hand starts to ring again and I jump, from the unexpected sound of it. It's Sienna, calling me back.

My thumb swipes immediately across the screen. "Sienna? What's wrong?" I ask, pressing the phone to my ear. I step fully inside the store, letting the door drift closed to muffle the street noise outside, the sound of cars passing by and people on their phones, having conversations of their own. I hear the shrill, unmistakable panic in my voice, and I think how, in the next instant, Sienna is going to ride me for overreacting, for freaking out about nothing. *Geez Mom. Relax. I'm fine,* she'll say, drawing that last word out for emphasis.

That's not what happens.

It's quiet at first. I just barely make out the sound of something slight like movement or wind. It goes on a few seconds so that I decide this must be a pocket dial. Sienna didn't mean to call me. The phone is in her pocket or her backpack and she called me by mistake. She doesn't even know she's called me twice. I listen, trying to decipher where she is, but it's more of the same. Nothing telling. Nothing revelatory.

But then, a man's voice cuts through the quiet, his words cold and sparing, his voice altered as if speaking through a voice changer. "If you ever want to see your daughter again, you will do exactly as I say."

I gasp. My eyes gape. I lose my footing, falling backward into the closed door. A hand rises to my mouth, pressing hard. I can't breathe all of a sudden. I can't think; my mind can't process what's happening at first. I pull the phone away from my ear, looking down at the display to see if I'm mistaken, if it's not Sienna's number that called but someone else. A wrong number. Because this can't be right, this can't be happening. This can't be happening to me.

But it is right. Sienna's number stares back at me from the display.

"Who is this," I ask, pressing the phone back to my ear, "and why do you have my daughter's phone?"

And then, in the background, I hear Sienna's piercing scream.

"Mommy!" she bellows. It's high-pitched,

9

frenzied, desperate, and that's when I know that this man doesn't only have Sienna's phone. He has Sienna.

Pure terror courses through my veins. Sienna hasn't called me *Mommy* in at least ten years. I can't stop thinking what horrible thing must be happening for her to lapse back into her childhood and call me *Mommy.* I'm completely powerless. I don't know where she is. I don't know how to get to her, how to help her, how to make this stop.

"Go away," Sienna commands. Her voice trembles, so that she doesn't sound like herself, who is usually so defiant, so sure. There is no mistaking her fear. "Leave me alone," she demands, crying now. Sienna falters on the words, her voice cracking, so that the execution doesn't carry the same weight as the words themselves.

Sienna is terrified and so am I.

"Sienna, baby!" I shriek. There is the sound of commotion, of muffled noises in the background — this man, I imagine, subduing Sienna, forcing a gag into her mouth so that she can't speak or scream, and Sienna fighting back from the sound of it, resisting him.

I realize that I'm not blinking. I'm not breathing.

Tears sting my eyes. "What are you doing to her? Who is this?" I demand of this man, screaming into the phone so that everyone in the store stops what they're doing to look at me, to stare, some gasping and pressing hands to their own mouths in shock, as if this nightmare is somehow collective. "What have you done with my daughter? What do you want from me?"

"Listen to me," the man says back, his modulated voice unshaken and sedate, unlike mine. I still hear Sienna's desperate cry in the background, a keening, weeping wail, though it's stilted. The sound of it is enough to bring me to my knees, and yet I don't know what's worse: the sound of Sienna's cry or the sound of it as it grows distant and then fades completely away.

"Where is she? What have you done to her? Why can't I hear her anymore?"

"You need to do exactly as I say. Exactly. Do you understand?"

"I want to talk to my daughter. Let me talk to my daughter. I need to know that she's okay. What have you done to her?"

"I have nothing to lose," the man says. "You're the only one with something to lose, Ms. Michaels. Now you need to shut up and listen to me because I don't care one way or the other if your daughter lives

11

or dies. What happens to her is entirely up to you."

PART ONE

ONE

The first time I see her in the hospital is in the ICU, shortly after she's come out of surgery. I stand at the sliding glass door, looking in on her lying on the hospital bed, hooked up to a central line, an ET tube, an ICP monitor, a Nasogastric tube, more. IV lines run into her veins, pumping her with fluids, with medicine like diuretics, anticonvulsants and morphine probably. Her head is wrapped with gauze. Beneath the gauze, just hours ago, I've been told, pieces of her skull were removed to relieve pressure on the brain. There isn't much to see of her face because her eyes are closed and she's all gauze and tubes, but what I can see of her is swollen and bruised.

She's not my patient. Another nurse, Bridget, stands in the room with her, tending to her, getting her settled, and yet I felt sick to my stomach when I first saw her lying there on the bed through the glass. I'd heard the mumble of voices already, the hushed tones whispering of what people say happened to her, of what brought her here.

I'm assigned to a few other patients today. We have thirty ICU beds at the hospital. We're broken down into pods, with ten beds in each and a nurses' station at the center of them. The nurse to patient ratio depends on how critical a patient is. Patients on ventilators or that are critically ill have a patient to nurse ratio of two to one, but with lower acuity patients, we might have as many as four. It's a lot to manage. It means that, despite our best efforts, errors sometimes get made, like last week when one of the nurses gave a patient someone else's morning meds by mistake. She realized what she'd done right after she did it, told the doctor and everything was fine, thank God. It doesn't always work out that way.

Bridget catches a glimpse of me over her shoulder. She stops what she's doing and steps out of the room to come stand beside me at the sliding glass door.

"Hey," she says as the doors drift closed. "Did you hear?" she asks, leaning in like she always does to gossip.

"Hear what?" I ask, and my heart kicks it up a notch as if in preparation for what she's about to say. I was late to work today. I had

16

a doctor's appointment this morning and didn't get in until noon. I should have been here sooner — the appointment was over by nine thirty — but after what happened, I walked the city for miles, considering taking the whole day and letting someone else cover for me, even though I only had shift coverage for a few hours. In the end, I came to work. I had to talk myself into it, but it was what I needed to do. I needed to act like nothing was wrong because if I didn't, there would be questions. Everyone would want to know where I was and why I didn't come in and besides, I thought work would be a welcome distraction. I was wrong.

"She jumped," Bridget says. "From a pedestrian bridge."

My breath hitches. It's all anyone is talking about, the woman who dropped over twenty feet from a bridge and just nominally survived. "I know. I did hear that. How awful. What's her name?"

"Caitlin," she says, and I muse over the name, becoming accustomed to it.

"Caitlin what?"

"Beckett. Caitlin Beckett."

Bridget speaks then as if giving me the change of shift report, though she's not my patient and it's not a shift change. She says that the patient is thirty-two years old, that

17

she came to our ICU from surgery, though she arrived at the hospital through the emergency room before having a decompressive craniectomy for cerebral edema caused by a traumatic brain injury. In other words, swelling around the brain was putting pressure on the brain. They had to relieve that or she would be dead by now.

Bridget goes on, saying more. At some point, I stop listening because I can't take my eyes off this woman. Caitlin Beckett. My mind gets trapped on the fact that she's only thirty-two. It's so young. I shake my head, feeling really appalled when I think about it. I am forty. The age difference is considerable, though when I was thirty-two, I was just coming into my own. At the time, I thought it was one of the best years of my life. I was married, with a child. I had more confidence than I'd ever had in my whole life. I knew who I was and I didn't have to worry about trying to impress people anymore.

Caitlin lies in an ordinary hospital gown — starch white with stars on it — beneath a blanket, her arms placed unnaturally at her sides. I feel sick inside, though I've seen everything there is to see working as an ICU nurse. This patient shouldn't upset me any more than every other patient, but she does,

18

for different reasons.

"Do you think she will make it?" I ask Bridget.

"Who knows," she says, looking around to make sure we're alone before she does. Hope is paramount to being a nurse. As nurses, we should believe that all our patients will live, though the survival rate for someone like this is generally poor. Most don't survive. Even if she was to survive, the odds of her having a good quality of life are not great.

"Is her family here?" I ask, putting stock in the likelihood that she will either die or come out of the coma as a shell of her former self.

"Not yet. They're still trying to find a next of kin."

I stare through the glass wall at her face. She looks peaceful, sleeping. She isn't. The bed she lies on is angled upward, so that her head and upper body are inclined. Beneath the gauze, her hair, at least some of it, would have been shaved in preparation for the craniectomy. I imagine her bald. Her lips form around the endotracheal tube, which keeps the airways open so that air from the ventilator can get into her lungs. Her coloring is off. It's waxy and wan where it isn't bruised purple. Her injuries look

19

horrific. A fractured hip, a broken leg, broken arms and ribs, more.

Bridget asks, "She's pretty isn't she?"

I frown. "How can you tell?" She's unrecognizable. It's impossible for Bridget to know what she looks like with the swelling, the bruising and the gauze.

"I don't know," she says. "I just can. It's terrible what happened."

I swallow. It takes effort because my saliva is thick and ropy. "Tragic."

"What makes a person do something like that?" Bridget asks, and I can't believe she's going on like this, to me of all people. But she doesn't know my story. She doesn't know what happened before. She doesn't know how much this upsets me.

When I don't answer fast enough, she says, "You know, jump from a bridge, kill themselves?"

I shudder at the thought, shaking my head. I feel her eyes on my face, searching it, and feel my cheeks and ears go red. "I don't know."

"Of all the ways to go, why that?" Bridget asks. I wish she would drop it, but she doesn't. She goes on, driving the point home, saying in a low voice so that no one passing by in the hall can hear, "What about carbon monoxide or a lethal dose of morphine? Wouldn't that be easier, less painful?"

She isn't trying to be insensitive. Not everyone knows my family's history with suicide.

I blanch. I say nothing because I don't have an answer and because I can't stop thinking about what it would have been like for her to fall, to slam into the earth from the height of the bridge. There is a metallic tang in my mouth all of a sudden. I press my fingers to my lips, willing it away. I can't stop wondering things like if she lost consciousness during the fall or if she was wide-awake when she hit the ground. Did she feel her stomach float up into her chest, her organs moving freely around her insides like on an amusement park ride, or did she feel nothing but the searing pain of impact?

Bridget excuses herself. She slips back through the sliding glass door to attend to the patient. For a minute longer, I stand there watching as Bridget shows something like affection in the way she rearranges the other woman's hands on her abdomen, setting her fingers just so, letting her own hand linger on hers. I read her lips as she leans over her and asks, "What did you do, baby girl? What did you do?"

I can think only one thing in that moment:
It's a wonder she survived this long.

Two

My shift ends at seven. I leave the hospital that night, heading east down Wellington for Halsted, trying to leave patients behind, to not take thoughts of them with me when I go. It's easier said than done. No matter how hard I try, some still come with me. As nurses, we're supposed to compartmentalize, to be detached, to mentally separate our professional lives from our personal lives, like sorting medication into a pill sorter, clearly divided with thick plastic tabs. We were taught this in nursing school, though it's not that easy and it's not something that can be taught — to care for and about our patients, but to not let ourselves get emotionally attached because attachment, they say, leads to burnout, which causes nurses to leave an already hemorrhaging profession. It's hard because as nurses, it's in our nature to be compassionate, and these two things — detachment and compassion —

are at odds with one another.

The sun set hours ago. This time of year, night comes early and fast. On the days that I work, I hardly ever get to see the sun. It's dark when I leave for work in the morning and it's dark when I go home.

I text Sienna as I walk, reminding her that I'll be late, and she replies with a quick, K. I ask if she remembered to close the front door and she texts back, Yes. These last few days, the door to our apartment has not been latching properly. It doesn't always stay closed. It would be just an inconvenience, except that there have been a string of break-ins in the neighborhood lately. Crime, in general, has been on the rise citywide. Carjackings. Armed robberies. Just last week, a woman was followed into her apartment building on Fremont. She was attacked, beaten and robbed in the stairwell. The assailant left her with a broken nose and a broken arm; he took her purse with everything inside, all her money, her debit and credit cards. She's lucky to be alive.

The police are still looking for who did it, which has me on edge. I can't stop thinking that there's this man out there somewhere, attacking women, and I wonder if he's had his fill for now or if he's already on the hunt for his next victim. The thought of it keeps me up some nights. It doesn't help that Fremont is only two blocks from where Sienna and I live. I've asked the landlord twice already to fix the door, but he's busy. He says he will but he still hasn't.

Did you lock it? I text Sienna about the door.

Yes, she says again, and I want to ask if she's sure, to tell her to double-check that the door is locked, but I don't want to come across as paranoid or give her a reason to feel scared, and so I let it go.

I say goodbye and slip my phone into my bag. At Halsted I turn left, making my way toward Belmont. Halsted is alive tonight, full of people heading home on the evening commute, so that the air is electric, buzzing with the sounds of voices and cars.

Outside it's begun to snow, a sudden blitz of big, fat snowflakes. The temperatures aren't abysmally cold because of the snow, but still I pull my hood over my head to stay dry, tuck my chin into the coat, plunge my hands into my pockets and walk faster.

The church sits on the north side of Belmont, looking dignified and majestic in this weather. It's picturesque with the snow coming down as it is, like something straight out of a Thomas Kinkade painting. When I come to Belmont, I wait for the 77 bus to

25

pass and then jog across the street for the church. The building is Tudor Gothic style with towers and steep concrete stairs that lead to three sets of solid, arched wooden doorways, which are surrounded by stained glass windows. The church connects to the parochial school, so that the whole campus takes up almost an entire city block.

I climb the steps, pull open the heavy wooden doors and let myself inside, grateful when the doors drift closed and the city slips away behind me. The inside of the church is worlds apart from the outside. It's quiet and warm, the lights are dimmed and the mood is calm and atmospheric. Up ahead, through another set of doors, sits the church's nave, where there are rows and rows of empty pews and ethereal stained glass windows.

Just before me, a woman stands alone in the narthex. She wears a white, thigh-length winter coat and a black winter hat, looking very put together while I'm in my gym shoes and scrubs from work. The scrubs are slate blue, soft and ridiculously comfortable, but not exactly on fleek. Sienna would never let me hear the end of it if she knew I was wearing my scrubs out in public again.

"You look lost," I say, smiling as I dry my shoes on the mat and come further in.

The woman is about my same age if not younger, a brunette with dark eyes and olive skin that complement the white coat. On her lower half are skinny jeans, tucked into the tall shaft of a pair of serious, rubber-soled winter boots with a fuzzy cuff, and I regret the gym shoes on a night like this, knowing that by the time I make my way home, the snow may be deep enough that it gets into my shoes.

The woman laughs to herself — at herself — a nervous laugh like a titter. "I think I am," she says, letting her eyes go around the room, where there are no signs, nothing and no one to tell her where to go. "I don't know if this is where I'm supposed to be."

"Are you here for the divorce support group?"

Another nervous, this time self-deprecating laugh. "Is it that obvious?"

I'm quick to reply, "No, of course not. It's just that I'm headed there myself, and I don't know of any other meetings in the building tonight. It's usually just our group." I take a breath, my tone changing. "You don't need to be nervous," I say, hoping I'm not overstepping but interpreting her posture, her body language. "I mean, it's okay to be. Everyone gets nervous their first time here, but there really is no reason to be. I'm

Meghan," I say, stepping close enough to reach out a hand that she takes into hers, which is somehow warm despite the weather outside, and I wonder how long she's been standing in the narthex, waiting for someone to come and help her. "Meghan Michaels."

The woman's expression changes. Her head lists and her eyebrows draw together, a look of something like disbelief washing over her face. Her eyes widen as if to take me fully in. "Meghan Michaels? Barrington High School, class of 2002?" she asks, and I nod dimly, my brain trying to catch up, to make the connection. I did go to Barrington High School, though that was a long time ago. It's about an hour from where I live now, but my parents left the suburban town a year after I graduated and I haven't been back much since, nor have I been good about keeping up with high school friends. "It really is you," she says, as if seeing the resemblance between me and my teenage self. "It's me," she says, her hand going to her chest. "Nat Cohen. Natalie. We went to high school together."

"Oh my God," I say, happy but shocked. Natalie Cohen. Nat. I haven't heard that name in over twenty years. She looks different, but then again we all do. Her face has thinned, becoming less round, and her hair is longer than I ever remember it being. She used to wear it in this short blunt bob for as long as I knew her, and I wonder when she made the decision to let it grow out. It looks gorgeous long. *She* is gorgeous. Nat was always pretty, but in high school, there was a tomboyishness about her that has since disappeared. She's aged incredibly well. There are no lines on her skin like mine, and shallowly I wonder if she gets Botox, fillers or other injections, or if she was blessed with good genes. Nat and I were in the same graduating class. We played tennis together, though she was always so much better than me.

I open my arms and wrap them around her, conscious of how nice it feels to be this close to something from my past. I soak it in; I hold on for a minute too long. Memories of high school surface, of simpler, happier times that make me nostalgic. As I release her, I say, "I can't believe it's really you. How have you been? Where are you living? Are you still playing tennis?" I can't stop myself from asking so much. I want to ask even more, but how do you catch up on twenty years, especially when we have only a few minutes before the meeting begins?

"I've been better," she says.

"God, of course. That was a dumb question," I say feeling insensitive, if not stupid, because here we are, headed into a divorce meeting. No one that attends these meetings is living their best life. We're all in limbo, trying to find ways to move on and be happy.

"You've let your hair grow out," I say because, even with a hat on, her long locks come inches below her collarbone. "I love it. It suits you."

"Thanks," she says. "That old shaggy bob had to go."

"You look amazing. Truly. How long have you been standing here waiting?"

"Ten or fifteen minutes. The truth is," she says, visibly relaxing now that she's with me, "I don't know that I should be here. I don't know that I *want* to be here."

I say, "No, I get it. You're not alone. My first time, I didn't even come in. I made it as far as the building but then, somewhere just outside, changed my mind. I got cold feet, turned around and went home. I was sure everyone would be insufferable, and we wouldn't have anything in common other than that we were all divorced. I came back, a few weeks later, and that time I stayed and I liked it and the people very much. They're not insufferable at all but friendly and kind. You'll like them, I think.

It's this way," I say, taking a step toward the stairs so that she'll follow. "Come with me, and we can catch up after the meeting, when we have more time. There's so much I want to ask you."

Behind us just then, the heavy church doors open again and I turn at the sudden onslaught of city noises infiltrating the quiet church. It's Lewis, another of the group's members, coming in. Out of the corner of my eye, I see Nat startle at the sound of him, her reaction disproportionate to the noise. I let my gaze go to her, though her own eyes are fixed to Lewis, watching as he stomps his heavy boots on the mat, snow clinging fast to him and reminding us of the storm outside. It's only when he removes the hood and she gets a better look at him — at his round, babyish face and benevolent eyes that belie his large size — that she settles, her body slackening, her fisted hands slowly uncurling.

We're supposed to get something like four inches tonight, though it's always so imprecise. It could be one inch or it could be ten.

"Beautiful night," Lewis says, stepping past us, and I can't tell if he's being facetious or not, though it is truly beautiful. There's something magical about the first snowfall of the season.

31

My eyes go back to Nat's as he disappears down the stairs. "That's just Lewis," I say, wondering what about his arrival made her so scared. "Sweet guy. His wife left him for some other guy when he quit his high paying corporate job to do something he found more fulfilling. Turns out she loved his money more than she loved him. What do you think?" I ask, nodding toward the steps. "You want to give it a try? You don't even have to talk. You can just listen," I say. Faye, the leader, is a therapist but, like the rest of us, is divorced. Her mantra is that this is a safe place to listen to one another, to offer support, to empower one another and to feel less isolated by our divorces.

That said, my first time here I was reluctant to open up. I came in planning to just listen and observe. I remember how I sat in my chair, looking out at the circle of faces around me, which were warm, open and receptive. It settled my anxious nerves and, when Faye asked that night if anyone wanted to share their story with the group, I felt my hand raise by instinct.

"I'm divorced," I'd said, hearing a small tremor in my voice, wondering if anyone could hear it but me. "Though I guess you know that already, because why else would I be here if I wasn't divorced?" I'd laughed at myself then. Others had laughed too — with me, not *at* me — and I'd found it to be encouraging. The words came more freely after that, and I was able to tell them how it had been months since I'd filed for divorce. "To say I've been having a hard time with it is an understatement, even though I'm the one who left him. I asked for this, in a sense. This was my doing." I took a breath, noticing that the tremor had gone away. "I think the thing that makes it so hard is that I don't know anyone who's divorced. It's strange, because something like 50 percent of marriages end in divorce, right? So how is it possible that it's never happened to anyone I know? It makes me feel like some kind of anomaly. No one knows on a personal level what I'm going through. I have great friends who are incredibly sympathetic, but I've felt myself pull away from them over the last few months. We just don't have as much in common anymore. Going through a divorce, there is so much to deal with, like raising a child alone, custody and visitation rights, changing my will, my name, getting rid of the joint bank account, trying to build my own credit because everything we shared was in Ben's name and so I don't have much credit history myself. I can't talk to anyone in my life

33

about this."

I remembered how I'd stopped there and inhaled a sharp breath, feeling self-conscious because I'd said far more than I meant to say, but also finding it was cathartic. "I'm sorry. I didn't mean to say so much."

"No," Faye said. "Don't be sorry. Don't ever apologize, Meghan. This is why we're here, to listen and support one another. Everyone in this room is dealing with these same issues too."

All around me, the circle of heads was nodding.

And then she'd asked me to tell the group a little bit about Ben. I wasn't sure at first how to describe him. When we met, Ben was a dream. We were in high school at the time, back when things like a career and children were so far in the future we didn't think about them. They didn't exist, even in our wildest imaginations. Fast forward over twenty years. I wasn't happy. Ben wasn't happy. Sienna, by default, wasn't happy. Ben and I fought all the time. He was so focused on work, and it upset him when I asked him to make family a priority too, because he read that as me being insensitive, as not supporting him or his career, which wasn't my intent. I just wanted Ben to pay more attention to Sienna and me. I started thinking then, more and more often, about how I'd be better off without him, because being alone and lonely was better than feeling neglected and ignored. But for years, fear of the unknown kept me from leaving him. The reason I finally did wasn't for me but for Sienna, because I didn't want ours to be the model of a marriage she saw. I wanted her to know that a marriage could be full of love, happiness and mutual respect too.

I say to Nat now, "Until I started coming, I could think of few things worse than walking into a roomful of strangers and imparting the details of one of the most painful experiences in my life. But now I've realized that what is worse is going through it alone." I pause to let my words sink in, and then I ask, nodding again toward the steps, "What do you think? You want to give it a try?"

"Okay," she says, giving in.

We head down the steps together to the parish hall, where the large round tables have been pushed out of the way to make space for a circle of black folding chairs in the center of the room. Faye has already gotten the meeting started when we arrive, and so we slip into the last two chairs, which are on opposite sides of the circle, and I watch from afar as Nat shimmies out of her coat and sets it on the back of the chair. She's quiet during the meeting. She listens, but she doesn't speak and I don't blame her.

At some point she takes her hat off, and it's then, when she sweeps a hand through her hair, pushing pieces back from her eyes, that I spy a bruise along the upper forehead, beneath the hairline. I do a double take when I see it, taken aback by the size of the bruise and by its bright red color as if fresh. Whatever happened, happened recently, maybe today. I stare at it longer than I should, wondering how the bruise came to be there. I've done my fair share of dumb, clumsy things before and maybe that's all this is.

But maybe there's more to it too.

Nat glances up just then. Our eyes meet. I swallow and force a guilty smile, feeling self-conscious for getting caught staring. By instinct, her hand rises up to the bruise. She feels it, running her fingers over the tender bump, and then plucks pieces of hair down to cover it. And then, as if worried that's not enough, she puts her winter hat back on.

I look away. I try and listen as others speak, but my eyes keep going back to Nat.

The bruise is gone but not forgotten.

When the meeting is through, I grab my coat and start making my way toward Nat, but before I reach her, another woman, Melinda, sidles up next to me and says, "Hey, Meghan, do you have a minute?" She doesn't wait for an answer, and I watch as Nat steals a glance at me before slipping her arms into her coat and making her way toward the stairs. "I wanted to ask you about the school where your daughter goes, specifically what the admissions process and entrance exam are like. My oldest will be going to high school soon, and we've just begun looking into private schools in the area. It's overwhelming to say the least."

By the time I finally make it upstairs, Nat has made her way to the entrance. She's too far away to catch, and so I can only watch as she pushes the heavy wooden doors open to the barrage of snow, which falls sideways and in. Just outside, she stops, taking in the faces of people passing by. She pulls up her hood and lets go of the door, which floats slowly toward closed, but before it shuts I see Nat merge with a group of passersby.

Later, I walk out of the church, back into the cold and the snow alone, my breath coming out like clouds when I breathe, wondering if I'll see Nat again and if she'll be back.

I think about the bruise as I walk, though not so much the bruise itself but the way Nat was so quick to hide it. I find myself worrying about her, wondering where she's going and who she's going home to.

The snow has built up significantly in the last hour or so, collecting on the sidewalks and streets. Cars and buses move slowly past. There will be a parking ban on some streets overnight, so that the city can plow before morning rush hour.

I take the Red Line home from the church, heading north. It's getting close to nine o'clock now and I feel uneasy, out at this time of night, worried about myself and worried about Sienna at home alone. I've never been afraid in this city, not until the recent spate of robberies and attacks, which has the whole neighborhood on edge.

I get off the Red Line at Sheridan and power walk from there, wanting nothing more than to get home, to be home and to see with my own eyes that the door to our apartment is shut and locked and that Sienna is okay.

THREE

The next day at work, I check in with the charge nurse for my assignment when I arrive and find out I'm assigned to two patients today, including Caitlin Beckett, the woman they say jumped from the pedestrian bridge. I say okay, walking away, feeling a little bit more than apprehensive. I was hoping I wouldn't be assigned to her, that I'd be assigned to the same patients as yesterday, and I want to argue that Bridget should be if, for nothing else, continuity of care, but today is Bridget's day off.

I set my things in a locker in the break room, and then I go to Caitlin's room. It's hard to look at her lying unconscious on the bed and not feel myself come undone. Just inside the glass doors, I come to a stop, letting my eyes run over her, staring at her awhile. Bridget was right; despite the gauze and tubes, you can see that she is pretty. She lies utterly still. Her skin is pale so that if I didn't know any better, I'd think she was dead. The only reason she's not is because machines breathe for her and bring nutrients and fluids to her. I've heard whispers in the break room already about what people think happened to her — gossip and unverified claims. We shouldn't gossip about patients, and yet we do. It's cathartic, a way to de-stress from a long day of work or to steel ourselves for a day to come.

This morning I listened in on a couple nurses talking about her in the break room. One said that when she jumped, she heard Caitlin just narrowly missed the train tracks and landed somewhere between them, on the rocks. "Do you have any idea how many times the train goes by every day?" she asked, meaning that if Caitlin landed on the tracks, she would have been hit by a passing train and that would have been the end of it. She wouldn't be here in our ICU fighting for her life. She'd be dead.

"Trains can't stop very fast," she went on, though it was all very theoretical because it's not the way it happened. "Even in an emergency. I've heard that sometimes it takes over a mile of track to stop once the brake is applied, because of the weight of the train and its speed."

"She's lucky then, that she jumped from where she did," another nurse, Natalia, said.

"Lucky?" Misty asked in reply, incredulous. The long-term effects of a traumatic brain injury can be profound, things like motor deficits, vision problems, difficulties with fine motor skills, difficulty thinking and remembering, more. "How can you say that? Have you seen her?" The answer was yes; we'd all seen her by then. I wasn't the only one who had walked by her room to get a glimpse of her through the glass. Others had too.

"If she really wanted to die, she should have picked another bridge to jump from, like one with semis and cars."

"Can you imagine being the driver of a car or train that hit her though?" asked Natalia. I had my back to them. I didn't want to contribute to the conversation, but that didn't mean I didn't want to listen, that I didn't want to hear what other people were saying about her. It was just before seven in the morning, right before the shift change and so the break room was more crowded than usual because of the change of shift. "What do you think it's like to know you're going to run into someone, to watch it happen, but not be able to do anything to make it stop?"

41

Erin told us then how her uncle is a freight train engineer. "Years ago there was a woman on his line, trying to commit suicide." She described how his and the woman's eyes locked before he hit her, about how, even after he applied the emergency brake, he had to wait endless, agonizing seconds, listening to the shriek of something like four thousand tons of train trying in vain to stop. Then the inevitable happened. The woman disappeared from view, slipping somewhere beneath him, and it was up to Erin's uncle to get out of the train when it finally did stop and go looking for her.

I wasn't sure I wanted to hear the rest. Erin said, "There are two things that can happen when a train runs into someone — one, they can be thrown clear from the train and sustain massive internal injuries, which they'll probably die from, or two, that they can go under the wheels and most likely be dismembered." She paused for effect. "That's what happened to this woman. The second one," she said, shaking her head at the horror of it, of what her uncle had to witness. "He has nightmares still, to this day. It's been six years."

"My God," said Misty. "That's awful. It wasn't his fault, and yet he'll have to live with that guilt his whole life, knowing he played a part in someone else's death."

I bristled at the thought. I couldn't stand to listen to it anymore and so I pushed myself off a bench and walked out.

My friend Luke followed. "Nice to see they're at it again," he said of the gossip mill. I smiled. Of the nurses on staff, Luke was the most like me. Age had something to do with it. He and I had ten or fifteen years on most of the other nurses, many of whom had recently graduated from college. As we headed down the hall together, he asked, "Are you feeling okay?"

I glanced at him, drawing my eyes together. "Yeah, fine. Why?"

"You're quiet," he said. I looked away, but I could still feel his eyes on me.

"Am I?" I asked, pulling a face because I was trying so hard to act normal.

"Yes," he said, and then, carefully, "You were late to work yesterday."

"Oh. That was no big deal. Just a doctor's appointment," I said, though Luke and I both know I wouldn't schedule a routine appointment on a workday, but he thankfully didn't pry.

Still, I could tell he wanted to say more, that he wasn't letting me off the hook so easily. "I saw you were wearing your wedding ring yesterday too," he said, taking me by surprise, and I felt guilty, caught, my face reddening. I didn't think anyone had noticed. "It's none of my business," Luke went on. "But —" he hesitated, treading lightly "— are you and Ben getting back together?"

"God no. It's just —" I struggled for words to say, coming up with, "Old habits, you know?" It was a mistake to put the ring on. I don't know what I was thinking. After all those months, it looked so foreign on my finger. I took it off as soon as I got home; I walked straight into my bedroom before Sienna could notice to put it back in the little modular tray in my jewelry box where it belonged.

"Yeah," he said, "I know. I get it. How's Sienna doing?" he asked then, changing the subject, and I was glad. I appreciated how often Luke asked about Sienna, how she is, how school is going for her, if I like her friends.

"She's good. Fine."

"Hey, I've been meaning to ask, how was your date?"

It takes a second. My date. I'd almost forgotten. Suddenly that felt like a lifetime ago, though the mundanity of it, the everydayness of his question, was welcome.

A few nights ago I had a date. His name was Alec. It was the first date I'd been on since Ben and my divorce. I met him on an online dating site, which I joined — albeit reluctantly — a few months back. I was wary of joining, but Luke and a couple other nurses at work convinced me to try. The truth is that Sienna is getting older. She grows more independent every day. Knowing she'll head off to college soon and I'll be alone for the rest of my life keeps me up at night.

The fact that Ben is dating again is what convinced me. It was the catalyst for my saying yes to a date with Alec. Ever since Sienna let on about Ben's girlfriend, she's taken up space in my mind. I'm not so sure I didn't go on the date to get revenge — putting on a dress I hadn't worn in years, one which was sexy with a shirred waist and a plunging, deep V-neck, thinking how good it would feel for a man to touch me again, to run his hand under the short skirt of the dress, to stare at me in a wanting way.

But it didn't. It felt strange, unwanted at the time and now, days later, inconsequential, so much that I'd already forgotten about him.

"Meh," I said to Luke with a shrug.

"Just meh?" he asked.

"Yeah, just meh. We didn't connect. It was awkward."

"That sucks. I'm so sorry, Meghan. His loss. The next one will be better," he promised, but I wasn't sure there would be a next one.

Now, in Caitlin's hospital room, the night nurse comes and gives me the change of shift report. We stand at the bedside, and she goes over her vitals, her medical history, medication and more. She is in a coma still, no better and no worse than she was yesterday. She's completely unresponsive to all external stimuli, which isn't unusual for someone in her condition. Patients like her can have different levels of consciousness. Some can be minimally conscious or in a vegetative state. They may flinch when we draw blood. They might grind their teeth, thrash in bed, cry or make other involuntary movements, but not this patient. She can't do anything on her own, not even breathe.

The only difference today is that sometime last night, after my shift ended, hospital staff located her parents. I find them in the waiting room, where they spent the night practically upright in recliners. I stand and watch them from a distance as they try to sleep. Their eyes are closed but whether they're actually asleep or not, I can't say. ICU waiting rooms have a very palpable tension to them, different from anywhere else in the hospital. For the most part, visitors are only allowed to see patients one or two at a time, for short periods of time. They wind up camping out in the waiting room, rotating between grieving, praying, crying, visiting, sometimes sleeping and eating, though that's rare. They look like zombies by the time they leave, and only sometimes do they get to take their loved ones with them when they go.

I let them sleep. I go back to the patient's room, but it's hard being alone with her. I go about my work, going through the motions, trying not to think about what happened before, about what brought her here. I check the monitor and her IVs; I check her vitals and administer medication, but, all the while, my eyes keep drifting back to her face, taking it in, making sure she's still unconscious. Only about a third of her face is truly visible — the rest is covered with gauze, tubes and tape that pulls unmercifully at the skin — so that she's practically unidentifiable. She could be anyone. I think of how peaceful she looks now and how contradictory that is to what happened.

Later, visiting hours begin and her parents come to the room. I have my back to the door when they arrive, but I hear the glass slide open and then a woman asks, her voice

47

tentative, "May we please come in?"

I turn to find them standing in the open door. Now that they're here, I get a better look at them. They're middle-aged, somewhere around sixty, both gray, though his is more like salt and pepper and hers is silver. They're well-dressed — her in jeans, a camisole and cardigan, and him in dress pants and a dress shirt, as if he just came from work — though all of it looks slept in and shapeless. They're practically the same height. They hold hands, clinging fast to each other, desperate for something to hold on to. She wears yesterday's makeup and it's smudged around the eyes. "We're Caitlin's parents," she says. "Tom and Amelia Beckett."

"Yes, please, come in," I say. "Good morning. I'm Meghan. I'll be taking care of your daughter today."

"It's nice to meet you," her mother says, but she's not looking at me. She's looking at her daughter now, taking in the gauze and the tubes, the drains, the IV lines as if seeing them for the first time. She sucks in a breath, pressing her fingers to her mouth, fighting tears. I look away so that I don't get choked up by her reaction. I feel responsible for it. Seeing a loved one like this is hard to digest. Being in an ICU is an adjustment; it can be overwhelming at first, for many reasons. The lights in the room are harsh. They do nothing for a patient's appearance. The sheer number of people coming into and out of the room every day is exhausting: residents and attendings, respiratory therapists, nutritionists, PTs and OTs, more. It's hard for families to remember who everyone is. They worry every new face is the harbinger of bad news. The constant buzzing and the beeping of the machines is unfamiliar. It can be frightening, because people don't know what they mean. They worry every sound a machine makes is something bad, potentially life-threatening.

"Can I touch her?" Mrs. Beckett asks as they come to stand at their daughter's bedside.

"Of course you can," I say, watching as she lays a tentative hand on Caitlin's arm, careful not to dislodge the peripheral line.

I tell them that she is stable, that nothing has changed overnight. The doctor will be in this morning and, sometime today, a respiratory and physical therapist. I explain how it's important that we keep coma patients moving as much as we can, to prevent their muscles from atrophying, their skin from breaking down. "Were you able to

49

get any sleep last night?" I ask.

"Some. Not much."

"Have you eaten?"

"Not yet."

"You should. You need to be taking care of yourselves, making sure you're eating and sleeping. A nurse will be here all the time, taking care of your daughter. She's in good hands," I say.

"My wife and I are grateful for that, for everything you're doing for Caitlin."

"Of course. Please don't mind me," I say, going about my business or trying to anyway, but it's hard. My concentration has been derailed by their presence, by their grief. I look away, gazing at the monitor as I say, "If you have questions about anything, you can always ask."

"How long will she be like this?"

"It's hard to say. It varies from patient to patient." It's hard to look at Mrs. Beckett when I speak. Her grief is palpable. Most people are in a coma for only days or a few weeks, before they start to slowly regain consciousness and move to something like a vegetative state, where they can breathe on their own or are minimally conscious. But comas like this can also last months or years, and some people never wake up.

Mrs. Beckett's eyes come to mine and she

asks, "What's it like being in a coma?"

"From what I've heard, it's different for everyone," I say, letting my gaze drift back to Caitlin, my eyes fixing on the placid, restful look on her face, but seeing flashes of something else: fear, shock, pain, dismay. I think again about the fall itself, of what it would have been like to tumble from that height. I linger on her desperation, a last-ditch effort to undo it, to stop herself, and then spinning, flailing, hitting the earth. I try to be unemotional and clinical, to think of her as I would any patient, but it's hard. I'm only human. I wonder if the fall and the impact hurt. I wonder if she was unconscious by then or if, in that moment, her nociceptors were insensitive to pain and she was conscious but felt nothing when she hit the ground.

"For some," I say, moving my eyes away, looking back at Mrs. Beckett's face, "it's like coming out of general anesthesia. They're groggy when they first wake up, but for them, the time they were unconscious passed by in the blink of an eye. For others, they dream."

"Nightmares?" she asks, visibly panicked, worried that's what's happening right now, that her daughter is trapped in her brain with nothing but bad dreams.

51

"No," I say, shaking my head, though it's a lie, because sometimes they do report having had nightmares while unconscious. "Just dreams. Sometimes lucid dreams. Sometimes it's hard for them to distinguish between the dreams and reality when they first wake up. It takes time."

"What are they like when they wake up?"

"It's a process. It's rarely spontaneous. There is a drifting in and out of consciousness. They might be incoherent at first. There may be memory gaps."

"Will she remember what happened when she wakes up? Will she remember that she —" she pauses, and then says *"—jumped."*

I don't know what Mrs. Beckett is hoping: that she does or doesn't remember. The latter would be fortuitous.

"It depends," I say. "I don't know. Some do and some don't."

Sometimes patients wake up with a black hole in their memory, spanning days or weeks before the accident or illness. They can't remember what happened to them or why they ended up in a coma, which would be a blessing.

Sometimes patients come out of a coma with flawed memories. They remember things that never actually happened. They make wild claims that can be blamed on things like lucid dreams or a disconnect with reality.

I look away, but still feel Mrs. Beckett's eyes on me. "Do you have children, Meghan?" she asks after some time.

I look back up and meet her gaze. "Yes," I tell her. "One. A daughter." I don't always like to talk about Sienna when I'm at work. I like to keep my personal life private. But being in an ICU room is a very intimate experience. Today, I only have one other patient besides Caitlin, and I'll split my day between them. For as much time as I spend with patients and their families, personal topics come up.

"Are you and your daughter close?" she asks, distracted, staring again at her own daughter's blank face, at the ghastly endotracheal tube in her mouth, taped to her skin to keep it in place.

"Yes. For the most part."

She confesses, "We haven't been close to Caitlin in many years. We didn't even know that she'd come back."

I swallow. It's not any of my business, but still I'm curious. I have to know. I ask, "Come back?"

Mrs. Beckett glances over her shoulder at her husband. She's getting choked up now and can't speak. Mr. Beckett looks at me and explains. "Caitlin moved to California years ago. As far as we knew, she was still there. The last we heard from her she sounded good, fine, happy. That was a couple months ago. We asked all the time when she was coming to visit, but she always said she didn't know. She had all sorts of excuses as to why she couldn't come see us. Work was busy for her. She didn't have enough vacation time. Airfare was expensive. She didn't know when she could get away."

"She was always so busy," the mother parrots under her breath, and I can tell it's a sensitive topic from the way she says it. She was hurt Caitlin didn't make time for them.

"What does she do for work?" I ask, wanting to know more about her and who she really is.

Mr. Beckett shrugs. "Various things. Whatever she could do to pay the rent, working a couple odd jobs at a time sometimes. Retail. Waitressing. She was a bank teller for a while, but that didn't work out. What she wanted was to be an actress. Thought she'd go to Hollywood and become a star."

"We supported her," Mrs. Beckett is quick to say, lest I think otherwise. "We didn't have the heart to tell her that the odds of that happening were one in a million, because maybe she was the lucky one." She looks at her husband then and asks, bottom lip quivering, her nose beginning to run. "Why do you think she didn't tell us she'd come back? Do you think she didn't want us to know?"

He shakes his head. "I don't know."

I find a tissue and hand it to Mrs. Beckett. "How long had she been back?"

Mr. Beckett shrugs. "Long enough that she had time to find an apartment."

"What if she thought we'd be disappointed in her? What if she felt she'd let us down, or she was embarrassed because things didn't work out like she wanted them to?"

He dismisses this. "Since when does Caitlin care what anyone else thinks? Caitlin is strong, she's resilient," Mr. Beckett says. He turns away from his wife and says to me, "Which is what makes this all the more devastating. We didn't see it coming. We never thought she was the type of person to try and take her own life."

He looks as if he wants me to say something, to explain why this is happening. I know that I have to come up with something to say to set their minds at ease. "I don't know that there is a type," I slowly say. We have had suicide attempts in the ICU before. I read a statistic once that said for every person who dies by suicide, there are twenty-five attempts. That fact scared me, especially when I thought of Sienna, of our family history and the mental health crisis that is happening these days with teens. It's an epidemic. I wanted to know more, mainly whether Sienna was at risk. There are personality subtypes of suicidal individuals, like how, in general, they tend to be dependent, anxious, impulsive. Often, they internalize their feelings versus letting them out. Sometimes people who commit or attempt to commit suicide have a diagnosed mental disorder, like depression or bipolar disorder, and some have an addiction. But not all. Men are more likely to kill themselves, but women are more likely to attempt it. But these are just statistics and risk factors. The truth is that anyone can take or attempt to take their own life. Maybe something terrible happened or they're just having a bad day. "So often these things take everyone by surprise. You can't blame yourself. You can't think that you should have known or done something differently," I say.

"Can I talk to her?" she asks.

"Of course you can," I say, "and you should. They say it helps, that people in a coma can benefit from the sound of familiar voices. There's been research on it."

"What do I say to her?"

"Anything. It doesn't matter. It's the sound of your voice that matters."

She nods, but she's slow to start.

"Caitlin," Mrs. Beckett says after a minute, and her voice cracks. She clears her throat and tries again. "It's me, honey. Mom. Your dad is here too," she says, and then she reaches for him and draws him closer to the bedside.

"Hi, pumpkin," he says, leaning down close, suspended above her.

Later, after her parents leave and I'm alone with her, I wonder if it's true, if she can hear me, if she can feel me, if she knows that I'm here.

I'm standing at the bedside. I have my back to the door, which is something they teach us as nurses, to keep ourselves between the patient, their visitors and the door, to always have a way out of the room. An escape route. If we feel unsafe, they tell us, leave the room and don't look back. Get help. There are things you learn as a nurse not because they taught you in nursing school, but through observation and experience — like keeping patients and families at an arm's length, never turning your back to them and never wearing a stethoscope around the neck because of one time a patient tried to strangle a colleague with it and she would have died if someone else didn't intervene.

I turn to leave Caitlin's room for the nurses' station when I see a man standing about ten feet away, just on the other side of the glass door. He stares into Caitlin's room, his eyes piercing and unkind, the type of gaze you feel all the way to your navel. It's the way he stares that makes alarm bells go off, because his stare is intimidating, practically predatorial; it defies social norms. Normal people don't stare like that. They don't lock eyes with someone and then not break it.

My whole body goes tight. I become motionless all of a sudden, frozen midstride, afraid to leave the room, to go out into the hall where this man is. I'd have to pass by him to get to the nurses' station, and I think how, during the day, the unit is unlocked; anyone can let themselves into the ICU. There's nothing to stop them.

I take a breath. I turn around, facing the patient, turning my back again toward the door. I tell myself it's nothing, just a friend of hers who's come to visit and he's upset, grieving, which is the reason for the way he looked at us.

But what if he's not? What if he's not upset or grieving, and what if he's not a friend?

All of a sudden I worry I've made a mistake in putting my back to the door. What's to stop him from coming into the room with us, from standing behind me and blocking my exit?

I have to leave the room while I still can. I take a breath and gather the courage to turn and go.

But when I look again, he's gone.

FOUR

I see the friend request on my phone first that night. I don't pay any attention to it. I scroll right past while standing in line at the convenience store on the corner after work. I drop my phone in my purse when it's my turn to pay, leaving it there as I walk carefully home in the dark through the snow, staying alert to my surroundings, carrying bags so heavy my arms burn from the weight of them.

Sienna is with someone in the kitchen when I come in, the front door slightly open because Sienna forgot to lock it and it didn't latch properly again. She's talking to a friend, whose voice is deep and masculine. The kitchen is in the way back of our apartment; they don't hear me arrive. I stop in the open doorway, thrown, because Sienna has never had a boy over before and I realize only now that we haven't had a talk yet about whether boys are allowed in the apartment when I'm not home. I don't know where I stand on that because, until now, I haven't had to think about it.

I listen in on the conversation, which is about math, but resembles something flirtatious.

"I suck at geometry," he says.

"No you don't," she says, her tone not quite like herself. I hold my breath so I can hear, remembering what it was like when I was her age. Seeing Nat at the meeting last night has spawned memories of high school. Not only have I been thinking about her, but about other people we went to high school with too, like my best friend Carrie Grant and Jason Murphy, who I was sure back then I wanted to marry or at the very least lose my virginity to, before I met Ben.

"This shit is like really hard," Sienna says to her friend. I bite my lip, leaning against the doorframe to offset the weight of the bags in my hands. Outside, the sky is dark, the darkness pouring in. Sienna hasn't turned on any lights other than the kitchen light, and so it's dim in the rest of apartment where the kitchen light doesn't reach.

I'm also not used to hearing Sienna say words like *shit,* which is how I know she's trying to show off for this boy. She likes him. I can tell. Sienna is sixteen. It was only a matter of time before she developed an interest in boys. "Besides," she says, "you slayed the last test. I got a C. If anyone sucks at geometry, it's me."

"That's not true. I just got lucky on that test. Circles are not my jam."

"Are they anyone's?"

"Simon Hall maybe."

Sienna sneers. "Simon Hall is stupid smart."

"He probably actually likes this shit."

"He probably does it on the weekends for fun."

They have a good laugh at Simon Hall's expense. The L goes rolling by, muffling their laughter. As far as I can tell, Sienna and her friend stop talking, waiting for the train to pass before they carry on. They pick up thirty seconds later, talking about things like chord and tangent lines and, from the way he explains geometry to my daughter — gentle, patient — I realize that this boy doesn't suck at math as much as he'd like Sienna to believe. He was being self-deprecating, which tells me he likes her back.

Sienna makes a mistake in her work. He corrects her, and she says, "Shit. I'm so stupid." I can hear the frustration in her voice. Math is not her cup of tea.

His kindness is endearing. "No, you're not. Anyone could have done it."

"You didn't," she says. There's a beat of quiet, and then, from out of nowhere Sienna says, "Gianna says a person can't be both pretty and smart," as if these things are mutually exclusive, and this boy tells her, "Gianna's an idiot. You're both." I feel myself smile because it's exactly what she was angling for: a compliment. She's never been shy.

From the kitchen comes a discomfiting quiet. I imagine their faces close together and I wonder if my daughter has ever been kissed. I wonder if she's done more than that.

Sienna would die if she knew I was listening in. I let the front door slam closed loud enough that there's no mistaking I'm home.

"Sienna?" I call out as if I don't already know where she is.

"In here," she says back, chair legs suddenly scraping against the maple floors. I follow the sound of her down the narrow hall and to the kitchen. Our three flat is a standard layout, living room with its large, protruding window in front, kitchen in back overlooking a negligible, communal yard, with two small bedrooms and a bath just off the hall between them.

Sienna is standing at the refrigerator when I come in. The door is open; she's reaching inside for the juice. Her clothes have become a source of constant irritation in recent years. Gone are the grunge days of my youth: the baggy, flannel tops and wide leg jeans. Instead, she wears this red tank top with spaghetti straps that's both cropped and low cut, showing far too much skin for my liking, and is out of place for this winter day. Admittedly, I bought the shirt for her, but with her word that she'd wear a cardigan or hoodie over it, which she's not. Her jeans are the distressed kind, with holes everywhere. They're high waisted, which covers some of the bare midriff. But still. There is a dress code at school. None of this is allowed, not cropped tops nor jeans, which means she changed since she's been home. Her friend has not. He's still in his school issued polo shirt and khaki pants, which also tells me he's quite possibly been here since school ended over four hours ago.

What have they been doing all that time?

"Mom, this is Nico," she says, barely looking over her shoulder at him. He sits at my table. He's man-size, a boy in a man's body.

I smile. "Hi, Nico. It's nice to meet you."

"Hi, Mrs. Long," he says. He's awkward but polite.

"It's Michaels. *Ms.* Michaels" Sienna cuts in because I went back to my maiden name after the divorce while Sienna kept Ben's.

She leaves the refrigerator door open as she pours herself a glass of juice. I come around to the far side of the room, setting the grocery bags on the table, glad to be free of their weight. I slip out of my coat, seeing that the heavy bags have left red troughs in my arms. "Meghan is fine, Nico. Sienna, you mind helping with these groceries?"

"Are you going to pay me?" she asks, cocking a hip as she sips her juice.

"How about I keep paying for your phone and we call it even?"

Sienna pouts, sticking that bottom lip out. She has naturally pouty lips. She has these beautiful bushy eyebrows, which are in high demand these days. Her whole look is enviable. She's what all the girls aspire to be: pretty and thin. I just wonder when her teenage sass will reach its peak and she'll come back down to earth.

"I'll help," Nico says, scootching his chair back and standing up. He's even taller when he's on his feet. It's been so long since there's been a man here, even if he is only sixteen years old. Which makes me wonder — is he sixteen? Or is he older than Sienna?

Nico unloads, laying items on the table that Sienna puts pokily away.

"Thank you, Nico. That's very kind of you. Can you stay for dinner? I have Italian beef in the slow cooker. It's ready. I just have to serve it."

"You should," Sienna says. "Her Italian beef kicks ass."

"Sienna."

"What?" she asks. "It does. It's a compliment. You should take it, Mom."

"I can't," says Nico. "It sounds amazing, but I've got to get going actually. Thanks for asking."

"Sure. Another time maybe," I say. I hang back in the kitchen, putting the last of the groceries away while Sienna walks her friend to the door and they say their good-byes in the darkness of the living room. I don't try and eavesdrop, but I notice how their voices become softened, inaudible from here, just hushed whispers and then a high-pitched squeal from Sienna that cuts through the quiet. Ah to be sixteen again.

"He seems nice," I say to her after Nico is gone.

"Mmm-hmm."

"Does he live close by?"

She shrugs. "I guess."

"You don't know?"

"I'm not a stalker, Mom."

"No one said you're a stalker, Sienna. I'm just trying to have a conversation with you. And hey, listen, I don't know how I feel about you having boys over when I'm not home."

She groans. "So you're saying I can't?"

"I'm saying I need to think about it."

That thin hip juts out again. She puts her hand on it, pouting. "You're such a helicopter parent."

The L goes rattling by. I watch it through the window, slowing down for the curve before speeding up again. The tracks run adjacent to our apartment. From almost everywhere, we can see it snaking around the side of the building, an industrial, rusty-bottomed eyesore that keeps the rent below market value. About every five or ten minutes the train comes. It comes all night, twenty-four hours a day, though starting around two in the morning, it's less frequent. Sienna and I have become accustomed to it. If anything, it's white noise now. But when we first moved in, months ago, after Ben and I divorced and I moved out of our charming condo on Webster, it was a nightmare. I'd wake up in the middle of the night believing the Red Line was in my living room. Or the apartment would shake so badly, I'd think the old building was about to collapse. We've had to make accommodations like hanging pictures with extra screws so they didn't keep falling and shattering against the wood floors, and stopping conversations midsentence so we're not screaming over the sound of the passing train.

"While we're on that subject," I say — meaning the subject of helicopter parents, since Sienna brought it up — "I thought we talked about wearing a cardigan with that shirt."

Sienna gripes, "It's like a hundred degrees in our apartment. Do you want me to die from heat stroke?"

"Or just wear a different shirt," I suggest.

It isn't until later — after I've served dinner and we've eaten, sitting side by side on the sofa with our plates held beneath our chins to catch the falling beef and au jus, and Sienna has gone to finish homework in her room — that I pull out a chair and sit down at the desk that's pressed up against the big window in the living room. Outside the street is quiet, peaceful. It's dark out, though the streetlights and the reflection of snow help brighten the world. In the brief lull between passing trains, I hear the noise of the city in the distance, the invariable sound of sirens and traffic that is always there.

I open my laptop. I check my email first and then I go to Facebook, where the friend request still waits for me. I open it to see that it's from Natalie Cohen Roche. Nat. I smile to myself, my heart swelling because I'm glad she found me on here. She wants to reconnect, to be friends again, which I'm so grateful for because it's a time in my life when I could really use a friend.

I take a look at her profile photo. In it, she stands on the edge of what might be Niagara Falls, or maybe just some other massive waterfall, looking happy, and I wonder how she went from that to attending a divorce support group with me. What happened to her in the years since high school?

I don't know, but I hope to find out.

FIVE

Mr. and Mrs. Beckett spend the first twenty-four or more hours in the hospital without interruption. When I come in the next day, they're still there, draped limply over the arms of two of the waiting room's spartan recliners with their eyes closed, though I can't tell if they're asleep or not. I stand on the other side of the room watching for a while, for the movement of their eyes to tell me if they're conscious. They're alone in the room. The TV is on, mounted in the corner, but it's on mute, the only sound the gentle hum of the overhead lights, which never go off.

At first glance, Mrs. Beckett appears to be cold. She wears her cardigan wrapped tightly around her so that the plackets overlap, her arms knotted against her. I turn away, using my badge to unlock and pull open the door to the ICU, where I find a blanket and bring it back to the waiting

70

room because I can't stand to see her looking cold. After everything, it's the least that I can do for her. I try not to wake her, but still, she stirs as I lay the blanket gently over her. Her eyes flutter open. She adjusts on the chair, centering herself, gazing up at me. Bit by bit she makes out my face, and first the recognition and then the panic take over. She thinks something has happened to Caitlin. That's why I'm here, that's why I've come: to tell her her daughter is dead, that she coded overnight and that, despite the doctors' best efforts, she couldn't be saved.

"What is it?" she breathes out, her hand going to her heart.

"Everything is fine," I whisper. "I brought you a blanket, Mrs. Beckett. I thought it might make you more comfortable. You looked cold."

It takes a second for my words to sink in. Only then does she glance down to see the white thermal blanket on her lap. She looks at it, taking it in, and then she lets her gaze go back to me, unconvinced. "Are you sure? Is everything okay with Caitlin?" she asks, and I feel guilty for making her feel like this.

"Yes. I'm so sorry. I just didn't want you to be cold. I didn't mean to wake you. Please," I say, "try to get some sleep."

I return to the ICU, where I get my as-

71

signments from the charge nurse, finding out I'm assigned to Caitlin again, which comes as no surprise, though I was hoping that Bridget would be, now that she's back. I put my things in the break room and then sit on the bench to change my shoes. Again today, the nurses are talking about Caitlin Beckett. She's still a hot topic.

I leave the break room, heading to her room, where I see the night nurse, Kathy, inside, waiting to give me the change of shift report. "How is she doing?" I ask, coming in, letting my eyes run over Caitlin. Even after almost twenty years working as an ICU nurse, the sight of her in bed takes me aback.

"About the same," she says, and I find comfort in that.

Kathy gives her change of shift report. After she leaves, I do my initial assessment, going through the motions. I take her vitals, administer medication, force her eyes open to check for a pupillary response, and then I check the urine output, which is how we watch for things like dehydration and kidney function. There is a urinary catheter in place, to collect urine directly from her bladder and bring it to a drainage bag beside the bed, which has to be routinely emptied. Caitlin wears an adult brief, too, that has to be regularly changed. She requires more care than a baby, and I wonder if she'll always be this way or if she'll ever go back to being the person she was before.

The Becketts look exhausted by the time they come to the room. Mrs. Beckett holds a paper cup filled with coffee in her hand. Her clothes — the same ones she's worn for days — hang limply on her; her jeans bunch in the knees.

"How did you sleep?"

"Not well," Mrs. Beckett says. "I can't sleep, not here, not with Caitlin like this," she says, letting her eyes go to the bed.

Mr. Beckett spent the night with her in the waiting room, but now he plans to leave, to go home, to shower, walk the dog and catch up on work. "Come with me for just an hour or two and take a nap in our bed," he suggests before he goes, but Mrs. Beckett shakes her head with a childlike mulishness to it. She won't go. She won't leave Caitlin alone. She lowers her tired body into a chair, bent on staying, and then later, after Mr. Beckett has left and she and I are alone, she turns to me and asks, "Have you ever known someone to do what Caitlin did?"

The question — the frankness of it or perhaps the fact that it hits a raw nerve — takes me by surprise. A knot forms in my throat. I try swallowing it away, but it's like a boulder: large, heavy and unable to be knocked loose. It chokes me, stealing my air, and I have to clear my throat to dislodge it. "You have, haven't you?" she asks because of my delay and my reaction. She softens, easing off. Her head slants and her eyes turn warm.

I grew up in the suburbs of Chicago. Not far from us, there was a highway overpass that crossed over the expressway. The year after I left high school for college, my little sister drove her car out close to that overpass. She parked on the shoulder of the road just before it, walked a hundred feet to the dead center of the bridge, climbed to the top of the concrete parapet and jumped.

When I tell her, Mrs. Beckett stares open-mouthed at me, as if this revelation binds us, as if it makes us kindred spirits. She looks to me in mild astonishment and says, "Then you, more than anyone, know what Tom and I are going through. You know what it's like. You can understand."

I nod, trying to stay unaffected but it's impossible. The truth is that everything about this stirs up memories of Bethany and brings back all the emotion I felt after she died. Lately, I've found myself thinking of her all the time, and about what it would have been like for her to stand at the top of that highway overpass and jump. After her suicide, I did research, looking into things I didn't need to see but I couldn't stop myself; it became an obsession, a form of self-sabotage, self-flagellation. Nothing I read did me any good, but I wanted answers. I wanted someone to tell me how my happy little sister could do that to herself. What I found out was that jumping from a building or a bridge is one of the more lethal forms of suicide. Unlike with an overdose for example, where there is a chance someone might find you and that you can be saved, jumping isn't something that can be stopped or undone. It's a manner of suicide exclusive to those who are most bent on dying. That fact, when I read it, broke me. Bethany didn't have any doubt. She wanted to die.

I swallow hard, asking, "You have other children besides Caitlin?" because I have to change the subject before I start to cry.

"Yes, two. Caitlin is our baby," she says, letting her gaze go down to Caitlin's face before reaching into her purse to pull out a small photo album. She flips through the pages and, when she finds the one she's looking for, she stretches the album across the bed to me.

"That's her," she says, pointing at the

photo. "That's Caitlin. I wanted you to know what she looks like," she says. I know, of course, what she looks like. I can see that for myself, but what she means is that she wants me to see what she looks like without all the gauze and tubes, which mask half her face while the rest is swollen and bruised.

I look down. The image I see throws me off-balance. I find myself staring at her face and her eyes, which are very much vibrant and alive. In the photograph, Caitlin Beckett is a confident woman, composed and practically bold. She strikes that pervasive hand-on-the-hip pose, her chin jutting out, her smile teasing and playful, and it's hard to reconcile the woman she was with the woman she is now. If I didn't know any better, I'd think they weren't the same. I swallow hard, my saliva thickening.

"She's a beauty, isn't she?" Mrs. Beckett asks, but she doesn't wait for me to respond. She goes on, harrumphing and saying, "Clearly, she didn't get it from me."

It takes a second to collect myself. I say, "She's lovely," and then I hand the album back. "Will you tell me about her?"

"About Caitlin?" I nod. Mrs. Beckett chuckles to herself. "Typical youngest child," she says, but the laugh is melancholic. "Outgoing, attention seeking. Charming and creative. If you were to ask the others, they'd say that Caitlin was Tom and my favorite, or mine anyway. She always got her way, or at least that's what the others would say."

"Did she always get her way?"

"I may have spoiled her, yes. Some. Not intentionally. But she was my last. My last to carry, to give birth to, to nurse. I coddled her more than the others, because after Caitlin, I would never do it again. There was a finality to it, which was hard for me, because I dreamt my whole life about being a mother. Each of Caitlin's firsts — first steps, first day of kindergarten — was also my last."

I grow solemn, thinking of Sienna. I can relate. These last few years, now that Sienna is a teenager, I feel her pulling away from me, her life going in a different direction than mine. It used to be that I knew everything about her, her friends and what she was thinking, but now I don't.

"Are your kids close?"

"No," she says. "They live on opposite sides of the country — one in New York and one in Seattle — but despite the physical distance, they've never been close. Caitlin is our only daughter. My relationship with her was different than the one I have with my boys, and I'm not sure but that they didn't resent her for it. You have a daughter too?" she asks.

"Yes."

"Just the one?" I nod. "Do you have a picture? I'd love to see what she looks like," she says. I carry my phone with me, in one of the many pockets of my scrubs. The phone is always on silent, though I check it throughout the day with some frequency, in case Sienna texts or calls.

"She doesn't like to have her picture taken," I say. "She's at that age where she scrutinizes every photo of her I take. None is ever good enough. She zooms in on the image until every pixel is magnified and then she comes up with some reason not to like it — her hair, her smile, the particular angle of her head."

I slip my hand into my pocket to retrieve the phone. I swipe through the pictures of Sienna on my photos app for one to share, finding one I love. When I do, I hand Mrs. Beckett my phone and then I watch her eyes, the way they study Sienna's face.

"I have no idea why she wouldn't like having her picture taken. She's stunning."

"Thank you," I say, slipping my phone back into a pocket.

"The blond hair must come from your husband," she wrongfully assumes. She wouldn't be the first to notice that Sienna looks nothing like either Ben or me, who are both brunette, while Sienna is a light blond.

"No," I say, and then I tell her the same thing I tell everyone, holding Ben's mom accountable, though she is more of a strawberry blonde. "My mother-in-law, we think."

Mrs. Beckett is thoughtful for a moment, and then she asks, "Is that what you wanted? Just the one child?"

The short answer is yes. I made a conscious decision to have only one child. I didn't struggle getting pregnant with Sienna, not at all. It was too easy. She was an accident, though we don't go around trumpeting that fact. I found out I was pregnant with Sienna before I was ready to have kids. It caught me off guard.

"When I was younger," I say, "I always thought I wanted a large family. I had this very idealistic, starry-eyed view of what motherhood might be. But Sienna was colicky when she was born. She cried all the time, and not just a fussy baby cry, but a screaming in pain type of cry. It was horrible to listen to. I couldn't soothe her for anything. She would cry in the middle of the night, so that I never got any sleep. I was working then, fewer hours, but still. My husband couldn't get up with her at night. He had to be at work earlier than me, and for longer hours. It didn't matter though, because even if he had offered to help, I would have insisted on doing it myself, because I'm her mother. She needed me.

"I remember that when Sienna outgrew her crib, I sold it. It was something subconscious. I didn't even think to keep it for another child of mine because on some level, I'd already decided there wouldn't be another child. I remember, too, seeing how frazzled our friends with multiple kids were. They had to be in four places at the same time, and their weekends were full of things that neither adult in the family wanted to do. By then, Sienna had moved beyond the colic, and Ben, she and I had some semblance of a normal life. I could sleep at night. We could do things together as a family." I pause for breath — feeling embarrassed that I've said so much — and then say, "It sounds selfish."

"No. Not at all. It sounds honest."

"It's good to know our limitations, I suppose."

"It's not as if it's a shortcoming. Raising

children is more work than anyone imagines, and you have something very special with your daughter, I imagine. A bond."

"I do," I say, letting my guard down because I like Mrs. Beckett, and because, despite the circumstances, she's easy to talk to, though I should know better than to let myself get close to patients or their families. I should know better than to talk so openly with strangers. I should have learned my lesson by now.

"Please don't tell my wife, but I've been doing some research," Mr. Beckett says later in the day. "Occupational hazard," he explains. "I'm an attorney."

"What type of research?" I ask.

"About falling. About how a person survives a fall like Caitlin did. I've been to the bridge," he says, "and when I saw how far she fell, I didn't know how it was possible. That bridge is unmarked, but the state, I've come to learn, requires a vertical clearance of twenty-three feet above the tracks. The fatality rate for a fall like that is high." Mr. Beckett sits back in the chair and I think that this must be a defense mechanism, a way to cope. Fact-finding as a means of avoiding the reality that his daughter might be in a vegetative state for the rest of her life or she might die.

"But Caitlin," he says, going on, letting his eyes run over her, "from what I've learned, had some advantages — her age, for one, and the fact that she's a woman. Older or younger people and men are more likely to die from falls like this," he says, very matter-of-fact, returning his eyes to mine to say, "Women are more resilient than men. Their weight compared to that of men saves them sometimes. You ladies are fortunate," he says, and then he pauses for effect, holding my gaze, and I wonder if it wouldn't be better if Caitlin was dead.

I'm drawing up warm water to flush her feeding tube. I turn my back to him, which makes me uncomfortable, to not have him in my visual field.

I try to be nonreactive, but my throat has tightened and gone dry. I empty 50 mL of water into the tube, pushing slowly down on the plunger, reminding myself to breathe.

"In the end though," he says, after some time, "it all comes down to luck. Some people can survive a hundred-foot fall or more. Sometimes you have that one lone plane crash survivor. Others die by falling six feet."

I let my eyes go to Caitlin's face. "She was lucky then," I say, but even I can tell how disingenuous that sounds.

I feel Mr. Beckett's eyes on me still, as if he wants to say something more, but he doesn't.

I'm alone in the room with him now. A friend came and took Mrs. Beckett down to the cafeteria to eat, though she wouldn't leave the building, which is what the friend suggested. Mr. Beckett had to practically force her to go, and I think the only reason she did was because her friend came all this way to see her and she didn't want to come across as rude. It was clear she didn't want to leave. She only did with Mr. Beckett's promise that he would call her if anything happened, if there were any changes, if Caitlin woke up.

"You said that Caitlin has an apartment in the city? Have you been to see it?"

"No." He looks back over his shoulder to make sure we're still alone and that Mrs. Beckett isn't coming back. "My wife," he says, bringing his eyes back to mine, "would like to go or she'd like me to go, to make sure that Caitlin didn't have a cat that might be starving or something. I told her Caitlin could hardly take care of herself, much less a cat." His words catch me off guard, and I can see that Caitlin was a letdown to him. She failed to live up to his expectations.

"I'm sorry," he says when I say nothing because I'm not sure how to respond. "That probably sounded cruel. I didn't mean for it to. What I meant is that Caitlin was still trying to find her way and that it's more important for Amelia and me to be with her now, rather than wasting time going to see her apartment. Our daughter is here. There's nothing for us to see there."

"Of course," I say. "I understand. You said you hadn't spoken to her since she'd been back?"

"Yes. That's right."

"How did you know where she was living then?" I ask.

He clears his throat. "We received a call from her work. Caitlin had listed Amelia as an emergency contact, which surprised us because we didn't even know she left California and was living here in Chicago. When she didn't show up for her shift and couldn't be reached, someone called to see where she was and if she was okay. Her boss gave us Caitlin's address."

I nod, wondering about the legality of that, if employers are allowed to just give personal information away, but ultimately it doesn't matter because sooner or later they would have found her. Caitlin's personal belongings were given to the Becketts at the hospital, and included things like the contents of her purse, which likely meant an ID and apartment key.

He says, "What I said before, I didn't mean for it to come out the way it did."

"It's fine. I didn't think anything of it."

"I don't want you to think that I'm disappointed in my daughter for the choices she's made. It's just that we have these lofty aspirations for our children. We want them to grow up to be happy, successful, independent. Caitlin struggled with that." He hesitates, thinking, and then decides to go on. "Please don't repeat this. I never told my wife about this but, a couple months ago, Caitlin called me. As far as Amelia knew, it had been six months since we'd spoken. Caitlin, I believe, was still living in California at the time. She wanted money. Caitlin was never shy about asking for money," he says, and again I hear the disappointment in his voice. "The requests were frequent because she was always between jobs or not making enough to support her lifestyle, and because Amelia indulged her as a child. Caitlin wasn't used to having to work hard. I said no when she called. I'd had enough of her requests. She's an adult, for heaven's sake. She should be able to support herself.

"But then," he says, and his tone changes from exasperation and disappointment to something else, something different and far more like remorse. "A few weeks before the suicide attempt, she tried calling again. I saw her call come in, but I didn't answer it because I didn't want to be put in a position to have to say no to her again. It wasn't easy for me because, as a father, I wanted to give her the world but I also wanted to teach her about having a good work ethic and being a responsible human. I let the call go to voice mail. She left me a message; I still have it. I never called her back, because I assumed it was money she was after."

He stares down at the white sheet, lost in thought, clearly affected. He reaches into his pants' pocket and pulls out his phone. His hands are shaking now and his whole demeanor has changed.

He checks again, over his shoulder, to make sure his wife isn't on her way back from lunch, and then he holds the phone out and puts it on speaker so that we can both hear.

He plays the voice mail for me.

Her voice, when I first hear it, throws me off-balance. It's not the way I expected it to sound. What I expected was something more bold or self-assured, but not this.

"Daddy," she says. Her voice is thin, reedy, like she's trying not to cry. It complements the woman on the bed before me: naked, frail and exposed. She lets that one word slip — *Daddy* — and then she goes quiet and I wonder if she's trying to compose herself or if she's deciding what to say next. What does she want to tell him? What does she want him to know?

My heart has started to beat harder inside my chest, waiting for her revelation. Before me, Mr. Beckett rubs at the lines of his forehead. His head drops, slumping forward, hanging heavy. He's no doubt listened to this voice mail a thousand times now, so that he knows it by heart, every word, her cadence, the rise and fall of her voice, every long pause.

The silence goes on, though it's not only silence because there is some white noise, static, in the background, like running water or the whir of a fan. Just as I start to think the voice mail will end like that, with that one word — *Daddy* — her voice comes to me again through the speaker, breathy now, desperate and emphatic, losing composure. "I'm in trouble. I need your help," she declares, and my throat constricts, my heart starts to beat even faster. She goes quiet again, and I wait with bated breath, wondering what she's going to say, watching as the phone's progress bar nears the end, the little dash traveling across the black line like a bullet train. She has less than eight seconds to say something — now seven, six — and I start to think that's all she'll say, that one desperate admission: *I'm in trouble. I need your help.*

But then, all of a sudden, there's noise in the background. The slamming of a door maybe, or something fell. A thud and then a voice — mumbled, just out of earshot, weak. I can't hear what the person says, nor can I tell if it's a man or a woman, but what I can hear is the way Caitlin draws in a sharp breath, her voice becoming instantly composed as she says, "No one. Just a wrong number."

I flinch, pulling back, caught off guard by her words.

No one. Just a wrong number.

The call ends all of a sudden and silence fills the hospital room. Mr. Beckett's head slowly lifts. He turns to me. There are tears in his eyes now and I wonder if they're from sadness or from guilt and I want to say something, to assuage that guilt, but don't.

"Money," he says, by means of explanation. "I thought she only wanted money."

He shakes his head, disappointed in himself. "Please don't tell my wife about this," he begs and I nod. I won't tell anyone. "You're the only one I've told." I don't know what to feel about this. I understand the need to unload, to get it off his chest. But why me? Why is he telling this to me? "I don't want her to know that Caitlin called." There is a moment of hesitation, a beat of silence, and then he says, "She'll think our daughter is practically dead because of me."

Later, I'm alone in the break room. It's a misnomer — break room — because we don't often get breaks. Most days we sit and we eat, but it's fast, shoveling food in quickly so we can get back to our patients, but some days even that is a luxury.

I'm sitting at a little round table, eating leftovers from last night, thinking about my conversation with Mr. Beckett.

The small TV on the counter is on; it always is, even when no one is here to watch it. I'm staring at the evening news when Luke comes in, singing untimely Christmas carols, though the little tabletop tree with its lights and garland that was on the counter has been put away until next year. Luke is almost always upbeat. He's one of only two male nurses on staff, which is typical — only something like 12 or 14 percent of nurses are men — though, contrary to popular belief, he's not gay. You don't have to be gay to be a male nurse. He's married to a woman, though he was single for so long that people came to their own conclusions about him. His wife is gorgeous too, like a goddess.

Luke stops midsong when he sees me and smiles, his dimples deepening. "What's on the menu today?"

"Spaghetti," I say, picking at it with a plastic fork. It's four in the afternoon, well after lunchtime, but is the first opportunity I've had all day to sit and eat.

"That sounds good."

I make a face. "It's not. It's cold. The microwave won't work."

"Again?"

"Still."

"I can take a look at it if you want," he says, which is typical Luke, to want to help people, to want to fix things.

I tell him not to worry about it and, at the same time, his attention drifts to the TV. "What are you watching?" he asks.

"The news," I say, as a breaking story comes on about another attack that happened in the city last night, this time on Grace Street, which is just two blocks from where Sienna and I live. My stomach churns. Luke stands beside the table and we watch in disgust as the anchor describes how the attack happened just after eight o'clock last night. This victim, like the others, was followed into her apartment through the back door, which she entered from the alley, climbing the back steps to the third floor. The assailant waited in the shadows for her to unlock the door. He stood silently by and let her open it. He came up from behind and forced her inside, but then, unlike in most previous times where the women were only robbed, this one was also raped. She never got a look at the man's face because it was dark in her apartment and because he came at her from behind, forcing her to the ground face down, telling her that he had a gun and that if she so much as thought about screaming, he'd end her life.

I push my Tupperware away. I can't eat.

Luke is quiet at first. He holds his breath before slowly releasing it, his anger palpable, and I know he's thinking about his wife and what he'd do if this man ever laid a hand on her.

He says, "Last week I got asked to cover for someone for the night shift." The night shift runs from seven at night until seven in the morning. "I said no, though Penelope and I really could use the extra money, you know?" he asks and I do know that. Luke has told me before about their financial situation. His wife is about ten years younger than him, pregnant and on bed rest for preterm labor; she's unable to work and so they're relying on one income for the time, which has been an adjustment for them. It's hard, especially with a baby on the way. "I don't like the idea of her being home alone all night. Each of the victims lived alone," he tells me, which is right, when I think about it, though I hadn't until now. "He watches them. He knows when they'll be alone."

His words are chilling. A shiver runs through me as I think how the entire city's sense of security has been completely upended by this one man.

I picture Sienna and my apartment. We have a back door too, like this latest victim. The back door leads to a small wooden deck that overlooks a communal backyard, which is shared by the building's tenants. Just beyond the yard is an alleyway. I don't often use the back door but if I did, that woman could just as easily have been me, tired, coming home from a long day of work. Most of the time, Sienna is home when I come home, but sometimes she's not. Sometimes she's with Ben and, on the nights that I work, Sienna is home alone.

Luke fills his water from the dispenser and leaves, and I shift my attention back to the news. Another story comes on, this one about a recent wave of suicides in the city. I reach for the remote, turning the volume higher. "Just last week," the anchor says, "a fourteen-year-old boy took his own life, because of cyberbullying. And, over the weekend, a Chicago police officer was found dead in his apartment from a self-inflicted gunshot wound."

The video then leaves the studio, going to an image of Lake Shore Drive, where a voice-over says the most recent victim is a young woman who tried to take her own life by jumping from one of the city's pedestrian bridges on the near south side. I stop eating. I hold my breath, my fork suspended midair. The image is wide at first — the skyline, Lake Michigan — and then it homes in on a bridge where a reporter stands, freezing cold, telling us that this is where the young woman jumped. The video then goes back to the studio, where the anchor interviews a psychologist. It's a split screen view. The psychologist is in an office somewhere, and he tells us the warning signs to look for in people who may be suicidal: talking about suicide, withdrawing from social contact, doing risky or self-destructive things. Across the bottom of the screen flashes a suicide prevention number. The whole news segment is unexpected and sad, and then the psychologist disappears and the anchor moves on to something uplifting — how one of the city's animal shelters will be waiving adoption fees this weekend in an effort to find the animals good homes — to end the newscast on something lighter. The shift is sudden, the anchor's segue practically glib: "This next story will cheer everyone up," she says, the sad look on her own face transforming into a smile on a dime, before we get a look at a litter of puppies that will make most viewers forget all about Caitlin. But not me.

Six

Someone is moving into the apartment downstairs. I see the moving truck arrive and double-park in the street. I stand at the window with my mug of coffee, watching as a couple of burly men haul boxes and furniture out of the truck and in through the doors of the three flat to the apartment below.

"What are you looking at?" Sienna asks, coming out of her own bedroom in a long sleeved blue polo shirt and the pleated khaki skirt she hates so much. Sienna is tall; she manages to hike the modest skirt up high enough on her waist to reveal more of the thigh than is intended. I smile to myself. She's nothing if not resourceful.

"Someone's moving in downstairs. Are you almost ready for school?" I ask, and she nods, slipping into a coat to leave, and I can't help but be cold for her bare legs on this winter day. She doesn't have to wear a skirt. Pants are also an option, but she hates the tan, twill, shapeless uniform pants even more than she hates the skirt.

Sienna goes out our apartment door and a few seconds later, I watch her emerge on the sidewalk below, holding the door open for the movers. It makes me happy; for as sassy as she sometimes is, she still has good manners. I follow her with my eyes as she walks down Dakin for Sheridan, where she'll catch the bus to school. Her commute is long, nearly forty minutes — two buses and a short walk — each way. She's been riding the city bus alone for years. City kids are resilient that way. Her school is a Roman Catholic college prep high school, one of the best in the city, though it comes with an exorbitant price tag, which Ben and I split.

I watch her out the window for as long as I can, captivated by her infallible confidence, but also scared of it. A little prudence would do her some good.

I sink into the sofa with my coffee, kick my feet up on the coffee table and open my laptop, grateful for a day off. I navigate to Nat's Facebook page. Now that we're Facebook friends, I'd like to know a little bit more of what she's been doing these last many years. Sienna gives me a hard time for still using Facebook. She thinks I'm a Luddite because I haven't replaced it with TikTok or Snapchat so that, like her, I can agonize over keeping up with my streaks. She likes to think of Facebook as the social media platform for middle-aged moms, and I'm not sure she's wrong.

I don't post much myself, not anymore. Still, when I look at it, my page is a history of faux-happy memories, like the picture of Ben, Sienna and me together, smiling beside the Millennium Park Christmas tree last year, when in reality Ben hadn't wanted to go, to venture into the Loop for dinner and to see the lights. I'd practically had to force him to and even when he did, he was still upset about it, mostly because of how much he hates tourists and holiday crowds, but also because his week was so busy and the last thing he wanted to do on a weekend was have plans. I remember how he walked three steps ahead of Sienna and me the whole night, and if he spoke two words to me, that was all. He only smiled for the picture because a stranger was taking it, and he didn't want to come across as rude in front of someone he didn't know, and so he'd stood in the middle of Sienna and me, arranging his arms around our shoulders and pulling us in so that our heads touched.

He smiled widely for the picture, the tree in the background giving off perfect holiday vibes. He'd gone so far as to snatch Sienna's Santa hat from her head for the photo and put it on his, and I remember how friends' comments all praised Ben — *He is SO funny. Love the hat, Ben! OMG he's too cute.* — though he couldn't get it off fast enough when the moment was through. He'd handed it back to Sienna and then turned and walked away, hands in his pockets, three steps ahead again, and I was grateful for the way Sienna looped her arm through mine and walked with me, though she shouldn't have had to do that.

Still, when I got home, I posted the picture to Facebook, because everyone was posting pictures of all the festive things they were doing that holiday season to Facebook — cutting down Christmas trees, pictures with Santa, ice-skating at Millennium Park — and I wanted to make the world believe that we, like them, were happy too. The truth is that social media is an optical illusion. It's an *un*reality, it's the very deliberate version of people's lives that they want you to see.

I haven't posted anything to Facebook since the divorce, though I haven't given it up altogether. I like to look because it's how

I keep up with family and friends.

Nat still hasn't removed her married name, Roche, from Facebook. When I get to her page, I click on the profile photo to enlarge it, seeing again that image of her standing beside some waterfall. In it, she's leaned back against the metal fencing, her elbows propped on the top rail. Water rushes urgently down behind her, seemingly moving in the static image so that you can practically feel the sprays of cold water that shoot up from the misty river below. Her hair blows in the wind, not enough to mar the photo, but enough that it adds life to it, that it makes her laugh, revealing a beautiful smile. Back in high school, I remember that Nat had a gap-toothed smile. The gap was slight and endearing and only added to her personality and charm, but I can see how, as an adult, it might have made her self-conscious. She's had it fixed and the result is nothing short of flawless.

I X-out of the profile image to reveal the cover photo beneath. This one is of Nat and a man. He's handsome, enough that I draw in a breath and hold it. My eyes run over the chiseled cheekbones and jaw, the slim nose, the close-set hazel eyes, the dirty blond hair — which is a combed-back crew cut, classic and clean — trying to decide if

I've seen him before, because there is something about his face that strikes a chord. I can't put my finger on it. Nat stands just to the back of him, her arms thrown around his shoulders from behind, hands clasped across his chest — her large wedding ring visible, platinum or white gold, the shank of it lined with small diamonds with a larger, round one in the center of the ring. Her chin rests on his shoulder and, while he's practically simpering for the camera, she gazes sideways at him, the look in her eyes one of utter adoration, like she can't tear her eyes off him. I don't blame her. I can't either. He's incredibly attractive. I feel silly, but even as I look at Nat in the photograph, my eyes keep returning to him. Unlike Nat, who's averting her eyes, he has a direct gaze that practically demands attention.

I was never the prettiest or the most popular girl in school, but even as a grown adult I've often wondered what it would be like to snag a man like that, to be able to hold hands and walk down the street with someone *that* attractive — which is not to say that Ben wasn't attractive — he was, very much so — but I don't know that Ben ever turned heads the way this man surely does.

I read her bio, saying how she attended Barrington High School. She works now as a teacher at a cooperative nursery school in Lincoln Park. I'm familiar with the school because it's one that I looked into for Sienna years ago, though enrollment was limited. After priority spots were taken, there was a lottery for the rest. We threw her name into the hat, but Sienna didn't get picked. If she had gotten in, I wonder if Nat would have ever been Sienna's teacher. We might have crossed paths either way. Fate is funny that way.

I scroll slowly back through Facebook, back through time, feeling like I'm snooping as I do, though I don't know why, because the reason people post things to social media is for them to be seen. If Nat wanted to keep her life private, she wouldn't put it online and she wouldn't have sent me that Facebook friend request.

That said, Nat is frugal with the photos she posts. There are some, but there aren't many. She and the man in the cover photo, Mr. Roche, posed beside a turquoise blue sea in some place like Turks and Caicos or Punta Cana, with one of those little overwater huts behind them, standing with stilts in the water. She and him at a concert. She and him on the Ferris wheel at Navy Pier

— a selfie — the setting sun and the city skyline behind them. In all, they're smiling. In every one, they look happy and very much in love, and I wonder what happened between them for their marriage to end in divorce. He hasn't been tagged in any of the photos and she never mentions him by name; there are only witty little captions like *Heaven on Earth* and *On top of the world*. I have no way of knowing who he is.

As I scroll — my feet kicked up on the coffee table before me, lukewarm coffee in one hand, the other on the laptop — the ping of an incoming message takes me by surprise. Automatically, the messenger box appears at the bottom right corner of my screen, insinuating itself onto the page without my having to open it. It's Nat. I feel a prick of guilt as if she knew somehow that I was on her page.

I hope you don't mind that I found you on Facebook.

A second later, another message appears.

I just wanted to say how nice it was to run into you the other day. It brought back such great memories of high school. I can't believe it's been over twenty years! Thank you, too, for talking me into staying for the meeting. I'm lucky I ran into you — for more reasons than one.

I smile to myself, leaning forward to set my coffee on the coffee table so I can type with both hands. So great seeing you too! I'm glad you stayed for the meeting. Did you like it?

I ask. I hope she did. I don't think she would have felt uncomfortable — as promised, Faye didn't call her out to share — but the meetings do hit close to home sometimes, whether you speak or not. Sometimes even something someone says can jog a painful memory.

A small version of her profile photo appears beside the message to tell me she's read it, and then three dots appear; she's typing back. I wait and then, when it's clear she's typing something long, I set the laptop aside, grab my coffee mug and go to the kitchen for a refill. Her message will be waiting for me when I come back.

But when I do come back, the dots are gone. The last message in the chat is mine. Whatever she was going to say, she deleted it and took it back, and I wonder why.

I try again, typing, I'm sorry I got caught up in a conversation after the meeting and didn't get a chance to talk to you before you left. Do you think you'll be back next week?

Her reply this time is quick. I'm not sure I can come, she says, and I wonder if she's not sure she can come because she has something else going on that night, or if she's not sure she can come because she didn't like the meeting and never wants to go back.

Or if she's not sure she can come because someone won't let her.

Ok, I type at first but I don't send it because it feels somehow caustic in its brevity. I don't want to come across as short or rude, though I'm reading too much into it, I know.

I delete my initial response. Instead I type, Would you want to grab coffee or a drink sometime? I'd really love to catch up.

It feels forward, bold. But I send it anyway and then wait for a reply.

SEVEN

The Becketts have taken a liking to me. On the days that I don't work, another nurse is assigned to Caitlin, but on the days that I do, they ask for me. Today for example, I wasn't assigned to Caitlin. I was given other patients, but when visiting hours began and the Becketts found Luke in Caitlin's room, they made a request to the charge nurse, who obliged.

"They must really like you," Luke said as we passed in the hall. He's incredible at what he does. He's compassionate, he has the world's best smile and a sense of humor to boot. A patient would be lucky to get to work with him.

"Don't take it personally. They're just used to me, I think," I said, trying not to read too much into it. They like talking to me. Mrs. Beckett and I have a bond, because we're both mothers. That's all.

"There's something strange about them,"

he said then, his words running down my spine, especially in light of the conversation I had with Mr. Beckett the other day where he played that voice mail for me.

I was walking away when he said it, toward Caitlin's room. I stopped and turned back. "Like what?" Luke stood three feet from me in pale blue scrubs with a white T-shirt beneath, a partial tattoo of a snake visible beneath one of the short sleeves. He's told me about the tattoo once before, a remnant from his wild youth, getting it when he was sixteen with a fake ID. By his own admission, Luke was a holy terror as a teenager. His parents were mostly absent, though his father was an alcoholic with a temper. He hit him and Luke's mom, not all the time, but sometimes, and then he would go on a bender and disappear. Luke told me about his past when I complained about something Sienna did — blowing her curfew or something relatively benign like that. He said, *It could be so much worse, Meghan. She's a good kid.* As a child, he told me, he drank, did drugs and some petty theft. When I asked why, he said he loved the rush of it, the thrill of taking something that wasn't his, and because no one could stop him, no one could tell him no. It gave him power and a sense of control that he didn't have in his own family, I think, where he felt powerless. Now Luke is the salt of the earth. He did a short stint in juvie, before eventually outgrowing that phase of his life. He went to college and became a nurse.

In the hall, Luke's arms were crossed, his stethoscope slung around his neck. He cocked his head. "I don't know. It's just a hunch. But something seems off," he said, about the Becketts.

I couldn't let it go. "How?"

He gave some thought to it. "The mom doesn't make eye contact when she speaks. And earlier, when she first came in, she cried or seemed to cry. But there were no tears."

The bruises and the lacerations on Caitlin Beckett's face are hard to look at. I don't think I'll ever get used to them. There are smash fractures and soft tissue injuries on her skull and face. Her nose and jaw are broken and she has two black eyes. She's missing teeth. The rest of her body is worse, a medley of broken bones, torn ligaments, contusions. Her limbs are deadweight. I can maneuver them any which way I'd like and they would fall when I lift them, if I were to let go.

Many of her injuries are overt. But there

are things the doctors don't know yet, like whether there is nerve damage and, if she wakes up, if she'll be able to do things like blink, chew, smile. She may need surgery to repair the damage, to restore whatever function is lost and to improve her appearance, should she live, so that someday she looks like some version of herself.

In the afternoon, the nursing assistant Marianne comes and I ask the Becketts to leave us so that we can give Caitlin a bath. I pull the curtain for privacy. I avoid looking at Caitlin's face as I remove her gown. I cover her with a blanket while Marianne and I wash, careful not to expose any more of her than I need to. Bathing a patient is an intimate experience. It can be uncomfortable for everyone. When I give bed baths to patients who are conscious, we talk or I talk, if they're nonverbal. I ramble on about nothing, about anything, to avoid the awkwardness. But with someone who is unconscious, it's quiet. Marianne and I stand on opposite sides of the bed, working from the head down. It's not always a job for RNs. We don't always have time to bathe our own patients, but when I can, I do.

We roll Caitlin onto her side to wash her back. I check her skin at the same time, looking for bedsores, and then we change the sheets, which, on an occupied bed with a patient who can't assist, is a challenge. When we're done, we place the soiled bedding in a bag and then I take it away to be washed. Marianne offers to do it for me but I say no thanks, that I need to check on another patient and will take it on the way.

The other patient is a woman named Marin Layley, who's seventy-one years old, being treated for a stroke, though she has a number of comorbid conditions too like high blood pressure, heart disease and diabetes. She's lucky to be alive, though she's not out of the woods yet. She's in the ICU for close monitoring and frequent neuro checks. She also requires insulin four times a day, which she's due for. In the room, I find her insulin pen on the medical cart, where I last left it, and give her a dose. In theory, insulin pens shouldn't be left out in the open like this — where anyone could conceivably come in and take it if they wanted — but we don't always have time to put them back into patient specific bins in the medication room after each use. Sometimes it's more efficient to just leave them out.

On my way back to Caitlin's room, I round a corner to find a man in the room with her. I stop in the middle of the hall, taking him in. He stands with his back to the door so that I can't see his face; I only see him from behind, the tufts of dark hair that appear from beneath the back closure of a hat.

But even from behind, I know who he is. He's the same man who was here in the hospital a few days ago, standing in the hall just outside Caitlin's room, looking in.

A feeling of unease washes over me.

Who is he and what does he want?

He stares down at Caitlin in bed and there is something about the way he stands, his body language or the way he looks down at her, that makes me uncomfortable. There is nothing affectionate or benevolent about it. He doesn't touch her. He doesn't stroke her arm or her hair. He just stares, as if looking down on a dead body in a casket. The man is tall and slender. His presence, him turning up like this, takes me by surprise, because I didn't see him arrive and because, in the time that she's been here, no one has been in that room to visit except for Mr. and Mrs. Beckett.

"Meghan," a voice says, and I tear my eyes away from the man to find Luke sitting at the nurses' station beside me, studying me from over the computer screen.

"Sorry," I say. "Did you say something?"

"I asked if you were okay."

I don't answer because I don't know if I'm okay. Instead I ask, "Did you see that man come in?"

"What man?" he asks, and I nod toward Caitlin's room.

"Him," I breathe.

Luke's gaze follows the direction of mine and he takes him in, letting his eyes run over the jeans and the black thermal shirt, a lightweight jacket that lies at the end of the bed. He shakes his head. "No, but I was on a call just now," he says and, as I watch, he reaches forward to set the phone back in its cradle. "Maybe ask Anna."

"I will. Thanks."

Visitors are supposed to report to the nurses' station when they arrive. There are signs all over the ICU, which are hard to miss. That said, during visiting hours, the unit is unlocked; anyone could enter without consent, unlike overnight, when employees have to swipe a badge to get in.

I slide down the long desk to Anna, who sits on the other side of it. "Hey," I say, and she glances up from another computer screen. "The man in 214," I say, leaning in to whisper, and she looks over my shoulder and into the room, which is directly behind me now. "Did you see him come in?"

"No. Is everything okay?"

"Yes, I think so," I say, keeping my feelings to myself.

Despite my misgivings, I have to go in. I turn away from Anna. It takes a second to gather courage, but eventually I step forward, toward the room. The man hears me coming. He throws a glance back over his shoulder and I get my first good look at him.

"I didn't know anyone was here," I say, stepping inside the room, hearing something like fear in my voice. The man wears a green trucker cap, the brim of which darkens his face, though his eyes are a vivid blue. Dark curls spill out from beneath the hat. There are subtle lines around his eyes and mouth and if I had to guess an age, I'd say forty. "Are you . . . are you family?" I ask, swallowing hard, taking in his bent nose, which looks like it had been broken at some point in his life and was never properly realigned.

There is a moment of hesitation, during which he takes stock of me. His eyes travel over my face, down my neck to my chest, to where my name tag sits, just above my left breast. I follow his gaze, staring upside down at my own name and feeling my heartbeats gain speed. My full name is on the name tag. Meghan Michaels. My picture is there too. The state requires it of all health-care workers, going so far as to say how the letters in our name must be of a sufficient size and easy to read, and the picture must be current. It's to protect patients, to ensure they receive care from qualified professionals, but who or what protects us from them?

I've heard other nurses articulate their fears before, about how this or that has happened to someone they know: a discontented patient or family member learns their name, finds them on social media, finds out where they live, or a drug addict tracks them down, mistakenly believing nurses have free and unrestricted access to pills. We don't. Our privacy is at risk and sometimes our safety is too.

His eyes come back up to my face, which they peruse before finding my eyes. His head cocks and he's slow to speak, but when he does, he says, "No. A friend." I wonder if even that is true.

My words are tremulous. "I'm sorry," I say. "Only family is allowed to be here." It's not the hospital's rules, but what Mr. and Mrs. Beckett wanted.

He says nothing at first. His eyes hold mine and I wonder if it's meant to be intimidating, because it is. I have a very physical reaction to his stare. My chest tightens. My heart rate changes, becoming faster so that I can hear the whoosh of blood in my ears. I feel his stare all the way to my core, and I want so desperately to look away, to turn around, to see if Anna and Luke still sit at the nurses' station behind me, to know that they're there and I'm not alone, but I don't. I keep my eyes on his, telling myself that I have no reason to be scared.

He breaks his gaze then, reaching for a coat lying at the end of the bed. "I was just leaving," he says. He takes his coat into his hands and goes to move past me, stepping too close on the way to the door so that I fall back, so our elbows don't collide.

"I need pictures of me as a baby," Sienna says first thing when I walk into the apartment that night. She's in the living room with the TV on, wrapped in a blanket, doing homework. It was a long, restless walk home from work, because I couldn't stop thinking about the man who came to see Caitlin at the hospital, specifically his ice-cold eyes and the way they stared at me, making me feel uncomfortable, if not scared. I kept thinking for the rest of the day that he might still be at the hospital somewhere. I saw him leave her room; I didn't see him leave the building. It was unlikely, but something I couldn't shake. I looked all around for him when I left work, wondering if he was there, hiding out in the ambulance entrance or in the loading dock as I moved down Wellington and past them in the dark.

"Hello to you too," I tease, hanging my coat on a hook. "My day was fine, thanks for asking."

"It's for a school project," Sienna says curtly. She's been in a mood lately.

"When do you need them by?"

"Now. The project is due tomorrow."

"Sienna," I say, disappointed because Sienna never used to leave things until the last minute but it's becoming more common now. It's a teen thing — the lack of motivation, the poor time management — but the subtle changes in her behavior are becoming more apparent all the time. If it's not the slip in grades, the irritability or the way she blows hot and cold, then she's pushing the boundaries, impatient to grow up. I don't like it and I wonder what I have to blame for it — hormones, boys, Ben, *drugs?*

"What?" she asks, quick to take offense. "I looked. There are like none here."

She's right. There isn't enough room in

our apartment to keep things like photo albums, and Sienna was born at a time where not everything was digital as it is now. The first few years of her life are chronicled in scrapbooks that I keep in the building's basement, where there are large metal cages for each tenant's things, which hold everything I took from my life with Ben that I wasn't able to fit into the living space.

"They're in the basement," I say, and then I tell her I'll get them because it will be easier than to explain where they are. I grab my keys, head out the door and lock up behind myself, moving down the stairs to the foyer. Once there, I unlock the basement door and pull it open to an oppressive blackness. I reach for the light at the top of the stairs, flicking it on, but nothing happens. I toggle the switch up and down, but the basement stays dark. The light bulb at the bottom of the steps must have gone out.

I can't go back up to Sienna empty-handed. She'll be upset. Grudgingly I decide that I'll be okay because there is another light downstairs, an exposed bulb with a string that hangs from the low ceiling just above the washing machine.

I steel myself. I take a breath and step into the darkness. I leave the door behind me open, held secure by a door wedge that's always sitting in the foyer to hold the door open for deliveries and such. I feel grateful for the foyer light, which pales as I descend, moving further away from it, down the stairs' bare wooden treads and to the concrete floor at the bottom of the steps.

The light is on the other side of the basement. There are rusty, steel weight-bearing columns between it and me, which I try not to run into, feeling blindly with my hands. I regret leaving my phone upstairs because I could use the flashlight on it. Instead, I feel around for the string in the darkness, managing to conjure up all sorts of terrifying thoughts in the five or ten seconds before my hand connects with it, such as: *What if I'm not alone down here? What if someone is here with me?*

I flash back to the man's eyes from the hospital, how they were haunted.

When I find the string, relief floods me, though the amount of light the exposed bulb gives off is practically negligible.

I look around to make sure I'm alone, and I am. The basement is small. The walls are cinder block and the ceilings are low. It can't be more than six feet from the floor to the rafters, so that taller men would have to duck so as not to hit their heads.

The metal storage cages are against the

opposite wall, creating dark pockets where the light doesn't reach. I go to the cages, finding ours. It has a padlock on the door. I spin the dial, entering the combination and then pull down on the lock to open it. I slip the padlock off, replacing it over the metal loop so I don't misplace it while searching for the scrapbooks. The cage door creaks as I open it. I step inside, unwanted thoughts suddenly filling my mind about getting locked in the cage, whether accidentally or on purpose.

How long would it take for someone to find me? If I screamed, would anyone hear?

I begin to search. The faster I find the scrapbooks, the faster I can leave. I roll our bikes out of the way to get to the plastic storage containers stacked three high behind them. The containers are labeled and while some labels are specific — *Christmas lights* — others are not: *Keepsakes.* I find one of the bins labeled keepsakes and lift the lid, setting it aside. I start rifling through things like a wedding album and pairs of Sienna's adorable baby shoes, tiny Sherpa lined boo-ties and black ballet slippers that fit in the palm of my hand. Thoughts of baby Sienna crush me and I find myself on a trip down memory lane, discovering a lock of hair from her first haircut and a cozy, wearable

118

sleep sack that stirs up memories of sleepless nights in the rocking chair in her room — a time when I wished her older so she'd sleep through the night, but that I would give anything to have back now. I press the sleep sack to my chest, smelling it, embracing it.

I'm somewhere faraway, deep in thought. I'm not in the basement at all but in Sienna's nursery with lullabies playing so softly from the CD player that they won't wake Ben. The room is darkish, save for the starry globe-shaped night-light that projects stars on the ceiling and wall.

The cage door behind me suddenly creaks.

Someone is in the basement with me.

I come back, spinning, searching the room with my eyes. No one is here but me.

I try telling myself there must be a reasonable explanation for the door closing, such as that the heat kicked on, air from the vent inching the cage door closed. It doesn't make me feel any less afraid.

I think again about the man from the hospital. Conceivably he could have watched me leave. He could have followed me home. He could have come into the building, slipping in behind another tenant.

I push the cage door back open, feeling desperate to find the scrapbooks and leave.

When I do, I scoop them into my arms, relieved. I inch the cage door closed and replace the lock. I move to the other side of the room to pull the string to turn the light back off. Darkness falls over the basement, rendering me practically blind. I shuffle to the steps, feeling with my hands, worse off than before because my eyes have adapted to the light.

When I get to the bottom of the stairs, I'm thrown by the closed door at the top of the steps.

I left it open. I know I did.

I stand there in a state of suspended animation, looking up at the door. It couldn't have closed on its own because it was held open with the door wedge. Someone would have had to move the wedge and deliberately close the door, which doesn't mean their intent was malicious or unkind. Maybe they didn't know anyone was downstairs and they thought the door was left open by mistake. They were trying to help.

I jog up the steps. When I get to the top, I reach for the knob and try opening the door, but it doesn't budge.

I try again, with more force this time. "Hello?" I call out, pounding a palm on the door.

I press an ear to the door. I try to listen,

though my pulse beats hard, blood rushing through my ears. I can't decide if there is someone on the other side of the door or not. I'm not so sure but that I don't hear footsteps or the faint click of the latch sliding into place on another door.

"Hello?" I say again. "Is someone there?"

I knock. I wrap my hands around the knob and jerk at it, feeling frantic and desperate, wishing again that I hadn't left my phone upstairs. The world around me is nearly black, the only light a sliver of it coming from under the door.

It takes time, but eventually I hear another noise in the foyer, something closer and more distinct, and it takes a second but I place it: it's the jiggling of a key in the little recessed, aluminum mailbox slots that line the foyer wall.

I knock on the basement door again and this time, from the other side, the knob mercifully turns. The basement door swings open like nothing, and I brace myself for who I might find on the other side.

Mr. Hilman, the elderly neighbor from the first floor, stands in the foyer looking wide-eyed and confused.

"What are you doing down there?" he asks. "In the dark?"

"I . . . I went down to get something from

121

storage. When I tried to come back up, the door was stuck. The light switch isn't working," I say, toggling it up and down to show him. "The bulb must have gone out." My voice shakes as I say it. I feel stupid, but also scared.

"Because this," he says, "was lodged under the door." In his hand, he holds up the door wedge, which is more than just a wooden block, but something modern and grippy, and I can't make sense of it, how it came to be on the other side of the door from where I left it. "That's why you couldn't open it. How long were you down there?"

"Just a few minutes," I say, feeling short of breath. "I don't know how that happened. I . . . I don't know what I would have done if you didn't get home when you did." Sienna would have come for me eventually. If enough time passed, she would have gotten worried or impatient and come looking for me. I wouldn't have been down there all night.

I thank him again. I let myself into the stairwell and start to climb. My breathing is still heavy. My heart pounds as I make my way up the last flight of stairs to my apartment alone. When I get to my front door, I slip the key into the lock. I've been gone much longer than I intended. Not just a few minutes, but more like fifteen or twenty. I turn the door handle and open the door. Sienna is on the sofa still, wrapped in a blanket, her feet kicked up on the coffee table, doing homework on her laptop. She has no idea how long I've been gone.

But then, she looks at me, gazing slowly sideways. I don't know if it's the heavy breathing or the whiteness of my skin that gives me away, but her face changes and she asks, "What happened?" as I close and lock the apartment door and then carry the scrapbooks to her, leaning forward to set them on the coffee table beside her bare feet.

"Nothing," I say, lying because I don't want her to worry and because I keep telling myself that maybe nothing did happen, maybe it was just the landlord, the mailman with a late delivery or another neighbor. Maybe someone came in through the front door, saw the basement door open and thought they were being good Samaritans by closing it. "I'm just tired. Hungry. It was a long, crazy day and it's catching up with me. There are the scrapbooks. Take whatever you need. I have to get something to eat." I keep walking to the kitchen, where I'll be out of view, because I don't want Sienna to see me like this. I don't want her to worry. I don't want her to think something is wrong.

I don't go for food right away; instead, I lean against the countertop, trying to get control of my breath.

Later, after I've settled down, Sienna asks me to look through the pictures with her. She and I snuggle together under the blanket on the sofa. We flip through the pages of the scrapbook, and Sienna asks questions like what Ben and I would have named her if she was a boy and if it was hard for us to get pregnant with her. The second strikes me as a strange question to ask, but Sienna says that Nico's mom and dad had trouble getting pregnant with him. "Isaac," I say, and then, careful with my words, "No. As with most everything about you, it was a breeze. You made it too easy."

"I like this one," she says, pointing to a picture of her and me together. In it, she's about two weeks old, sound asleep in a pink one-piece against my chest while I sit, reclined in a chair, my head turned, smiling sleepily for the camera, which is to my left. Sienna's scalp is smooth, with tiny, ultrafine blond hairs that get caught in a beam of light coming from a window across the room. Her mouth is open like a baby robin's and her eyes are closed. She's peaceful and asleep. We both look so content.

"Me too," I say, as Sienna rests her head on my shoulder and I turn the page.

I try to lose myself in the moment, to forget about what happened before.

But the one thought that keeps nagging at me is that, even if the landlord or another neighbor closed the basement door, thinking someone left it open by mistake, why would they put the door wedge under it?

I can't shake the thought that someone tried to trap me downstairs.

EIGHT

I see her through the window of the restaurant the following night. The restaurant was my suggestion. It's an intimate coffee shop slash wine bar just off Halsted, which used to be one of my favorite places to meet up with friends back when that was something I still did.

My phone rings on the way. I answer the call.

"Is this Meghan Michaels?" the woman on the other end of the line asks, her voice hard to hear over the noise of the city.

"Yes," I say, holding a hand to the opposite ear to block out the noise.

"Hi Meghan, I'm calling from Dr. Berry's office about your recent mammogram."

"Is everything okay?" I ask, my voice hesitant, knowing it's not, of course. They don't call with mammogram results unless there's a problem.

"There was an asymmetry on the right

breast, which is most likely nothing to worry about. Most of the time, it's not cancer. Still, we're going to need additional imaging studies to be safe."

"Okay," I say, feeling anxious, and she gives me a number to call for a different radiology office than where I've been, one with different equipment.

I put the phone away when we're through, trying not to think about it for now — as she just said *Most of the time, it's not cancer.* Still, easier said than done. I walk fast, dodging pedestrian traffic, but end up getting caught at a red light just before the intersection. I stand at the light, watching through the glass where Nat waits for me, seated at a table on the enclosed patio that stays open year-round, kept warm with a fire and heat lamps. She sits beside a massive stone fireplace, facing out onto the street, under a set of clear string lights. Through the glass, the whole scene looks inviting and snug and warm.

As I wait for the illuminated walking person to tell me to cross, I watch her in the near distance, her hands folded around a mug, staring blankly out into the night, her mind seemingly somewhere else. Behind her, a waiter carries a tray of drinks past a young man who slips into a coat, getting

127

ready to leave.

The light turns green. The walking hand appears, and I cross, bypassing people in the way because I'm already fifteen minutes late and feeling guilty for it. I sent her a message on Facebook and told her that I got caught up at work and was running behind, but the last time I checked, three blocks away, she hadn't read the message yet. I was worried she would give up and leave before I arrived.

When I get there, I pull the door open and let myself in through the main entrance, weaving between tables and chairs for the patio. "Hey," I burst out with, coming up behind her in a rush. "I'm so sorry I'm —"

And then I freeze because, at the sound of me, she jolted, the mug in her hands getting shaken so abruptly that coffee sloshes over the edge and onto the table. "Oh my gosh," I'm quick to say, springing into action, coming around to the other side of the table, where there are napkins, which I reach for, using them to sop up the mess. "I'm so sorry," I say again, more gently this time, studying her as she lowers the mug to the table and then lets go of it, and when she does, I see how her hands gently shake.

"It's fine," she says, bringing them to her lap where I can't see them.

"I didn't mean to startle you. Here, let me get you another coffee," I say, my eyes searching for the waiter, who's a few tables away, taking another customer's order. It wasn't the whole cup that spilled, but this was not the first impression I was hoping to make after all these years, and I want to remedy that.

"No," she says. "You don't need to do that."

"Are you sure? I feel so bad."

"Please don't worry about it."

I lower my arm. I set my bag on the floor and sink into a seat. I had the presence of mind to change into something before I left work, and so I'm in jeans and a blouse instead of the frumpy scrubs she saw me in the other night. "It was my fault," she goes on. "I'm such a klutz. Always spilling things and hurting myself." She chuckles, though her laugh feels unnatural, strained. She looks away from me and, at the same time, tucks a strand of hair behind her ear. It's an instinct, a habit. She doesn't realize what she's done, but with her hair out of the way, there it is again, up close and personal this time: the bruise. My eyes go to it.

Nat brings her own eyes slowly back. She catches me looking at the bruise. Right away, she releases her hair from behind an ear and tries to hide it, but it's too late. I can't unsee what I already saw.

I swallow. What I want to ask is how she got the bruise, but instead I say, more staidly this time, "I'm really sorry I'm late. I hate to be late," thinking how good it feels to finally sit down after a full day of being on my feet. "I got caught up at work and couldn't get away."

"Busy day?" she asks. Her hair hangs long now, like dark curtains around her face, spilling over the shoulders of a black mock neck shirt that comes clear up to her chin.

"Yes. Very," I say.

"What do you do?"

"I'm a nurse. Critical care."

"Oh wow. Meghan. That very admirable. But it must be stressful too?"

"Yes, it is," I say. "But rewarding. I like to help people." I leave it at that because as a rule, I don't talk about my patients outside of work. Other nurses do — anonymously — but it's a HIPAA violation nonetheless because, even without saying a patient's name, someone else might pick up on identifying characteristics and know who the person is. Most of the time, I'm a stickler for rules. I don't like to break them but, rules aside, not talking about my patients is a good habit for keeping work

130

out of my personal life.

"I can't remember. Did you always want to be a nurse?" she asks.

I smile. "Either that or an astronaut. Until I learned that astronauts have to wear diapers in outer space and then suddenly it didn't seem as desirable a career choice."

She laughs and this time, there is an ease about it.

She slowly sobers and says, "You must see all sorts of horrible things though. Sick people and death. It has to be hard, especially after what happened with Bethany." My throat tightens at the mention of my sister's name. "I'm sorry," she says. "You probably don't want to talk about that."

"No," I say, "it's okay."

"I heard what happened," she says. Of course she did. Everyone we went to high school with knew that the year after I graduated, Bethany killed herself. "I wanted to reach out. I can't even remember if I sent a sympathy card."

"I'm sure you did."

Nat would have been a freshman in college at the time, like me. I can't remember if or where she went to school, but if she went away, it would have been hard for her to come back for the funeral. And anyway, Nat and I were friends, but it wasn't as

131

though we were best friends. We were teammates. We had a friendship in the locker room and on the court, but we never got together to hang out on a Friday night. Once I started dating Ben in high school, I spent more time with him than my friends anyway. Ben was there at the funeral with me, standing by my side through the services.

After I returned to college, I abandoned all aspects of my past life except for Ben and tried to forget what happened, as if that was possible. My parents left my childhood home, citing too many painful memories, and there was never a reason to go back. Even Ben's parents eventually gave up on Midwest winters and left.

"I heard you married Ben Long."

"I did," I say, and then I give a short, wry laugh and add, "You can see how that worked out."

"I'm sorry."

"Don't be. I should have known better. Almost no high school relationships last. It was naive to think ours would be different. Did you know Ben in high school?"

"Not really. We had a couple classes together, I think. I'm not sure we ever talked."

I nod, realizing how long ago high school

suddenly feels. So many years have passed that many names and faces have become hazy if not altogether gone. "What do you do for a living?" I ask, changing the subject, though I already know what she does because I saw it on Facebook. After I finished looking at Nat's Facebook page the other day, I went to Instagram to see if I could find out more about her there, but no luck. She isn't on Instagram as far as I could tell.

"I'm a teacher."

"What grade?"

"Preschool. Four-year-olds."

I smile. "Aww. Little ones," I say.

"Yes. They're the best."

"Where do you teach?" I ask, and she tells me about the co-op preschool in Lincoln Park. "Do you have kids yourself?"

"No. My husband and I wanted to wait until we were married for a few years to have kids," she says, her hands back on the table now, fingering the handle of her coffee mug, and then her voice drifts and I catch her drift: their marriage didn't last that long.

The waiter comes. I order a chai tea, though after the day I've had and the news I just received from Dr. Berry's office, I could use a glass of chardonnay. *Most of the time, it's not cancer,* the woman on the phone had said, but what she didn't say is that sometimes it is.

I consider it for a minute — ordering wine — but with Sienna waiting at home and work in the morning, the last thing I need is a foggy head or a wine headache. "What are you drinking?" I ask Nat, wanting to get her another coffee to make up for the one she spilled, but she demurs.

"If I have another coffee, I won't sleep tonight."

"Decaf?" I suggest.

She looks to the waiter and says, "I'll just have some water, please," and the waiter says of course and leaves.

Beside us, the fire in the fireplace crackles. Orange flames dance behind the screen, licking the air.

"The irony being," she says, coming back to the conversation, and I look away from the fireplace and to her, "that we wanted time for us, for our marriage to blossom before bringing kids into the equation. I should be grateful, I suppose, that I had time to figure out who he really is before having children with him."

Without meaning for them to, my eyes go back to the bruise and, though I can't see it behind the panels of hair, I still know it's there.

She catches me looking.

134

"It's awful, right?" she says.

"What is?" I ask, playing dumb because I feel guilty that I've been caught staring again.

"This," she says, gingerly pulling her hair somewhat back to reveal the edges of the bruise to me. The revelation is brief, and then she covers it up again, positioning the pieces of hair back into place to hide the wound.

I pull a face. "Ouch. What happened?" I ask, trying to react like the bruise is brand-new to me, like this is the first time I'm seeing it.

"The other night," she says, reaching for and fiddling with the edge of a paper napkin, reluctant to meet my eye, "I got up in the middle of the night to use the bathroom. I was half out of it. I'd had a glass of wine before bed, but that's no excuse. I was totally sober. I don't know what happened. I lost my bearings, I guess. I was disoriented from sleep, or I stood up too fast, something like that. Anyway, in the darkness, I miscalculated, walking straight into the doorframe instead of through the open door."

I grimace. "That must have hurt."

She shakes her head. "It didn't, actually. It stunned me because I wasn't expecting it, but it didn't hurt." She pats at her head again, makes sure the hair is where it belongs. She looks at me, and then she looks away again, her voice lowered as she says, "I keep trying to cover it up because I don't want people to get the wrong idea."

"Like what?" I ask.

She shrugs. "I don't know, that someone is hurting me or something."

A beat of silence follows. I want to ask if someone is hurting her and, if so, if it's her ex, the handsome man in the Facebook images I saw. Mr. Roche. But then, before I can, the waiter comes back with our drinks, going on and on about how he didn't know if she wanted bottled or tap water, and, by the time he leaves, the moment is gone.

"Do you still talk to anyone else from high school, besides Ben?" she asks, and suddenly it doesn't feel right to dredge up the bruise again.

"Not really."

"Mandy Cho?" she asks and I shake my head. In high school, Mandy was my doubles partner, though we didn't talk to one another off the court. We had opposite strengths — Mandy was a big hitter, while I was a pretty consistent returner — and so the tennis coach paired us together, not because we were friends but to balance our strengths and weaknesses. "Do you?"

"No. Not much. I lost touch with just about everyone after high school. It was my fault. I'm terrible at keeping up with people."

"What about Emily?" I ask because Emily Miller was Nat's closest friend in high school.

"Some. She calls every couple months."

"It's hard, right? Everyone is so busy. How is your family?" I ask. "Are they still in Barrington?"

"No, not anymore." She changes topics. "This place is nice," she says about the restaurant. "You said you've been here before?"

I nod, taking a tentative sip of my tea, testing to see how hot it is. "It is. Yes. A friend found it years ago and I've been coming ever sense. Quaint, quiet." The drinks and food are good, but it's mostly the vibe I like: the soft, warm lighting; cool jazz playing in the background; the atmosphere.

I ask what she thought of the meeting the other day.

"It was nice. It felt good to be surrounded by people in a similar circumstance for a change."

"That's one of the reasons I love it too."

She asks, "How long have you and Ben been divorced?"

"About a year," I say, and then I tell her what I told the others my first time at the support group: how I was the one who filed for divorce and how I did so for my daughter, Sienna, because I couldn't stand for her to see Ben and me fight anymore.

She changes positions on the chair. "My family and friends absolutely love Declan," she offers. "They were enamored the first time they met him. They think he's *the perfect guy,* as if there is such a thing. Sweet, charming, attractive, with a great job that pays well." She takes a breath and I hold mine, hoping she'll say more, and she does. "It's hard to talk about Declan with them because they have this preconceived notion of who he is, and what I say is at odds with that notion. I don't think they believe me when I tell them."

"Tell them what?"

"What he's like."

I take another sip of my tea, too fast this time so that it burns my tongue. "What is he like?" I ask, trying not to react as I lower the mug to the table.

She reaches for her ice water, running her fingers through the beads of condensation on the outside of the glass. I watch her, waiting for a reply that doesn't come.

"I'm sorry," I say, shaking my head. "You

don't need to answer that. Would you rather we talk about something else?" I ask because I can tell this conversation is making her uncomfortable, and I don't want to do that. It's been twenty-some years since we've laid eyes on each other. The last thing I want is to come on too strong.

"No," she says, sliding her glass away, looking slowly up. "It's okay. This is actually good for me, I think, to talk about Declan with someone who doesn't know him for a change. I considered a therapist but the wait lists are months long, and there's something nice about talking to someone you actually know, to someone who gets it, to someone who's in a similar position, instead of someone who is getting paid to listen to me, you know?"

I smile. "I do. I know. It's the same reason I found that group. Misery loves company, right?"

She nods, though it's brief. "Right." She reaches for the glass of ice water again, lifting it into her hands, biding time, deciding whether to say more or to let the conversation drop. A man and a woman pass by beside her then, stealing her attention, and she waits — watching as they slip past, happy and laughing, him helping her into the sleeves of a long winter coat — before bringing the glass to her lips. She takes a sip and sets the glass down on the tabletop. Her eyes come to mine.

"He's been cheating on me, with some younger woman, but that's not the worst of it." She pauses, gaining courage. "Declan is a lawyer, an associate at Tanner & Levine in the Loop. He'll be up for partner in another couple years, which is a big deal — huge really — but it's not without pressure and personal cost. It's a seven-year track, which he's been aspiring to since the day he started working at the firm, five years ago. It was a career change for him. Now he bills something like two thousand hours a year, which means twelve-hour days and weekends a couple times a month. He's incredibly smart. Persuasive. A hard worker. He's very good at what he does. But . . ." she says, swallowing hard, her eyes suddenly averting, shying away from mine. Her voice sinks low so that it's hard to hear over the sound of music through the sound system, and by instinct I lean forward in my seat, watching her face, though she stares out the window as she confesses, "He can get mad sometimes. He —"

She stops what she's saying midsentence. She goes silent, her mouth still formed around the word, not producing sound, the rest of her thoughts trapped somewhere in her throat. I watch as her posture straightens, as her spine lifts from the chair's backrest. Her face changes too, the color whitening, blood draining, going blank.

"Nat? Is everything okay?" I ask as I follow her gaze to the corner window, where, on the other side, a dark form retreats.

On the glass is a small cloud of condensation as if from someone's breath.

A chill rises up my spine as I watch the fog disappear. I look back to see Nat's eyes blink hard, and when she swallows again, I watch the forced movement of it in her throat, like dislodging a rock. "I — I'm sorry," she says. For one fleeting second, she breaks her gaze to glance at me and then her eyes go back to the window, which is empty now save for the onrush of pedestrians, bundled up in coats and hats, moving down the street. There's a vibration to her voice when she says, "I completely forgot. A friend is sick. I promised her I'd drop off dinner tonight. She has the flu. I have to go."

She takes her napkin from her lap. She tries to drop it on the table, though it misses by an inch and flutters to the ground just beside it. Standing up quickly, Nat reaches for the coat from the back of the chair, jabbing her arms into it though she's anxious and so the movement isn't fluid; it takes two or three times to find the armholes.

"Now?" I ask, looking at my watch, seeing that it's already after eight o'clock.

"Yes," she says, though it's not lost on me how she's still looking out the window and won't meet my eye. "Well, I was supposed to be there an hour ago. She'll be wondering where I am. If she's even still awake."

She digs in her bag and hands me a twenty, which I try to turn down but she won't let me. "Please. Take it," she says. "You were so kind to suggest this. I feel like a jerk for leaving so fast. But . . ."

"Your friend is sick. I understand. Please, go," I say. "We can do this another time."

She picks her way around tables and chairs for the main entrance, squeezing through chairs backed too closely together, disappearing somewhere I can't see.

A few seconds later I watch out the window as she appears in the night, her hat on, a fur-trimmed hood pulled over it. She risks a glance down the street and then waits for a small group of people to catch up to her before merging with them, her head down, walking fast.

I leave the cash on the table. I follow her out into the night, letting the door drop

142

from my hand, my eyes sweeping the street for signs of her or for the amorphous shape in the glass.

But they're gone.

Just outside the restaurant, I send a quick text to Sienna to let her know I'm on my way, and then I put my phone in a coat pocket because I need to have my wits about me. It's just after eight o'clock. The attacks those other nights happened right around this same time, and I'm on edge already, thinking about what Nat just said, or almost said — *He can get mad sometimes. He* — She never had a chance to finish what she was going to say before something on the other side of the window stole her attention. I fill in the blanks for myself.

He has a temper. He loses control. He hits me.

I think back to about four or five years ago, when I took care of a woman in the ICU who had suffered a brain hemorrhage as a result of domestic abuse. Her name was Anne, and her husband brought her in through emergency himself, claiming a misstep on the basement stairs, except that I could see how nervous she was, how she couldn't look me in the eye, how she — like Nat — blamed herself for the supposed fall:

I'm so clumsy. I'm such a klutz. My feet slipped right out from under me. I was going too fast. I'm so stupid. She was wearing socks and the basement steps, she said, were a gleaming hardwood. She slipped, her head somehow managing to ricochet off the wall before hitting the floor. She thought she was fine — just a bump on the head — until the blinding headaches began and she started to vomit. Her husband stood attentive by her side, doting on her, reluctant to leave the room even when we asked him to for an exam.

Alone, she was loath to say what happened at first, but as nurses, we're trained to look for signs of violence, and I saw them. In time, with gentle prodding, she came clean, saying how he'd beaten her with a hockey stick while their two children — ages three and six — watched on, huddled together in the corner, crying hysterically, begging him to stop. That said, she didn't want to get him in trouble. She loved him. She pleaded with me not to tell anyone, saying how he was sorry. He told her he'd never do it again and she believed him because she wanted so badly for that to be true.

I called the police, but there was only so much they could do because Anne didn't press charges, and then after, I worried I'd made it worse because her husband knew she'd opened up to me about the abuse. Instead of pressing charges or leaving him, she and the children stayed and I read an article sometime in the last couple of years that made me physically sick: how he'd been arrested after finally succeeded in beating her to death.

I remember I was upset. I remember, too, that Ben blamed her, the victim, because she hadn't left when given the opportunity. She stayed and chose her fate. He said something glib like *You can't save them all,* but I wondered for a long time after if I could have or should have done more, but what?

I put it out of my mind for now. I keep walking. The walk home is windy and cold, though the other night's snow has melted, daytime temperatures surging past freezing only to fall again when the sun goes down. The streetlights are on. The shops and restaurants are open, the lights inside all ablaze, which comes as a comfort. On these busy streets, I don't feel worried or scared.

But when I get to my little residential street, things change. The world around me becomes suddenly quiet and dark, and I start thinking about the women who were attacked in recent days, wondering if they were like me: cold and tired with aching feet, eager to be home, and if they let their guards down too soon, which is easy to do when home is within view.

I glance back over a shoulder to make sure I'm alone, and I am, as far as I can tell. The sound of my footsteps echoes down the street. I slip my hand into my bag, feeling blindly for my keys. I can't find them at first and I get mad at myself for not taking them out of my bag back on Broadway, when there were people around. I should have thought ahead. I should have been more careful, more prepared. My search feels futile — Where the hell are my keys? — and I start to wonder if it's possible they fell out of my bag at some point in the night, if they're somewhere at work or on the restaurant floor.

Just as my anxiety kicks in, my fingers curl around the keys.

My walk home takes me past two boarded-up, derelict buildings and a somewhat skeevy parking lot before I get to Sienna and my apartment. The parking lot sits beneath the L tracks just adjacent to our building, and even in broad daylight is dark and dingy, the tracks overhead blocking the sun from getting in. The parking spots are owned by local residents, but some rent theirs out for cash on apps like SpotHero when they manage to find street parking for their own cars. It's a nice side hustle, but it invites strangers into the neighborhood, which I don't like.

I walk fast past it as the L soars by overhead, deafening me. I try not to dwell on the one car that sits idle in the parking lot with its headlights on.

I walk faster, jogging up the steps to Sienna and my building, slipping the key into the lock, letting myself into the foyer, where the wind makes its way in with me, rustling the pages of a newspaper that sits abandoned in the corner, behind the open door.

I press the door closed so I know I haven't been followed in. I start climbing the steps to our apartment. When I'm between the first and second floors, I hear a man's voice coming from higher up, which is where Sienna and I live. Ours is the only apartment on the third floor.

My heart rhythm hastens.

What is a man doing at our apartment?

I take the steps two at a time, my bag slipping from my shoulder to the crook of my arm. I leave it there, not wanting to take the time to push it back up. Suddenly Sienna is all I can think about. I need to get to Sienna.

I round the corner and see her first, and practically heave a sigh of relief because she's okay. She stands there in the open doorway in her pajamas, a pair of plaid, flannel boxer shorts and a boxy, cropped T-shirt that reveals a small amount of pale midriff, her feet bare, one foot balanced on top of the other, her arms knotted across her chest. She's already washed up for bed. Her face is bare, sans makeup, her hair thrown into a messy topknot, and if I had to guess, she's not wearing a bra.

Sienna sees me. Her head and her eyes come to me, gazing over this man's shoulder. He stands in the hall just outside my front door with his back to me. "Mom," Sienna says, a lilt to her voice as the man spins around so that I can see his face. He's an actual man — not some teenage boy like the other day — but a grown adult, thirty-five to forty years old if I had to guess, wearing jeans, a blue button-down, and he meets me with an uncurbed smile that I don't return, that I can't return because smiling is the furthest things from my mind.

"What's going on?" I ask, breathless. I hear the strain in my voice as I step past him, putting myself between him and Sienna. I don't wait for someone to tell me what's going on. Instead I ask, "Can I help you with something?" trying to ascertain how he got into the building in the first place and what he's doing at my apartment door, talking to my teenage daughter alone. I thrust my bag up onto my shoulder and cross my arms, wishing for more height to have greater leverage.

"I'm Evan," he says, extending a hand that I don't take, thinking that he's some kind of salesman, and how inappropriate — if not illegal — that he's gotten into our apartment building at this time of night to try and sell us something we don't want or need. There isn't a No Soliciting sign on the front door that I can remember, but one would think a locked door would suffice.

"What can I do for you, Evan?" I ask, a tartness to my words that doesn't sound like me.

"Mom," Sienna says, and I hear the disapproval in her voice, the embarrassment, because of how I'm acting and because I still haven't taken the man's hand. In fact, I don't take his hand, and ultimately he withdraws it, humbling. As he slips his hand into the pockets of his jeans, his smile fades.

"I'm sorry," he says. "I don't mean to impose. My wife and I just moved into the

149

apartment downstairs. We got some of your mail by mistake. I came to return it."

I draw in a breath, thinking of the movers I saw the other day, hauling boxes and furniture inside. I look back to Sienna. Said mail, I see now, is in her hand. It was hard to see at first because of the way her arms are crossed, but she uncrosses them and waves the envelope in my face. I look at it and then I let my eyes go back to the man.

I take a step back, into the apartment, bumping into Sienna, who falls a step back herself and then turns and retreats further into the living room. I reach for the door to close it. "Thank you for bringing the mail up. That was kind of you," I say, and then I actually close the door, putting a stop to any further conversation.

I watch the man's expression go flat as the door closes, though my pulse thrums in my neck and my heart beats with such force that I need to sit down.

"That was so embarrassing," Sienna declares when the door is closed and the dead bolt locked. I turn to face her as she drops down onto the sofa, kicking her feet up on the edge of the coffee table so it slides forward an inch, taking the rug with it, buckling the wool. "Did you really just kick him out?"

I don't answer her. Instead I ask, "What were you thinking, Sienna?" I still stand, staring at her aghast from the other side of the coffee table. "You know better than to open the door to a stranger."

"He's not a stranger. He's our *neighbor,* Mom," she says, which he is, but she didn't know that when she opened the door for him, and either way, he's still a stranger; we don't know him. "Besides," she goes on, very blasé as if she has no idea what could have happened to her tonight if that man had different intentions, "I thought it was you. You said you were on your way home so when he knocked, I thought it was you."

She's right. I did. I texted her maybe twenty minutes ago from outside the restaurant to let her know I was on my way. But still, the thought of Sienna opening the door to a stranger scares me. She should know better and I thought she did, but now I'm not so sure anymore.

"You didn't have to be so mean to him," she says.

"I wasn't mean."

"You weren't exactly *nice.*"

Fair point. I wasn't, but he caught me off guard. I was scared for Sienna's sake. "Listen," I say, "next time use the peephole, okay? It's there for a reason."

151

"What reason?"

"To keep us safe."

"From what?" she asks, and again, her optimism scares me a little, that feeling that bad things happen to other people and not her.

"There are bad people out there in the world, Sienna. Not everyone has good intentions. There is a man out there attacking women in their own homes. You watch the news — you know that. You have to be more careful. You can't trust everyone you meet. Okay?" I ask, and she says okay back, but her eyes are on her phone, and I'm only fifty percent sure she's listening.

NINE

The next morning, I pick up my mail on the way out of the building, dropping it into my bag to make room for today's to fit. As I walk to work, I overhear two women just ahead of me talking about another attack in the city last night and it unmoors me. I didn't turn the TV on this morning. I didn't read the news. I didn't know about this latest attack. There have been so many now I'm losing count. They say he wears a black mask when he goes after women, so no one has gotten a good look at him.

It's been weeks now and still no one knows who he is.

At work, the police come.

I've just come back from a quick lunch to find two male officers standing inside Caitlin's room. I come to a dead stop before the nurses' station when I see them. My feet stop moving all of a sudden and my body has a very visceral reaction at seeing the police. The uniforms. Their hulking bodies. Guns and tasers on their vests.

All other thoughts are quickly dispelled from my mind. The only thing I can think about is why they're here. We have had police in the ICU before, but not when it's a suicide attempt because there's nothing illegal about trying to take your own life.

The officers are in the room, speaking to Caitlin's parents. There is another man there too, in his thirties if I had to guess, standing behind Mrs. Beckett with a hand on her shoulder, the gesture warm, intimate. He knows her; he's not with the police. Through the glass, everyone looks very bleak. One of the officers has his back to me, while the other is angled sideways, his hands resting on the chest of his load bearing vest while the other officer does the talking.

I brush up beside Luke in the nurses' station. "What's happening?" I ask in a quiet voice. "Why are the police here?" I hold my breath, afraid of what he might say.

He looks at me. "They're saying now that maybe it wasn't a suicide attempt after all."

I pull back. The air leaves my lungs and the hallway turns suddenly warm.

"What do you mean?"

He blinks hard, and I know what he's going to say before he says it.

"They think that maybe she was pushed."

"Pushed?" I ask, like I don't understand the meaning of that little one-syllable word. I say it again and then again in my mind until it loses meaning. *Pushed.*

"Yes," he says, quite calm in comparison to my own reaction, yet he's had a few minutes to sit with it, to live with the knowledge of what the police know, to bat it around in his mind. "Pushed."

"By who?"

"No one knows."

The Becketts look up as I enter the room. They're adrift, their minds a million miles away from this hospital room. The police have left, but the other man is still here, standing propped against a wall, his arms crossed against a dark crewneck sweater. His gaze lifts when I come in; our eyes meet and I see the resemblance right away. He's a younger version of Mr. Beckett in height and body shape, but with Caitlin's features: the same dark hair and eyes.

"Meghan," Mr. Beckett says, rubbing at his forehead before zeroing his heavy eyes in on me, and it strikes me how utterly done in he looks, with both mental strain and

155

physical exhaustion.

"Can I get you anything?" I ask.

"No," he says, with a curt shake of the head, and I try not to read into the brevity of his reply. Mrs. Beckett turns away, saying nothing. She sits on the chair beside the bed, pulled up close to it with her back to me so that I can't see her face. "Meghan, this is our son. Jackson."

"It's nice to meet you," I say, coming further into the room where the air is different all of a sudden, charged.

"You too," he says, pushing himself from the wall. "I've heard quite a lot about you from my parents."

My eyes go to Mr. Beckett, who says, "We told him how much you've been doing to help us and how you're a godsend."

"It's nothing. I'm happy to help."

"Well, we're grateful. Jackson," he tells me, "flew in this morning to be here, to be with Caitlin. He landed just a couple hours ago and came straight from O'Hare."

"It was nice of you to come," I say.

"I'm just sorry I couldn't be here sooner." Jackson steps closer to the bedside, coming to stand behind Mrs. Beckett. His hands fall to her shoulders, offering comfort. I watch him, watching the way his eyes go to Caitlin in bed. I search in vain for signs of emotion, of sadness, of disbelief, finding none, but maybe he's just being stoic. It's been days since she arrived at the hospital and, I shouldn't judge, but I think how, if Bethany were still alive and something like this happened to her, I wouldn't have hesitated; I would have been on the first plane I could find.

"You're here now, and we're grateful. Caitlin would be too," Mr. Beckett says, and I wonder if anyone but me notices the way Jackson quietly sneers at his father's words — *Caitlin would be too* — something cynical rising to the surface before it disappears.

My mind goes back to what Mrs. Beckett told me in confidence days ago, how Caitlin and her brothers aren't close, how her own relationship with Caitlin is different than the one she has with her sons, and how she isn't so sure but that they don't resent Caitlin for it.

Jackson must feel me looking at him because his eyes move swiftly to mine, too quickly to anticipate, and he catches me staring.

"Our oldest, Henry," Mr. Beckett goes on, and I look to him, embarrassed and grateful for somewhere else to focus my attention, "wishes he was here too, but he's in the middle of a trial and can't get away. Jackson

157

was in London for work when it happened," he says. "He got here as soon as he could."

"You must be exhausted if you've just come from London," I say, thinking of the long flight and of jet lag.

He shrugs. "Nothing a little caffeine won't fix."

I nod, looking back to Mr. Beckett. "I saw the police here earlier," I say, treading lightly.

The Becketts are at first reticent. The three of them exchange a glance, but it's Mrs. Beckett who turns to me and asks, "Did you hear what they're saying?"

In the last couple hours, the gossip mill has been at it again. It's all anyone is talking about, how Caitlin Beckett was pushed from the pedestrian bridge. I've heard it again and again — at the nurses' station, in the break room. *Did you hear? The police were here. Caitlin Beckett didn't jump after all. She was pushed.* Eyes glinted as they spoke. *Dear God* and *How awful,* people said, but their voices betrayed them. They were less compassionate and more gossipy, everyone eager to find someone who hadn't yet heard so they could be the one to break the news.

Every time I heard it, I bristled, thinking of the final shove that drove her over the edge.

"Yes," I say, swallowing. "I did. It's awful. I'm so sorry. Are they certain?"

"Yes."

"Do they know who did it?" I ask.

Mrs. Beckett shakes her head as Jackson releases his hands from her shoulders, stepping back. There is this vacant, wooden expression on her face, though it's not quite the same grief she's been wearing on her sleeve the last few days; it's something different. She turns away from me again; her eyes stray to her daughter on the bed. She scootches forward to the edge of her seat, stretching a hand to move a section of dark hair that's fallen on Caitlin's forehead, gently sweeping it aside and then staring for a long while at the stillness of her daughter's face.

"The police don't know. There was a witness. A woman who saw Caitlin on the bridge that day. Someone else was there," Mr. Beckett says, and my heartbeats quicken at his words.

"Why would anybody do this?" Mrs. Beckett asks, holding back tears.

This time, it's Mr. Beckett who places a hand on her shoulder. "I don't know, honey. I don't know," and then to me he says, "She, this witness, was in a car on Lake Shore Drive, driving past. She didn't get more

159

than a few seconds' look, but she's certain there were two people on the bridge that day. She didn't actually see Caitlin get pushed, otherwise she would have called the police right away, but she saw something happening on that bridge, something contentious. And then she drove on and forgot all about it because it's a big city and altercations happen all the time, and she wasn't entirely sure it wasn't just two people screwing around."

Mr. Beckett's phone rings then. He takes it from his pocket, looking down at the screen. "I'm sorry," he says, "but I have to take this. It's for work." He excuses himself, stepping out into the hall to take the call.

Mrs. Beckett turns to me, picking up where her husband left off. "This woman didn't give it another thought until that segment the other day on the news, about suicide in the city. I didn't see it but I heard about it. She knew our Caitlin didn't jump like they said. Something else happened on the bridge that day. The police looked into it. Caitlin was living with a friend, but she had started working with a Realtor just a few weeks ago. She was looking into condos to buy. Caitlin was putting down roots. Who thinks of the future and does things like looking for condos to buy if they're suicidal?"

She locks eyes with me, and I see something new in them now. Shock, anger and fear, but even more than that: relief. Her daughter wasn't depressed like she thought, and she didn't have a desire to die. "They're saying it was an attempted *homicide,* Meghan. Not a suicide attempt after all. Which means Caitlin didn't try and take her own life like we thought." There's a long, pregnant pause and then she says, "Someone else did."

My stomach clenches. Homicide. *Murder.* It sounds so brutal, so cold-blooded when she says it that my mouth turns suddenly acidic, tasting like vinegar as saliva collects under my tongue and in my mouth.

"Do you think it's possible someone lured her to that bridge?" she asks now, speculating.

"Maybe," I say, my shoulders rising up into a shrug.

"Do you think whoever did this was there, waiting for her to come?"

I shake my head. "I don't know." Now that the police are involved, they will focus on finding who did this. Twenty-four hours ago that was irrelevant, but now it's the only thing that matters, aside from keeping Caitlin alive, though as the days pass and every day I come in to find her still unconscious, I wonder if she'll always be that way.

"What is it, Meghan?" she asks, and I realize I'm not looking at her anymore, that my eyes have strayed and I'm staring at the bare white wall, somewhere faraway.

"There was a man here the other day," I say, meeting her eye. "He came to see Caitlin." As I say it, I think of his eyes again, the way they traveled my body to my name tag, looking at it with interest.

"A man?" Mr. Beckett asks, returning to the room just then, coming to stand beside his wife, concern manifest in the lines of his forehead. I should have told them about this man before, and now I wish I had, that I hadn't kept that to myself.

I watch as he slips an arm around the small of her waist, drawing her close. "You didn't tell us," he says, and at first, it sounds like an accusation and maybe it is.

"No. I didn't. I'm sorry," I say, my face hot. "I didn't think it was worth mentioning. He said he was a friend."

"What was his name?"

"He didn't say. Visitors are supposed to report to the nurses' station when they arrive, and if he had, we wouldn't have let him in. I'm so sorry," I say.

"Well, what did he look like?" Mrs. Beckett asks.

I describe the man for them. I tell them about his dark, curly hair, the blue eyes, the bent nose. The Becketts' bodies stiffen, growing taller. They look at one another and decide, "We don't know anyone who looks like that."

Mrs. Beckett's voice quivers when she speaks. "What did he want?"

"To visit, I assumed, but I told him only family was allowed in Caitlin's room and that he'd have to leave, and he did." It wouldn't have been hard for him to find Caitlin's room without reporting to the nurses' station. There are thirty beds in our ICU, ten beds broken down into three pods. There is a whiteboard at the nurses' station, where the charge nurse sits, designating assignments. For purposes of privacy and to avoid HIPAA violations, patients are listed by initials only, but that would be enough for someone who knows her to recognize her by, if the whiteboard was visible to him. It's not exactly on display, but it's not inconspicuous either. Anyone passing by with decent eyesight could see it.

Aside from that, the doors are made of glass. They're easy to see straight through. The hallway can be chaotic at times. In fact,

163

it's often chaotic. The nurses' station is a central hub. It's located in the center of the pod and is where everyone congregates. At any given time, there are people milling around it, so it would be easy to see how a person could slip by and no one would notice, no one would think twice.

Mrs. Beckett looks at her husband and says, "We should tell the police," and he agrees.

Throughout the whole conversation, it's not lost on me how Jackson still stands with his back to the wall, quiet, listening, seemingly unaffected. If I found out just a short while ago that someone tried to kill my sister, I'd be outraged.

That night, I'm in the break room. It's just after seven o'clock and I'm exhausted and het up from the day. I quietly gather my things to leave. Beside me, Luke does the same thing.

I catch a glimpse of the mail I took from my mailbox this morning on the way into work. I didn't look at it this morning; I just stuck it in my bag. Now, a small red envelope sits on top with my name on it, written in an all-caps, very manly print, and the thing that draws my attention to it is that there is no address, no return address and no postmark.

Luke says goodbye, to head home for the night. I say goodbye too, but I'm distracted because my mind is miles away now.

Luke leaves and, alone, I reach for the envelope. I slide a finger under the flap to open it. Inside I find a torn sheet of white computer paper. The front is blank, but when I turn it over in my hand, the back robs my lungs of air.

In jagged, masculine handwriting with all caps and black ink, it reads *BITCH,* the horizontal stroke of the *H* written so forcibly that a hole lances the page.

The break room door opens all of a sudden and I jump, almost dropping the note. Luke returns. "Almost forgot this," he says absentmindedly, sweeping something up off the floor. I don't see what it is. I barely register him because my eyes are hung up on the note, on the handwriting, on that awful word.

Who could have sent this? Even more, how did it come to be in my mailbox if there is no postmark? It didn't go through the post office. Someone put it there. Someone was at my apartment. Someone got into my mailbox somehow and left this note for me.

"Meghan?" Luke asks, and my eyes jerk up to find him standing close. There's a mischievous twinkle in his eye. "What's that you've got there, a love note?" he teases because of the red envelope, I think.

"Yeah right. I wish. But no," I say, thinking on my feet, "it's just a letter from an old friend." My words are terse, my throat tight. I need water. Air. I can barely breathe. I force the note back into the envelope though my movements are careless, rushed, and it takes three attempts to get it in, the corner of the page catching on the envelope's flap.

BITCH

His expression turns thoughtful, concerned. "Is it bad news?" he asks.

"No, why?"

"I don't know," he says, reading me. "You just seem upset."

"I'm not. No. I'm honestly fine, just tired," I say, making a false front of being fine, and he believes me, I think.

"Okay. If you're sure."

"I am."

"I'm going to head out then. Have a good night." He pauses. "You want me to wait for you? I can walk you home?"

There's a part of me that almost says yes, because I'm afraid to be outside alone, because of this note and because of everything else that's been happening. I glance up and our eyes meet, and I think what a

166

relief it would be to have someone like Luke in my life to confide in, to assure me that this note is a mistake and that everything will be okay, to walk me home and make sure I get inside safely.

But then I think of Penelope alone, waiting for him to come home.

"No," I say, taking a deep breath, my words more grounded and self-possessed. There will be people on the street as there always are. Rush hour commuters. The only place without foot traffic is my own street, which I will take fast. It's just a short stretch, and then once I'm in the apartment, I'll be fine. "Thank you, that's sweet, but I'll be okay. I might treat myself and take a cab," I lie, hoping he buys it.

His eyes are still on me. They're warm, keen, searching.

"Can I tell you something?" he asks after a minute.

"Of course. You can tell me anything."

"You won't think I'm weird?"

"Well, that depends on what you're about to say," I say, trying to keep things light, witty, though it's completely contradictory to how I feel.

"It's just that I worry about you and Sienna," he admits. "Not that you can't take care of yourselves — you can — but, I don't know — all these stories on the news. This fucking madman going after women. I lose sleep over it some nights."

"You lose sleep worrying about Sienna and me?" I ask, but as soon as I do, I think that I've misinterpreted what he was trying to say and feel embarrassed. He loses sleep thinking about this madman, not about Sienna and me.

But Luke nods. I wasn't wrong. He does lose sleep worrying about Sienna and me.

Ben has never said that. Despite all the women being attacked in our city, he's never once expressed concern for Sienna and me, and the fact that one of us is often home alone.

Luke says then, as if going back on what he said, "Not that you need some man to take care of you. That's not what I mean. You're stronger than anyone I know, Meghan," and, in that moment, something inside of me changes.

I've never thought of Luke as attractive, not that he isn't, but I've never thought of him as anything but a coworker and friend. I've never thought what it would be like for him to take me in his arms, to press his body into mine, to run a warm hand the length of my hair, to follow me into my apartment, to stay the night with me so I didn't feel so alone or scared.

Just as quickly as it enters, I eliminate the thought from my mind, feeling wrong for even thinking it. Luke is Penelope's husband. I have no right to thoughts like those.

My voice is light, dismissive. I make an offhand gesture with my hand. "You don't need to worry about Sienna and me, Luke. Don't get me wrong — I appreciate it — but honestly, we're fine. Divorce or not, Ben is always keeping an eye on us, to the extreme," I lie. "Some days, it's intolerable. He means well, but I wish he would leave us alone."

"Okay," Luke says, suddenly self-conscious I think, and I feel guilty for a different reason, watching as he backs away toward the door. "Just be careful out there."

"I will. You too."

Luke leaves. I watch as the door drifts closed.

I throw the letter away before I go, pressing down with a bare hand, forcing it to the bottom of the trash can so no one will see it. I wash my hands after.

Out of sight, but not out of mind.

TEN

Standing alone in my kitchen, I send Nat a direct message on Facebook. I try and keep it breezy because I don't want to overwhelm or put pressure on her, but I've been thinking about her all day and the way things left off at the restaurant, with something outside frightening her enough to make her leave. All day at work and then later at home with Sienna, eating dinner and helping her with homework, I've replayed her words in my mind — *He can get mad sometimes. He* — before she cut abruptly off and practically ran from the restaurant, concealing herself in a passing crowd. I think of all the ways to finish that sentence. *He has a temper. He hits me. He scares me. He might kill me.*

Now I just want to hear from her. I want to know that she made it home okay. I wonder where home is for her, how far she had to walk, and whether her ex knows where she lives.

Is your friend feeling any better? I ask in my message, though I wasn't born yesterday. I don't for a second believe she left because she was taking dinner to a sick friend, and I understand, but I feel bad that she felt she had to lie to me. I know we've lost touch over the years and that we weren't the kind of friends in high school who told each other everything, but I'd like to think she feels safe with me and that she knows she can trust me. I would have rather she told me what was going on. I would have walked her home myself to make sure she got there okay.

I check and check again all night, but she never reads my message and she never replies.

My ex-husband Ben stands just inside my apartment, stealing all the oxygen from the room. The hostility between us takes my breath away sometimes, and I find it hard to remember a time when we were happy together. Those cozy moments on the sofa and the intimate moments in bed — did they really happen or did I only imagine they did?

"Is Sienna almost ready?" he asks, looking through or past me because he has this way of never meeting my eye anymore.

171

"Yes. Just give her a minute."

He's pissed that Sienna isn't ready. What little patience he has wanes and he goes to stand at the window, looking out at the street below. "I'm double-parked," he says gruffly, turning back to glance at Sienna's closed bedroom door, his not-so-subtle way of telling me to tell her to hurry up, which I won't because I refuse to be servile.

"I told you she's almost done."

"She has thirty seconds," he says, checking his watch, and not for the first time since he's been here.

"And then what?" I ask, calling his bluff.

Tension hangs in the air like early morning fog. I wait for Ben to say something, to threaten me with a call to the judge, but this time, he doesn't.

"Is that a new shirt?" he asks instead, looking at it with something like disdain. I glance down at my shirt. It's nothing fancy but it is nicer than what I'd usually wear around the house. I put it on after work, slipping first out of my scrubs and then standing, braless, in my bedroom before the floor-length mirror, staring at my breasts, wondering if the right one, in particular, looked any different than usual, as if I could somehow see the cancer itself, a prickly thistle beneath the skin. I regretted that I

172

hadn't been better with self-exams over the years. I just turned forty a couple months ago; this was my first mammogram, which scares me because if it is cancer, who knows how long it's been there. Standing before the mirror, staring at my reflection, I pressed my fingertips to the breast, feeling around, but feeling inept; I didn't know what I was looking for or if I'd know it if I found it. Eventually I gave up and went to my closet, searching for something to wear.

I put effort into my appearance on the nights Ben comes for Sienna. The last thing I need is for him to see me looking exhausted and slovenly in my work scrubs. I want him to see I'm doing fine — no, better than fine — I want him to see I'm doing *great.* Tonight I'm wearing a black-and-white floral shirt with a pleated neckline and satiny fabric, and jeans.

Since the divorce, Ben pays child support, which is equivalent to 20 percent of his income because I'm the custodial parent, or the one who gets Sienna for the majority of the time. He gets her for a few days every other week, which he was fully on board with because his work and travel schedule preclude him from being a full-time parent like me. Still he gripes about the amount of child support he has to pay, which goes toward things like Sienna's education, food, shelter, clothing, all of which he was happy to contribute to before the divorce. But now it's as if he thinks I'm using his money for new clothes for myself.

His is a loaded question. What he really wants to ask is did I use Sienna's child support payments for my shirt?

Even without the 20 percent of Ben's income, Sienna and I do fine financially. I don't make nearly as much as him, but I make enough to support us. Our apartment is affordable and I'm smart with the money we spend. It also helps that my grandmother died sometime after the divorce, leaving me with a significant portion of her nest egg that I was grateful not to have to split with Ben — though he was bent out of shape about it, as if she intentionally timed her death to coincide with the signing of our divorce papers. I've used some of the inheritance on expenses, but most I've put away in the bank while I figure out what to do with the rest, though Sienna's college education is at the top of the list. Still, it's nice to know I have an emergency fund if Sienna and I ever need it. I don't lose sleep over money like I used to. If something terrible happened — if I lost my job or if I found out I have cancer, for example —

we'd be fine for a while.

"It is," I say. "Do you like it?"

Ben shrugs. "It's okay." He looks at his watch again. "It's ten after five. She should be ready when I come to pick her up. I shouldn't have to wait. This is cutting into my time with her."

"Give her a break. She was at school all day, Ben."

"She could have packed last night. She could have packed *before* she went to school. This is fucking ridiculous." With a humph, he steps past me, brushing past my arm for Sienna's bedroom door and knocks. "Come on, Sienna," he barks through the door, "let's go."

"Geez, Dad," Sienna says, opening the door with her duffel bag over a shoulder, "relax. Is the apartment on fire or something?" I hold back a smile and then I watch out the window as they leave, seeing how Ben walks two steps ahead of Sienna to the car, and I think how much I hate the time she's away from me, when I'm not there to keep her happy and safe.

When they're gone, I find a bottle of wine and an empty glass, carry them and my laptop to the sofa. I give myself a generous pour and then sip from the glass as I go to

Facebook to see if Nat has replied, and she has.

I lied to you.

That's all it says, four little words sent less than ten minutes ago.

When? I type back, hoping she's still online.

She is, because her reply is immediate. My friend wasn't sick the other night. I didn't leave to bring her dinner.

The vagueness of her statement practically begs me to ask. Why did you leave?

Declan was there. I saw him in the window. He was watching me.

I draw in a breath. Those words — *He was watching me* — undo me, and I go cold at reading them, my glass of wine suspended in my hand midair. I knew someone was there that night. I'd seen the dark shape in the glass and saw his breath on the window. But still, reading her words, having her confirm what I thought, sends gooseflesh rising up my arms.

The L draws near. I feel the vibration of the earth first before I even hear the train coming. A second later, my eyes go to the window and there it is: a smear of light appearing out of the darkness, crossing over the street before rolling past the apartment. The floodlit train passes by too fast for me to see the faces of people inside but I wonder if, sitting stagnant in my apartment with the lights on and the curtains open, riders see me. I rise from the sofa. I go to the window, grabbing for the dark flax curtain panels to close them.

I sit back on the sofa. Did you make it home okay? I type.

One and then two minutes pass, but she doesn't answer. I think that maybe she's gone, that she's logged off Facebook, but the little green dot beside her image tells me she's still active.

Are you okay, Nat?

I don't know, she types then, and I practically hear the hesitation, the unease and fear through the computer screen.

Where are you?

I'm fine, she says in lieu of telling me where she is.

Please tell me where you are.

She types back that she's on Broadway, just outside some stand-up comedy club, and I wonder why, if something has happened so that she can't go home.

I ask her for the intersection or the address, which she is reluctant to give because she doesn't want to inconvenience me. You don't need to come, she says. Really. I'm okay.

I'm coming, I say with some finality, feeling grateful that Sienna is with Ben tonight so I can help. I'm already on my way, I add because if I am, then she can't try and talk me out of coming. I google stand-up comedy clubs on Broadway and find one, and then I slip into my coat and hat and leave, hurrying out of the building and down the street to Sheridan, where I'll have more luck finding a cab. It takes a few minutes but eventually one comes and, when it does, I slide into the back seat, giving the driver the address. Traffic is heavy tonight. It backs up at intersections, creating a jam. I get frustrated, checking Facebook to see if Nat has messaged me again, but she hasn't. From my apartment, it was just over a mile to get to her and, in retrospect, I should have walked because I'm not saving any time in a cab.

"Just drop me off here," I say to the driver somewhere before Belmont, because I don't have the patience to wait for the light ahead of us to turn green. I pay him and slip out, looking quickly before crossing the street. I jog the rest of the way down Broadway, searching for Nat as I approach the comedy club, where there is a line of people waiting to get inside.

I don't see her at first. I think she's gone, that she left.

But then I find her. She's not at the comedy club. She's two doors down, standing in the recessed entry of some shoe repair shop, which is closed. The entry is deep and there is a red awning that provides some shelter from the elements, but not enough to keep the cold entirely out. Nat looks freezing, pressed into a corner to avoid the wind, her arms folded around her. Behind her the store is dark, though neon signs in the window emblazon her face in hot pink, bright white and a vivid orange.

I try to keep my face neutral when I see her, to be nonreactive.

I try to keep the shock and horror at bay. I tell myself the neon lights make it look worse than it really is, but I'm not sure they do.

"Nat," I breathe, and her eyes rise to mine. Her bottom lip is swollen to twice its size. This didn't just happen because a cut on the lip has scabbed over, but it happened recently. There is a swollen lump on her cheekbone that's purple and raw. "What happened?" I ask, my voice soft, slow and sedate as I step forward, slipping into the recessed entry with her.

There are tears in her eyes. "I did something stupid," she says.

"What?" I ask, but I regret it almost immediately, because what I should have said was no — *No you didn't do anything stupid* — because victims of abuse always blame themselves for what happened, but nothing she did is deserving of this.

"You're going to think I'm an idiot."

"No," I promise. "I won't."

With reluctance she says, "Declan called yesterday. He asked me to meet him at our old condo after work. He was crying on the phone. I can't remember the last time I heard him cry. He's always so stoic. I asked him what was wrong and he begged me to come home, to come back to him. He said he was sorry, that he couldn't live without me, that he was getting help and would never hurt me again, would never cheat on me again. He promised, *on his life,* he said."

"And so you went home to him?" I ask. "And he did this?"

"It's my fault," she says. "I should have

known better. I upset him." I hate that she would think she was to blame for this kind of abuse, though I know it's normal for victims of domestic violence to think this because it's what their abuser wants them to think — that they did something so egregious as to deserve physical punishment.

"How is it your fault, Nat?" I ask. "He's the one who hurt you. He did this."

"When he called," she says, "he said he wanted another chance and I said okay because, to be honest, I love and miss him too. I believed him when he said he would never hurt me again, because he sounded so broken down and gutted on the phone. I'd never heard him sound like that. He left work early, which he never does. He brought home flowers and takeout and at first everything was fine. No," she says, thinking back in an almost nostalgic way, a sad smile playing on her lips, turning the swollen one even more deformed, "it was better than fine. It was just like the old times. He was the Declan he used to be, when I first met him. Loving, funny and sweet. He started a fire and I opened a bottle of wine, and we ate dinner on a blanket on the living room floor in front of the fire. It was romantic. We talked for hours, we laughed. We made love," she says, pausing there, reminiscing. "He was so tender, so attentive. He took his time. When we were done, we laid there holding one another, and he said he'd been thinking about us starting a family, and how he wanted more than anything to have a baby with me."

Suddenly she sobers, any vestiges of wistful memories disappearing. "But I knew I couldn't do that, not with the way he sometimes is. I brought up what he said about getting help. I asked about the therapist and how it was going, and that's when he told me that he wasn't actually seeing a therapist, that he'd thought about it but decided that it wasn't something he needed to do after all. He could control his temper himself." She pauses for breath and to collect herself, and then goes on, "I should have known better. I shouldn't have said anything. I shouldn't have second-guessed him."

"What did you say?"

"I asked him if he really thought that was a good idea, and wasn't it worth seeing a therapist at least once before making the decision not to go."

"It's a smart question, Nat," I say gently. "It wasn't wrong of you to ask."

"Yeah, well, apparently it was, because the

mood in the room suddenly changed. He stood up and threw what was left of his dinner at me, and then he screamed, *Why do you always have to go and ruin everything? We were having a perfectly good night and then you went and fucked it all up again. You're so fucking stupid, Nat. You couldn't just keep your dumb mouth closed.* He hit me," she says, her fingers brushing against her lip before moving to her cheek. Tears prick my eyes and I force them back. That someone could speak to her — to anyone — like this makes me sick. She takes a breath, holds it and then slowly exhales.

"He's not wrong, you know? I should have known better than to bring it up. If I would have just gone with the flow, if I could have just enjoyed our time together and not questioned him or dredged up sensitive topics, he wouldn't have gotten so upset."

"Nat," I say. "It's not your fault. Where are you staying now? Do you have your own apartment?"

She shakes her head. "No. With a friend and her husband," she says. "They have an extra room. I've been with them for a few weeks."

I think back to what Nat told me at the restaurant the other night, how no one believes her when she tells them about

Declan because they find him to be so charming. To quote her words, they think he's *the perfect guy.*

"What did she say when she saw your face?" I ask.

Nat turns shy. It takes a second for her to reply and when she does, she says, "I lied to her. I couldn't tell her that Declan did this, so I told her I slipped and fell down the stairs on my way to catch the L. She believed me." Some L stations are elevated and others are underground, with steep, concrete steps and poor lighting. It wouldn't be hard to think that someone could lose their footing on the unforgiving stairs and fall and, if they did, the end result might look something like this: a bruised cheek, a swollen lip.

The similarity to my former patient, Anne, and her claim that she fell down the basement steps is upsetting. I think back to Anne and how her husband ended up killing her eventually, and how I regretted not doing more to help while she was still alive. Leaving an abusive partner is the most dangerous time for someone like Nat. I remember reading that somewhere. For men who wind up killing their spouses, the inciting incident is, most often, when a woman leaves or threatens to leave. It's one of the reasons women stay in abusive relationships for as long as they do, because they're afraid of what might happen if they leave.

"What about people at work? Do they think the same thing? That you fell?"

"I didn't go to work. I called in sick because I didn't want my students seeing me like this. They would have been afraid. I went to the museum instead. I just walked around all day alone, looking at things, wondering how my life ended up like this."

"You can't go back to him, Nat. Ever. No matter what he says, he won't change."

She says, "I know," but it's meek and I want to ask if she does — if she *really* does — but it's not my place, and I don't want to overstep and push her away because as far as I can tell, there isn't one person in her life she can talk to about Declan except for me.

A question comes. "How did he know where to find you the other night, when we were at that restaurant?"

Her eyebrows pull together, the neon sign still emblazoning her bruised cheek. "What do you mean?" she asks, confused.

"You said he was there, watching you. How did he know where you'd be? Did you tell him?"

Her face changes. Her eyes enlarge and her jaw goes momentarily slack. Her words are slow, staccatolike when she speaks. "It was just a coincidence, I thought."

This city is big. It's sprawling, spanning over twenty miles north to south along the lake. There are upwards of a hundred different neighborhoods and something like three million people who live here. It's not impossible to run into someone coincidentally, but the odds of it happening are slim.

"Maybe," I say, "but maybe not. Have you checked your phone? Do you know if he ever installed one of those tracking apps on there?" Sienna and I have one called Life360, which lets me track her phone so I know where she is. Sienna hates that I have it, but it was one of my stipulations when she got her phone, especially with her long commute to and from school. I promised at the time that I wouldn't use it to snoop on her and her friends, but only in case of an emergency. To be fair, I turned my location on so she, too, could see where I am at all times. *It's just a precaution, to keep us safe,* I told her and, as always, she asked what was so bad and scary out there that we needed to be kept safe from. The list is endless.

"I don't think so," Nat says now, but she takes her phone out of her bag for good measure to check. "How would I know?"

"May I?" I ask, reaching for her phone, which she easily gives after unlocking it for me. I scroll through the list of apps. There isn't anything obvious, like Life360, though I come across the Find My app, which is standard on certain phones. It's a catchall location sharing app, where you can find a missing phone or iPad just as easily as people.

I search under People.

It says, so completely unambiguously that I feel my heart start to race as a chill runs down my spine: *Declan can see your location.*

I quickly toggle off the option to share her location. And then, by instinct, I spin around, looking back over a shoulder, overwhelmed by the sudden feeling of being watched. I wonder if Declan can see us now, if he knows where she is, if he followed her here. The street behind me is full. It's dark out and the people move in all directions; I can't take them all in. The line waiting to get into the comedy club has started to move too, drifting forward. There are cars and buses driving past and people standing and walking on both sides of the city street. And then there are bars and restaurants with windows, some as large as garage doors that lift when the weather is warm, so massive a person could be sitting anywhere inside the restaurant and be able to see somewhat out.

Declan could just as easily be inside one of the restaurants as in a bus driving by. I turn back to look at Nat, trying to put my thoughts into words that won't scare her. "What is it?" she asks, her face practically white, her eyes reading my own face. "What's wrong?"

"You've been sharing your location with him this whole time. He's known all along where you are. I turned it off," I say, returning the phone, "but he knew exactly where you were the other night. It wasn't a coincidence that he found you. Maybe you should go to the police, Nat, and file a restraining order."

"What good would that do? A piece of paper won't stop him."

She's not wrong. Still, I say, "I just think it's good they know what you're up against."

"Someone will serve that to him. He'll know what I've done, that I reported him. It will only make him mad, Meghan. It will only make things worse."

I nod, too afraid to force the issue in case she's right. I don't want to be the reason something terrible happens to her.

"I should go. My friend will be wondering where I am if I'm not home soon."

"Okay," I say, offering to walk or ride with her, but she says she's okay, that she'll go it alone. "Are you sure?"

"Yes."

I'm full of misgivings, fear. "I don't feel comfortable with that. Please," I beg, "let me walk you home."

"No. I'm fine. I can do this," she says, and reluctantly I say okay because Declan has taken so much and I don't want to take her autonomy too.

I watch her hail a cab. I wait for it to arrive and then I stand on the curb just behind her, watching her get in. She pulls the door closed and waves at me through the window, her face hard to see through the glass. She breaks her gaze, saying something to the driver. Before the cab pulls away, I rap on the window to get her attention. "Send me a message when you get to your friend's house, okay? So I know you made it there." She nods.

As the cab takes off down the street, I watch its taillights for a long time until I can't tell which lights belong to it anymore.

I don't think about my own safety.

I take for granted that she is the one in danger and that I am safe.

189

■ ■ ■ ■

I decide to forgo a cab and walk back to the apartment. The night is crisp but the cold air feels good on my face, as does the movement, because I'm anxious, and the idea of going back to an empty apartment, where I'll do nothing but sit and worry about Nat, isn't appealing.

I walk along Broadway almost the entire way. The city is loud and busy tonight. Even the weather can't keep people inside. I'm grateful when Dakin Street comes and I can slip away from the hustle and bustle of Broadway for something quieter, though it's also then that the fear sets in, that ever-present knowledge that there are murderers out here and that there is a man somewhere on these very streets assaulting women. I reach in my bag for my keys, grateful to feel the weight of them in my hand. The apartment door key, in particular, is honed and though it's not like I could kill someone with it, the pointed end would do damage. I single that one out, holding it in a hammer grip as I walk under leafless trees, past two and three flats and dark cars parked along the street. I pay attention to my surroundings, though the darkness muddies my vi-

sion. It's hard to see, but my hearing, on the other hand, is more tuned in. At first there is practically nothing, just the usual city noise: the sound of sirens in the distance like a woman's piercing cry, the rasp of a car door opening and closing.

It's windy tonight. On the sidewalk beside me, trees sway, their naked limbs like hands. The wind itself makes noise, hissing as it whips around the edges of the buildings.

As I near the abandoned buildings on the street, I hear something in the distance, something different than I'm used to, something haunting and keening like an elegy. The sound is so inappreciable at first that I don't know if it's there or if it's not. If I'm only imagining it.

I hold my breath. I listen closer and in time the sound becomes more distinct.

Somewhere behind me, someone is whistling.

I whip around. On the horizon is the contour of a man, I think, from the shape and size of him and because women don't whistle when they walk alone at night. We do everything we can to be inconspicuous.

My breath catches. I turn back around, looking straight ahead at my apartment building in the distance. Over time, the sound edges closer. The whistle disappears

and is replaced by silence at first, and then the distinct sound of footsteps, jogging as if to catch up, kicking up loose gravel that sails in my direction.

My throat tightens. I readjust my grip on the key.

I can tell from the heaviness of his steps, from the way they advance on me, cutting the distance faster than my own legs can go, that I was right. It is a man. A woman would know better than to follow another woman this closely at night.

My legs move more quickly now. My breath changes too, becoming shallow.

It takes everything in me not to look back, not to run.

There is no end to the number of rules women are supposed to follow at night regarding their safety — be observant, stay off your phone, adjust your routine so you don't always take the same route, wear comfortable shoes that you can run in and carry mace or a Swiss army knife. Or better yet, don't walk alone at night, especially if you've been drinking, because alcohol lowers your awareness and your reaction time and makes you an easy target — and yet men can do any damn thing they'd like and it's fine.

I move to the edge of the sidewalk to give

this man more room to pass, but he doesn't. He soldiers on at the same pace, following a hairbreadth behind me, so that my own pace changes and I walk somehow even faster, my shoulders squared, thinking he will touch me or worse, and I think about those women who were attacked in recent days and if the same thing happened to them in the moments before they were assaulted.

Not a second later, I think about Declan Roche. I picture his face.

I think about what I just saw on Nat's phone: *Declan can see your location.*

What if he was watching Nat and me as we conspired in the entryway under the awning?

My throat tightens. I think of her beaten face and wonder to myself, if he could do that to Nat, to a woman he supposedly loves, what he could do to me, a complete stranger?

As my building draws near, fear gets the best of me and I spin around, saying, "What do you want from me? Get away."

My hand shakes as I brandish the key like a knife.

I don't know which of us is more surprised.

Luke, my friend from work, stands before

me, frozen on the sidewalk. His eyes go wide and shock fills his face. He's pulled back from my faux knife, which I lower, my heart hammering inside my chest.

"Meghan," he says, reaching out a hand as my knees buckle and I stagger forward, grabbing a hold of his arm to catch myself. "Oh my God," he says, his voice dripping with compassion and remorse. "I'm so sorry. I didn't mean to scare you."

I regain my balance and just barely get out, "It's fine," but the words are terse, breathless, anything but *fine.* I take a minute, and then I let go of his arm but still, my heart hammers inside of me and my eyes burn with tears, from fear, from relief, which I hold back, not wanting to cry in front of Luke because I don't want to make him feel bad. It's not his fault that I feel this way. As a man, he has no way of knowing how it feels to be a woman walking these streets alone at night.

"Are you okay?" he asks, shame and empathy in his eyes. "I didn't know that was you."

"Yes," I say, but we both know that's not true.

"Shit," he says, taking me in. "I feel like such a jerk. I'm so sorry. I wasn't paying attention."

"It's fine," I say again, fighting to catch my breath, to get control of my voice so that it comes our less brusque. "I thought —" I start to say, but I stop myself, shaking my head, because I don't want to put into words how I thought Luke was going to hurt me. I don't want to make him feel more guilty than he already does, and saying it aloud somehow makes the possibility of it even more real. It could have happened. I could have been attacked just like that.

Luke's breath is visible when he speaks. "I wasn't looking where I was going. I was on my phone, texting Penelope," he says, and I see the phone then in his hands, the glow from the screen bright as an incoming text arrives and I catch a glimpse of it upside down, feeling embarrassed for him. Fuck you, it says. He takes in the text, wincing, and then he moves his eyes to mine.

"What happened?"

"She's pissed about something I've done. Again."

I watch the wind move his hair and I ask, softening, "About what?"

Luke slides his phone into a pocket and says, "It's nothing."

"It's not nothing. You're upset."

"Maya," he says, explaining, "was scheduled to work the night shift last night, but there was a last-minute emergency with her mom." Maya is another nurse at the hospital. I don't know her well because she always works the night shift, but I know that her mom has dementia and that Maya takes care of her. "She had no one to cover for her, so I stayed until someone could come in. It took a couple hours." As nurses, we're supposed to call in sick three hours before our shift so there is time to find coverage, which makes sense on paper but that doesn't mean last-minute emergencies don't sometimes crop up.

For our patients' safety, we're also mandated to stay until we've completed the handoff to an incoming nurse, which means Luke would have had no choice but to stay until another nurse arrived. "Penelope got it in her head that I was late because I was with another woman. I can't convince her otherwise."

"I'm sorry," I say, meaning it because I've been there myself, stuck at work when I had someone waiting for me or somewhere else to be. "I'm sure it's just the hormones speaking. Lying around in bed all day alone would be unbearable." Penelope is something like seven months along in her pregnancy. She's been on bed rest a couple weeks and already it's been hard.

"I know. It would be, especially in our little apartment. Did I ever tell you how I took her to see a house not too long ago, before the doctor put her on bed rest? A single family home in Roscoe Village."

"I don't think so."

"I did. I thought I would surprise her. I thought it would make her happy. There's no room in our apartment for all the things a baby needs. We're bursting at the seams."

"They're so small and yet they require so much."

Luke nods. "I know," and then he says, going back, "I don't think Penelope liked the house."

"No? Why not?"

"She said it was too expensive," he tells me and, chances are, it was. With Penelope unable to work, Luke is always picking up extra shifts to make more money. I worry about Luke sometimes and the way he describes his marriage to Penelope. I worry she emasculates him, that she makes him get down on himself because he doesn't have a six-figure salary and can't provide for her in the way another man could, in the way Luke wishes he could.

"There are other houses," I say, but I can see in Luke's face that his heart was set on that one. "Maybe after the baby comes, you can keep looking. Where are you coming from now?" I ask. Beneath a winter coat, Luke wears jeans, the mock neck of a dark, half-zip sweater visible through the opening.

He shrugs. "Nowhere." Luke and Penelope live just a couple blocks from me in a one-bedroom apartment. I didn't know it when Sienna and I first moved into our apartment, until we ran into each other at Whole Foods. "I've just been walking. Penelope and I both needed some time to cool off."

"Oh," I say, imagining a heated exchange between the two of them at home, followed by the hostile texts. *Fuck you.* I can't judge. Ben and I have been there too but a high-risk pregnancy makes it all worse. "It's cold to just be wandering." I say, but I hesitate then because, in light of Penelope's belief that he was with another woman last night, I don't want to add fuel to the fire. But then the wind picks up, chilling me to the bone, and I wrap my arms around myself and ask anyway, "Do you want to come inside and talk?"

"I don't want to put Sienna out," Luke says, though I see in his eyes that he is considering.

"You wouldn't. She's with Ben."

He looks at his watch. I don't even know what time it is, but it has to be after nine. "If you're sure. It's getting late though. I don't want to be a nuisance."

"You're not a nuisance. Come inside, where it's warm. I'll make some tea and we can talk."

"Okay."

I turn and climb the concrete steps that lead up to the door, catching a glimpse of my reflection in the front door glass to see that I'm alone. I turn back. I find Luke still standing on the sidewalk, three steps below, his hands in the pockets of his jeans, gazing up at me. "On second thought, I should probably go home." He's quiet, thoughtful for a beat, and then adds, "I might pick up some ice cream on the way as a peace offering."

I smile, though I feel a jab of disappointment at the thought of going inside to a dark and empty apartment alone. I would have relished the company, the conversation so that I didn't have to be lonely myself, so I didn't have to think and worry about Nat.

But Luke going home with ice cream as an olive branch, despite knowing he didn't do anything wrong only reaffirms what I already know: Luke is a good guy.

"You're right," he says. "Lying around in bed all day alone would be unbearable."

Ben never did that. He never saw things from my point of view.

"But so, too, is working a fifteen-hour shift," I say. "Penelope is lucky to have you. I hope she appreciates it."

He shrugs, humble. Maybe she does, maybe she doesn't.

I say goodbye, waiting for him to turn and walk away, back the way he came. But Luke stays put, saying as he nods toward the door, "You go first, so I know you're in," and I appreciate it, not wanting to be left outside alone because, for all I know, someone else is close by and overheard what I just said: that Sienna isn't home and that I'm alone.

"Good night."

"Good night."

I let myself into the foyer. I push the door shut, giving it a gentle tug to be sure it's closed all the way. Even with Luke just outside watching, you can never be too safe.

ELEVEN

The next morning I get the urge to go to the pedestrian bridge. The urge is sudden, but it's not from out of nowhere, because I find myself thinking about Caitlin and what happened all the time, dwelling on the fall itself and wondering what it would have been like to drop from that height.

The day is cold. Ice forms on the inside of the windows in Sienna and my apartment. The sun is out, but the sun, this time of year, is deceiving. It can't be more than twenty-five or thirty degrees.

I bundle up before I leave, putting on a coat, a hat, gloves and boots, heading out through the door and then walking down two flights of stairs and out the front of the building.

I walk through the snow to Sheridan, where I pay my fare, climb the grimy, narrow, semi-exposed steps, and then I wait, shivering — with my chin tucked into the neck of my coat — on the wooden platform for the train to come. The platform is narrow, an island wedged between tracks, with little if any protection from the elements. For the longest time I worried about Sienna up here alone on the narrow platform, always reminding her not to stand too close to the edge. She could lose her balance or someone could plow into her by accident, and she could fall.

The platform is quiet now. Rush hour has passed, early morning commuters already at work, and I don't know which I'd prefer: being up here with strangers, or being alone.

A couple minutes pass and then the Red Line rolls in along an S curve, brakes squealing as it jerks to a stop. The doors open and I get on. I look around, letting my eyes run over the nearly empty car, counting the people on the train. There are three including me. I give thought to getting off, to waiting for another train to come — calculating the time I'd have to wait and whether that train would be just as empty — but before I can decide, the doors close and the decision is made for me. The train lurches forward. I stumble into a seat and the train continues on, along the elevated track until eventually it slips underground, moving through dark, choked tunnels beneath the city.

I get off at Roosevelt. I make my way out to the street and then head east on Roosevelt for the Museum Campus. From there, I follow the nearly desolate path further south to Soldier Field. In the summer, this path would be busy with families, with runners, bike riders and museumgoers, but as it is, it's almost completely uninhabited. The emptiness takes my breath away, and I wonder if I've made a mistake in coming.

I cut past Soldier Field. When I reach it, I travel through a long, shadowy underpass beneath Lake Shore Drive, bringing me closer to the bridge. The entire commute takes about an hour so that, by the time I step out from beneath the underpass and see the bridge just ahead, my teeth are chattering and I'm so cold that, despite a pair of leather gloves, I can barely feel my hands.

The bridge. It's not much to look at. You almost don't see it until it's there. There's nothing pretty about it, nothing fresh and modern like the light blue sinuous curves of the pedestrian bridge at 43rd Street. This bridge is wooden and austere; it's a necessity only, indispensable but old and ugly, providing lakefront access to residents who live here.

I feel a surge of emotions wash over me seeing the bridge. I regret coming all of a sudden; this was wrong. I could still turn back and I consider it for a split second, but then I don't, not when I'm this close. I don't usually do this kind of thing. I don't let patients dominate my days off and I don't get wrapped up in their stories. I don't let them affect me in any personal way, though it takes effort not to. I have to be careful.

The bridge slopes gently upward. It's not a hard climb, but still my breathing is heavy. I hold fast to the corroded railings and climb the ramp to the top to where the bridge spans six railroad tracks. Once there, I tent a hand to my eyes to block out the sun.

At the center of the bridge, a single bouquet marks the spot where Caitlin went over the edge. I walk to it and squat down beside the flowers, which are wrapped in cellophane and half-dead. Their petals wilt, losing color, turning pale. I wonder who left them.

I glance over my shoulder to be certain I'm still alone, and I am, as far as I know.

A semitruck soars by just then, blaring its horn at something, and I jump. I turn toward the rush of road noise. I see cars in the distance, traffic easily moving in excess of forty-five miles per hour on Lake Shore Drive. I think about what Natalia from work said, that if what happened had happened on a different bridge — one that went over the street and not the train tracks — she'd be dead and not fighting for her life in our ICU. Natalia was right. If it had happened on Lake Shore Drive, things would be different. Traffic isn't always heavy on Lake Shore Drive, but it is constant. There would have been no way for a driver to anticipate something like that and no time for them to react to a falling body.

I stand up. I step past the flowers to get closer to the edge of the bridge. I lean down, looking over the railing to the tracks beneath, feeling suddenly light-headed from the height. It's disorienting and overpowering, a sheer drop. I can't even begin to estimate the distance to the earth. I find myself thinking again about what happened when Caitlin landed, wondering if it would have hurt when she hit the ground or if she would have been unconscious by then. I thought the same thing about my sister Bethany for years. I wondered if she would have been dead before impact or if she died sometime after. I wondered if it hurt.

I think about the person who found Caitlin. I've heard it was a lineman, someone who was already here inspecting the tracks and came across her body. I think about this lineman a lot, and about what he saw, the condition of her body.

All of a sudden, I'm not alone.

I jerk, hearing the hollow screams of kids passing through the Lake Shore Drive underpass, going the opposite direction and away from me. I look, but the voices are disembodied. I can't see them. They're just kids — I can tell from the sound of them — being silly, playing around, listening to the echo of their own voices in the underpass, which should bring some humor to the situation, but instead, the sound of their piercing screams undoes me.

The ground beneath me suddenly seems to move, and I jerk my eyes back, grabbing hold of the railing as a train appears, bearing down on the tracks beneath me. I grip the bridge's ledge even tighter to keep my balance, having to tear my eyes away from the train as it passes by below.

I've never been any good with heights, but this is something different, something even worse because of what happened here.

I risk a glance back down. One thought comes to mind when I see it from this angle: She should have died.

There's movement in my peripheral vision just then, immediate and unanticipated. My head swings to the right, to the ramp that leads up to the bridge, where a man appears, stopping at the top of the ramp to take stock of me. My stomach tightens and I feel caught, taking in his thick, warm-looking brown parka, his bare head, the brown hair that stands upright in the wind. I think the thing that worries me most is how he lingers at the end of the bridge, hanging patiently back, watching me. It crosses my mind to leave, to go the other way so I don't have to walk past him. But that would make things worse.

The pedestrian bridge is part of a path that leads to the Museum Campus and then all the way to Northerly Island if you follow it long enough. When the weather is nice, people walk or bike, but it's too cold out for that now. The kids are gone from the underpass. They've moved on to somewhere else. I look around. The vastness, the barrenness of the space is overwhelming.

Jackson Beckett begins a slow walk along the bridge, his hands in the pockets of the parka. "What are you doing here?" he asks as he reaches me, and I feel guilty for having come. I can't come up with an answer to save my life, because everything I can think of — how curiosity got the best of me and I had to see it for myself — sounds insensitive. "It doesn't matter," he says, letting me off the hook. "It's a public bridge. Anyone can be here."

He looks away from me, toward the skyline, the modern skyscrapers a sharp contrast to the steel rails of the rail yard. "It was brave of you to come, though, when there's a murderer on the loose," he says before correcting himself, "Sorry. *Attempted* murderer," his tone too light, too offhand for the situation, his breath visible in the cold. He sets his bare hands on the rusty railings and leans over, looking far down over the edge of the bridge, taking it in, unfazed, unlike me, by the height. I look at his hands, holding tight to the bridge railing. He's married, a wedding band on his ring finger, and I wonder about his wife and what she's like, and if the Becketts have grandkids. First impressions aren't everything, but my gut tells me there's something about him not to like.

"Terrible what happened, isn't it?"

"Yes. Awful," I say, opening my mouth for the first time. I'm not usually like this. I can almost always come up with something to say, but his demeanor, his choice of words, makes it hard. "Your poor family," I say.

"You must all be completely beside your-selves."

He lifts himself back up, quiet at first.

"Do you think she'll make it?" he asks then, as if asking if there is snow in the forecast rather than if his sister will live.

"I . . . I don't know," I say, caught off guard by his bluntness. "There's certainly a chance, though there's no way to know for certain." He stares, saying nothing, as if expecting something more. "What I some-times tell loved ones is to hope for the best but prepare for the worst, just in case. It's good to be prepared, I think. To consider all the possible outcomes. It's good that you came when you did. People have a hard time forgiving themselves if something ter-rible happens and they don't get a chance to say goodbye."

He harrumphs. "Yeah well, I didn't come for her. I came for my parents. They asked me to come and so I did. They don't live far from here, you know?" he offers then — and I say no, that I didn't know that — before turning to lean his back against the edge of the bridge, fighting off the cold. "They have a townhome on Indiana," he says, pointing in the general direction, and my eyes go there, west of the bridge, further away from the lake. "You can see Soldier

Field and Grant Park from their deck."

"That must be nice," I say, knowing that views like that don't come cheap. If they really can see Soldier Field from their deck, then their townhome must be incredibly close. It makes me wonder if that's the real reason Caitlin was in the area that day, if she came to see them, though, according to the Becketts, they didn't know she had come back from California. But maybe she was nosing around or maybe she did come, but no one was home, or she got cold feet, changed her mind and left. "Is this where you grew up?"

"No," he says, taking in the buildings in the near distance, just beyond the rail yard. "No, this neighborhood wasn't what it is now twenty years ago. It's changed, with loft condominiums taking over old warehouses, and luxury townhomes being built. I grew up in Hyde Park," he says, and I nod. "It was sometime after Caitlin, Henry and I left that they sold the old house and moved here, to be closer to Dad's work. He'd had enough of the commute. It used to take him almost an hour to go eight miles. Now, when the weather is nice, he can walk."

I nod. City traffic is the worst. I can't think of anything to say, and so, unthinking, I fill the void with, "My ex-husband and I had our wedding reception at Promontory Point," which is in Hyde Park, a peninsula extending out into Lake Michigan with sweeping skyline views — wishing a breath later that I hadn't been so quick to disclose personal details about myself.

Ben and my wedding was relatively small as weddings go, less than a hundred guests, though the space — a charming vintage building with French doors, stone verandas and breathtaking views — was everything I wanted. The pictures, now packed away in a box in the basement, were exquisite.

"Promontory Point." He laughs under his breath. "My buddies and I used to hang out there back in high school, usually up to no good. In fact," he says, sobering, "I was just there last weekend with a friend. It is beautiful, even in winter."

"I don't doubt it," I say. I've never been in winter, but I imagine what it would be like to stand on the large boulders beside the lake, to take in the white of the snow against the dazzling blue of the lake and sky.

"I should go," I say then, using the brief lull in conversation to my advantage, "I'm sure you want to be alone up here. I'm sure you weren't expecting company."

"Don't leave on my account."

"My daughter," I say this time, "will be home from school soon and will wonder where I am."

"Sure. Yeah. Of course."

I say goodbye. As I walk away, along the bridge and down the ramp before disappearing beneath the underpass, I feel his eyes on me.

It isn't until I'm halfway home, back on the L, the Red Line soaring through a narrow tube at the bottom of the Chicago River — which I try not to think about because if I did, it would make me claustrophobic and I'd think about running out of air, about drowning — that I realize: Jackson Beckett arrived from London only two days ago. He couldn't have been with a friend last weekend at Promontory Point when he was in London for work.

Someone isn't telling the truth.

TWELVE

My head pounds the next night as I slip out through the hospital's main entrance and onto Wellington. The sky is dark. There is snow in the forecast; it's supposed to start sometime after midnight, which means that up above, dense clouds paper over the stars, blocking them from view. The sun set a long time ago, but because of the dearth of windows in the ICU, I didn't see it happen. I didn't see the sun rise or the sun set, so that it's almost possible to pretend it was dark all day.

I find two ibuprofen in my purse and take them as I walk west on Wellington toward Sheffield. My commute home is about a mile long. If I walk at a good pace, which I do, I can make it in fifteen minutes. This makes standing on the L platform, waiting for the train to come, not worth it in my opinion. I'd rather keep moving. I stay warmer that way. It feels like I'm making progress and, either way, whether I take the train or walk, I get home at roughly the same time.

When I come to it, I turn right onto Sheffield. Sheffield is the street I always take when I'm going straight home from work. There's comfort in familiarity. I've walked this route so many times I could practically do it with my eyes closed. It's the most direct route and takes me the whole way from the hospital home, passing by low and midrise apartment buildings mixed with shops, restaurants, doctors' offices, Wrigley Field. Anyone who knows anything about baseball knows that Sheffield Avenue, behind Wrigley Field, is one of the best spots to stand and catch home run balls.

My mind is elsewhere. I'm not thinking about where I'm going. I'm not paying attention to where I'm walking. My eyes are unfocused, looking where I'm going but not ingesting what I see. I almost don't see her. I almost walk right past in my haze, but then I hear a man's cruel words hurled like darts in the air — *What the fuck, lady. Why don't you watch where you're going?* — and I look. It's not as though I haven't heard words spoken in this city like that before, but the coldness of strangers, the way people speak to and treat one another, stuns me. This man is in his fifties or sixties. He looks expensively dressed, though the buttons of his black suit coat are strained over a large abdomen and he's losing his hair. He's turned toward a woman, and he points a hard-hearted, pitiless, practically inhumane finger at her, so close it almost touches her nose, saying, "What the hell is wrong with you?" before mumbling, "Idiot."

Just before him, I make out Nat's shocked face as she stands there, getting shamed in public and reprimanded like a child. Her shoulders round forward, her skin becoming mottled and red, fighting tears. Nat carries a large, black duffel bag over her shoulder, which looks cumbersome enough that she might have clipped the man's shoulder with it walking by or stepped on the back of his fancy leather shoes. Something like that, something accidental and benign. Not the worst aggrievance, and yet he's made her feel stupid for it. I read her lips. "I'm sorry. I'm so sorry," she mouths, shaking her head as he pulls down on the lapels of his suit coat, straightening it, and then turns away without another word.

Once he's gone, Nat seems anxious to get away. I don't blame her. I see it in her eyes and in her body language. Her eyes flit like hummingbird wings, searching for a place to go, finding one. She turns quickly, attempting to duck into a nearby restaurant, except that on the way in, she struggles to get the large bag through the door.

I make my way to the door. I come up from behind, holding it open for her.

"Thanks," she says, but it's offhand and brisk because she hasn't looked to see it's me holding the door open for her. All she can think about is getting away from strangers' eyes.

"Nat," I say, and only then does she stop and turn to look, her eyes settling on my face, studying it. Nat's lip is still swollen today, though the dried blood has been washed away. The bruise looks worse. It's spread closer to the eye, and I think about the man on the street just now, laying into her, and wonder how anyone could do that when she looks like this.

Her words are clipped. "Meghan," she says, stepping back out onto the sidewalk, instead of into the restaurant where it's warm and brightly lit. She folds her arms across herself and asks, "What are you doing here?" as I let go of the door, letting it drift closed. Nat pulls her eyebrows together so that her forehead pleats. Her words are not unkind but there is some reservation to them, an undercurrent of distrust that I

216

can't blame her for, not after all she's been through.

"That man was an asshole. Whatever happened didn't deserve that kind of reaction," I say, and then, "I was just on my way home from work. I walk past this place almost every day." I say it as justification for my being here, so she doesn't think I've been following her. I can see why she would. "The hospital where I work is only a couple blocks away," I say, pointing arbitrarily in the direction from which I came. I lower my arm. "That man shouldn't have spoken to you like that. It wasn't right. There's something wrong with him, not you. I hope you know that."

She nods, but I don't know if she believes me.

"I'm glad to see you," I go on. "I didn't hear from you last night. You were going to send me a message and let me know you made it home." I'd looked for her message first thing this morning, standing barefoot in the kitchen waiting for the Keurig to warm. I looked again later in the day.

"I'm sorry," she says, and I feel guilty for even mentioning it. I don't want to make her feel bad. "I know. I forgot."

"No, it's okay. Don't apologize. I'm just relieved that you're okay," I say, though the

217

luggage is hard to ignore. I eye the large duffel bag, wonder if her life's worth is in there, all of her possessions, everything she managed to take when she left Declan, and ask, "Are you okay?"

She nods, her hair falling in her eyes, where she leaves it.

"Are you going somewhere?"

"Yes."

"Where?"

"I . . . I don't know," she says. "I haven't decided."

My head lists and I say, "I thought you were staying with your friend."

"I was. But . . ." She pauses, tears suddenly pricking her eyes. "I don't know," she says again, shaking her head, looking away. She can't look at me as she says, "I don't think that's going to work out."

I set a hand on her arm. "What happened, Nat?"

She's reluctant to say. I wait and eventually she does. "My friend, Kristy, told me her husband said it was time to ask me to leave. I think I was in the way. I overstayed my welcome."

"Oh God," I say, thinking how awkward that must have been for her and what it would have been like to be asked to leave by a friend. "I'm so sorry."

"Don't be. It's not your fault. She felt terrible about it, but I get it. Three's a crowd," she says. The look on her face tells a different story. She swallows hard, and then I see it in the downcast eyes: a mix of sadness and despair.

"When did this happen?"

"This afternoon. She said I didn't have to leave right away, that I could stay until I found an apartment or somewhere else to go, but I didn't feel comfortable staying, once I knew I wasn't welcome."

"No, of course not. I get it. I would have left too. Did you eat dinner yet?" I ask. I haven't eaten in hours and the smell of food is prevailing on me. "Do you want to grab a bite?"

"I'm not hungry," she says, and she wouldn't be, not after what she's going through. Food is the last thing on her mind. "I should let you go. I shouldn't keep you like this when you have your daughter waiting for you at home." She turns to go.

"No, wait," I say, stopping her. "She's not. Sienna is with Ben. I don't have to leave. Do you have another friend you can stay with, Nat? Or money for a hotel?"

"Yeah," she says, shrugging a shoulder, "sure."

"Who?" I don't want to overstep, but I

219

remember what she said the other night in the restaurant, how she couldn't talk to anyone about Declan because they were all biased toward him. They liked him too much to believe the things he was doing to her. It's not lost on me now that the only person in her corner is me, someone she hasn't seen in over twenty years. My memories of Nat from high school have faded over the years, but I have vague memories of her as fun loving and easygoing with an infectious smile. She was captain of our tennis team, a leader. People looked up to her. Now she seems practically meek and I hate that a man did this to her, that he changed her very essence. I don't know him, but still, I hate him for it.

I regret that she and I fell out of touch and wish now that I'd made more of an effort to stay connected over the years.

"There is a hostel close by," she says.

"A hostel?" I ask, aghast. There is one on this street in a brick midrise. I walk past it almost every day. From the outside it looks nice, but when I think of migrant travelers, of dorm-style living or shared bathrooms and amenities, it doesn't sound appealing.

"That's all I can afford," she says. "It will be fine."

I think back. The other night at the café,

she told me that her ex, Declan, is a lawyer, an associate at a law firm in the Loop, but that soon he would make partner. Nat, on the other hand, teaches preschool. This makes him the obvious breadwinner. He should be paying alimony and the payments should be significant enough that she could get back on her feet, that she could rent an apartment or at the very least, afford a few nights in a hotel.

"You must have money from the divorce. Alimony payments?"

"Declan has our money."

"What do you mean?"

"I mean I don't have access to it. He has all of it." Dividing assets is a divisive time and never does anyone get exactly what they want, but they should get *something,* and Declan already has their apartment or house. There is no possible way a judge would have given him all the assets. Nat has a job. She earns an income. Where is that, the money she makes?

"I . . . I don't understand. He can't do that, Nat. Some, if not half, of that money is yours. Have you talked to your lawyer? If Declan is keeping your money from you, that's illegal."

"I don't have a lawyer."

"You represented yourself in the divorce?"

I ask. A person can represent themselves in a divorce. It's not always a good idea though, especially if the divorce is contentious. My heart breaks for her, thinking she somehow lost everything in the divorce, including her home, her money, her right to spousal maintenance payments.

"No."

"I'm confused, Nat."

She's reluctant to explain.

"Nat?" I ask, and eventually she tells me.

"Declan and I aren't divorced."

I'm taken aback. "I . . . I thought you were. You never filed for divorce? Why Nat?" I ask.

Again her eyes fill with tears. "Because I'm scared. Scared of what he'll do, of how he'll react if he knows I'm leaving him for good. But until I do," she says, "he has all of our money and I have none of it."

"What about a credit card?"

"No," she breathes, wiping her eyes and her nose with the back of a sleeve. "Nothing. He took that away a long time ago." I take her by the elbow and pull her closer to the building, where we have a few feet of space to ourselves. Her voice is quiet as she says, "At first he just gave me cash and told me to buy whatever I needed, and it was a luxury, not having to balance a checkbook, pay bills or even think about money. He said I had so much going on that I didn't need to worry about our finances; he would handle it, and it was a relief. But then later, when I asked for my debit and credit cards back, because you can't just buy everything with cash, he said no, that as it turned out, I was irresponsible with money. I couldn't be trusted. He keeps me on an allowance. If I need more money than he gives, I have to ask for it, and then he decides whether I can have it or not." She speaks in the present now and I realize that this isn't something he used to do. This is something he does now. She's still reliant on him for money, which keeps her completely dependent on him. For food. For shelter.

"That's what men like him do. It's a form of entrapment, Nat. It's one of the many reasons women stay in relationships like yours or keep returning to an abusive spouse. For money. Shelter. Because there is a very real fear of being homeless or broke. You were brave to walk away from him," I say, reaching out for her hand, "but now we need to figure out your finances. We need to get you what's rightfully yours. You need to file for divorce. We can talk to my attorney. She's amazing."

"If I'm so brave, then why do I always feel

scared?" she asks, her dark eyes begging. She's not looking for an answer, though I know exactly why she would feel scared, because she's always looking over her shoulder for him. "I don't feel brave. But," she says, recovering, "a few weeks ago, I went to the bank. I opened an account in just my name, and I filled out the paperwork so my paychecks get deposited there instead of into the account with Declan. I have my own money now. Not much, but some," she says, "and I've been saving."

"That's great."

"I'll be fine. I'll get through this," she says, though her eyes tell a different story.

"I know you will."

She forces a tight smile. If she's only been saving her own money for a couple weeks, on a teacher's salary, she has maybe a thousand dollars saved, tops. A hotel in the city could cost two or three hundred dollars a night and a hostel, though less, isn't ideal. I worry that if Nat doesn't have anywhere else to go, if she can't afford food to eat, then she'll go back to Declan for lack of options because that's what women in her position do.

My mother once told me that I was born to be a nurse because it was in my nature to help people. It makes it easier that Sienna is with Ben tonight and I'm the only one home. I have to work all weekend. I'd agreed to take on a few extra shifts for another nurse, because I could use the money and Sienna wasn't going to be home anyway. I didn't think it would matter. Now I regret it. But it will be fine. We'll figure something out. I know Nat and, if the situation were reversed, she would do the same for me.

"Come stay with me," I say.

She's visibly taken aback by my offer. "That's so sweet," she says, eschewing it at first, "but I can't ask you to do that, Meghan. I can't impose on you like that."

"You didn't. I offered. And it's not an imposition at all. Please," I beg, because I know that if she doesn't come with me, things may turn out very badly for her.

I couldn't live with myself if they did.

In my apartment, Nat says, "I told you the other day that Declan has been seeing another woman."

"You did. I remember."

"I almost feel sorry for her. She doesn't know him like I do. She doesn't know what she's gotten herself into." She stands, shifting positions, and then says, "I thought about talking to her, about letting her know what he's really like and trying to stop her before she lets herself get too close to him."

"Did you?"

"No," she says, looking out the open window.

"Why not?"

She brings her eyes back to mine. "Because I didn't know if she'd believe me. And because I kind of hate her too. Part of me thinks it's what she deserves, for Declan to hurt her," she says, and then she pauses, thoughtful, and a knot forms in my stomach, thinking of partners who cheat and of people who sleep with married men and women, and wonder if they are deserving of some terrible fate. "That's awful, right? I shouldn't think like that."

"No," I tell her. "It's okay to be upset. You're only human. We all have thoughts like that."

"I found her."

"You did?"

"Yes. I found her number in his phone. I called a couple times, but when she answered, I hung up. I couldn't bring myself to say anything. I shouldn't be jealous," she says, though I can see she is and I can't blame her. He's still her husband. She loved him once.

I don't know what to say. I can't blame

her for the mix of emotions, for feeling hurt and betrayed, but also wanting to help this woman, to save her from the same fate.

"Tell me again how you and Ben met," she says, changing the subject.

We're standing in the living room as the L approaches outside. Nat starts when she hears it and I tell her, "It's okay. It's just the train."

Still, it takes a moment for her to settle, for her to see the incoming lights and to attribute the change in her heart rhythm to the train and not to Declan. The sound isn't him. He isn't coming for her.

Not yet anyway.

I lay the sofa cushions on the floor. I reach down to pull out the sofa bed as her phone dings the arrival of an incoming text. She glances quickly at it as I watch, her eyes reading over the message before she puts her phone away, her eyes going outside again, as if looking for someone.

I wait for the train to pass and then say, to answer her question, "We had a class together. Honors English, junior year." I think back, hearkening back to happier times. "We didn't meet in class though. I assumed he had no idea who I was. He was too cool and I was too insecure. But then one day, I got a job at that little frozen yogurt place in town," I say. "When I went in for my first shift, I discovered that Ben worked there too. We became friends. He was different than I expected. He was funny and kind, and not all wrapped up in being popular and liked.

"One day after work, Ben and I stayed late to study for finals together. He'd worked there long enough that the manager trusted him to close. I remember how magical and romantic it felt, being there with Ben in the empty shop with all the lights off except for the storefront windows. Ben walked me to my car after we studied and locked up, and to this day I still think about the way our hands brushed by accident against each other and how, somewhere in the middle of the empty parking lot, I pulled shyly back, but Ben reached for me in the darkness, taking my hand into his, holding it."

The memory overwhelms me. My throat tightens and I wonder, not for the first time, how Ben and I went from that — a budding relationship full of love and potential — to where we are now.

Nat's phone dings again and she reaches for it, darkness covering her face. "Who is it, Nat?" I ask this time, putting Ben out of my mind.

"Declan," she admits, her eyes rising up

over her phone to come to mine. "He's been texting all day."

"What's he saying?"

"That he's sorry. Begging me to forgive him, begging me to come home."

"How did you reply?"

"I haven't. Not yet."

"Good," I say, reaching for a bed pillow from the floor and pulling a pillowcase over it. "Good for you, Nat. That's the best way to handle it, I think." *Not yet.* That worries me. There is a part of me scared that she will go back to him, even after all he's done to her. "You can block him. Then you won't see when he texts."

I lay the pillow at the head of the bed. "I know. The thing is," she begins, her discomfort palpable. I move to the window, drawing the curtains together as she says, "it made him mad when I didn't reply. It enraged him actually. The tone of his texts goes from begging forgiveness to threatening and mean."

"Can I see?" I ask, turning back to Nat as she hands me her phone.

I'm so sorry for the other night baby. I didn't mean to hurt you. It's been killing me all day. I feel terrible about what happened. Please come home. Let me make it up to you. It will never happen again. I love you. I will go to therapy if that's what you want. I will do anything for you.

We can go to therapy together. Marriage counseling. It would be good for us. We can get back to the way we used to be.

I can't stop thinking about you, baby. I'm nothing without you. I can't eat, I can't sleep. I keep fucking things up at work because I can't focus on anything. All I can think about is you.

Please answer me Nat. Please don't shut me out.

Where are you, Nat?

Where the fuck are you?

You are nothing without me. You'll regret this.

You fucking bitch. ANSWER ME DAMNIT.

As I stand there with her phone in my hands, the phone pings. Another text message arrives, one that makes my skin crawl. I will find you, it says. I will bring you home where you belong and once I do, I will never let you leave. I'll lock you in a room if I have to. You are mine, Nat. Never forget that. I own you. Nothing can keep us apart.

"What does it say?" Nat asks. I say nothing. There are no words. She asks again, "What is he saying this time?"

In an instant, I hold down on the text message to delete it.

"Meghan?" she asks, realizing what I've done.

"Nothing you need to see."

I look slowly up from the phone to find a tear move down Nat's cheek. I reach for her hand, promising her, "You're safe here, Nat. He won't find you here."

But even I have trouble believing that.

Later, in my own room with the door closed, I reach for the string to lower the blinds on my window before changing out of my clothes and into my pajamas. My bedroom, like Sienna's next door, sits on the side of the apartment that faces west. Our view from the third floor skims over the roof of the two flat next door and onto the street, which is nowhere near as good as having a view of the skyline or lake, but still feels fortuitous for the sunlight and privacy.

I fasten my hand around the string, but before I give it a tug to lower the blinds, I look outside to see if the night's forecasted snow has begun to arrive, and it has. There are flurries, visible in the halo of light given off by a nearby streetlight.

As I lay down to sleep, I wonder if Nat really is safe here like I promised.

Or if in bringing her here, none of us is safe anymore.

THIRTEEN

It's hard to get up in the morning.

It's hard to leave, to go into work. I always hate working on weekends but today in particular, it's hard to leave the safety and warmth of the apartment. I leave a note and then slip quietly out, making as little noise as possible. It's then — walking to work in the dark, early morning commuters absent because it's the weekend and everyone else is fast asleep, so that the streets are dead, practically dystopian — that I start thinking about the note I found in my mailbox the other day, the one I've worked hard to put out of my mind until now. *BITCH.*

I try telling myself that I wasn't the intended recipient, but my name on the envelope disproves that. I try to convince myself it was just a mean prank, but the fact that someone broke into my mailbox to leave it calls that into question. Someone wanted to scare me and they did.

I make it to work without incident, though I arrive to the news that someone from the hospital, a pharmacy technician who everyone adores, was attacked last night. It's all anyone is talking about because she's someone we work with, someone we *know*.

"I heard he followed her to her apartment from work," Misty says as a small group of nurses stands in the break room, feeling like we've had the collective wind knocked out of our lungs, because this is far too close to home.

"I heard her fiancé, who she lives with, was out of town and so she was alone for the night," says Natalia, which makes me uneasy because this man must have known somehow that she would be alone.

"Does anyone know how she's doing? Is she okay?" I ask, though it's a dumb question to ask because of course she's not okay. I think of Hannah, who is young and friendly, if not a little shy, leaving the hospital last night and walking home by herself, which is the same thing I always do, and it makes me wonder why her and not me.

It could have just as easily been me.

When visiting hours begin and Mr. and Mrs. Beckett come into Caitlin's room, the police are with them.

"Are you Meghan Michaels?" one of the men, a detective from the way he's dressed, asks and I nod, wary, feeling anxious. Not yet ten o'clock and already it's been an inauspicious start to the day. "Mr. and Mrs. Beckett tell us there was an individual here the other day to visit Ms. Beckett."

"Yes," I say. "There was."

This man is everything I would expect of a detective: intense and austere. He's tall, of average weight. He wears a suit, dark and fitted with a gun in a hip holster. I don't see the gun at first, not until he moves the front panels of the coat by accident, and then I do.

"We've gone through Ms. Beckett's phone records to see who she was in contact with over the last couple of weeks," he tells me, and I bring my gaze from the gun to his eyes, which are observant and alert. "I'd like to show you some pictures and see if you can't identify the man who was here. Would that be okay?" he asks, and I wonder if I shouldn't have told them about the man after all, if I should have kept that to myself and stayed as far from this as possible.

"Of course," I say, my mouth dry. "Whatever I can do to help."

"Is there somewhere we can speak in

private?"

I say yes. I lead the detectives to a small bereavement room, reserved for families to grieve. Mr. Beckett tries to follow, but one of the detectives asks him and Mrs. Beckett to wait there, with Caitlin, until we come back.

In the room, the detective tells me to have a seat, and so I pull out a chair and sit at a table across from him while the other man stands at my back, making me uncomfortable for many reasons, including his physical size.

I watch as the detective places a photo lineup on the table. Before me are six images of six men, each of them similar looking though my eyes go right to the one. It's a mug shot, like the rest, taken from the front with an almost identical, featureless wall behind him so as not to distract from the face. In it, he's in his own clothes, not a prison uniform, though there's no denying that this is a mug shot, taken from the shoulders up, so I only see the neckline of a white undershirt, but I see his eyes, which are hollow and angry.

My stomach tightens. I can't decide if it's guilt or fear. This man will be accused of attempted murder because of what I say. If they can find him, he'll get in trouble. He'll be arrested. He's not a good man; clearly he's been arrested for something before, which tells me he's done something illegal in the past.

"Do you recognize any of these men?"

I pick up the picture. I hold it in my hand, taking in the dark, curly hair, a small tattoo on his neck that I hadn't noticed until now, the cold blue eyes. "This is him."

"Are you certain?"

"Yes," I say. "I have no doubt. It's him."

He takes the picture from me. "Thank you for your help, Ms. Michaels." He gathers the rest of the pictures. "We're through here," he says. "You can go."

I don't leave right away. I hesitate, thinking how I could go back to Caitlin's room and keep this to myself, but it seems like a missed opportunity not to tell the police about Jackson Beckett.

"Is there something else, Ms. Michaels?" he asks, his eyes coming to mine, sensing my hesitation.

"I'm sure it's nothing. Just a misunderstanding."

He recenters himself on the chair, folding his hands over a manila folder with the pictures inside, in no rush. His voice is firm but encouraging. "Why don't you tell us and let us decide."

I nod, though still unsure if I'm making the right choice, if I'm doing the right thing. I'm not sure if this will come back to hurt me. I take a breath. "It's just that I was under the impression that the Becketts' son, Jackson, arrived from London a couple days ago, though it seems he's been here longer than that."

"How do you know?"

"He told me. I don't even know if he's realized it by now. We were talking, and he let it slip, how he was with a friend at Promontory Point last weekend though as far as his parents know, he was in London at the time and didn't arrive until the middle of the week. I'm not sure it matters. The Becketts are under so much stress and they're not sleeping. It's just," I say, pausing for air, "I don't know why he would lie about being in London if he was here in the city. And there seems to be some friction between him and Caitlin, some sort of resentment. Animosity."

"How do you know?"

"Mrs. Beckett told me."

The officer nods, thoughtful. He takes a business card from his pocket and hands it to me. "If you think of anything else, call."

I go back to Caitlin's room alone, tucking the business card into the pocket of my scrubs, having trouble meeting the Becketts' eyes at first because of what I've just done.

"Did you identify him?" Mrs. Beckett asks, rising from the edge of the bed as I come in. Jackson is here now. He must have come while I was gone and he stands, leaned against the wall, though I can't bring myself to look at him. "Was he one of the men in the pictures?"

"Yes," I say, and her face grows pale, a hand going to her mouth. "Who is he? Do you know?" I ask, wondering if the Becketts have seen the pictures the police showed me before, if they know something I don't.

Mrs. Beckett nods, unable to speak. It's Mr. Beckett who says, "An ex-con. Milo Finch. The officers asked if we knew him, if we knew why he might have been in touch with Caitlin. We didn't. He's been out of a jail all of a month, and in that time, he's violated parole. He left California without permission. He failed to report to his parole officer. The police have been looking for him." Mr. and Mrs. Beckett exchange a glance before she sinks back to the edge of the bed, reaching for Caitlin's hand as he goes on. "They think he followed her across the country, that he came here looking for her."

Mrs. Beckett says then, as if thinking aloud, her words catching me off guard, "I keep wondering if he isn't the same man you see on the news, the one who's been attacking those women."

"He's not," Mr. Beckett says, as if he somehow knows, but he's just postulating.

"How can you be so certain?"

"It's different, Amelia. Those other women were raped in their own homes. Caitlin was pushed from a bridge, and there were no signs of sexual abuse."

"But maybe she ran from him, Tom. And maybe he followed her there."

I dwell on the idea. It's not impossible to think that it's the same man. I attach weight to the conversation Mrs. Beckett and I began the other day. "You think this man, this Milo Finch, chased or lured Caitlin to the bridge that day? You think he's the one who pushed her?"

"Yes," Mrs. Beckett says. "I do. And maybe he's the one who's been raping those women."

All the police have to do is find him and it will be through. It doesn't matter what I just told them about Jackson. Milo Finch will be arrested. A jury will convict him. It seems so open and shut, if the police can find him.

I step out into the hall, moving toward the nurses' station. I haven't gone more than a few feet when I hear, "Meghan," and I turn back to see that Mr. Beckett has followed me out, looking older and far more disheveled than when he first arrived in the hospital over a week ago. "Can I speak to you for a minute?"

"Sure."

"That voice mail I played for you the other day, from Caitlin," he says, coming to stand too close, and I realize how very relevant it is all of a sudden, the last-ditch, pleading, *Daddy. I'm in trouble. I need your help.* He turns around to be sure Mrs. Beckett and Jackson are still in the room and that the glass door between them has closed, which it has. He turns to me, leaning in even closer and it takes everything in me not to fall back. "I was hoping we could still keep it between you and me. It's meaningful, in light of what we now know, but it's not as if that message is going to help the police find this man, and I don't want Amelia to know Caitlin reached out for help and that I dismissed it."

"Of course," I say. "Whatever you want."

He smiles, but it doesn't reach his eyes. He reaches out to set a hand on my arm. "Thank you, Meghan. I hope you don't think less of me for asking."

"No. Of course not," I say, but I do. The request shows him in a bad light. "I understand. And like you said, it wouldn't make a difference now."

On the walk home, I search for Milo Finch on my phone and find him. Milo Finch is a former restaurant owner and a registered sex offender, who was found guilty of possession of child pornography and sentenced to five years in prison.

I tell myself again that he's not a good man. I shouldn't feel guilty for turning him in to the police.

That said, I wonder where he is now. I wonder if, when the police find him, they will tell him it was me who identified him.

FOURTEEN

That night after work, Sienna calls.

"You'll never believe it," she says, squealing, her voice giddy and high so that I all but see her smile through the phone.

"What?" I ask. I'm in her bedroom, straightening up for her, which I sometimes do when she's with Ben. Nat is in the living room now. She had dinner waiting for me when I came home from work, which was nice for a change, to have someone cook for me. We sat at the small kitchen table and ate and talked about how, when she has enough money saved, I'll help her look for an apartment though, in the back of my head, I wondered what was to stop Declan from finding her there.

"Dad got *Dear Evan Hansen* tickets!" Sienna screams into the phone now. "Fifth row!"

I flatten, air coming out of me like from a balloon. Of course he did, I think. I thought about doing that too, but the cost for tickets is outrageous, and if I was going to get them, it was going to be for Christmas or her birthday and not just an ordinary day.

"When is the show?" I ask.

Sienna screams, "Tomorrow night!" into the phone and then says, "Can you believe it, Mom? This is so fire. I can't wait to tell Gianna and Nico."

"Wait up," I say. "Tomorrow night? Tomorrow is Sunday, Sienna. You come home tomorrow afternoon."

"I know," she says. "Dad told me to call and see if I can spend another night with him so that we can go. He said he'll drive me to school Monday morning. You don't need to do anything. Pleeeease Mom," she begs. "It's just one night and I'll be home Monday."

"Okay," I say after a second, because what choice do I have? Sienna would hate me if I said no to *Dear Evan Hansen*. She'd never forgive me. It's one of those Broadway in Chicago shows and is only here for a few weeks. She won't get a chance like this again. Ben knows this. Maybe it's just a coincidence that he managed to snag tickets for a Sunday evening, or maybe it was designed to pit Sienna against me, to keep her from me and to get under my skin.

"You're the best," she says as I move into her closet to collect her dirty clothes from the hamper.

"Just remember that the next time you want to do something and I say no."

"I will," she says, and then, "By the way, Dad has a girlfriend," she lets drop as I pull clothes out of her hamper. She says it so very casually — *Dad has a girlfriend* — like she's telling me she has math homework or a chemistry test to study for. I back away from the closet, lowering myself to the edge of her bed to catch my breath. I'm quiet for a minute, processing her words, and because of it, I think, she says, "You can't be all butt-hurt about it, Mom. You're the one who divorced him."

I wince. It's reasons like this I hate letting Sienna spend time with Ben, not that I have a choice. He puts ideas in her head. He brainwashes her. He wins her over with things like *Dear Evan Hansen* tickets and then sways her in his favor, because that's the kind of thing Ben would say, how *I* divorced *him*. I did, but it's not the whole story.

"You know I hate that word," I say.

"What word?" she asks.

"Butthurt."

I can practically see Sienna roll her eyes

at me through the phone. "Are you mad?" she asks after a second.

"No," I tell her, "but just please stop saying it."

"Not about *butthurt,* Mom. About his *girlfriend?*"

"Oh. No," I lie, moving back to the closet because it's a distraction. "It's fine." Ben should have told me about his girlfriend himself and let me process it without Sienna on the other end of the line. I ask, "Is she going with you tomorrow night?" I picture that. Ben, Sienna and said girlfriend at the gorgeous Nederlander Theatre, posing for a requisite picture together beneath the marquee on Randolph Street.

But Sienna says, "No. He only got two tickets and he wants to take me."

I bite my tongue. *How sweet.*

"What's she like?" I ask.

Sienna says. "I dunno. Fine, I guess."

"Is she there now?"

"No. I forgot to tell you, but I met her last time I was here."

"Oh," I say, but what I really want to ask is: Is she pretty? Is she prettier than me?

All of a sudden I have so many questions — How did they meet? How long have they been dating? — but I button my lip. It's none of my business.

I tell Sienna about Nat, about my old high school friend, who will be staying with us for a week until she can find her own apartment. A week is optimistic, but I don't say that to Sienna. Nat wouldn't be able to find, apply for and be approved for an apartment in that time, and I don't know that she has the money to do so. It might be more like two weeks or a month. It's not ideal to have a houseguest in our little apartment for a month, but we'll make do.

"I wanted to be here to introduce you two. I thought we could hang out tomorrow night and order pizza, but you'll be at *Dear Evan Hansen* now, which is fine," I say, emphasizing the word *fine* because I don't want to guilt trip her. It's that this is not how I imagined things playing out. "It's just that I work Monday, Sienna. You and Nat will both be at home without me." I don't know exactly what time Nat's school day ends but it can't be all that different from Sienna's. I won't be home until seven thirty at the earliest. In theory they'll spend hours together before I come home.

"That's so weird," Sienna groans, and I don't argue with her, because she's right. I don't like it either, but such is life. Nat is an old friend. She and Sienna will get along fine for the short time before I get home.

I'm excited for them to meet because they'll like each other, I think. I like too that Sienna can know a bit of my past, my history before her and Ben. I was once a teenager too. She forgets that sometimes.

I end the call with Sienna, telling Nat I'll be back before carrying Sienna's laundry basket down to the basement. Alone, in the near darkness of the basement, Declan's texts return to me, slipping into my mind, unsought and undesired, getting under my skin and making it crawl.

You fucking bitch. ANSWER ME DAMNIT, he had said in all caps, shouting.

And then, with an almost equally disturbing placidity: I will find you. I will bring you home where you belong and once I do, I will never let you leave. I'll lock you in a room if I have to. You are mine, Nat. Never forget that. I own you. Nothing can keep us apart.

I turn slowly around, looking into the darkened recesses of the basement to be sure I'm alone, that no one is hiding there. I throw the laundry in the wash and I leave, jogging up the stairs. I'm not gone more than two or three minutes.

Nat is standing with her back to me when I come in, looking out the dark window at the street, her hair hanging long and layered down her back.

The L has just finished passing by, the movement of it still making the apartment hum. She doesn't hear me come in. I have the empty laundry basket in my hands, so I kick the door closed, too hard on accident. It slams, startling Nat, who wheels around. That's when I see that she's on her phone, which she pulls away from an ear as she comes to face me, looking guilty. Pale. She must have thought she had more time.

I pull my eyebrows together. "Who are you talking to?" I ask.

"No one," she says. "Just a wrong number."

But as she brings the phone to her eyes to press End, I don't believe her. I know she's lying. It's not no one. I know in my heart that it's Declan and that she called him when I went downstairs to throw the laundry in.

I'm not mad, but I am sad. My heart hurts for her. I read a statistic once that said the average person goes back to an abuser seven times before leaving for good.

Seven times.

"It was just some guy," she goes on. "He said he was looking for someone named Justine."

I go along with it. "He must have misdialed."

I don't ask right away. I wait a second. I try to be subtle, while lowering the laundry basket to the floor. "Have you heard again from Declan? Any more texts?"

"No," she says with a quick jerk of the head, avoiding my eye. "No more texts."

Seven times, I think again, wondering how many times Nat has already gone back to him, knowing it's been at least once in this short time since we reconnected.

But it's not my job to doubt her. I'm here to support her, to be a friend. "Good," I say. "That's good. I'm glad that's stopped. How about some wine?"

"I'd love some," she says, putting her phone away.

I lower myself into the armchair, which is wide and plush, the color of rust. I pull my legs into me and say, "You never told me how you and Declan met." Nat is quiet and almost instantly, I regret that I asked. "I'm sorry. We don't have to talk about it if you don't want."

"No," she's quick to say before taking a small sip of her wine for liquid courage. "It's okay. It's just that . . ." Her voice trails.

"It's hard, I know."

"Yes. It is." She takes another sip of her wine and then goes on. "We met at the party of a mutual friend. My friend introduced us and we hit it off. We talked for hours that night and then, a few days later," she says, "he called and asked me to dinner. By our third or fourth date, I started imagining a life for us together. It was premature, I know, but I'd never met any man like him, one who I was so compatible with. I was a late bloomer. All of my friends were married by then, and I felt a rush — the pressure — to find someone to settle down with. I was scared of being alone, but I also fell head over heels in love. We dated for only five months when he proposed. There was never any hesitation or doubt in my mind. I immediately said yes."

"What was it like the first time he hit you?" I ask, knowing I'm close to overstepping my bounds, but I can't help myself. I have to know.

Nat doesn't baulk at the question. She takes a second to collect her thoughts and then says, "It was instantaneous. Blindsiding. And then it was done and he was so sorry and so full of self-loathing. He cried, sobbed like a child, and I was left to comfort him, to assure him it was no big deal and that things like that happen, though they don't. We'd only been married a few weeks then and had an argument over something inane like household chores. In the middle of it, he was walking away and I said something stupid because I just had to get the last word in, when he wheeled around and hit me. I don't know which of us was more stunned or appalled."

"And then it happened again?"

"Yes. But not right away. At first moments like that were infrequent, so that I could almost convince myself that each time was the last. In time they became more regular and as they did, they changed him. He realized how powerful it made him to make me feel small, and I think it was cathartic too, taking his stress out on me." She lifts the wineglass to her lips. She doesn't drink from it. "Each time I came up with some excuse as to why it had happened. He'd had a bad day. He lost a trial. A client fired him or someone else was chosen for partner over him. Each time, I told myself it would never happen again."

"Do you regret marrying him?" I ask. She must, after everything she's been through. Except that I know she's still in love with him too.

"Sometimes, yes. But I didn't know who he was when I did."

She drinks her wine, slowly finishing it. "Can I get you more?" I ask.

"No. Thanks." She leans over to set the empty glass on a side table. "What do you regret?" she asks.

The vastness of her question takes me aback, though it was fair for her to ask, a tit for tat. I'm quiet, musing on it, wondering how to respond. I could lie and say that I have no regrets, and she might believe me. But after everything that Nat has told me over these last few days, after how open and transparent she's been, the least I can do is be honest with her.

I take a long sip from my wine. "I have regrets," I say, lowering the glass, "but my biggest regret has nothing to do with Ben. A long time ago," I confess, "I did something bad."

Nat baulks, like she doesn't think perfect Meghan Michaels could ever do anything bad, but I have. I have secrets just like everyone else. "What?"

"You're going to think I'm a terrible person if I tell you."

"I won't. I wouldn't ever think that."

I swallow hard, afraid of how this might color her opinion of me. But Nat has told me so much and she's been so open about her marriage to Declan. I know I can trust her with this, and it will be a relief to let it out, to unburden my soul of this secret I've kept for years.

"I've never told anyone about this," I say. "The only person in the world who knows is me and, well, some pretty blond guy who bought me a drink at Guthries back in May of 2007."

I don't need to say more, to explain. Nat can do the math and see what I'm getting at, but I tell her anyway.

"It was weeks before Ben and my wedding. We'd had a fight. I don't even remember what it was about anymore, but I remember that we both said some things we didn't mean and, in retrospect, I got my first glimpse of the man he would one day become — thoughtless, touchy, easily provoked. I told him I didn't want to marry him anymore and, at the time, I believed it. I was so angry and what made it worse, I think, was that Ben didn't try and talk me out of it. He accepted it and said something very cavalier like how it was probably for the best. I went so far as to give him the engagement ring back. I called the banquet hall to see if I could get a refund on the deposit, which they declined because the wedding was weeks away. I was heartbroken," I say. "I called friends then to see if they could hang out, to comfort me, but no one was free on such short notice, and so I went to a bar alone to wallow in self-pity and get drunk."

"Guthries," she says, and I nod. Guthries. This cozy little unostentatious bar off Addison, not far from where Sienna and I live now. I can't walk by it anymore and not think of that night, though the memories I have are fragments only, disconnected pieces, and I don't know for certain what's real and what time and my imagination have only dreamed up.

He was cool, that I remember. Laid-back, humble and easy to talk to. I liked talking to him. I have no idea what we talked about, but there was an ease to him that made me feel at home.

We talked for a long time, sitting on stools at the bar, watching the sky darken out the window, turning from steel to purple to black like a bruise. At some point, he set his hand on my leg and my breath caught, watching his fingers twiddle with the gauzy cotton fabric of my skirt.

My heart sang when he slowly lifted his gaze to mine, when he leaned in to tell me about his apartment, which was just a short walk down Addison.

"It will be more quiet there," he said, his breath hot on my ear. "I can't hear you over all this noise."

I knew he didn't want to talk, but I said okay because I didn't want to either.

He lived on the third floor of a midrise building. We took the stairs, holding hands, quietly climbing. Just inside his apartment, he pressed me against a wall and lifted my skirt to my waist. I don't remember much after that, though I spent the night with him when we were through, sleeping beside him. He held me, his strong arms wrapped around me from behind, which I liked because even though I knew it was, it didn't feel like a meaningless hookup.

The morning after, I awoke before he did, got dressed and slipped quietly out, pulling the door gently closed. I walked home as the sun was rising, a chill to the spring air. I knew I would never see him again, though I didn't regret what had happened between us. Maybe some part of me already knew that something special had happened that night, something momentous, something that would stay with me for a lifetime to come.

Sometime later that day, Ben showed up unannounced at my apartment to apologize, accepting full blame and admitting that he had been an asshole and was completely in the wrong. I forgave him. We kissed and made up. I called the banquet hall to see if the room was still available, and it was. The wedding was back on. Three weeks later, Ben and I tied the knot.

Two weeks after that, I saw the two faint pink lines on a home pregnancy test. Ben and I hadn't exactly been celibate and so the odds were fifty-fifty, but the guilt, the what-if — the possibility that the baby wasn't Ben's — weighed heavily on me. There was a short window where I could have confessed to what happened. We had, after all, been on a break and I'd done something rash, which Ben might one day understand and forgive me for.

But I didn't tell him. I kept it to myself, and the window of opportunity closed.

After Sienna was born, I brought Ben's toothbrush and her to a lab. I had them tested. They were not a match.

I vowed to never tell either of them, and, in time, I came to forget myself that they were not biologically related. I started to believe the lie that Sienna's blond hair came from Ben's mom. I told it so many times, eventually it just rolled off the tongue whenever someone pointed out the disparity between Sienna, Ben and me.

"I'm glad you told me. I'm glad you trusted me enough to tell me," Nat says now, and then she says softly, "But that was a long time ago, Meghan. What's done is done. You have to forgive yourself and let it go. Ben got something special from this too — a daughter he loves."

I nod. Nat is right. He did, when I think about it. If it didn't happen like it did, Ben and I would never have had Sienna.

"I'm glad you're here, Nat," I confess, reaching for her hand. I don't tell her this, but I'd been feeling so lonely since the divorce. With Ben gone, Sienna growing up quickly, and friends practically nil, it was only a matter of time until I was completely alone.

How fortunate it is, I think, that Nat and I came into each other's lives at just the right time.

Fifteen

The Becketts push to ramp up security for Caitlin. They want someone watching her all the time, every minute of the day, now that they know an ex-con is looking for her. She's far more vulnerable than other patients. Her life is at risk, they say, and maybe it is, though it's just not feasible that an RN or a CNA can commit to standing guard in her room — we're short-staffed as is, which is nothing new, though the shortage is worse now than ever before — and the hospital can't pull a security guard from somewhere like the front desk or the ER, because they're just as needed there and are equally in short supply.

That evening, after I've given my end of shift report to the night nurse and am getting ready to leave, a young woman steps into the ICU, slipping in before someone has a chance to lock the door for the night. It's just after seven o'clock. My shift has been over for a few minutes. I've gotten my things already — my coat and my bag — and I stand at the nurses' station saying my goodbyes.

I turn at the sound of the door opening, watching as the woman steps cautiously through the doorway. Her hair is fine, a dark brown that's practically black, very mono-tone, which suggests to me an at-home box dye. She has long, straight bangs that sweep sideways across a small forehead before get-ting tucked behind an ear on the opposite side. Her small body is practically lost in an army surplus jacket, the olive drab arms overtaking her wrists and hands. The body of it is too wide, and I wonder if she picked it up from a thrift store, which is something Sienna and her friends are into these days: thrifting, seeing how far their allowance can stretch.

"Can I help you?" I ask, calling gently out to her. I smile, trying to take the edge off. She smiles back, but it's perfunctory. No sooner does she smile than the smile is gone.

She steps hesitantly up to the desk. "I'm, um," she says, slow to find her words, "look-ing for Caitlin Beckett."

Up close I see that gold hoop earrings hang from her earlobes. The cartilage is pierced — a thin, minimalist hoop hugging the helix — as is her nose, where a tiny gold stud pokes out of the crease. Her skin is fair, pale even, which is completely contradictory to the dark hair. She's young and lovely, with a heart-shaped face, wider around the forehead and eyes, narrowing at the chin.

"Visiting hours just ended," I say, and then I ask, "Are you family?"

"No," she says, shifting from one foot to the other, crossing and then uncrossing her arms, constantly in flux, "a friend."

"I'm so sorry," I say, hating to be the one to tell her, though the Becketts are more adamant than ever that no one can see Caitlin but them. "Only family is allowed to see Ms. Beckett. But if you want," I offer, "if you give me your name, I can let Mr. and Mrs. Beckett know you stopped by. I'm sure it would mean a lot to —" I start to say, but my voice drops off because, at the mention of their names, she stops listening. She stops moving. She plants both feet firmly on the ground beneath her, standing centimeters taller.

She gives me a hard blink. "They're . . . they're here?" she asks in a low tone and I feel her words somewhere deep inside of me.

"Yes, of course," I say. "Why?"

I see her larynx move in her throat as she swallows.

Her eyes start to stray, leaving mine. As I watch, they pass slowly over the unit, studying the faces of people at the nurses' station, and then moving on through the hall. Visiting hours are ending now, the night nurses encouraging loved ones to leave. It's a process. Some go right away at a nurse's first request, but others take more nudging. Regardless, people emerge from patient rooms, carrying coats and purses; this woman watches them all, looking through the glass and into the rooms.

She finds Caitlin's. It's not that hard, because of its adjacency to the nurses' station and because of the ICU's very design, which is intended for visibility. It's important that the medical staff can see inside of them, in case of an emergency.

I don't have to see the Becketts for myself to know that she's found them. I see it in her response, in the deep breath that she draws swiftly in and holds in her lungs. As I watch, her eyes squint, sharpening the image before her like the turning of a camera's lens, bringing objects closer and into focus.

I let my gaze go then to the Becketts, to see what she sees. On the other side of the glass, they sit, administering to Caitlin as they've done for all these days that she's been here, though I'm not used to seeing it like this, from outside the room instead of inside of it with them. It feels intrusive, like I'm some sort of voyeur for watching, but at the same time, I find it's impossible to look away.

The night nurse isn't there, nor is Jackson. The police were here earlier, talking to the Becketts, but they've left too. For now, it's just Mr. and Mrs. Beckett in the room with Caitlin, and their movements, their gestures are tender and affectionate. It takes my breath away at first and I stand there, moved by how endearing the whole scene is to someone on the outside looking in.

Mrs. Beckett sits perched on the edge of the bed. She holds a washcloth in her hands, gently wiping the visible parts of Caitlin's face with it. Gauze is still wrapped around Caitlin's head, though it's been unwrapped and rewrapped to check the incision, and between it and the endotracheal tube taped to Caitlin's face, pulling at the skin, there isn't much for Mrs. Beckett to clean.

When she's done, she sets the washcloth aside and reaches for a tube of ChapStick, which she sweeps across Caitlin's lips, moisturizing as best she can around the tube. All the while, Mr. Beckett sits in the chair beside her, leaned in, his hand on his wife's knee. He takes the ChapStick from her when she's done with it, replaces the cap and sets it aside, and then he reaches for Mrs. Beckett's hand. The intimacy between them, as a couple and as a family, is undeniable and I feel a stab of envy because the relationship I have with my parents is something less.

The woman's voice is apoplectic when she speaks.

"Caitlin would have fucking hated this," she says, the jaggedness of her words cutting into me like a knife.

"Hated what?" I ask, pulling back, tearing my eyes away from the Becketts to bring them to her, though she's so taken with what's happening in the room that she doesn't return my gaze.

"This. Them," she says, louder now, her voice seeping with disgust, making a dramatic sweeping gesture with her arm to indicate the whole scene, "hovering over her."

My eyes go back to Caitlin's room and I watch now as Mr. Beckett pushes himself from the chair and rises to his feet. He comes to stand behind his wife. His hands settle on her shoulders, his thumbs digging in, massaging them. She lets her own hands fall away from Caitlin and to her lap. She sags back, leaning into him, her exhaustion manifest after all these endless days of never leaving this place, of administering to Caitlin, of sleeping in the waiting room at night or, more likely, not sleeping. Mr. Beckett says something to her. I can't hear him, but I see his lips move and then I watch as she firmly shakes her head — an adamant no — and I know that he's trying to talk her into leaving, that he's trying to convince her to go home with him for the night and sleep. But she won't have it.

I bring my eyes back to this young woman's face, searching her eyes. "Why would she hate this?" I ask.

Of course I can see why she'd hate the fact that she was unconscious, wearing an adult diaper and urinating into a bag. But that's not what she means.

She looks at me, turning her head in slow motion. "Don't fall for their charade."

"Their charade?"

"They're not who they pretend to be. Caitlin hated her parents. Both of them, but her mother especially. She would die if she knew what was happening right now."

I look back into the room. Mr. Beckett is leaving now. He's slipping his arms into a coat and moving toward the door, with his back to Mrs. Beckett. Mrs. Beckett still sits by the bedside, readjusting a pillow and then drawing the thermal hospital blanket up to Caitlin's neck. It won't be long until the night nurse asks her to leave too, and I imagine how Mrs. Beckett must relish these last few minutes before she has to leave for the waiting room. She draws the blanket higher than I would and I think how easy it would be to suffocate an unconscious person if you wanted to, if not for the glass walls and the nurses' station so close by, though most of the time everyone is so busy they wouldn't even notice something like that. It's only the screaming of medical devices indicating changes in heart rhythm, in blood pressure and other vital signs that might call attention to what's happening inside the room, though even those are often false alarms and don't actually require immediate attention.

I turn back to ask the woman why Caitlin hated them so much.

But she's gone.

A blast of Arctic air hits me when I push my way out the building's main doors.

I carry my coat. I hold it in my hand, clutching it, because I can't be bothered to slow down and put it on. That would take time, precious seconds that I don't know that I have. I rush out the door, gasping, momentarily dazed by the shock of cold air that greets me as my eyes sweep the street.

I may have lost her already. It might already be too late.

My arms aren't bare — I wear a boxy, cropped cardigan over my scrubs — though the winter air slips easily through the weave, the plackets of the cardigan blowing open as I sprint down the parking lot ramp and toward Wellington, scanning the adjacent sidewalk and street for the woman's jacket. It's just after rush hour, but the streets are still overrun with buses and cars that back up at busy intersections where pedestrians cross, stopping the flow of traffic. There are people everywhere. It's hard to know where to look first.

The sky is dark. The sun set hours ago, though the buildings and streetlights are aglow, and every car that drives past gives off a glaring halo of light that only makes it harder to see. From behind, everyone looks almost the same in winter coats and jackets and hats, and it's not lost on me how the woman who came into the hospital was short and petite, meaning that anyone taller or more wide would block my view of her.

I move down Wellington, and only now, a block from the hospital, do I stab my frozen arms into my coat, my fingers numb as I struggle to grab a hold of the zipper and pull it up. My eyes water from the cold. My nose runs. I wipe it on a sleeve.

It gets somehow even colder the further I go from the hospital. The wind picks up, whipping around the edges of buildings so that I can hear the howl of it like a coyote at night. The taller buildings provide protection from the wind, but the minute I step past them, into the openness of a street, the air sucks me in like a vacuum and it takes effort to hold my ground, to not succumb to the wind.

Somewhere close by, from the front porch of a two or three flat, comes the melancholic knell of a wind chime getting battered to death by the wind.

I head east toward Halsted, though I have no way of knowing which way the woman went. She could just have easily gone west to Sheffield. I take my best guess and, as it turns out, I'm right, because in the small huddle of people waiting for the light to turn green at Halsted and Wellington, I make out the army surplus jacket.

The light turns green, and I worry it will turn red again before I get there, or that the flow of cars turning right onto Halsted will stop me from crossing. Pedestrians have the right of way, but that doesn't mean cars, especially impatient rush hour drivers anxious to get home, always oblige. I break into a jog, feeling relieved when I enter the intersection. The woman walks fast. She has her hands in the pockets of the coat, the hood thrust over her head, and her head down. I watch from behind, refusing to lose sight of her. As I watch, the hood of her coat blows off, revealing the near-black hair. She gropes for the hood with a bare hand, yanking it back on again, but it's no use; the wind tears it immediately off. We're walking into the wind now, sloped forward, leaning into it for leverage, but still it's a slog.

"Excuse me," I call out, but my words misfire. The wind pilfers them and carries them somewhere behind me, back toward the intersection at Wellington and Halsted. I try again, louder this time, practically shouting, but it's no use. There are at least six people between this woman and me, and I have to shove my way through them to try and catch up.

I'm breathing hard from exertion though I close the gap. When I'm close enough, I reach out for the woman's arm, but she's walking faster than me and so I just barely manage to pinch the back fabric of her jacket. It's enough to get her attention, enough that she slows and turns from the sensation of being touched.

At first, I think, she's under the impression that someone touched her by accident, but then her eyes take me in and they widen with recognition and surprise.

She comes to a full stop on the sidewalk and turns to face me. "You're that nurse, right?" she says. I nod as she crosses her arms, the wind blowing her hair from behind so that it wraps around her face now like octopus tentacles. "What are you doing? Are you *following* me?" she asks, incredulous, as we stand, two boulders in a raging river, dividing the water's flow as people move around and past us, no one too seemingly inconvenienced.

"No," I say, embarrassed by the accusation.

"Then what are you doing?" she asks brusquely.

I search for words. "You left so fast. I didn't get a chance to ask you —"

"So you are following me."

"Yes. I'm sorry." I feel stupid. "I should have said yes, that I am following you, but not in the way you think."

"What do you want?"

"Who are you," I ask, letting my voice soften, "and how do you know Caitlin?"

"What are you," she asks, "the fucking police?"

"No," I say, shaking my head. "I'm just a nurse."

"I didn't know nurses asked so many questions." She regards me for a minute, and I don't think she's going to answer. I think she's going to blow me off, turn and walk away.

But then she says, "She was living with me."

"Caitlin was?"

"No," she says, "Princess Kate," which leaves me feeling obtuse. She's mocking me. "Of course Caitlin."

"You were roommates?"

"Yeah," she says. "I placed an ad online looking for a roommate and she found me."

"You didn't know her before?"

"No."

"What was it like to live with her?"

"Fine. I guess, though the last couple weeks, she was all uptight. She stopped answering her phone. When I asked who she was avoiding, she said collection agencies, and maybe it was. She would leave for days at a time until I thought she was gone for

271

good, and then she'd come back, out of the blue."

"Where would she go?"

She shrugs. "She was seeing someone I think," she says. "Maybe she was staying with him. Is that all you want to know?" she asks. She doesn't wait for an answer. She starts to walk away and it's a reflex when I reach out to stop her with a hand on her arm, which she shrugs instantly off.

"Sorry," I say, pulling my hand back. "No. There's more. I want to know what you meant back there, at the hospital. When you said that Caitlin hated her parents. What did you mean by that?"

She rolls her eyes, which is not unlike something Sienna would do. "It's not that hard to understand."

"No, you're right. I get that," I say, talking fast, worried she'll lose interest in me and try leaving again before the conversation is through. I should have phrased my question another way. "It's just that it surprised me. From the way Mrs. Beckett talks, she adores Caitlin. I never imagined there would be any animosity between them."

"Well you imagined wrong." The woman turns away. But then, almost immediately, she turns back and deadpans, "You're so worried about someone getting into Caitlin's room that shouldn't be there. But what if the danger is already inside?"

It's not that I think Mrs. Beckett pushed her off the bridge. Of course I don't think that, and I know that if the police can find Milo Finch, he'll be arrested.

But still, my breath hitches. My voice gets caught. I say nothing back. I can only watch as this woman turns again and disappears into the night.

A gust of wind comes in just then. The rush of winter air assaults me, the wind agitating my hair before slipping down the collar of my coat, touching skin. I pull my hood up over my head and tug the coat's zipper higher.

I hear my name shouted from somewhere behind me.

Meghan.

I spin around. There is a crowd of people on the sidewalk behind me. The light at the intersection has just turned green and they cross the street all at once, moving toward me in a pack. I take them in, searching each individual windblown face when Mr. Beckett breaks through the crowds.

My heart pounds and my legs go numb, watching as he moves with confidence as he walks, weaving around people, somehow

273

unsusceptible to the cold.

"I thought that was you, but I wasn't sure," he says when he reaches me, his eyes going the same way the woman just went, and I wonder if he can see her, if he knows who she is. "I saw you from back there," he tells me, making a dismissive gesture to somewhere behind him, on the other side of the intersection, and I wonder: From back where? How long had he been watching me? Did he see that she and I were talking?

He brings his eyes back to mine. He smiles and asks, "Is this how you get home, Meghan?"

I try to keep my voice from shaking, but it does anyway from the cold and nerves. "Yes," I say, though that's not true.

He smiles again, clearly pleased. "We can walk together then. I'm headed this way myself and I wouldn't mind the company."

I swallow hard, my saliva thickening. "Okay," I breathe out, my breath visible in the cold, as we turn and move down the sidewalk together, closer than I would like because of the crowds.

"Do you always walk home alone like this?"

"Yes. It's a short walk. It's not far and is good exercise."

"I don't know how safe it is to walk in

274

this city alone at night anymore," he says. I keep my gaze on the sidewalk. Still, I feel his eyes on me, searching. "You'll have to forgive me, Meghan. Once a father, always a father. Raising a daughter, it's in my nature to be protective. But you have a good head about you and I'm sure that you're smart, careful, that you stay on busy streets when you're alone. That said, it sure is cold," he says, pressing his hands further into his coat pockets.

"You get used to it," I say, though that's a lie. You don't ever get used to cold like this. In the coming days, meteorologists say we're likely to enter a deep freeze thanks to a polar vortex coming in from the North Pole, with possible overnight lows of negative twenty degrees, and a wind chill that is even more grim, more like thirty or forty degrees below zero. It isn't atypical for January and Chicagoans are a hardy bunch; brutal temperatures like these rarely bring us to our knees, but that doesn't mean we like it.

"Do you?" he asks disbelieving. "Because I've lived in Chicago my whole life and I've never gotten used to cold like this."

"It helps to keep moving. The faster I walk, the better. It keeps the blood flowing."

He chuckles. "I like that about you, Meghan. You're very smart. Very astute. And you always look on the bright side of things."

We come to Broadway, just a few blocks east of Sheffield, which will take me home.

"I try," I say, "but don't always succeed. I can be quite the pessimist too. I'm this way." I step past him for Broadway, anxious to leave him, to be alone, "I'm sure I'll see you tomorrow."

But Mr. Beckett says, looking around, taking in the intersection before his eyes come back to mine. "I'll walk with you awhile, I think. I know you're a smart girl and chances are you'll be fine, but I'd just feel more comfortable if I stayed with you a little while longer. I'd never forgive myself if something happened to you."

My throat tightens. "Oh no," I say. "I can't ask you to do that. Really, I'm fine. I do this all the time. It's so cold out. You should get home."

"No, I insist," he says. "And besides, as you can imagine, I'm not too eager to go home to an empty house. I like talking to you. I like your company. Amelia does too. I don't know what we'd do if we didn't have you."

"I'm just doing my job."

"Don't sell yourself short, Meghan. You've

gone above and beyond." We wait for the light to turn green, and when it does we cross the street, heading north on Broadway. "Do you live by yourself?" he asks and I'm made uneasy by his question. I search for words, which should be easy to find. Do I or do I not live alone? "Pardon me for being so blunt, but I've noticed you don't wear a ring."

"No," I say, my voice diminished. "I don't live alone. I live with my daughter."

"Right, of course. I remember you said you had a daughter. Raising little girls is not for the faint of heart. You're divorced then?"

"Yes."

"For how long?"

"Almost a year."

"What happened?"

"I'm sorry," I say, "but if you don't mind, I'd rather not talk about it."

Again I feel his eyes on me, gazing down from where he stands, at least six inches taller than me. "Of course. My apologies." He changes tack. "Listen, Meghan. I'm glad I ran into you like this. I've been wanting to talk to you about Amelia. I don't know who else to talk to about this. I'm worried about her."

"That's understandable," I say.

"She's not doing well."

"No. She's not. I can see she's having a hard time with this, as any mother would. But the hospital has counselors and chaplains available. It might be good for her to talk with someone, if you think she would, if you think it might help."

"Maybe," he says, nodding, "though Amelia is a private person. I don't know how she would feel about speaking to a counselor. We're all quite private in fact, which is why I appreciate you using discretion when speaking to others about us. The police have an investigation to do, but we don't need too many people probing into our personal lives."

"I . . . I wouldn't."

"No?" he asks. He knows it's not true. He did see me speaking to Caitlin's roommate earlier. He knows who she is. I shake my head, but it's weak and in my silence, he says, "I received a call from that detective this morning. He had something interesting to say."

"What's that?" I ask, feeling my heart rhythm change.

"He said that the other day, when you were looking at mug shots together, you told them something about Jackson." My jaw clenches, my throat narrows, making it harder to swallow, harder to breathe.

"I'm sorry," I say, feeling caught and also stupid for thinking the police would be more discreet with where they got their information.

"I don't blame you, Meghan. I appreciate you looking out for Caitlin like that. I spoke to Jackson. I asked him if what the police said was true, and it is. He wasn't in London like he said. He was here, in Chicago," he says. "Turns out he's been in Chicago many times this year and we haven't known. He's kept it from us and from his wife, telling us that he was in Toronto or Detroit or some other place for work. I haven't told Amelia yet. She has enough on her mind for now and shouldn't have to worry about this too, but Jackson has been seeing a woman here in the city. He's been having an affair. Being in London for work was only a cover story."

"Oh. I'm so sorry."

"Yes. I am too. It caught me off guard. I thought Jackson and his wife were happily married. They've been married five years and, lately, Amelia has been nudging him for grandchildren, which I don't think will happen now." He's quiet for a minute. "I didn't expect him to go and do something like this. I thought I raised him to be better

279

but, he fell in love, he says."

I say again that I'm sorry. "We can only know so much about the people in our lives."

"That's true. That's very perceptive." He pauses. "The reason I asked you not to talk about our family with others, Meghan, is because people tell stories. They tell lies," he says, going on. "For example, Amelia used to teach fifth grade. She loved teaching. She had a real passion for and a knack for it — it was what she was born to do. It was what she dreamed of doing, ever since she was a child. She taught in the public schools for years, until something terrible happened."

I turn to face him, my attention piqued. "What?"

"A student of hers lied. She told her parents that Amelia hurt her. There was no truth to it," he's quick to say, lest I think otherwise, which I do. My mind immediately goes there, to Mrs. Beckett hurting a student of hers, but Mr. Beckett goes on, explaining. "What happened was that this student had gotten in trouble for misbehaving in class and it just so happened that this same student had fallen and bruised her arm at recess that day. When her parents asked about the bruise, she said Mrs. Beckett did it, that Amelia had grabbed her by the arm when she was yelling at her, fastening down on it, squeezing hard. Amelia never touched the girl."

"What happened?" I ask as we walk together down Broadway.

"The girl's parents told the principal, who had no choice but to call DCFS. But being indicted by DCFS comes with consequences. Rumor got out that Amelia was being investigated for suspected child abuse of a student. It was completely unfounded and unsubstantiated of course — other kids attested to the fact that they never saw Amelia lay a hand on his child — but despite having her name cleared, Amelia was embarrassed. Her coworkers and the parents of the children she taught never looked at her the same. Amelia left her job, which was hard on her. I suggested she look for another position in a different school, a different district — a fresh start — but Amelia wasn't sure she ever wanted to step foot in a classroom again. What was to keep this from happening again?" He takes a breath before going on, deciding whether to say more. "Amelia has had many letdowns in her life, and her relationship with Caitlin has been much the same, a series of disappointments."

"How so?" I ask as we step into the intersection at Barry, crossing, letting traffic wait for us.

"Just as with teaching, all of her life, Amelia dreamed of being a mother," he says. "She wanted a daughter more than anything. She and her own mother had been incredibly close. They were practically inseparable until her mother had a heart attack and died. Amelia envisioned having a similar relationship with Caitlin, but that didn't happen.

"Caitlin was always a difficult child," he says, and as he does, I turn to see a change come over his face, his voice infused with something like resentment or disgust. "I hate to speak negatively after everything that's happened but, as a child, Caitlin didn't enjoy being told no. Unlike other children who might pout or slam a bedroom door, she would fly into a rage and pull out all the stops to get what she wanted. There was nothing she wouldn't do. With Caitlin, it was pathological," he says, giving the full picture of the woman who lies unconscious on the hospital bed, one that bears scrutiny. "Caitlin was eleven or twelve when the investigation with DCFS happened. She caught wind of it and used it to her advantage, realizing how easily a lie could ruin

282

her mother's life. Every time Amelia told her no — no she wouldn't buy her more candy or clothes — Caitlin would make like she was being hurt. *Let go, you're hurting me,* she'd cry out in public until people looked. Amelia and I tried to make light of it. Caitlin, we told ourselves, was an adolescent with a still-developing brain. She didn't know what she was doing. She didn't know the consequences of her words and actions.

"Once, when she was angry with Amelia for something I don't even remember what anymore, it was that inconsequential — she picked up the phone and dialed 911. She told the dispatcher that her mother was hurting her. The police came, because they had to and, for a second time in her life, Amelia was investigated by DCFS.

"For all of Caitlin's life, Amelia and I would tiptoe around her, afraid to do anything that might set her off. But she had Amelia, in particular, in an emotional death grip, because Amelia wanted more than anything to be close to her, to be her confidante and a good mom. You have a daughter. I'm sure you can understand. We have two sons, but Caitlin is our only daughter. Amelia would do anything to earn her affection and love, which was parceled out by design. Imagine," he says, "loving

283

this tiny little human so much and so unconditionally, and then one day, she turns on you and becomes the source of so much pain." I can't imagine it. I can't bear to think of it. Sienna has her moments but she could never hurt me like that.

"Every time Caitlin behaved in a certain way," he pauses, thinking his next words through, "it broke Amelia's heart and pushed her closer to the edge."

I wonder what he means by that. But before I can ask, he changes course, saying, "I'll definitely mention the counselor to Amelia though and see if I can't talk her into giving it a try. It would be good for her to talk to someone."

He reaches out all of a sudden then, setting a hand on my arm, stopping forward motion. The sensation of his hand on my arm — the firmness of it and the breach of personal boundaries — discomfits me. My breath hitches. I turn to face him, looking up.

"The thing is," he says, his face suddenly grave. "I don't know what Amelia will do if Caitlin dies. She won't survive it."

I pull back. I don't know what to say, how to respond. My mind searches for words, something comforting that doesn't give away my own discomfort.

"I don't mean to unload on you like this," he says because of my silence, his eyes holding mine, studying them before the faint, throttled sound of a ringing phone, heard barely over the sound of traffic and the wind, interrupts us. "I'm sorry," he says, breaking his gaze, reaching into the pocket of his pants to produce the phone, letting his eyes run over the name on the caller ID. "Speak of the devil. It's Amelia," he says, and then, "I can call her back later," as if he's just going to slip that phone back into his pocket and keep talking to me, keep walking with me.

"No," I say, too eagerly, and then more staidly, "No. You should take it and make sure she and Caitlin are okay."

"Yes," he says, giving it some thought. "You're probably right. You'll be alright on your own from here?"

I nod. "I'll be fine. I do this all the time."

As I walk away alone, I think how what he said — about Mrs. Beckett not surviving if Caitlin were to die — sounded almost prophetic.

SIXTEEN

That night I have bad dreams. Angsty dreams, like that the apartment is on fire and I'm late to school and can't find my class. It goes on all night so that I don't get any restful sleep. I'm tired the next day at work as a result. I go through the motions, keeping to myself and avoiding people as best I can because I'm not in the right mind for conversation.

Around five o'clock, I step out into the hall to text Sienna.

I had texted her this morning too. This morning, I waited until I was at work because I didn't want to text too early and catch her when she was still with Ben, having breakfast together or on the drive to school. How was the show? I'd asked and, at the time, she texted almost immediately back in all caps.

SO GOOD.

I'm glad you enjoyed it! I said, hoping it didn't come across as insincere. I was glad she enjoyed the show. I just felt envious that she shared the experience with Ben, and I regretted not having splurged to buy the tickets first.

I slipped my phone into the pocket of a cardigan then, keeping it on silent but vibrate so that if Sienna needed something, I'd feel it pulse in my pocket.

The day got away from me, so that only now do I find the time to check back in.

How is everything going? Are you and Nat getting along okay? I ask, because today is the day that they will be alone and meeting for the first time. The situation isn't ideal. I know that and feel guilty for it, but there is nothing I could do in light of *Dear Evan Hansen,* and the last thing I wanted was to take that experience away from her and say she couldn't go.

I hold the phone in my hand, waiting for a reply that doesn't come.

Nat was still getting ready when I left for work this morning. I left the apartment before she did, telling her to lock the door from the inside because she didn't have a key. She was going to work herself and Sienna would be home before either of us, so she'd be there to let Nat back in.

287

Now, after a few minutes of waiting in the hall, I reluctantly return the phone to the pocket of my cardigan and get back to work, though Sienna's lack of a reply troubles me.

An hour later, I steal another look at my phone. It's after six o'clock now and Sienna still hasn't replied. My anxiety intensifies. I'm sure there is a reasonable explanation (maybe, I tell myself, she and Nat are hitting it off so well that she hasn't bothered to look at her phone), but still I send Nat a quick message too, asking if everything is going okay and letting her know that I'll be home soon.

The next hour lasts an eternity. I can barely focus during my change of shift report to the night nurse.

I walk quickly out of the building when my shift ends. I speed walk home, bobbing and weaving around pedestrians, dropping down and stepping into the street to get around slower foot traffic. I try calling Sienna three times but she never answers. Her phone is often on silent because, if it wasn't, it would go off all day with the deluge of friends' texts, but her phone is almost always in her hands, too, which means that if she was looking at it, she would see that I was calling.

I race down Sheffield, cutting the corner

when I come to our street. I see the three flat in the distance, but I can't get there fast enough. My legs don't move as quickly as I would like.

I run my eyes over the exterior of the building. From the outside, the living room is completely black and I don't understand why it would be. The light should be on. Sienna and Nat should be in there, eating dinner together in the living room and getting to know one another.

I feel it in my gut.

Something is wrong.

I dash up the outside steps. I jam the key in and let myself into the building. I climb the stairs toward the third floor. Somewhere just beyond the second floor, I get a view of our front door, which is open. My heart starts to race. I walk somehow faster, taking the steps two at a time now, rounding the top of the stairs and pressing the door open with my hand. I come in to the sound of Sienna's music, which is loud.

"Sienna!" I call out but she says nothing back.

It's dark in most of the apartment. But in her bedroom at the center of it, Sienna's desk lamp is on, the light from it weak.

I drop my purse just inside the front door, hearing the contents spill. I leave them. I make my way to her room, finding Sienna standing at the edge of her bed with her back to me, unpacking her overnight bag. Relief overwhelms me. She's here. She's fine.

I take a breath, letting my heart settle before I speak.

"What time did you get home?" I ask, rapping on the door with my knuckles.

Sienna spins around. "What the —" she asks, dropping the shirt that she was holding to the floor. I've startled her. She didn't hear me come in over the sound of her music.

"Sorry," I say, holding my hands up as a sign of peace. I make my way to her Bluetooth speaker to turn the volume down. "I didn't mean to scare you. I thought you heard me come in. We have neighbors you know. I'm not sure they're as big of fans of Beyoncé as you."

She rolls her eyes. It takes a second for her to catch her breath.

"I thought I was about to be murdered," she says, that word — *murdered* — taking on a whole new meaning in light of everything that's been happening.

"That's not something to joke about, Sienna," I scold. "You left the front door open by the way."

"No I didn't," she says, defiant as always, as if I didn't just see the open front door.

"Yes, you did. You have to make sure it's closed and locked," I say, which reminds me to send another note to the landlord to have it fixed. "I texted you over two hours ago. Why didn't you reply?"

"I didn't see it," she says. She looks at her phone and, only now, sees my text. "Sorry. I fell asleep after school. I got like three hours sleep last night." Of course she did. The show would have gone late. Ben, she tells me, took her out to eat after the show. By the time they made it back to his place, it could have been approaching midnight.

But I can't think about that now.

"Where is Nat?" I ask, watching as Sienna's face clouds over in confusion. "My friend," I prompt. "The one who is staying with us. Is she not home yet?"

Sienna shakes her head. "I didn't see her. She never came." I worry Sienna is wrong. I worry that Nat *did* come but that Sienna was asleep and Nat couldn't get in downstairs. Nat might have buzzed to be let in. Sienna might have slept through it.

I want to be angry. But I can't be, not yet. My first priority is finding Nat, figuring out where she went when she couldn't get into the apartment.

I race back out to the living room for my phone so I can check Facebook to see if Nat messaged. It's still dark in the living room and so I go to the lamp and turn it on, twisting the switch. Light fills the room.

And that's when I see, in the glow of the floor lamp, that the sofa bed has been remade, the cushions and throw pillows replaced on the seat. The coffee table has been slid back into place and Nat's large duffel bag, which has taken up residence in front of the TV for over two days, is gone, the only proof it was ever there the matted section of rug.

My hand rises to my mouth. I lower myself to the arm of the sofa.

I think back to my patient, Anne, whose husband beat her to death. I followed the murder trial. I went to it one day, sitting at the back of the courtroom because I wanted to see his face. The day that I went, there was a homicide detective on the stand. He described how Anne's husband left her to bleed out internally after the beating. I know from my own work that bleeding out internally can be sudden, painful and severe, or it can be slow — a silent, sly death, a trickle of blood until the total blood loss is so severe it's beyond hope. I deliberated for days after the trial and then for weeks about which way Anne died — sudden and painful, or slow.

Did she go into shock? Did her organs fail? Did her children watch?

I think about Ben's decree when I first heard about Anne's murder, how I can't save them all. Maybe he was right. Maybe I should have listened. Maybe I shouldn't have tried.

"Mom?" Sienna asks, coming up behind me, her hand on my shoulder a comfort. "What's wrong?"

Nat left. She left this morning sometime after I left for work, taking all of her things with her. She had no intention of coming back, and I wonder when she made the decision to leave, sometime this morning or in the middle of the night?

Or did she know even sooner than that?

She went back to him, to Declan.

Fear grips me from inside.

No good can come of this.

I send her a message on Facebook.

Where are you, Nat? Let me help you.

All night long, I stay awake, worrying about her. I constantly refresh Facebook but she doesn't read my message. I go to her Facebook page and find myself looking again at her husband, Declan, and, this time, when I see his handsome face, I feel sick inside, my stomach tightening. When I think of all the things he's done and said to her, he's not attractive after all, but ugly. Vile. I wonder if he made good on his threat, if, when she came home, he locked her in a room as promised, tied her to a bed or worse. A moan rises up from inside of me as I picture Nat with something like zip ties on her wrists, bound to the spindles of the bed with a fresh black eye, a broken nose, bruises on her neck — retribution for her leaving. A reckoning.

I wonder if when he's through with her, he'll come for me because I helped her. I kept her from him.

I think of Sienna in twenty years.

I think of what I would do if a man ever hurt her like that.

I'd kill him, I think.

Night lasts an eternity, but eventually morning comes. The sun rises. Life goes on.

In the morning, I watch Sienna get ready for school. Standing in the kitchen with my coffee, I see her reflection in the mirror through the open bathroom door. She puts on makeup, though not much because she's perfect without it. Flawless skin, long, thick lashes. The teen years pass by with turbo speed, and I think again of those long, sleepless nights when she was a baby and how I'd give anything to have them back.

Once she leaves, I shower, grateful for the day off. I'd be worthless today if I had to work. Sometime after nine, I bundle up in my coat, gloves and hat and head out into the cold. Christmas is coming and I haven't even begun to shop. I'm not in the mood for it, but right now I could use the fresh air and the distraction.

I don't have many people to buy for this year, which is an upshot of divorce I suppose. I won't be buying for Ben or his family. But there is Sienna of course, my parents, and I like to pick up some small things for a few of the nurses at work. I go first to a cozy corner boutique, and then I make my way to a cheeky little home decor store with magnets and coasters and vintage art that makes me laugh. I'll find something there for Luke and the rest of my colleagues.

My phone starts to ring as I open the door to walk into the store. It's buried in the depths of my bag and is difficult to find. I shove aside a wallet and a cosmetic bag, knowing the search is likely futile. I will never get to it in time.

My fingers make contact on the third or

fourth ring. I fish it out of the bag, but as soon as I do, the phone goes quiet. I'm too late. A missed call notification from Sienna appears on the screen. I'm taken aback. I physically stop in the open doorway and stare down at her number on the display. Doubt and confusion fill my thoughts because it's just after ten o'clock in the morning and Sienna is at school, or rather, she should be. Sienna texts from school sometimes, sneaking her phone when the teacher isn't paying attention — Can I hang out with Gianna today? I lost my water bottle. Did u buy tampons? My stupid calculator won't work. — but she doesn't call. My mind goes in a million different directions thinking how, if she was sick, the nurse would call and, if she got in trouble at school for something, then the dean would call. Sienna wouldn't ever be the one to call.

I don't have a chance to call her back. Almost immediately the phone in my hand starts to ring again and I jump, from the unexpected sound of it. It's Sienna, calling me back.

My thumb swipes immediately across the screen. "Sienna? What's wrong?" I ask, pressing the phone to my ear. I step fully inside the store, letting the door drift closed to muffle the street noise outside, the sound of cars passing by and people on their phones, having conversations of their own. I hear the shrill, unmistakable panic in my voice, and I think how, in the next instant, Sienna is going to ride me for overreacting, for freaking out about nothing. *Geez Mom. Relax. I'm fine,* she'll say, drawing that last word out for emphasis.

That's not what happens.

It's quiet at first. I just barely make out the sound of something slight like movement or wind. It goes on a few seconds so that I decide this must be a pocket dial. Sienna didn't mean to call me. The phone is in her pocket or her backpack, and she called me by mistake. She doesn't even know she's called me twice. I listen, trying to decipher where she is, but it's more of the same. Nothing telling. Nothing revelatory.

But then, a man's voice cuts through the quiet, his words cold and sparing, his voice altered as if he's speaking through a voice changer, "If you ever want to see your daughter again, you will do exactly as I say."

I gasp. My eyes gape. I lose my footing, falling backward into the closed door. A hand rises to my mouth, pressing hard. I can't breathe all of a sudden. I can't think; my mind can't process what's happening at first. I pull the phone away from my ear, looking down at the display to see if I'm mistaken, if it's not Sienna's number that called but someone else. A wrong number. Because this can't be right, this can't be happening. This can't be happening to me.

But it is right. Sienna's number stares back at me from the display.

"Who is this," I ask, pressing the phone back to my ear, "and why do you have my daughter's phone?"

And then, in the background, I hear Sienna's piercing scream.

"Mommy!" she bellows. It's high-pitched, frenzied, desperate, and that's when I know that this man doesn't only have Sienna's phone. He has Sienna.

Pure terror courses through my veins. Sienna hasn't called me Mommy in at least ten years. I can't stop thinking what horrible thing must be happening for her to lapse back into her childhood and call me *Mommy.* I'm completely powerless. I don't know where she is. I don't know how to get to her, how to help her, how to make this stop.

"Go away," Sienna commands. Her voice trembles, so that she doesn't sound like herself, who is usually so defiant, so sure. There is no mistaking her fear. "Leave me alone," she demands, crying now. Sienna falters on the words, her voice cracking, so that the execution doesn't carry the same weight as the words themselves.

Sienna is terrified and so am I.

"Sienna baby!" I shriek. There is the sound of commotion, of muffled noises in the background — this man, I imagine, subduing Sienna, forcing a gag into her mouth so that she can't speak or scream, and Sienna fighting back from the sound of it, resisting him.

I realize that I'm not blinking. I'm not breathing.

Tears sting my eyes. "What are you doing to her? Who is this?" I demand of this man, screaming into the phone so that everyone in the store stops what they're doing to look at me, to stare, some gasping and pressing hands to their own mouths in shock, as if this nightmare is somehow collective. "What have you done with my daughter? What do you want from me?"

"Listen to me," the man says back, his modulated voice unshaken and sedate, unlike mine. I still hear Sienna's desperate cry in the background, a keening, weeping wail, though it's stilted. The sound of it is enough to bring me to my knees, and yet I don't know what's worse: the sound of Sienna's cry or the sound of it as it grows distant and then fades completely away.

"Where is she? What have you done to her? Why can't I hear her anymore?"

"You need to do exactly as I say. Exactly. Do you understand?"

"I want to talk to my daughter. Let me talk to my daughter. I need to know that she's okay. What have you done to her?"

"I have nothing to lose," the man says. "You're the only one with something to lose, Ms. Michaels. Now you need to shut up and listen to me because I don't care one way or the other if your daughter lives or dies. What happens to her is entirely up to you. Now," he says, and I know in my heart that this is Declan. This is an act of vengeance for my having had Nat, for harboring her, for turning her against him.

Panic grips me. "What?" I beg. "I'll do anything. Just give me my daughter back."

"I need you to wire ten thousand dollars to this account."

My heart all but slips right out of me. Ten thousand dollars. A ransom demand.

He doesn't wait or ask if I'm ready. In the next breath, he fires off bank account and routing numbers and I race, desperate, to the woman who stands open-mouthed behind the cash register, motioning like a mime for paper and a pen. She searches the counter for them, but it's another woman, standing to the side, a customer in line, who goes inside her purse and finds them for me.

"I . . . I didn't get it. Please, say them again," I plead, and he does.

"You have five minutes to wire the money."

"Or what?" I ask, panic in my voice. "I . . . I can't do that. I need more time. I can't do this in five minutes."

"Five minutes," he says again, "and then she dies."

The line goes dead. When I pull the phone away from my ear, Sienna's number is gone. Vanished. It feels predictive, prophetic. I moan. It's primitive, animal like. My hand goes to my mouth, my knees buckle beneath me so that I would collapse if not for a stranger's hand on my back, propping me up.

I don't have time to go to pieces.

In five minutes, Sienna might die.

There is a hand on my shoulder, which I shrug off. People are talking. Asking me questions. Incessant questions, while others stand quietly aside, their mouths agape. *Is everything okay? Ma'am? Ma'am? What do you need? Should we call the police?*

Four minutes and forty seconds.

I step away, finding space. I pull up the bank's app on my phone, my fat fingers pushing the wrong buttons in my haste. If it wasn't for my grandmother's inheritance, I wouldn't have this kind of money and I thank God for it because I don't know what would happen if I didn't.

Would Sienna die?

Four minutes and twenty seconds.

There is no time to think it though. There is no time to call the police. I picture Sienna bound and gagged. This man is a monster; there is nothing he won't do. I won't risk it. A call to the police would take precious time that I don't have, and for what? They would never find Sienna in that time.

Three minutes and fifty-five seconds.

My heart palpitates. The pounding in my chest is almost too much to bear.

I enter the recipient's information and select where I would like to wire the money from, which is my savings account, where my grandmother's inheritance sits collecting minimal interest because I haven't invested it yet. I select the amount to send, and then I schedule the wire and hope it sends, watching the time pass by on my watch.

One minute and twenty seconds.

One minute and ten seconds.

One minute.

The Wi-Fi isn't strong and I worry it will fail, that I'll lose the connection before the money can send. If that happens, there isn't time to try again.

Regret fills me.

I shouldn't have let her go to school today.

I should have kept her home.

I shouldn't have gotten involved with Nat in the first place. I shouldn't have put her safety before Sienna's.

This is my fault. It's my fault this is happening.

I move around the store with my phone in hand, everyone backing away, giving me a wide berth, trying to find a spot with better Wi-Fi, and eventually I do. Eventually the wire transfer goes through.

I fall to my knees, sobbing.

The voices return. *Ma'am. Is everything okay? What can we do? I've called the police. They're on their way. Do you need something? Water? Someone get her a glass of water. Give her room. Ma'am.*

I can't respond. I'm in my own head thinking how this isn't the end of it. I don't know what he'll do now that he has his money. Will he let Sienna go? Or will he keep her?

Only then do I think to check the location sharing app to see where he has Sienna.

I hold my breath as the app loads. I expect it will tell me she's down some alley or moving seventy miles per hour on the expressway. I wait in fear because if he took her this morning as she was on her way to school, she could be in Wisconsin or Indiana by now. Michigan even.

But that's not where the app says she is.

Sienna, it says, is at school.

My mind spins. I don't understand. I can't make sense of it. It isn't just that Sienna's phone is at school because the call came from her phone. I heard her voice in the background. No, the app is wrong. It hasn't updated or my connection inside this store is slow. I click on the button for it to refresh and then watch as two little purple arrows chase each other around and around the screen, updating, and when they come to rest, the words at the top read: *Last updated now.*

According to this app, Sienna has been at school since 8:02 this morning. According to the app, once she arrived at school this morning, she never left. She's been there the whole time.

He has her right there on school grounds.

I press myself to standing. I run outside

to hail a cab while calling 911. When the dispatcher answers, I say, "Someone has my daughter," and then I tell him what happened and what I know, and the dispatcher says that he will send police to the building. He asks questions about Sienna, like for a physical description. He wants me to stay on the line with him, but I tell him I can't. "Please," I beg. "Tell them to hurry."

As the cab pulls away from the curb, I hang up and call Sienna's school. An automated calling system answers and I have to wait to press nine to be connected to the school secretary. It's torture. She drones the name of the high school when she answers. I cut her abruptly off.

"I'm calling about my daughter. Sienna Long. Is she there?" I say. "I need to speak to her." It's not that I expect Sienna to just be back in class now as if nothing has happened. But I don't know what else to say.

The woman puts me on hold. Time becomes eternal.

I consider every worst-case scenario in this moment. Sienna is being held in a car or a van in the school parking lot. She's locked inside the custodian closet or a mechanical room or some other restricted place where students aren't allowed to go. She's hurt. She's dead or dying as I wait on hold for

305

the secretary to get back to me.

I can't stand it. I end the call and call immediately back, wait for the automated calling system to answer and then press nine again. When the secretary answers, droning the name of the school, words rush out of me. "This is Meghan Michaels again calling about my daughter, Sienna. You had me on hold. Please," I say, fighting tears, "I need to speak to my daughter."

In the next moment my fears are confirmed.

"Yes, Ms. Michaels. Sorry it took a minute. I called down to her class. I spoke to Mr. Pruitt, but he said that Sienna didn't show up for third period. Have you tried calling on her cell?" she asks, as I press my fingers to my mouth, nodding because I don't have it in me to speak.

"Ms. Michaels? Are you still there? Ms. Michaels?"

"Yes," I breathe, and then I pull the phone away from my ear and press end.

In the back of the cab, I cry.

Sienna has been taken from me. The only thing in the world that matters is gone.

The police arrive at the school before I do. As the cab pulls in, I find two police cruisers in the circle drive of the parking lot. Students walk past, heading out for an open period, noticing the cars. I pay the cab driver, throwing too much money at him, and then run out of the car and past the students, tugging in vain on the main door handles, but they're locked. I have to wait to be buzzed into the building, stating my name and reason for being here before the secretary will let me in.

I find the police officers standing in the main office, surrounded by the school principal, the assistant principals and the secretary, everyone looking grim. "Mrs. Long?" one of the officers asks as I enter, and I say yes, not bothering to correct him.

"Someone has my daughter," I cry out.

"She's on her way," he says.

My head snaps. "What?" I gasp.

"Your daughter is on her way."

I don't have time to ask questions, to process it. Because from around the corner, I see her. Sienna. Her backpack is on. There are books in her arms. She is physically intact. There are no cuts, no bruises, no gag. Her face is neutral, placid, fine. Confused.

I leave the office, running gracelessly to her, my arms outstretched like the wings of a plane.

"Mom?" she asks, coming to a dead stop just short of me. She looks at me before letting her eyes to go the police, her surprise unambiguous. "What are you doing here? What are *they* doing here? What happened? Is everything okay?"

"You . . . you weren't in class," I sputter, taking her into my arms, holding her so I know for certain that she is real, that she's really here, and not only a mirage.

She lets me hold her for a brief moment, and then she steps back so she can look at me. "I . . . I was with Mr. Garcia. I was retaking a math test. I . . . I have a pass," she says, looking back and forth between the secretary, the principal, the police officers and me, brandishing it in the air for us to see.

I start to cry again.

It was all a lie.

"It's called a virtual kidnapping," the police officer says to me as I sit in the police station on Addison, filling out a report with Sienna by my side. "Scammers target people and prey on their worst fears, coercing them into quickly paying ransom for a loved one's release."

"What about the money?"

The money, he tells me, is most likely gone. It's already been accepted and once that's happened, it's virtually impossible to get back. But he will look into it.

"This man called me from Sienna's phone. I heard her voice in the background. How?"

"It wasn't your daughter you heard. It was someone pretending to be her, or a recording even. In stressful situations like this, it's easy to mistake the voice. As for the call coming from your daughter's phone, it's called spoofing or, more specifically, caller ID spoofing. The attacker uses technology called VoIP to change the caller ID to something familiar, something personal." He waits a beat and then says, "Everything is specifically done to scare and manipulate you."

I feel stupid, ashamed and violated. "And I fell for it," I say, dropping my head into a hand.

The officer says, "It's easy to do. They can be very persuasive, and the amount of time you're given to wire the money is so short, there is no time to think it through or to investigate. It's very intentional, but often random. The attacker might make a dozen calls like this a day in the hopes that just one person pays the ransom fee."

"But if it's so random, then why Sienna? And why me?"

He shrugs. "You were unlucky."

But I'm not so sure. I have a hard time

believing this could be so arbitrary, so indiscriminate. It felt much more intentional than that.

Someone wanted to hurt me.

SEVENTEEN

Sienna and I walk down the street, drawn together by the crowds so that our arms touch. I want to wrap my arm around her, to take her by the hand like I used to when she was young and I worried that if I didn't hold on to her, she'd get lost or drift aimlessly into the street, but I don't think sixteen-year-old Sienna would like that very much.

We decide on something quick, a deli on Clark, so we can take our food to go and then go back home, sit on the sofa and eat. Sienna orders a panini and me the minestrone soup, and then we stand on the far end of the counter, waiting for our food to come up. I stare at Sienna while she stares at her phone as we wait, lost in TikTok, and normally I'd tell her to put it away and talk to me, but today I don't because the latest TikTok trend has her laughing and I love to hear that: her laugh. It's so pure. I remind myself that there are far worse things in the world than TikTok.

I breathe in, forcing myself to enjoy the quiet and the warmth of the deli, the imagined sense of safety.

Behind us, the front door opens. I turn to look as a young couple walks in, a chill from outside following them in as the door drifts lazily closed, a rush of wind carrying a small stack of napkins from a nearby table to the ground.

I see the napkins fall before something outside catches my attention and I look, gazing out into the darkened night. The deli is well lit; from inside, it's hard to see outside where it's dark. My eyes run over the glass, searching. I almost don't see him at first. My gaze goes right past him and if not for the reflection of light that catches his eye, I'd miss him altogether, but my eyes double back, and the longer I stare, a face begins to form, the features coming into focus, his body something like a vignette, faded and with indefinite edges.

My breath quickens. I say to Sienna, trying to keep my voice smooth, "I'll be right back."

"Where are you going?" she asks, not looking up from her phone.

"I think I see someone outside that I

know. Just stay here, okay? Wait for our food. I'll be back." All I can think about in this moment is keeping Sienna safe. It's not her he wants. It's me.

Sienna's eyes rise up over the phone and go to the glass. She squints, as if trying to see through something opaque like a glass of milk. "Where?" she asks, not seeing him because he's stepped further back from the window.

"Just stay here."

I walk to the door. I pull it open, stepping outside into the cold night. At the same time, he turns and drifts someplace more dark and sequestered — an alley just beyond the deli — looking back so that I'll follow and I do because I worry that if I don't, something might happen to Sienna.

I come to the alley laden with back entry-ways and service delivery bays, a network of black metal fire escapes that are harder to see in the near dark of night. I turn and enter, the street, with its lights, people and traffic, fading away.

Milo Finch comes to a stop about ten feet into the alleyway.

"What do you want from me?" I ask, keeping my distance, wrapping my arms around myself.

"You can relax," he says. "I'm not going

to hurt you."

"How do I know that?"

"If I wanted to hurt you, I'd have done it by now. It's not like I haven't had the chance."

I don't know that this makes me feel any better. I don't know if I believe him either. He knows my name. He read it on my name tag at work. He saw me working at the hospital and, if he wanted to, he could have hung around after and followed me home from a shift. He might know where I live. For all I know, he followed Sienna and me to the deli tonight.

"The police are looking for you. They think you're the one who pushed Caitlin Beckett off the bridge."

"And why would they think that?"

I skirt around the truth. "They know you've been following her. If you do anything to me," I say, "they'll know it was you."

He harrumphs, looking at the street behind me. "I'm not scared. To be honest, I wish it was me who pushed her off the bridge. Though, if it had been," he says, bringing his eyes back, "I would have made sure she was dead before I left." His words are so cold, they take my breath away. "If there is any justice in the world, she won't survive this. That woman took everything from me."

"What do you mean?"

He looks away again and I don't think he's going to say. He's quiet, contemplative. He stands inches taller than me, looking down, and I become aware of not only the hatred in his eye, but something more like sadness or grief.

"She worked for me a long time ago. I used to own a restaurant in California. For over ten years, I worked hard, building it from the ground up. It was my passion, my life's work, and she was a waitress I hired, that I took a chance on because she didn't have experience working as a waitress, but she seemed eager and proved at first to be a quick learner. Worst decision I ever made."

"What happened?"

"She worked for me for only a couple months before I fired her. I had to. She gave me no choice. I caught her stealing from me, voiding orders so she could take the cash. She was lucky I only fired her, because I could have called the police and pressed charges. Any normal person would have just moved on and gotten another job. Instead she held a grudge. She wanted to get back at me and she did." He takes a long, slow breath before exhaling, and I wait, holding my own breath, for him to go on, and in time he does. "Late one night, she broke into my home. My wife and son were out of town for the night. I'd left a window on the first floor open, which I sometimes did for the cross breeze and because I didn't think about someone breaking in while I was asleep. My mistake. My bedroom was on the second floor. I slept with the door closed, not that it would have mattered because I'm a deep sleeper." In my mind, I picture this, a woman removing the screen from outside, sliding the window open and crawling through in the darkness of night. "She downloaded stuff onto my computer while I was asleep."

"What kind of stuff?"

"Really sick stuff. Obscene. Pictures of little girls," he says and my stomach sours, feeling sick. Child pornography. I might not believe him, I might think he was making this up, if I hadn't already gleaned certain things about Caitlin Beckett myself, like how she will lie and hurt people to get what she wants. "She sent those images from my email to people I knew, and then left out the window, back the way she came. I slept right through it. The police came the next day, before I was even out of bed, because someone I knew, a friend, had called. They searched my house. They took my computer. They found what they were looking for and no one believed me when I said it wasn't mine. Why would they? I wouldn't have believed me either. The evidence was there."

My throat is tight. Child pornography is a very serious crime. You don't just get a slap on the wrist. It's life changing.

"That woman is merciless," he says. "I spent five years of my life behind bars. I'm a registered sex offender now, which means I can't step foot in a park and every time I try and find a job, they run a background check. The best I can get is as a general laborer when I have a master's degree in culinary arts. My life is over. That woman ruined it, and what's worse is that my wife took our son and left because she believed I had those things on my computer. I lost my family, my business, my reputation, everything. My son is eight now. My wife won't let me see him because I'm unfit to be a parent, or so they say. I haven't seen him since he was three."

I press a hand to my mouth, shaking my head, my heart aching for him. I think how, when Sienna was three, she was just learning how to use the potty all by herself. She couldn't get herself fully dressed or tie her shoes, but by the time she was eight, she was in third grade, reading chapter books and she knew how to ride a bike and to swim. Between the ages of three and eight there are hundreds of milestones. First day of preschool, first day of kindergarten, first lost tooth. He missed them all.

"When I got out of jail, I went looking for her," he goes on, holding nothing back. "She thought she could get away with it and, for a while, she did. But I found her living out near L.A. in Alamitos Beach and then as soon as I did, she took off. I didn't give up looking for her."

It's why she left California. It's why she came suddenly back to Chicago, without letting anyone know, because he'd been released from jail and was looking for her. It explains the voice mail she left on Mr. Beckett's phone, the last-ditch, pleading, *Daddy. I'm in trouble. I need your help.* Because this man was after her, because he had tracked her all the way across the country from California to get revenge, to take back everything she took from him — his life.

"Why are you telling me this?" I ask. I don't feel afraid anymore.

"Because there is no legal recourse for what she's done. I can't prove it and I can't get my life back. But if there is any justice in the world," he says again, "she will die."

From the way he looks at me, I can't help but think he's asking me to kill her.

"Mom," I hear from behind then, a lilt to the end of it suggestive of a question. *Mom?* I spin around, seeing Sienna's bemused face in the entrance to the alleyway, spotlighted by a beam of light from a nearby streetlight. She clutches our bag of food in her hands, her head cocked, her posture slouching and uneasy.

With my back to him, he leans in to breathe into my hair, "There is nothing worse in the world than losing a child," and I go rigid. "If there is any justice, that woman will die."

He brushes past me as he leaves, giving Sienna a wide berth.

I catch my breath and then go to her. "Who was that man?" she asks, her eyes following him as he moves down the street.

I take out my phone to call 911, to tell them where he is, so they can find and arrest him. If nothing else, he's violated parole. The police are looking for him. I start to dial, pressing the nine before my conscience stops me. Milo Finch violated parole over a crime he didn't commit. He did time and he lost his family as a result,

319

which is far worse than any punishment the police or a jury could ever pass down.

I put my phone away, watching as his figure disappears in the night.

"Just someone from work," I say, refusing to look at Sienna because I don't want to lie to her face, but I also don't want to tell her the truth, how that man wants to kill a patient of mine and I don't blame him.

EIGHTEEN

I haven't stopped thinking about Nat. Every minute of the day, she's still on my mind.

Sometime after midnight, I pull up Facebook on my phone to see if she has messaged yet, but she still hasn't. I don't have any new messages, and the last message I sent to Nat, I notice, isn't there. It's gone. In fact all the direct messages between Nat and me are gone.

I decide to go to her Facebook page. I want to see the pictures of her and Declan again. I want to see his face, his eyes. I look up her name but the search yields no exact results. There are Natalie Cohens and Natalie Roches, but no Natalie Cohen Roches, and all of these profiles want me to add this person as a friend, meaning we aren't already friends. I search each of the profiles, looking for that image of Nat standing beside Niagara Falls, but never find what I'm looking for.

Either she or Declan deleted her Facebook page.

Someone doesn't want me to find her.

In the morning I reluctantly let Sienna go to school, though I ride the bus with her and walk her inside, where I get assurances from the school principal that the school is safe and that my daughter is safe. Sienna herself looks at me and says, "It's okay, Mom. I'm fine," and I give in, knowing that despite these assurances, I'll still worry about her.

As I walk away from Sienna's high school, I look back twice, wondering if I've made the right decision in leaving her there.

I think about Nat then and the things she told me about herself, like how she works as a teacher at the cooperative nursery school in Lincoln Park, and that her husband, Declan Roche, is an associate with the law firm Tanner & Levine in the Loop.

I can't go home because I'll sit there and worry about Sienna all day. Instead I pick up coffee and head to Nat's nursery school, where I stand outside on the snowy street, watching as students arrive with their parents and nannies before rushing giddy and laughing into the building, happy to be at school — quite unlike at Sienna's high school, where the students moped in, tired and crabby.

I stand on the other side of the street, waiting until everyone has gone in, and then I cross the street, doubting Nat will be here — doubting Declan would ever let her leave — though I try anyway, because maybe someone at the school knows where she lives or knows some way to get in touch with her. I try pulling on the door handle but the school, like Sienna's, is locked. There is an intercom on the outside of the building, which I step up to, pressing the button, hearing it buzz.

A woman answers. "Can I help you?"

"Hi, yes," I say. "I was hoping to speak with Mrs. Roche. I'm a friend."

"Who?" she asks, unable to hear me over a passing truck.

I lean into the microphone, saying louder, "Mrs. Roche. Nat. Natalie Roche."

"And you said she's a teacher?" the woman asks, though I hadn't said that, and as she does, a knot forms in my stomach. I wouldn't think that there were more than ten teachers here and maybe only a few more support staff, not so many that it would be hard to know or remember them all.

"Yes," I say. "She's a teacher. Four-year-old preschool." And then it occurs to me that teachers don't always change their name when they get married. "She might go by Nat Cohen or Natalie Cohen," I say, wondering if she goes by her maiden name at school.

If Nat's Facebook page hadn't been deactivated, I would have a photo to show this woman. But as it is, I have nothing.

It doesn't matter. The woman's voice comes to me again through the intercom, saying, "I'm sorry, but we don't have a teacher here by either of those names. Are you sure you have the right school?" and with that, I start to doubt myself, to wonder if I've somehow made a mistake. Because there are other cooperative preschools in the neighborhood plus other Lincoln Park preschools that are not part of a cooperative. Nat could teach at any of them.

I thank the woman for her time and leave, feeling worried for Nat and dejected.

I could go to the police. But what would the police do? I don't know where Nat lives. They couldn't even do a standard welfare check if I said I was worried about her and her safety.

I start to walk home, but somewhere along the way, another idea comes to me. Instead of going home, I take the Red Line into the

Loop, looking up the address for Tanner & Levine on my phone as the train swerves along the elevated track before soaring underground just south of Fullerton, the winter scene disappearing, pitching us into darkness.

As the train rasps through the snug tunnels, I steel myself for a meeting with Nat's husband, Declan, thinking about what I will say to him when I finally meet him face-to-face.

I get off the train. I take the stairs up to street level, and then I walk to the tall, black building that houses Tanner & Levine. I let myself in through the revolving door. Someone in the lobby tells me which floor to find the firm on and then directs me to the correct elevator bank. I ride the elevator up to the forty-third floor and, when the doors open, let myself in through a set of glass doors to the modern, elegant office, feeling my heart hasten to know that Declan is somewhere within these same walls. I look around, letting my eyes roam, searching for him. The space is airy, bright, which is contradictory to how I'm feeling. Floor-to-ceiling windows line the wall, looking out over Lake Michigan. Under different circumstances, it would be beautiful.

"May I help you?" a receptionist asks, gazing up over a computer screen. I let my eyes go to her. She is young, pretty, impeccably dressed, so that I feel underdressed in my jeans and winter boots, though that doesn't matter. What I'm wearing is the furthest thing from my mind.

I step in, making my way up to the desk, my eyes in flux, searching the face of everyone I see. "Hi," I say, hearing my voice tremble. I take a breath, trying to get it under control. "I'm here to see Declan Roche," I say, expecting that she'll ask if I have an appointment with him, to which I'd have to say no because I don't. But somehow I'll have to persuade her to still let me see him.

But that's not what this woman says. Her face darkens. "Is he . . . a paralegal?" she asks, cocking a head so that her long straight locks fall longer on one side.

"No," I say. "He's an attorney." Soon to be partner, I think, finding it almost impossible, given his stature, that this woman wouldn't know who he is. By Nat's accounts, Declan has been at the firm for years, climbing his way up the legal ladder. But, I think then, that this law firm is massive. There must be over a hundred attorneys and maybe this receptionist is new.

Maybe that's why she doesn't know who he is.

"Declan Roche you said?" she asks.

"Yes."

"Are you sure you're in the right place? This is Tanner & Levine."

"Yes, I know," I say, hearing the edge in my voice, thinking how Sienna would be embarrassed by it. "I am in the right place. This is where he works." The receptionist just looks at me, deciding what to say, how to respond. I stare back, trying my best to stay calm but feeling my heart race. When she says nothing, I ask, "Can you check? Please? Because I think that maybe you're mistaken. I think he does work here."

Reluctantly she nods, reaching for a list beside the phone. The list is pages long, with the extension for each office. She goes through it, a long manicured fingernail sweeping across each page, down the list of names. "Declan Roche you say?" she asks, and I say yes.

"Sorry," she tells me when she reaches the end, "but there is no one here by that name," and I want to argue, except that as she was looking at it, I read the list of names upside down for myself and saw how it skipped from Rafferty to Schaabar.

My world spins. I widen my stance, because I feel suddenly like the office is moving around me.

She was right. I was wrong. He's not here. He's really not here. There is no Declan Roche at this firm.

"If that's all . . ." she prompts, putting her list away, her voice drifting.

My words are a whisper. "Yes. That's all. Thank you for looking."

I turn to go. I feel dizzy, weak. I can't make sense of this, because I know for sure, I remember explicitly, that Nat said her husband worked at Tanner & Levine. It's possible I might have made one mistake — that I might have confused where Nat worked — but it's impossible that I would have made two. Which means only one thing. Nat lied. But why?

And then it happens. I see something on the way out. Brochures for the law firm in the reception area, the name Tanner & Levine written across the front of them. A small stack of brochures sits fanned out on a side table beside magazines like *Newsweek* and *The Economist.*

They catch my eye as I walk past, and I gasp because there is an image of a man on the front of the brochures. I see his eyes first and then his smile, and the recognition hits.

On front of a threefold laminated brochure is an image of Declan Roche.

"It's him," I breathe.

I feel validated. I *am* right. I'm not losing my mind.

I swoop down to pick one up. "This. This is him," I say, my voice too loud, conveying too much enthusiasm, as I carry the brochure to the receptionist desk, pointing sharply at it. "This is Declan Roche. I was right. He does work here."

The woman takes the brochure from me for a closer look, letting her eyes run over his handsome face. "Okay," she concedes, nodding. "Let me call down to human resources and see. Why don't you have a seat."

I take a seat on one of the smoke gray lounge chairs, my heart palpitating because it's only a matter of time now until I really do come face-to-face with Declan.

What will I say to him? What will he say? What will he be like? I think he will be charming because that's the way all sociopaths are. But I know better than to believe that. I think of the things he's done to Nat, the things that he's said, the text messages I've read.

You are nothing without me.

You fucking bitch.

It doesn't take long. Less than a minute.

"Ma'am?" the receptionist asks. I look sharply up. My heart pounds and I think that she is going to tell me that he's on his way. I set the magazine aside and press myself from the chair to go to her. "I'm sorry," she says, setting the phone back in its cradle, "but as it turns out, our marketing department created that brochure. That man doesn't actually work here. We don't know who it is."

I blink once, twice and then three times.

"I . . . I don't understand," I say, stammering. "His picture is on your brochure."

"It's a stock photo," she says, and though she doesn't mean for them to, her words come as a punch to the gut.

A stock photo. I feel physically sick.

Stock photography. Images bought online, which means one of two things: that Nat is married to a model or, more likely, that every single picture on Nat's Facebook page was doctored using stock photos of this same man. Microstock images are dirt cheap. You can buy them for something like a dollar each, and then make alterations on programs like Photoshop to make it look like he's in Punta Cana or riding the Ferris wheel at Navy Pier. She can insert herself into them, make believe they're husband and wife. She must have found dozens of photos of this same man to use, on some website like Shutterstock.

Heaven on Earth.

On top of the world.

Why would she do this? Why would she pretend to be married to this man?

The receptionist slides the brochure across the desk to me and I spin it around so that I'm looking into this man's eyes, the world around me growing dim. I tune everything else out — the ding of the elevator, footsteps, a cough — and focus on him and only him. His eyes are seductive, a strange but beautiful combination of green and brown with flecks of gold. The color of them is one thing, but it's that undeniable effect that his eyes are watching me, following me no matter which angle I look from. And then there is his smile, a simper really, smug but also incredibly sexy, and I'd bet my life that the day I first saw him on Nat's Facebook page isn't the first time I've ever seen him. He looked familiar even then, though I couldn't place him at the time, and now I think what happened was that I saw him on an ad for the law firm or for something else. Because he's a model. He's not her husband.

"Are you okay, ma'am?" the receptionist asks, and I realize that I've lost all sense of time. I wonder how long I've been standing here staring at the brochure, my jaw slack, speechless. "Is there anything else I can help you with?"

She is smiling when I lift my gaze to hers, a polite albeit uncomfortable smile, and when I look down at the brochure again I see what I failed to see before, how his placement, the way he sits, the way his hands are positioned and the angle of his head, are an exact duplicate of Nat's cover photo on Facebook, except that Nat herself — her arms thrown around his shoulders from behind, hands clasped across his chest to show off her dazzling wedding ring, chin resting on his shoulder and eyes that gaze sideways, are gone. Excised.

Because they were never there to begin with.

"No. No thank you." I stagger away from the desk, taking the brochure with me. I don't know what I'll do with it. Finding this man would serve no purpose because he is not Declan. Declan is someone else.

The cold air outside is an insult.

I weave my way around people back to the train. I feel lost, hopeless, bemused.

It's as I'm riding the train back home that an idea comes to me. I find Emily Miller on Facebook. Emily Miller is an old high school friend, one Nat said she still talks to from time to time. With a name like that — and not knowing her married name — it's not easy, but I scroll through a myriad of Emily Miller's Facebook profiles with dwindling hope until I find the right one: Emily Miller Cease. She lives in Portland now. Her page is private, but I can see that she and I have mutual friends from high school. I send her a friend request but also a direct message, saying,

Hi Emily, It's Meghan from high school. I'm trying to find Nat Cohen and was wondering if you might have her phone number or know another way to get in touch? Please call.

I leave her with my phone number.

Later that night my phone rings, the number a 971 area code. I swipe to answer, pressing the phone to my ear. "Hello?" I ask.

"Meghan. Hi. It's Emily Cease," she says, and then, "Emily Miller. From high school."

"Emily. Hi. Thank you so much for calling me back. I can't tell you how much I appreciate it." Emily and I weren't great friends in school, but we didn't dislike each other. We just didn't know each other well. We didn't have many classes together or things in common or a reason to be friends. She was more into theater than sports, and I remember how incredible she was, how she had aspirations of being on Broadway one day. I wonder how that panned out.

Under different circumstances I might ask. But instead I get right to the point. "I'm trying to get in touch with Nat Cohen. You two were so close in high school, I'm hoping you might have her number."

There's a beat of silence.

When she speaks, her voice is solemn. Grave.

"I thought you knew. I thought everyone knew."

My world is spinning already but I don't know why. I lower myself to a chair, waiting for the bottom to fall out. "Knew what?"

"Nat is dead. She died nineteen years ago, Meghan. She and her whole family did."

"What?"

"It's awful, I know."

"How?" I breathe out.

"A car crash."

I'm rocked by disbelief.

"I'm sorry to be the one to tell you. Truly. If it helps, they say that she died quickly, that she didn't feel any pain." I can't find the words to speak. "Are you okay?" she asks.

"Yes," I manage to get out, and then, "Thank you, Emily. Thank you for letting me know."

We end the call and I sit there on the chair, stock-still.

It's not surprising that I didn't know that Nat was dead. After my sister Bethany's death, my parents moved away from our hometown. I never went back. I cut ties with almost everyone from that time in my life. It was the only way I knew to move on from my sister's suicide.

With shaking hands, I Google her name, *Natalie Cohen,* and then because that's too broad, too general, I add the words *Illinois* and *car crash.* I press enter and a new page loads. Each headline is a shocking betrayal.

Six dead in fiery wrong-way crash

Wrong way crash kills mother, father and their three kids

Recent college graduate with a bright future among those killed on Illinois tollway

Community mourns a family lost in deadly crash

I think I will be sick or pass out, I don't know which. On the kitchen chair, I spread my legs wide, hunch over and drop my head between them to increase the blood flow to my brain. I close my eyes. I breathe, in through my nose, out through my mouth, wondering if I should call Sienna, who's in her bedroom ten feet away, for help, but I don't want to worry her. I think about the breathing techniques they taught me before Sienna was born. I breathe out through pursed lips.

When I can, I sit back up. I lean back in the chair and look at the search results on my phone. I choose one of the headlines and read the article in its entirety.

All five members of the Cohen family were killed around 3 p.m. Sunday afternoon when their minivan collided with a van on Interstate 90 that was going the wrong way. The driver responsible for the crash, thirty-two year old Marcus High, was drunk at the time of the incident, with a blood alcohol content of more than twice the legal limit. He was also killed.

There is a picture. It's dated, circa early two thousands. Mr. and Mrs. Cohen stand on the left, him in khaki pants and a white shirt, her in nice jeans and a warm tan blouse. On the right are two teenage boys, twins maybe, one with glasses, one without, both tall and lanky in jeans and neutral, coordinating polo shirts.

And there in the center of them all stands Nat Cohen with her short, blunt bobbed hair and gap-toothed smile, in a jean skirt and a turtleneck.

My chest tightens. My mouth is suddenly dry, though my hands are wet with sweat.

Who is this woman who's been living in my home, who I've been telling my secrets to?

NINETEEN

The days pass. Christmas comes and goes. The brutal winter makes itself right at home. The snow is no longer magical but persistent, never-ending. It doesn't get warm enough for it to melt. The closest it gets to melting is dirty brown slush that we bring home on our shoes and into the apartment. The windows in our building are old and drafty; the winter air gets in and we are always cold, the days gray, spring an eternity away. I go to work and I come home, each day a carbon copy of the day before. Nothing changes.

Time passes and the police still haven't found my stolen money. It's not for lack of trying. The bank account, they've learned, the place where I wired the money to, belonged to a man named Joseph Minor. The police tracked him down to a dilapidated home just west of Washington Park. Joseph Miner is a drug addict and, at first when they told me, my heart leaped because I thought the police had found the person who did this to me. But I was wrong. Mr. Minor didn't do it because, when the police spoke to him, he confessed that he had, in essence, rented out his identity — his name, his social security number — for cash, for money for drugs. Someone else — a woman, he said — paid him off and then used his identity to set up the quasi-anonymous account, and I don't have to think long or hard to know who did it. She did. The woman I only know as Nat, using a voice changer app to make herself sound like a man on the phone and setting up the account online so she didn't have to go into the bank, so no one would see her and there would be no evidence. I tell the police it was her, but without a real name or a picture of her, it's like tracking down a ghost.

I look for her everywhere I go. At work. On my commute to work. Sitting in my living room staring out the window at the street. I watch the L pass by and wonder if she's on it. I never see her, but I think she's out there somewhere, watching me. I feel it all the time, this overwhelming, paralyzing feeling of being followed, pursued. There are nights that I know she's lurking in the shadows, walking behind me, following me home from work. I never see her. It's a gut feeling only, but I trust my gut, those times that my nerves scream out and the tiny hairs on my arms stand on end. I hear footsteps behind me, but every time I turn around to see, she's gone, slipping into gangways, into the alcoves of stores, into covered bus stops or blending in with other people on the street.

She's toying with me.

As the days go by, my indignation grows. She lied to me. She stole ten thousand dollars from me. She made me believe she was my long-lost friend. I let her into my home. I told her my secrets. And yet, I don't know who she is.

It wasn't just that. There's more. Because one day not long after she disappeared, I went into my jewelry box, which I keep on the dresser in my bedroom. I don't often wear jewelry, but Sienna asked for a bracelet to borrow, and when I opened the box, I felt sick. My wedding and engagement rings, which have sat untouched in one of the little modular trays since Ben and my divorce, were gone. The velvet tray lay empty.

I don't wear those rings anymore but they're worth thousands of dollars and even more in sentimental value. Right away, I told the police and reported the crime, but the only thing the police could do was file a report and then keep tabs on jewelry stores and pawnshops to see if she tries to sell them, but so far no luck.

I start to lose hope that I will ever see her with my own eyes. I try to distract myself with other things. I go on a date with a man I meet online, telling myself I need to move on and forget about *Nat* and everything that happened. I need to forget about my divorce and about Ben. I need to put it all behind me. I need to find a way to move on with my life, to find peace and happiness. What's done is done.

Easier said than done.

Today is a workday, but I've taken the morning off to go for an appointment on Wabash in the South Loop for my follow-up mammogram, to have the asymmetry on the right breast checked. I don't usually schedule appointments on days I work, but it was the only time for weeks that they could get me in and I didn't want to put it off any longer.

I change into the hip-length gown and then follow the mammographer into the room. After it's done, I sit, anxiously waiting for her to come back with results from the radiologist. If they're still inconclusive, we'll do an ultrasound and then go from there. I'm all nerves.

"Good news," she says when she comes back. "Everything looks fine."

"You're sure?"

"Yes. We're sure. The breast tissue was most likely superimposed when the first mammogram was done," she says, "making it look different than the other breast. It happens. It's common, but nothing to worry about. You don't need to have another mammogram for a year."

I smile, feeling lighter and in good spirits. It doesn't last long.

It's as I'm leaving the physician's building that it happens.

I step out of the building and onto Wabash. And that's when I see her crossing the intersection at Wabash and Cullerton, her dark brown hair hanging long over the back of the white winter coat, a pair of skinny jeans tucked into the tall shaft of her winter boots, the ones with the fuzzy cuff.

My heart stops. It's her.

I call out with the only name I know for her. "Nat!" I scream, cupping my hands around my mouth, though she's not Nat because Nat is dead. "Nat Cohen!" The woman turns and for a moment, our eyes lock. As they do, she visibly straightens. It might just be a coincidence that I've run into her here, but I'm not so sure she hasn't been following me and that this time, she just happened to get caught.

Who is she and what does she want with me?

Quickly I start making my way toward her. As I do, she turns the other way and runs. I give chase.

The street around us is filled with people despite the weather, everyone all bundled up in coats and hats, making it hard to tell who is who and were it not for her white coat — an outlier among almost exclusively black — I'd have lost her by now.

My anger surges as we race down Wabash. Seeing her has brought back all the emotion so that I feel humiliated and indignant all over again. This woman lied to me. She took advantage of my generosity. She came into my home under false pretenses and I fell for it. She stole from me.

All of a sudden, my rage reaches new heights.

The adrenaline spikes and I run faster.

At 18th Street, she turns sharply right. She cuts close to a brick building, throwing a glance back over her shoulder to see if she's lost me, which she hasn't. She runs fast, faster than me, the distance between us increasing. I keep her in my range of vision. We cross Michigan, Indiana, Prairie Avenue, running past businesses, a warehouse, apartment buildings and parking lots. I elbow people by accident as I run and am met with curt words like, *Watch it, Excuse you* and *What the fuck, lady?*

Houses appear. Massive houses. 18th Street becomes Calumet Avenue and still I run. I run down Calumet, past brick townhomes on one side of the street, high-rise apartments the other, some recognizable from all the times I've traveled down Lake Shore Drive, which is just a stone's throw to the east. Everything here is packed densely together, creating pockets to hide. Parked cars line both sides of the tree-lined street in the Prairie Avenue District, which is much sought after and where the most affluent Chicagoans lived before the Gold Coast was built. Under different circumstances I might stand to take it in, to admire it, the architecture and the history, but as it is, it's all a blur, and the only thing I'm really aware of are the many hiding spots and the many places to escape.

The street in front of me is devoid of life, nearly everything white. Winter is a wasteland.

I've lost her. I stand in the middle of Calumet, arms outstretched, spinning, my eyes wildly searching the street. When I come to a stop, dizzy, breathless, the townhomes to my right have patios that sit just slightly beneath ground level, access to them limited by a black wrought iron fence, which would be easy to climb, to then hunker down on the patios behind bulky outdoor furniture covered for the winter with polyester tarps, and hide.

I start drifting right when movement in my peripheral vision grabs my attention. I turn. To my left is a walkway. It's wide and open, heading under a bridge. From the bridge's underpass, I see a flash of white. I'm wrong. She's not hiding on the patios. She's gone the other way. I run toward the flash of white, as if dashing after *Alice in Wonderland*'s white rabbit, along the sidewalk and then under the bridge.

On the other side of the underpass, a ramp appears to the right, going up. It's a pedestrian bridge, over the rail yard.

Here, the beauty of the Prairie Avenue District fades and it's industrial. It's loud with traffic, which soars past on the adjacent Lake Shore Drive. The area is not as maintained. Things look aged. The deck of the bridge is a composite of wood and something else, but the railings are a rusted metal, reddish brown, flaking off. Less desirable parts of the city encroach on this, so that I wouldn't feel safe here alone, at this time of year, if I was in my right mind.

But I'm not. I'm not alone and I'm not in my right mind.

The pedestrian bridge goes to the right and then the left, climbing. Beneath us is a series of train tracks with four Metra trains on them, stopped further back and empty. There is a wooden platform just below, which is basic; it doesn't have a building or sell tickets. A rider would have to purchase those once on the train. The platform is empty.

She is fast. I'd never catch her but fate intervenes when, in her haste, she trips. She falls forward to the ground, catching herself with her hands, letting out a short cry of pain or shock.

On her hands and knees on the ground, she turns and looks back over a shoulder. Her eyes rise to mine, measuring the distance between us, which gives me the opportunity to close the gap, and I do, reaching out to grab her by the hood of her winter coat as she tries to stand up. She tries to pull away, to shrug out of the coat to free herself, but either I am physically stronger

346

or my resolve is stronger. She manages to stand up, but I hold on tight, not letting go.

"Who are you?" I ask, pinning her between my body and the bridge railing so she can't get away so easily. She backs a half step away from me, bumping into the edge. "Who are you?"

The answer is cheeky. "Nat Cohen."

"The fuck you are," I snap. "Nat Cohen is dead."

Her laugh is dry. "I didn't know if you'd fall for it, if my story would bear scrutiny, but it did. Don't feel too bad about it, Meghan. I don't talk to many people from high school either. They could be dead and I wouldn't know."

"But why? Why would you do this and who is Declan?"

"Haven't you figured it out by now?"

"Figured out what?"

"Declan doesn't exist."

"But the bruises and your swollen lip," I say in disbelief. She snickers and it dawns on me what happened, the reality of it a blow. How stupid I've been. "You did this to yourself. You let someone hit you or you hit yourself so that I'd think you were being abused, so I'd take pity on you."

Her reply is a cruel smile. The answer is yes. She did something like slam her own face against something hard enough to sustain a black eye, a bruised forehead and other injuries.

My jaw goes slack. "Why?"

What kind of sick person would do such a thing?

The same type of person who would fake a kidnapping and steal ten thousand dollars from me.

She doesn't say. She only shrugs. In her silence, I say, still finding it hard to believe, "But that night at the restaurant, he was there, outside, looking through the window. I saw what you were looking at, the condensation on the glass." I didn't imagine it.

She stares, looking smug. "The timing was fortunate. I couldn't have planned that better myself." It takes a second before I realize what she means, that while *someone* was at the window, it was unrelated — a man looking into the restaurant to see how crowded it was or if a friend had arrived, something like that — and she used it to her advantage to make me believe her husband was there.

I shake my head, going through everything that happened, trying to understand it. "But the Find My app on your phone. It said Declan could see your location. And the awful texts from him that night," I say, thinking back to that night when the text messages came rapid-fire — You fucking bitch and I own you. "I don't understand. I was with you when they arrived. You couldn't have sent them to yourself."

I'm so desperate to make sense of it, not wanting to believe that I could be so easily fooled.

"Couldn't I?"

"Did someone help you?" I ask. Someone would have had to help her, unless it's possible she has two phones and was able to schedule the texts in advance.

"Why would I tell you that, Meghan? You think I'm going to tell you all my secrets?" she asks, and I feel stupid because that's exactly what I did. I told her, a stranger, my secrets. I didn't think I was the type of person who could so easily be a victim of manipulation. I thought I was smarter than that. I think back, going back in time. She did her research. She studied me. She knew the way I walked home from work every night. She knew that sometime after seven o'clock, I'd be walking north on Sheffield that same night the horrible texts from Declan arrived. She put herself there, on my route, when I'd be passing by, and then she did something to piss off the man who screamed at her, creating a scene so that I'd notice her, so that I'd take pity on her, so that I'd welcome her into my home.

Everything was premediated. Everything was done with purpose.

"Why are you doing this to me? Why are you following me? What do you want from me?"

"I like you. I miss talking to you, I miss *you*. Under different circumstances, we could have been friends."

My laugh is barbed and cynical. "You like talking to me? The only thing you ever told me were lies," I say in disbelief. The sad thing is that I liked talking to her too. I was so relieved to have finally found a friend I could be open with and trust. "Do you know how many nights I lost sleep worrying about you, thinking he'd hurt you or worse? Nothing you said was real. The thing I don't get is why. Why did you do this? What did you have to gain from it?" Was it just an intricate but well-devised plan to steal from me? She pretended to be someone I knew because the odds of gaining my trust were in her favor. She appealed to my compassionate side, and I let her into my home so she could help herself to my things.

"I'm calling the police," I say, boring a hand into my bag for my phone, trying to keep this woman between my body and the edge of the bridge so she can't leave. The police will come and I'll tell them what she's done. "You're not going to get away with this."

"Call them. I dare you," she says, and in that moment, as the sun peeks out from behind a cloud, the light catches on her hand and I look at the bright, shiny object on her finger and gasp.

My ring. My wedding band, which I know is one hundred percent mine because it's not like other wedding bands but is one of a kind. On the inside is a message inscribed from Ben, one that doesn't ring true anymore. *You and me forever.*

The engagement ring isn't here, but still, she has the impudence to wear my wedding ring, to not only steal from me but to flaunt her loot in public like it's hers.

"Give me my ring. Give me my fucking ring," I shriek, feeling something in me start to snap.

"You mean this ring?" she laughs, holding her hands up but out of reach. She thinks this is funny. She's not sorry for what she's done to me, for how this has made me feel. She's completely without remorse.

I step closer, trying to take my ring from her, to wrench it off her finger if I have to. She steps further back, laughing at first, but

351

there's nowhere to go. She backs into the bridge's rail and her face tightens. She makes a grave mistake then. She puts a foot on the bottom rail, lifting herself up, rising higher, trying to gain leverage, distance, to shimmy away from me somehow, to get her feet disentangled from mine so she can get past me and run away with my ring. But it's a mistake. Because the upper rail now comes to just below her hip, and she's unbalanced. I can see in her panicked eyes how she regrets the decision, but she can't undo it because I'm standing too close, not letting her back down. She's fighting now, making an attempt to shove, to knee me away, to get her feet back on the ground, but it's difficult because of her position. She hasn't gained leverage but lost it instead, and so she screams, "Take it. If you want it that bad, take the fucking ring," twisting it over her knuckle, hurling it to the bridge deck and then reaching back to hold tight to the rusty railing just behind her. In anger and in spite, she says, "No wonder your husband didn't love you."

I blanch at the hateful words. Why is she doing this? What have I done to her? I think of everything I told her about Ben, all those intimate confessions. She violated, preyed upon, exploited me. She pretended to be my friend, to need me, just to take advantage of and steal from me.

"No wonder your sister killed herself," she says, hoping to stun and immobilize me with her words so that she can get away.

A train roars in the distance.

"Haven't you figured it out by now?" she goes on. "You're the common denominator. Everyone just wants to get away from you. Now get your fucking hands off me or I'll tell them what you told me. I'll tell them who Sienna's real dad is and how you're a wh—"

With that, something in me snaps.

I rear back. I push. It's reactive, provoked. I don't even think about what I'm doing, only how good it feels, how cathartic, my anger dissipating with each thrust. The first time she only jerks back and then recenters herself, aggrieved and in disbelief, saying, "What the fuck?"

But after the second time, her arms flail at her sides like helicopter propellors, trying to find her equilibrium, a toehold, an anchor. She doesn't. Her knees lock, but still gravity and imbalance pull her over the edge. I watch it happen in slow motion. As she falls backward, her eyes go wide like full moons. Her hands reach out, grabbing at the air, but in the next second, I can't see her face.

She's over the edge and what I see when I look down is graceful almost. She falls with ease, a lissome gymnast tumbling through the air.

She screams.

The landing is forceful. It's driving and abrupt. She slams into the earth with a dull thud. I jerk, blanching, and then I stare at her lying face down beside the tracks, her scream suddenly silent, her arms bent under her, hair swirled around her head, strands lifting in the wind, the only part of her that still moves.

My heart is in my throat. I cling to the cold railing with my hands, staring down, open-mouthed, gawping, gasping, over the edge. I can't catch my breath.

She's dead.

I pushed her.

I can't wrap my head around it. It's not possible. This can't be happening, this can't be real.

But it is. I see her on the ground before me, blood starting to appear, tiny rivers of it that flow through the rocks beside the train tracks, cardinal red in contrast to the milky pastiness of the ballast.

I look around, searching. The earth is a void, my only saving grace. There were no witnesses. No one has seen what I've done.

The only sign of life is in the cars that soar by on Lake Shore Drive, too far away and moving at too high of a speed to see what's really happened here.

But soon people will come. A pedestrian or a train will pass by and find her, and then more people will come to lift away what's left of her and to see what a dead body looks like.

I sweep my wedding band up from the deck of the bridge and slip it on my finger so I don't misplace it.

I have to go before someone finds me here.

PART TWO

TWENTY

It's hard to be at work. It's hard to focus when my mind is all over the place. I thought about taking the day and calling in sick, but I've taken days in the past and don't want to let them go to waste because eventually I might need them. And besides, I remind myself as I have so many times of late: I have to act like nothing is wrong, like caring for Caitlin Beckett doesn't upset me more than any other patient, though it does, for different reasons. Because I'm the one who pushed her from the bridge.

Late in the morning, I make my way toward her room. She's been in the hospital for just shy of two weeks now, every day the spitting image of the last. Nothing changes, so that I've become complacent, thinking she will never wake up, though still, every day for the last ten or so days, I've said a little prayer on the way into work that I'll arrive to the news that Caitlin expired overnight. But so far no luck. I shouldn't ever wish another person dead, but I do because if Caitlin dies then I won't get in trouble for what I've done.

I'm not a bad person. I've just done something bad.

I step into Caitlin's room, feeling a tightness spread across my chest as if the air is too thin in here, the oxygen lacking, making it hard to breathe. I wash my hands and then make my way to the monitor to check her vitals.

Mr. Beckett sits on a chair at the foot of the bed. He has a leather portfolio spread open on his lap, a yellow legal pad on the inside with the words Tanner & Levine printed on the top binding. I do a double take. *Occupational hazard,* he told me once, when he was doing research into the bridge and the likelihood of surviving a fall from it. *I'm an attorney.* I didn't put two and two together. I didn't consider that he was an attorney at the very place Declan Roche supposedly worked. That said, it explains how the firm name rolled so easily off Caitlin's tongue the first time she told me about her husband in the coffee shop where we met. I think how scared she pretended to be when I arrived that night, how her coffee spilled, and I remember what Mr. Beckett said the first time we met, how Caitlin thought she could go to Hollywood and become a star. She is quite the actress.

Mr. Beckett stares down, jotting something on the pad while Mrs. Beckett sits beside the bed. There is a magazine open on her lap but she doesn't look at it, letting her eyes rest instead on the lines of her daughter's face, reading them. The bruises on Caitlin's face are healing now. They're not gone, but her body is in the process of breaking down the blood, of reabsorbing it so that they have a brownish tinge to them and are no longer black-and-blue. Her broken bones are healing.

I look at her. I think about the last conscious minutes I spent with her as I often do when I'm in the room with her. For as hard as I try, I can't escape the image of her arms as helicopter propellors that day on the bridge, spinning, trying to pull at the air, to thrust herself forward so she wouldn't fall over the edge, but then she did anyway and I could do nothing but watch.

I stare at Mrs. Beckett now as she looks at her, at Caitlin — at Nat — whatever her name is. I think of the things her husband has told me. I see the love in Mrs. Beckett's eyes and wonder if Sienna treated me the same way her daughter treats her, I could still love her. I could, I think, because that's what unconditional love is. I don't know if there is anything Sienna could do that would make me not love her.

As I'm watching, my gaze going back and forth between Caitlin's and her mother's faces, it happens.

At first it is only an almost inappreciable ripple beneath the eyelid, the gentle lapping of waves against a shoreline, skimming the rocks and sand, so that I could almost convince myself it didn't happen.

I stare, waiting for it to happen again, and it does.

Caitlin's eyes blink open. It's slow, cautious. The light above her is bright, blazing down like the Florida sun. Her gaze is soft, unfocused and glazed. Her eyes settle on nothing. She doesn't move her head.

Mrs. Beckett's voice is urgent. "Tom. Tom."

But it's too much stimulation, too much noise, too much light. It happens so fast that Mr. Beckett's head snaps up from his work a split second too late, after Caitlin's eyes have sunken back shut.

"Did you see that?" Mrs. Beckett asks, only now looking at him as he sets his leather portfolio aside and rises to standing.

"See what?" he asks, but he doesn't wait

for a reply. "No," he decides. "I didn't see anything. Sorry, I was —"

"Her eyes," she insists. "She opened her eyes. You saw it Meghan, didn't you? You saw her open her eyes." Mrs. Beckett is staring at me now, her expression pleading with me to say yes, that I saw it, that she didn't imagine it, that she isn't losing her mind.

But I can't speak. I can barely breathe. My heart beats with such ferocity I feel suddenly dizzy, suddenly flush.

She wasn't supposed to wake up.

She was supposed to die like this, in a coma.

"Meghan?"

I muster a nod, but it's not necessary.

Because a second later, Caitlin opens her eyes again, more fully this time, and this time, when she does, her eyes find mine.

Twenty-One

Mrs. Beckett takes Caitlin by the hand, sliding her own under it and gripping gently. "Squeeze, baby," she pleads, standing suspended above her, looking down. "If you can feel my hand, squeeze."

We hold our collective breath. We wait, me frozen beside the IV pumps, Mr. Beckett at the end of the bed, everyone watching the two pale, delicate hands clasped together under the harsh ICU lights, one firm, the other limp.

Nothing.

Ten seconds pass before Mrs. Beckett gently squeezes Caitlin's hand again, as she leans even further down, staring wide-eyed into the still, brown eyes and says, "It's me, Caitlin. It's Mom. If you can hear me, if you can feel me, please, just squeeze my hand." Mrs. Beckett tightens her grip on Caitlin's hand as if to demonstrate what she means.

Caitlin's eyes are open now, like marbles that stare up at the ceiling, unblinking.

We watch the joined hands again, my own eyes agape, waiting for a spasm, a quiver, a twitch, but still, there's nothing, and I practically heave a sigh of relief as Caitlin's eyes sink slowly shut again, buying time. It's not like she can speak with the ET tube running down her throat and past her vocal cords, but if she could, I wonder what she would say and if she would say I'm the one who pushed her off the bridge.

"We should call the doctor," Mr. Beckett says, practical, businesslike. I feel his eyes on me, and it takes a minute to process, but then I think that yes, we should, *I* should, because I'm her nurse and it's my job to do things like that, to assess her and to call for the doctor. If this was any other patient, I'd be reacting already, taking the appropriate action and not standing frozen, anchored to the ground as I am now with my heart in my throat.

The reality of what's happening hits like a tidal wave.

She's waking up. She's coming to.

Caitlin Beckett pretended to be someone she's not. She lied to me, she made me trust her, she stole from me. I don't know what type of crime that is exactly, whether theft, larceny or something else, but it's nonviolent, punishable by probably a short time in jail and a meager little fine.

I, on the other hand, pushed her off a bridge. That's so much worse. It's attempted murder and I couldn't even claim self-defense because she didn't try to hurt me, not physically anyway. My life was never at risk. I could go to jail for something like twenty years, if not for the rest of my life. And I have a child — I have Sienna. In twenty years, Sienna will be thirty-six years old, an adult, not that much younger than I am now, and I think about the last twenty years of my life, all I have done and experienced, and then I think of Sienna doing it and experiencing it without me. Going to college. Meeting the man of her dreams. Falling in love. Getting married. Getting pregnant. Having children. Bringing new life into the world and then watching it bloom and grow.

I think of the things I told her. I think of the last words she spoke to me before I pushed her off the bridge.

I'll tell them what you told me. I'll tell them who Sienna's real dad is and how you're a wh—

Whore.

I have so much more to lose than she does.

"Meghan?"

My head snaps up. Mr. Beckett's voice brings me back to reality, to the present. He's watching me and I know I have to do *something* and so I step forward, my legs shaking and weak. I'm not so sure the Becketts can't hear my pulse, the surge of blood as it rushes through my body, so fast it makes me dizzy. As the Becketts watch, I move to the bedside. I lean down and force Caitlin's eyes open to check for a pupillary response, sweeping my penlight across her eyes, when what I really want to do is remove her from life support, to extubate her, to yank the endotracheal tube out and watch her die.

I back away from her. "Let me call the doctor," I say, which I do and, in time, he comes. He does an exam and orders tests to check different aspects and function of the brain and her awareness. He orders continuous infusions of a sedative as needed to keep her comfortable until she's ready to be weaned from the ventilator.

Caitlin doesn't open her eyes again for the rest of the day, at least not that anyone sees.

What I know about coming out of a coma

is that it's a process, split seconds of awareness and lucidity followed by a slip back into the dark void of unconsciousness. This is the way it often happens and is the way it will likely happen with Caitlin. But then — if I'm lucky — there are things like locked-in syndrome, which is so much worse and is what I hope for every time I think of her and her marble-like eyes staring blankly up at the ceiling: that she will be locked in.

It's rare but it happens. Locked-in syndrome is when a person's mind might function to the full extent, their cognitive abilities are still intact — they can hear everything happening in the room around them; they feel pain and all external stimuli — but their muscles don't work right. They don't work at all. The person is paralyzed, wholly incapable of movement except for the vertical movement of the eyes. In other words, a fully functioning mind is trapped inside a nonfunctional body. It's hell when you think about it, to be able to hear and think, but not scream. To have an itch but not be able to scratch it. I've read accounts of people suffering from locked-in syndrome, of them listening to doctors and nurses and loved ones talk openly about taking them off life support, letting them pass peacefully away because no one knows, no one understands that there is still life behind the eyes. Most don't ever recover. Many don't survive it. There are often complications, like aspiration or sepsis, and if I'm really lucky, she will be locked in and something like that will happen to her: she'll aspirate, get pneumonia and die.

I shouldn't think like that. I'm not a monster.

It doesn't have to be that way.

She could live too and, if that were the case, she would eventually be transferred to a skilled nursing facility for care because she couldn't stay here in our ICU for the rest of her life. That wouldn't be so bad, not for me, not for her either, not when the alternative is death. A skilled nursing facility could better meet her needs. I think about her living out the rest of her life like that, with the ability to hear and feel, blink and think, but not much more, and there is some satisfaction in it, imagining how she could ruminate for the rest of her miserable life on what she did to me and others, and live to regret it. The staff at the skilled nursing facility might be able to teach her to communicate with her eyes, but even if they could, it could be elementary, rudimentary at best. She would never be able to tell them what I've done and, even if she could, it would be so easy for me to dispute it, to say that she's mistaken or that someone misinterpreted what she was trying to say.

I'm in the room with her. It's early the next morning, before visiting hours have begun. Caitlin's eyes are closed and, at first glance, she looks unconsciousness.

But then I think of everything I know about this woman, about everything I've learned over these last few weeks, and wonder if it's possible she's bluffing, if she's only trying to pass for being unconscious. I wouldn't put it past her.

We assess patients' brain function and consciousness using the Glasgow Coma Scale, which I have done at every shift that I've cared for her. The Glasgow Coma Scale measures things like motor responsiveness, verbal performance and eye opening, though verbal performance can't be assessed on an intubated patient and so the highest she can score is 10 out of 15.

I start my assessment. Caitlin doesn't open her eyes like a fully conscious person would, and so I have to speak to her, to see if she responds to the sound of my voice, though I'm reluctant. I don't want her to respond. I want to pretend for as long humanly possible that she's completely

370

unconscious and unresponsive.

I blame myself. I got complacent. I got too relaxed. I took for granted that she would never wake up, but she has.

"Caitlin," I say in a forced whisper, standing by the edge of the bed. There is no response and so I lean closer and say it again, unhesitatingly this time, not expecting her to respond.

"Caitlin."

Her eyes fly open. I jerk suddenly back, plowing into the medical cart behind me, where items get jostled but nothing falls.

My heart pounds, a blast beat on the drum.

From two feet away, I watch Caitlin's face. Her open eyes stare up at the ceiling tiles.

The next step is to assess whether she responds to pain. I don't want to touch her, but I drag myself back to the bedside to pinch a couple inches of the trapezius muscle between my thumb and index finger. I pinch lightly at first and then gradually harder, and this time she reacts, her arm subconsciously flexing, bending at the elbow as if to pull away from the pain. I step back again, letting go. She can move, which comes as a letdown because it means she's not locked in.

I tally the results in my head. Today she

scores a seven on the Glasgow Coma Scale.

She was at a three when she came in, which is as low as a person can get.

She's getting better.

In the break room alone, I try to catch my breath, to think.

Caitlin Beckett is improving. It's only a matter of time now until the respiratory therapist comes to try and wean her off the ventilator. Once Caitlin can breathe on her own, she will be able to speak, and I wonder what she will say and if her memories are still intact.

The TV on the break room counter is on; it's the midday news and they're saying how the police are getting closer to finding the man who has been attacking women in the city, and I should be relieved, grateful — I should turn the volume up so I can hear it better — but my mind is somewhere else, and though I notice the voice of the reporter, I have my back to the TV and am only hearing her words at surface level. I don't mentally absorb them because I'm thinking about Caitlin and what I've already done and of what I need to do, because I can't take any chances. *The latest victim fought back. Scratched him. Debris from fingernails. DNA.*

I need to kill her.

I need her dead.

It's not that I want to do this. I'm not a killer. I save people for a living. The idea of taking a human life is unthinkable. I can't imagine anything worse, but I have so much to lose if she lives.

That said, it's possible. I *can* kill her. If you work in a hospital long enough you know that some medical mistakes are inevitable. Every nurse has made them in his or her career. I certainly have. We used to hear horror stories back in nursing school, and I remember when I first started working at the hospital, how I went into every shift just hoping and praying I didn't accidentally kill one of my patients that day. We're human, and everyone makes mistakes, but some mistakes are worse than others, more egregious, things that range from improper documentation to administering the wrong medication, maybe one meant for another patient, and sometimes it's okay, there are no adverse effects, but sometimes someone might have an allergy to a certain medication and die as a result. Even something like improper documentation can have fatal consequences if a nurse doesn't document a medicine a patient takes and someone else also administers it. Some mistakes have ripple effects like that, and then before you know it, a patient has overdosed and died.

There is a shortage of nurses in the workforce these days. Burnout from the pandemic is real. In the last few years, it's led many to rethink their career choice and to leave the profession en masse, which puts even more pressure on the rest of us. While the number of critical care nurses has been depleted, the number of patients continues to grow. They still come, despite the fact that we don't always have enough room or resources to care for them as well as we should. It's a known fact that inadequate nursing staff is directly aligned to patient mortality. The fewer nurses we have, the more responsibilities we have. We're spread thin. We're physically exhausted and emotionally drained. As a result, mistakes happen. It's not necessarily due to bad doctors and nurses, but systematic health-care problems. It wouldn't be my fault. It would be the fault of the system. What people don't know is that fatalities from medical errors are one of the leading causes of death in America, though they don't tell you that. Instead, it's misrepresented as something else like cardiac arrest, when in reality it was something like a fatal drug mix-up; a programming error; the injection of air into the arterial line to cause an embolism or infusing something like potassium too fast.

What I wonder is if a nurse makes a mistake that results in the death of a patient, is she criminally liable?

I might lose my job. I might lose my license.

I'm okay with that, if it means keeping me out of jail.

TWENTY-TWO

The next day, the decision is made to wean Caitlin from the ventilator. Once she's off it, she won't be sedated anymore and will be able to speak.

Liberating someone from a ventilator is a process. It's not something that happens right away. We have to be sure a patient can breathe on their own before we extubate them. It can take up to an hour or more, and sometimes, at the end of that, we find that they're not ready for extubation and it has to be delayed — which is what I'm hoping for, that when the respiratory therapist changes the ventilator settings or after we extubate her, Caitlin has trouble breathing and has to be reintubated. Caitlin is taken off the sedative first, so she's fully conscious.

The respiratory therapist changes the settings on the ventilator, and for the next hour we watch to make sure there are no difficulties and that Caitlin can breathe on her own; that her breathing is not too rapid or shallow; that she stays properly oxygenated and things like that.

I have trouble breathing the whole time.

Caitlin passes the spontaneous breathing trial with flying colors.

Everyone is thrilled about this but me.

Caitlin is getting better.

Everyone thinks she will live, though no one knows in what capacity. The long-term effects of a traumatic brain injury can be significant. People with TBIs can suffer from motor deficits, nerve damage, vision problems, difficulties with fine motor skills, difficulty thinking and remembering and more.

Talking is hard for most people when they first come off a ventilator. Their voices are hoarse and they can breathe on their own, but they're still weak and there is often brain fog from the sedatives and from the time spent on the machine. It's hard to think and to form words at first, but eventually most do.

I've been losing sleep thinking about that, running over and over again in my mind what will happen if and when Caitlin is able to string words into sentences and tell everyone what I did.

Today when I come into her room, she's

377

awake. Her eyes are open like little slits and her head is turned toward the door so that she sees me come in, her head and her eyes following me across the room, though there's no recognition at first, and my only remaining hope is that she doesn't remember what happened and that she doesn't know who I am. It's not wishful thinking. People with head trauma lose their memories all the time.

Caitlin and I are alone in the room together for now. The Becketts were here earlier, but they're gone, setting up a room in their house for Caitlin for when she comes home. Poor Mrs. Beckett must relish the thought of having her daughter back, of caring for her, though it's premature. Caitlin won't be leaving the hospital right away and even when she does, she won't be going home but more likely to an acute rehab facility for treatment, where she will work with speech therapists, PTs and OTs and there, if not here, she will say what happened to her. The police will come and ask questions and sooner or later Caitlin will tell them that Milo Finch didn't push her off the bridge like I suggested, but that I did.

I can't stop thinking about it. It's all I think about anymore, about what happens when she tells them what I did.

I tell myself there were no witnesses. No one saw me push her off the bridge. The only witness was too far away — in a car on Lake Shore Drive — to get a good look. If Caitlin remembers, it will be her word against mine and will be easy to blame on the head injury. I'll say that she's confused, that she only thinks it was me on the bridge with her because of all the time I spent with her while she was unconscious. She heard my voice in the room with her. She's twisting things around in her head, putting me on the bridge with her instead of in the hospital room. Things like that happen.

I could get away with that. I could convince people of my innocence.

Except for a few things. The first being that mammogram appointment. There is evidence that I was within a mile of the pedestrian bridge the same day she was pushed. And if it all comes out, how Caitlin pretended to be Nat to steal from me, then I had motive: revenge.

If Caitlin tells everyone that Sienna is not Ben's daughter, all it will take is a paternity test to prove it. That won't just be my word against hers. There will be physical evidence that her word it true.

I'll never get away with this.

Her eyes are on me now, her gaze less vacant than it's been and more fixed. I go through the Glasgow Coma Scale again and this time, when I ask, "Do you know what happened to you?" she replies.

It's inarticulate at first, but then she gets visibly agitated.

"You. *You,*" she says.

My throat tightens.

It's happening. She's forming words. And not just any words, but incriminating words, words that will ruin me if I let them, if I don't figure out a way to shut her up.

"I . . . I what?" I ask, my voice trembling, and in the next instant her hand latches down on my wrist. I gasp, trying to pull away, but she won't let go at first. I have to use my left hand to wrest my right from her, and only when I manage to get it free, do I let my gaze go back to her face, where her eyes are wide.

I turn and walk quickly from the room, my heart racing inside of me.

There are people milling around the nurses' station. I seek refuge instead in my stroke patient Mrs. Layley's room, feeling hot all of a sudden, a heat that spreads over my neck and face and though I can't see myself, I imagine my skin is red.

Just inside Mrs. Layley's room, I pluck at

my scrub top, pulling it away from the skin so that it billows and the air gets in. I try to breathe. I go to the sink. I wash my hands, letting the cold water run over them, taking a moment to catch my breath.

"Hello," Mrs. Layley says, and I know I have to go to her, that I can't just stand here and hide out in her room.

I go to the bedside, trying to smile, to be mentally present for Mrs. Layley, but it's practically impossible because all I can think about is Caitlin.

Her wide eyes. The expression of her face. The way her mouth formed around the word, trying it on for size, like a baby first learning to talk. I could be wrong, but I think her broken body moved too as she said it, that she pulled just barely away from me in bed, slithering like a worm to get away as if she was afraid.

She could have meant anything by it. *You* are my nurse. *You* are here.

There could be a dozen things she was trying to say.

Or she could have meant exactly what I think she did. It could have been quite implicit.

You pushed me off the bridge. *You* did this. *You* will never get away with it.

There is dampness beneath my arms and

I'm grateful for the dark scrubs or it might be visible.

"How are you feeling, Mrs. Layley?" I ask, but as she tells me, fighting to get the words out because her speech and comprehension have been affected from the stroke, I'm only thinking how I have no choice, how I have to do it, how I have to kill her and how I have to do it soon because if I wait too long, I'll miss the chance. It will be too late. Caitlin gets better every day, and it's only a matter of time now until she reveals all.

I tell myself that she's not a good person. She lied to me. She pretended to kidnap my child. She stole from me. She hurt her own parents. She told lies about her mother. She framed a man with child pornography and ruined his whole life. She has no virtue, no integrity. The world would be better without her in it. *If there is any justice in the world,* Milo Finch said, *she won't survive this.*

But how would I do it?

I mull it over. I bat it around in my mind. And that's when the answer comes to me, sitting there in plain sight, on the beside cart by Mrs. Layley's bed and from the moment I lay eyes on it, I know I've struck gold.

Mrs. Layley's insulin pen.

Insulin is a lethal drug. It comes with a

warning. Too much of it can kill, enough that people use it to commit suicide sometimes. It's opportunistic. But I'm desperate. And I'm already rationalizing in my mind how I could get away with it, how I could chalk it up to an egregious mistake, how I gave one patient's medicine to the other by accident. It happens. It happens more than people know, that nurses give medication to the wrong patient. Because we're understaffed and overworked and we don't always remember or have time to do things like scanning wristbands before giving medicine, intentionally skipping those safeguards that are meant to keep everyone safe, for the sake of time.

It's conceivable that I could move a decimal when calculating the dose too, that I could give Caitlin much more than Mrs. Layley would ever take and chalk it up to another mistake.

In theory, insulin pens shouldn't be left out in the open like this. We're supposed to keep them in patient specific bins in the medication room, but that's not always the most efficient because patents on insulin need it many times a day. We don't have time to be running back and forth to the medication room all day. It's become common practice for nurses to leave them unsecured in patient rooms or to carry them around in a pocket.

As a result, they get lost. I hear nurses at the nurses' station from time to time, troubled by lost insulin pens, looking for them, wondering where they left them. When they can't find them, they request a replacement from the pharmacy because patients like Mrs. Layley can't go without insulin without becoming hyperglycemic or developing ketoacidosis, and it's never a big deal. The pharmacy just replaces them.

I take the pen on my way out of the room, slipping it in my pocket as I leave.

TWENTY-THREE

I feel the insulin pen through the pocket of my scrub bottoms. It's not actually visible. I keep telling myself that it's not, reassuring myself. If anything, it's just a small bulge that no one would ever notice, but I look down at it from various angles to be certain it's not obvious.

I'd be lying if I said I wasn't scared or that I didn't have my doubts. I do. I'm not a murderer. It's not that I want her to die, it's that I keep thinking what will happen to me if she lives. Her life and mine are incompatible.

I think through the likely outcomes of giving her the insulin. Bradycardia. Pulseless electrical activity. Death. It's not a guarantee. There are variables of course because everyone is different. For example, it could take twenty units of insulin to kill a person or nine hundred. There's no way to know for sure how her body will respond, though this is regular insulin and not long acting; my guess is death will come relatively quick.

Caitlin is asleep, but she wakes up when I touch her, her eyes slowly opening, and I know that if I hesitate, I will lose my nerve. She grimaces, pulling back from the light, getting acclimated to it as I grab her by the arm, thinking, in that last second, about loyal Mrs. Beckett and the day, years ago, that police showed up at her front door because Caitlin accused her of child abuse. I think about what it would feel like to have your reputation tarnished, to be dragged through the mud by someone you love, by someone you would do anything for. I think of Milo Finch and the day the police came for him, taking him away in handcuffs, his family and freedom gone, his life forever changed because of her. None of it is provable.

She'll heal. She'll get physically better and walk out of the hospital an innocent woman if I let her, while I'll go to jail and she'll go on to ruin someone else's life.

I give the insulin in the back of the upper arm because it's easiest to get to. She winces and recoils from the pain of the injection.

"I'm sorry," I say, and I am, though I'm not sorry for what I'm doing. I'm sorry that she's not the person I thought she was. For a moment, I let my thoughts go back to the night I met her at the divorce support group meeting and how grateful I was to have found a friend. I think back to how I embraced her that night in the church, how I held on too long, feeling nostalgic and longing for the past and for simpler, happier times. She preyed on my loneliness and on my desperate need for a friend.

She was never my friend.

My hands tremble as I turn the dial on the pen and inject her for a second and then a third time, having to wrench her arm back into place because she fights harder each time.

When I'm done, I drop the pen back into my pocket.

I move the call button out of reach, stepping away from the bedside.

My breathing is heavy, lumbering, and my chest pounds. I hear the blood pulse past my eardrums. What have I done? It can still be undone, I tell myself, but I don't want to undo it. I want it to be over. I want her to be dead. I breathe in. I breathe out, knowing I have to find a way to relax, that I have to be patient because it won't happen right away. It will take a little time, her condition worsening before she goes into cardiac arrest and all the while, I have to act like nothing is happening, like nothing is wrong.

I force myself forward again. I silence the alarms in the room. Eventually she'll become tachycardic, her heart rate high, and I don't want anyone to know because they might try and save her too soon. I can't take any chances that she survives this. On our unit, we don't have teletechs sitting around, analyzing heart rhythms. Instead, as nurses, we're trained to pick up on subtle differences on an ECG or to listen to the alarms. Caitlin watches me as I silence hers, her eyes fully open and I wonder if she knows what I've done, if she knows what's happening to her and if she's scared.

I leave the room because I can't just stand here for the next hour and watch it happen. I have to go about my day. I have to act normal. I go to check on my other patients. I take vitals and administer medication, but, all the while, my mind is on Caitlin, wondering what's happening in her room, if she's experiencing heart blocks by now, the electrical signals slowing down, failing to conduct.

I leave one patient's room, stepping into the hall for the nurses' station to make a call. At the same time, I see Luke coming in the opposite direction. He smiles and I think he's just going to pass by, but then he says, "I've been meaning to talk to you. Penelope has a friend," at the last second before we pass, gently grabbing a hold of my forearm, turning me to face him. We're just outside of Caitlin's room when he does, and, because of my positioning, I'm forced to look in, to see sweat on her forehead, her skin turning red. "Dan — Daniel — Murphy," he says, though I can barely hear him because I'm thinking about Caitlin and wondering if anyone else can see the sweat but me.

"Earth to Meghan," Luke says, teasing. I blink my eyes into focus, forcing them on him. "Did you hear me?"

"I'm sorry, no," I say, shaking my head. "What did you say?" I ask, knowing that if Luke were to turn his eyes a little to the right, if he were to move his gaze just another couple feet, he would see into her room. Would he also notice her sweating or am I only being hypervigilant?

"Is everything okay?"

"Yes. Why?" I ask, stepping away from the glass, further into the hall so his eyes will follow.

"I don't know," he says, cocking a head. "You seem distracted."

I force a laugh that's anything but genuine, the sound of it unpleasant to my ear. "I'm totally fine," I say, overemphasizing the word *fine,* making it lack credibility.

Luke holds my gaze too long. "Are you really?"

I clear my throat and collect myself. "Yes. Honestly. I'm fine," I say, my words more grounded, more like myself. "I'm sorry, I just dazed off. Long day. What were you saying before?"

"I said I think you and he would make a good match. Penelope's friend, Dan Murphy. What do you think?" he asks, a grin forming on the edges of his lips. "A double date?"

"Penelope is on bed rest."

"We'll have you and Dan over to our place. I'll cook, I'll do the dishes, so that Penelope doesn't have to lift a finger."

"Spoken just like a man who's never been pregnant or on bed rest before. I'm sure she'd love that."

"She's going stir-crazy, Meghan. I'm sure she would. Think about it, okay? Let me know later. Just don't wait too long to decide because he's *quite the catch,* as Penelope says," he says, putting air quotes around the words. "If you wait too long, you might lose your chance."

"Okay."

"You promise?" he asks, lingering too long

when I wish he would leave.

"Yes. I promise."

When he walks away, the relief is profound.

But it's short-lived. Because at nearly the same time, the doors to the ICU open and I brace myself, imagining the Becketts coming back to visit at the wrong time, seeing it happen, watching their daughter die.

TWENTY-FOUR

Her heart slows. She goes into cardiac arrest. It's not V-tach but pulseless electrical activity, where the electrical activity in the heart is too weak to make the heart contract, to pump blood to the rest of the body. She has no pulse and the amount of electrical activity in the heart is not enough to keep her alive.

I'm in the room when it happens, watching as she loses consciousness, as she becomes unresponsive, as she turns pallid.

I do nothing yet, though my nerves scream out and my brain is on fire.

She's dying.

By the grace of God, the Becketts haven't returned from their house. They're still there, or they're somewhere in-between, like in a cab, the hospital lobby, or riding the elevator to our floor. I look out into the hall to be sure no one is there, that no one is watching Caitlin die, and then I let my eyes return to her, stepping to the bedside to check again that there is no palpable pulse.

Death from pulseless electrical activity happens within minutes, so that by the time I decide to call a code blue, she will already be edging towards death. Within five minutes of the brain not receiving blood and oxygen, her brain cells will start to die, and once that happens, there will be no reviving her.

I stand watching for as long as I can, to be sure that the damage is substantial and irreversible and then I know I have to attempt to resuscitate her. I have to make it look like I want to save her life as I would any other patient. I call a code blue, screaming it out into the hall, and then I start chest compressions, which are passive at first until a witness arrives and I put more effort into it, feeling Caitlin's ribs break under the pressure of my hands.

A code blue is not a gentle process. CPR is violent. It's an assault. Bad things happen to patients in an often vain attempt to save lives. Of the people who go into cardiac arrest in the hospital, most don't live and of those who do, many have a permanent neurologic disability and few live meaningful lives. It's awful, but I have to make peace with that. I can't feel guilty this time for allowing a patient to die.

People come running into the room, bringing the crash cart. Natalia takes over with chest compressions. I've mustered tears and am visibly upset.

"What happened, Meghan?"

"I gave another patient's insulin to her by mistake," I admit, breathing heavily, knowing that after she's dead, there will be an autopsy. They'll find the insulin in her system. Lying would only make things worse; it would make me look guilty. But being honest will go a long way in the future. There will be leniency. The fallout won't be as bad because there are systems in place to protect nurses who make genuine mistakes, so long as they tell the truth.

I say when and how much was given. I admit to having miscalculated the dose too, to moving a decimal point, and the room becomes instantly frenzied. Organized chaos, everyone cramped into a small space, so hyperfocused on their own task, but working toward the same goal.

Only I have a different objective.

They want her to live.

I need her to die, and she does.

The time of death is called. People step back and let their breath out at once. Someone turns off the machines and they fall silent. An ease descends on the room like fog, a brief moment of inactivity before everyone drifts away, back to whatever they were doing before Caitlin went into cardiac arrest.

I stand there, motionless for a while as people leave and others come in to express their condolences and ask if I'm okay, as if the loss is mine, as if I'm bereaved.

Alone in the room with her, I try telling myself this is just another patient, any other patient who died. But the reality of what I've done starts to sink in and consume me until I'm sure I see her heart beat through the thin bedsheet, an almost negligible rise, the barely audible *thump-thump, thump-thump,* and I have to pull the sheet back to see that she is dead, that she's *really* dead, pressing my fingers to the carotid to feel for a pulse, her skin paling now, cold to the touch and something like a silicone cake mold.

She's dead. She is really dead.

Someone steps in to tell me that the charge nurse wants to speak with me. I knew this was coming — it was inevitable — and that it will be the first of many conversations in the coming days, but it doesn't stop me from feeling overcome with dread.

"What happened, Meghan?" she asks when I go to her, and I fall apart, I lose myself completely. I sob, sputtering some version of the truth.

She's consoling. "It was an honest mistake, and the fact that you owned up to what happened will go far. But, Meghan," she says before I leave. "I'd get a lawyer just in case."

I leave her office, taking off for a nearby fire escape, which no one ever uses. When I come to it, I press my hands against the panic bar, rushing through the steel door and into the stairwell. I climb up, walking at first and then running up the steps, taking them two at a time so that I'm breathless, my legs filling with lactic acid by the time I reach the top, where I stop, bending at the waist, putting my hands on my knees. I turn and drop down on the stairs, gasping, wheezing, tasting my lunch in my mouth — sour now, saliva mixing with stomach acid — rising up my throat, collecting inside my cheeks and under my tongue. I fight the urge to be sick. It takes effort, conscious thought. I close my eyes; I breathe in though my nose, holding the air in my lungs, exhaling through my mouth. Again and again. I lean my head against the wall, grateful that it's cold against my face. My entire body starts to shake, an unrelenting convulsion like an epileptic fit. I'm hot and sweating but cold at the same time, like all the times I've woken up with night sweats, soaked in my own sweat but cold and shaking from the drying moisture on my clothing, sheets and skin.

I can't let anyone see me like this.

I can't let Sienna see me like this.

With unsteady hands, I reach into the pocket of my scrubs to find my phone. I stare at the image of Sienna for a long time, and then I type a text for her, Hey. I think carefully through my next words because Sienna is astute and she knows me better than anyone.

I think I'm coming down with something. Do you want to see if you can sleep at Gianna's tonight? I don't want to get you sick.

It's so unlike me, to pass Sienna off on a friend, to suggest she invite herself to sleep over at someone else's place. If Sienna had suggested something like this, I'd have said absolutely not, that it's rude.

But I can't see her right now. I can't look

at her after what I've done.

Sick how? she asks.

I don't know. Stomach flu maybe. Just text Gianna, ok? Let me know what she says.

This is weird, Mom. I can't just invite myself to her house.

I know. I'm sorry. But you have the ACT next week and the winter dance next weekend. You can't be getting sick. Do you want me to text her mom and see if it's ok?

No. That's embarrassing. I'm not five.

Ok. Then text her.

I set my phone on the stairs beside me. Eventually I'll have to get up. Eventually I'll have to leave. There are things to do before I can go home for the night, my only saving grace that it's after seven now and the night shift has come in; the day shift is leaving.

It only takes a minute and then Sienna texts back to let me know that she will be sleeping at Gianna's, and I'm relieved. I need Sienna gone. I need the apartment to myself. I need to think, to fall apart, to worry, to cry, all in private. I don't bother asking if Gianna's parents will be home, which generally I would. Normally I'm a stickler for things like that, always insisting that I get confirmation of a parent's whereabouts before I'll let Sienna stay with a friend overnight. I was sixteen once; I know what sixteen-year-olds do when left alone for any extended time. But tonight that's the least of my concerns.

Ok. Have fun. Love you.

It takes effort to leave the stairwell. I have to talk myself into it, to getting up, walking down the stairs and going back to the unit to finish what I need to do.

The medical examiner comes for the body. From a distance I see it get wheeled away, using the staff elevator, because not everyone needs to know that not all patients leave through the front door. Mr. and Mrs. Beckett follow, their hands clasped, their faces tired and grave, and I shrink back at seeing them, into a shallow recess in the wall, hiding because I can't see them now. I can't speak to them. I don't know what I would say if I did. Still, I watch them, my eyes following for as long as they can. Mrs. Beckett's tears are subdued and I wonder for a minute if she's sad, or if I've done her a favor and instead of grief there is relief.

When I finally leave the building, I walk slowly home. My guilt starts to get the better of me, my conscience screaming. I feel transparent, like anyone could look at me and know what I've done.

The night is cold. Way off in the distance, a siren screams, drawing near. I've lived in Chicago for almost half of my life and this is nothing different, nothing new, and yet it takes almost nothing to convince me that this siren is coming for me, that, after I left work, someone at the hospital figured out what really happened, what I did, that it was intentional. They called the police, and now the police are looking into it. They're investigating Caitlin's suspicious death.

The siren's wail gets closer. It moves in, approaching until it's there, just over my left shoulder, and I don't know what's louder: the siren's blare or the pounding of my own heart. I'm too afraid to look back and so I duck into an alley, pressing my back flush against a brick wall, beside an acrid Dumpster with a colony of feral cats living under it, watching the police cruiser soar past, and it's only then, when it's gone — the siren quieting from the distance — that I slip cautiously back out.

I stop at the liquor store on the corner because we have only wine at home and tonight I need something stronger than wine.

It's practically nine by the time I finally get home. It's pitch-black outside, the moon a waning crescent, and I'm not scared, I'm not even thinking anymore about the man who has been attacking women in the city. I'm only thinking of Caitlin.

She was not a good person, I remind myself every time the guilt creeps in.

I did everyone a favor. I did what I had to do.

I slip the key in and let myself into the building. I start making my way up the stairs, my steps plodding, my legs heavy as if weighed down by bricks. The plastic bag brushes against my leg, the vodka inside wrapped in a brown paper sack that rustles with every step.

I reach the third floor of the building. When I come to the landing, my back is to the door and my focus is on my keys, on singling out the key to the apartment so I can let myself in and close and lock the door behind me.

It's as I'm rounding the top of the stairs that I see movement in my peripheral vision. I startle, my head jerking suddenly up to find a dark form crouched beside the door. I scream, falling back, and it takes a moment to gain clarity, for the image before me to become crisp: the man sitting on the floor beside my door, on the threadbare maroon carpeting, his long face, the square jaw with its sharp angles and corners, the narrow eyes and his hair, brown but growing gray near the roots with a prominent widow's peak.

"Fuck. Damn it, Ben," I cry out, throwing my hand to my heart as my ex-husband, Ben, rises up from the ground, carrying his coat over an arm. "What are you doing here?" I ask, one hand to my heart, breathing hard.

"Sorry," he says, keeping his distance, looking sheepish. "I didn't mean to scare you."

My heart is wild inside of me. My words are brusque as I step past him so I can let myself into the apartment, close the door and lock him out, so I can be alone. "Sienna isn't here," I grumble. "Check your calendar. It's not your weekend with her."

"I know," Ben says, and I feel the weight of his hand on my arm as I step past. His grip is firm, physically stopping me. "Sienna texted," he says, his voice soft and civil, unlike mine. "She said she was worried about you, Meghan. That you were acting strangely. I told her I would check on you and make sure everything is okay."

I hesitate. I'm reluctant at first, but then I turn slightly, gazing up to meet Ben's eye. "I'm fine. I'm just not feeling well," I tell him. "Stomach flu maybe. If you don't mind," I say as I pull my arm away, "I just need to go inside and go to bed."

I take a step toward the door, but this time Ben helps himself to my bag, slotting a finger into the visible brown paper sack to reveal the bottle of Smirnoff inside. He gazes up, his eyes reading my face. "I didn't know vodka was the standard remedy for the stomach flu."

I pull the bag abruptly back, out of his reach.

"Hey," he says, his voice soft, sweet, practically cooing now. He cocks his head, his eyes going back and forth between mine, and he's not patronizing, I don't think, but genuinely worried. "Why are you so jumpy? Is everything okay?"

I fold my arms across myself, the bag of vodka hanging by the bag's handles from around my wrist. I feel myself tighten up and get defensive. My words are hostile. "Let me guess," I say roughly. "You're going to tell the judge about this?"

But Ben only flinches, looking physically pained. "No, Meghan," he says, shaking his head, the lighting in the hallway throwing shadows on his face. "I wouldn't do that, and even if I wanted to, there's nothing to say. You're an adult. There isn't anything in the custody agreement that says you can't have a drink after work." He takes a step forward, and this time, his hands come down on my shoulders and they're warm, firm, buoying. He bends at the knees, lowering himself so that we're practically at eye level now. "I'm not worried about that. I'm just worried about you."

I try to be strong, stoic, but exhaustion and emotion overwhelm me and tears come. I don't mean for them to, but they come anyway, and Ben's face changes, softening. I'm not one to cry. I never have been. I'm the type to keep my feelings inside and so this is something different for him, something new and unexpected, a side of me he's rarely seen.

Ben hesitates at first — not sure, I think, what to do — but then his knees straighten. He rises back up to full height, folding me into his arms, and I feel myself surrender, the dam breaking, water rushing through. I'm reluctant at first but then I lean my head against his chest, grateful for its strength, for the substantiality of it, for the rhythmic beating of his heart, which calms and steadies me. Ben runs a hand along my hair, and for a minute I feel safe. "What's going on, Meghan?" he asks, breathing the words into my ear. "You can talk to me," he says, and I give in, because Ben, despite our differences, despite what's happened to us over the last few years, knows me better than almost anyone, even sometimes better than I know myself. He's seen me at my best. He's seen me at my worst.

I pull slowly back, wiping at my face with the back of a sleeve. "It was a bad day," I say. "I lost a patient." I shake my head. "I . . . I didn't want Sienna to see me like this. I just wanted to be alone."

"I'm sorry," he says, and it feels like he is. It feels like he's being genuine. "I know how hard you always take it when a patient dies. It's what makes you such a good nurse, Meghan, how you never get used to it. You never get complacent."

I almost say how it was different this time, how I fucked up, how it's my fault she's dead, but I stop myself, letting Ben still believe for a while that I'm a good nurse and that what happened was beyond my control. For a minute, we stand there in the hall, not speaking, until he says, "Well," as he stretches an arm into the sleeve of his coat. "I just wanted to check on you, but I know you want to be alone and I don't want to impose," he decides, and suddenly I don't want him to go. I'm afraid to be alone with my thoughts.

"Do you have to?" I ask, my hand, by instinct, reaching for his. Before me, Ben is visibly taken aback. Seconds pass before he responds, and in that time, I'm sure I've made a mistake, that I've misread the situation, that I only imagined a moment between us.

But then he says, "No," easing his arm back out of the sleeve and folding his coat over an arm. "I don't have to go. I can stay if you want me to."

I nod. "I do." I turn my back to him, feeling his hand on the small of my back as I open the door to let us into the darkened apartment. Once inside, I cross the living room for the lamp. I turn it on, adjusting the brightness so that it's not too bright, and then turn back to face Ben, who is pushing the front door gently closed and locking the dead bolt. Ben is tall, over six feet with an athletic physique, his biceps visible through a thin white shirt, his jeans straight.

He turns away from the door, catching

me staring. "You can just throw your coat on a chair. Do you want something to drink? I have beer."

"A beer would be great."

I nod, carrying the vodka down the dark, narrow hall and to the kitchen. I take it out of the bag and then pour a couple shots into a lowball glass and fill it with Coke. I take a long sip and then send a quick text to Sienna, saying, You didn't need to text Dad. I'm okay. A second later though, I worry about the tone of the text, that it sounded brusque. I don't want Sienna to think I'm upset that she texted Ben, because it was genuinely sweet and well-intentioned.

I send a second text. I appreciate that you did though. Thank you for thinking of me. Have fun with Gianna tonight. I love you.

I take another drink from my glass, standing at the kitchen counter to see if Sienna texts back, but she doesn't right away, and I'm glad because it means she isn't on her phone and that she's enjoying her friend's company.

I take another sip and try not to think about Caitlin. I try hard to forget about the way her skin felt under my fingers after she died. I think instead about the awful things she did to me and others, how disingenuous she was. What she did was reprehensible.

She sought me out, she learned about my past so that she could impersonate a friend to slip easier into my life. She knew everything about me, and she used my desire to help people to her advantage, playing a victim so I would protect her, so I would take pity on her, so that I would take her in. I can't think of her as the woman she's been these last few weeks: helpless and unconscious with a family who loves her despite every awful thing she's done to hurt them.

I have to remember the woman she was before.

The one mistake I make, as I grab a beer from the refrigerator for Ben, tuck my phone under an arm and carry the two drinks out to the living room, is that I don't stop to wonder how she knew so much about me.

In the living room, Ben stands with his back to me. He looks out the window for the street. He doesn't hear me come in and so I hang back and watch him for a moment, finding it hard to believe that he is here in my apartment when Sienna isn't home, that he came for a reason other than to pick her up, but that he came to check on me.

The old Ben wouldn't have done that. The old Ben wouldn't have gone out of his way like that for me. Suddenly all of the bad feelings I've had for him these last few months soften. I look at them in another light. What if Ben wasn't the only one to blame for our marriage's collapse? Looking back, it was easy for both of us to get complacent after so much time together. There was a laxity and a lack of effort on both our parts. We weren't putting as much effort into our relationship as we did when we were first together. What if it was my fault as much as it was his?

"Here's your beer," I say, coming further in. "Do you want to sit?"

He turns slowly away from the window. Behind him, on the other side of the glass, it's snowing again. Ben crosses the room, stepping around the narrow edge of the coffee table. He lowers himself onto the leather sofa, our hands touching by accident when I pass him his beer. "Thanks," he says, and though I deliberate on where to sit, eventually I lower myself to the sofa beside him instead of opting to sit in the armchair alone.

Ben looks down at the beer, holding it by the neck. It's Guinness, which is what he always drinks, and it's not lost on him. "I didn't know you like Guinness."

"I don't."

"Oh," he says, as if thinking I bought the Guinness for someone else.

But I correct him. "Old habits die hard," I say, blushing because I don't drink beer, not often anyway. I bought this unintentionally at the grocery store a month or so ago. It was one of those things you do without realizing you're doing it because, when we were married, I bought six-packs of Guinness for Ben all the time. When I got home and unpacked the bags, I couldn't believe my mistake. I almost thought about throwing it away. I would never drink it, but it seemed a waste because someday someone might.

I never thought that someone would be Ben.

He throws back the beer, taking a long sip, and then, wiping his mouth on the back of his hand, asks, "Will you tell me your patient's name? The one who died."

I don't want to talk about her. I don't want to think about her.

"You know I can't."

"Nice to see you're still a stickler for rules," he says, and I smile, liking the banter. I like the way that, even after months apart and all the bad feelings between us, he can still poke fun at me. "What happened exactly?" he asks, draping his arm over the back of the sofa, sobering. His arm brushes against my shoulders and hair, triggering something inside of me. It's been so long since I've been this close to a man. The smell of Ben's cologne is strong and familiar, reminding me of home, and I flash back to our life together, to getting ready for work in the same small bathroom each morning, breathing in the scent of his cologne.

"Cardiac arrest."

"How old was she?"

"Thirty-two," I say, seeing the way he watches me, studying me.

Ben can tell that the conversation is making me upset. His tone changes, and he says, "I shouldn't have asked. Let's not talk about this," as he breaks his gaze, and I appreciate his willingness to let the conversation go.

I'm still in my scrubs. I regret that I didn't change when I first came home, that I didn't put on something else like jeans and a blouse or run a comb through my hair before getting our drinks. "I'm a mess. I should change," I say, making an effort to stand up, but Ben brings his arm around from behind the sofa to set his hand on my thigh. It stops me all of a sudden and I sink back against the seat, watching his hand on my leg. His hand is still at first, though it gives off heat, the warmth of it taking the chill out of the room and warming me through. I expect him to move his hand, but he doesn't. Instead he strokes my knee with a thumb, just a small sweeping motion that I feel all the way to my core. I stare, silent, at Ben's hand for a while, not reacting but not pushing him away either, letting him touch me, remembering how, at the frozen yogurt shop where we used to work when we were in high school, I fell in love with Ben's strong hands, with the deft way they would punch numbers into the cash register, which stirs up something inside of me now, nostalgia and something else.

My heart accelerates, a caged bird wanting to fly.

"No," he says. "You don't need to change. Stay. It's just me." He takes another sip from his beer. "What time is Sienna coming home?" he asks.

Our eyes meet as I say, "She isn't. Not tonight. She's sleeping at her friend Gianna's."

I see the movement of his Adam's apple in his throat when he swallows.

Ben reaches out to touch my hair, his fingertips softly grazing the outer rim of my ear. My breath quickens and I feel his breath on my skin when he speaks. "I've missed this," he says. "I've missed you."

He holds my stare, regret in his eyes. His gaze goes to my lips, and I think back to the first time Ben and I kissed. I was seventeen at the time. It wasn't my first kiss. I had kissed guys in my life by then, though they had been mostly regrettable, mostly drunk at high school parties where I had only hazy memories of guys rubbing against me in the dark, sticking their tongues into my mouth, and me mistaking it for love.

But I had never had a kiss like Ben's before. That night, his lips were soft and gentle as a breeze at first, sweeping against mine, rousing my senses, so that I lost touch with myself and my surroundings all of a sudden. I was buoyant, floating as we stood together in a dark corner of a parking lot, where the glow from a nearby streetlight couldn't reach and people driving past couldn't see us.

"Sienna said that you've been seeing someone," I say, though I almost don't because I don't want to know. I don't want to ruin the moment, but a part of me wonders if there isn't a woman waiting back at his condo for him, if she isn't lying alone in Ben's and my bed and if this isn't just a courtesy because Sienna asked him to check up on me.

"I was," he says, running his hands down

my hair, "but that's over."

"I'm sorry," I say, but if he's telling the truth, then I'm not sorry. I'm glad. "What happened?"

"To be honest?" he asks, looking sheepish as he takes another drink from his beer. "She was jealous of you."

"Of me?" I ask, pulling back, laughing gaily. "But you and I aren't together anymore. What did she possibly have to be jealous of your ex-wife for?"

"Oh I don't know," he says, but it's teasing, playful. He does know. "Maybe almost two decades and a child together. It's hard to compete with that. It didn't help when she found a picture of us in a dresser drawer by accident. I caught her looking at it, and though she said she wasn't — that she was just curious to know what you looked like — I could see she was mad as hell that I kept it."

I let it go to my head, both the fact that Ben kept a secret picture of me hidden in his dresser drawer and his girlfriend's reaction to it. "How could you tell?" I ask. "What did she do?"

"She asked a lot of questions about you. Your name, how we met, what you're like."

"What did you tell her?"

"The truth. That you're selfless, compassionate, but guarded. That you have a tough shell, but that once someone finds a way in, there's nothing you won't do for them." I'm touched. I've never heard Ben speak like this, I've never heard him put into words how he sees and feels about me. "I didn't tell her how beautiful you are. I didn't need to. She could see that for herself," he says while slipping his hands beneath the hem of my shirt as goose bumps rise up on my arms. He hesitates and then asks, "Have you dated anyone?"

"No," I say, but I'm distracted by his hands, feeling my body edge closer to his, my heart quickening. "Well, yes. I mean I did. I went on a date with some man I met online. It sounds desperate, right? Online dating."

"No. People do it all the time. I thought about giving it a try too. It's not exactly easy to find nice, normal, single women when you're forty."

"No, it's not. Not nice, normal, single men either. They either live with their parents or they're divorced, which makes you wonder what's wrong with them." I laugh then. "If that's not the pot calling the kettle black, I don't know what is. Is it strange that we're talking about this? About dating other people?"

"Yes and no," Ben says. "It's something we can relate to, something we have in common, even if it is awful to imagine my wife in bed with another man. Is this okay?" he whispers softly now, his hands moving up my bare ribcage, and I nod, my breath shallow, my heart going wild inside of me. His gaze goes from my eyes to my lips and back up to my eyes as I bite down on my own lower lip, lost in the color of his eyes and the shape of his mouth. Thinking only about how much I want him to kiss me, to lay me back on the sofa, and how I want to feel the weight of him as he lays himself down on me. I want to lose myself in this, in him, to forget about everything that came before this moment. The divorce. Caitlin Beckett. What I've done.

"Ex-wife," I say, "and I wasn't sleeping with him. It was just dinner and even that wasn't good. The food, the conversation, all of it."

"Ouch. Poor guy. What was his name?"

"Alec," I say, thinking back to how in person he didn't come close to resembling the man I saw online and how I felt terrible and shallow, but also completely misled. I decided to stay and give him the benefit of the doubt, and ended up regretting it. "What is your girlfriend's name?"

"Was. She's not my girlfriend anymore."

"Sorry. What was your girlfriend's name?"

"Caitlin," he says, and I immediately stiffen, coming close to choking on my own saliva. My back arches, lifting up from the sofa's backrest and I lean forward to set my drink on the coffee table, not trusting myself to hold it. The L goes flying by at the same time and I thank God because it buys me time. I don't have to speak. I don't have to respond. The walls of the apartment close in on me, the room suddenly short of oxygen.

Caitlin.

It could be a different Caitlin. There must be tens of thousands of women named Caitlin in the world.

But in my whole life I've only ever known one.

"I don't want to talk about her though. Or *Alec*," Ben says with something like disdain as the L disappears and the apartment quiets.

At the same time, my cell phone vibrates against the coffee table, the sound reverberating.

I startle at the noise. "Leave it," Ben breathes softly into my ear, leaning into me now so that I descend from the physical force of him, tilting back against the sofa,

417

its square arms digging into my back, hurting me.

I try to sit up against the weight of him, but he resists, bearing down on me, lowering himself between my legs, the size of him suddenly suffocating. "It's probably Sienna," I say, but he's disinterested, his lips on my neck as he drives his hand under the lacy edge of my bra.

"I'm sure she's fine," he drones.

"Please. Let me just make sure."

Ben's sigh is audible and aggrieved. He drags his hand out from under my shirt, though he hesitates then, his strong arms on either side of my head, propping him up but at the same time, boxing me in. He watches me a minute before sitting up, before allowing me access to my phone, and in that moment I see a glimmer of the man I married, the one who is selfish, irritated and easily provoked. I can see in his eyes that he wants to tell me no, that Sienna can wait for us to finish before I read her text.

He pushes himself from the sofa, rising beside it.

"Where are you going?" I ask, pulling down on my shirt to fix it.

"Bathroom," he says.

I wait for him to go before I reach for the phone, listening as the bathroom door

418

closes and locks.

I glance down at my phone then, using my face to unlock it. I was right; the text is from Sienna, just two tiny, diminutive words.

I didn't.

I draw my eyebrows together. I don't know what she means at first. What didn't she do?

I can hear Ben in the bathroom now. It won't be long until he comes back and I don't want him to be upset I'm still on the phone, and so I text quickly back, What didn't you do?

In the next room, the toilet flushes. I hear the rush of water as it comes pouring out of the bathroom faucet and into the sink. In my hand, my phone vibrates again and I look back down, my stomach clenching at the words.

I didn't text Dad.

My hand goes to my mouth.

Ben.

I think of what he just said: how he was dating Caitlin.

Was he a part of this? Did he help her pull

it off? But why? To hurt me, to get back at me for the divorce?

I wonder if he told this woman private things about me, like how my sister's death devastated me. Ben knows me so well. He knows everything about me. He knows I wouldn't be quick to trust a stranger, to let a stranger into Sienna's and my home, but an old friend was a safe bet, and an old friend in danger was a slam dunk.

Bile rises up inside of me as the thumb turn lock moves on the bathroom door. The sound of it subtle, slight.

Still, I draw in a sharp breath as I turn back to watch the door handle slowly spin. Ben pulls open the door. Light from the bathroom radiates out, his large, imposing frame filling the small doorway.

He turns off the light. All at once, the room behind him darkens, and I realize that there are only three units in this building and it's possible no one but me is here tonight and that no would hear me if I screamed.

"Is she okay?" Ben asks, his head slanted, his arms at his sides. He crosses the room in three steps and, as if by instinct, I rise up from the sofa, stepping back and away from him.

Sienna didn't text Ben. He came on his own.

Did he know that Caitlin was dead? Did he somehow know I killed her? But how?

"Meghan?" he asks.

"What?"

"I asked if Sienna is okay."

What if they hadn't broken up after all? What if they were still dating?

A little while ago he asked about my patient. He asked how old she was. He specifically said *she.*

I never told him my patient was a woman.

I'm short of breath. "Yeah," I say. "Fine."

Ben also has Life360, for the nights Sienna stays with him. He can track her location just like I can. He could have watched her leave our apartment. He could have followed her little avatar in real time as she walked the three blocks to Gianna's.

He would have known that I was alone.

"Meghan?" he asks again.

"Sorry. What?" I ask, a lump in my throat now.

I don't know what to do. I can't call the police, because Ben is watching. I couldn't get to my phone in time. I couldn't press the numbers without him stopping me.

And what would I say without confessing to what I did?

"What did she want?" he asks, coming closer. I can't move as Ben's arms rise to sweep my hair back and out of my eyes before he cradles my face in his hands. He tilts my head back, forcing my gaze up to his dark eyes, and I realize how quickly he could break my neck if he wanted to; he could sever the spinal cord and there would be no time to react or to fight back.

What if she told him that Sienna is not his? What if he already knows?

I try to control the quiver of my voice. "She has a headache actually. She's not sleeping at Gianna's after all. She's coming home."

His thumb sweeps along my throat, brushing over the trachea until I imagine his hands around my neck, applying pressure, cutting off the airway until I can't breathe. "That's too bad," he says, and from the way he looks at me, I can't tell if he believes it. "I thought we'd have more time." Still, he's not deterred. If anything, he's more decisive. His hands slide to the small of my back, drawing me swiftly into him as the L passes by again, and I think of all the people on the train watching through the open window as his lips skim over mine, moving down my neck, as he unknots the drawcord on my scrub bottoms.

"Me too," I say, pulling back, trying to infuse my words with disappointment as his hands fall away from me. "But I think that you should go, Ben. I'd hate for Sienna to come home and see us like this."

Ben stands, three feet away, cold and unexpressive. His posture straightens and he runs his hands through his hair, his dark eyes holding me captive. He's positioned between me and the door, and I wonder if I ran, if I could get to it, if I could unlock the dead bolt, turn the handle and get out of the apartment before he grabbed me by the hair or the wrist and yanked me back.

I don't think I could. The apartment is small, cramped. There is no leeway, no elbow room. I'd have to pass by too close.

And even if I could get out of the apartment, he would catch me somewhere before I could get help or get out of the building. Or he'd shove me down the stairs from behind. No one would find me for a while.

Sienna, despite what I said, isn't on her way home. For the next ten hours at least, I'm alone.

"No, you're right," he says, his voice sedate. "I should go. I don't want Sienna to get the wrong idea about us."

He watches me another ten seconds at least before he turns to leave.

After he's gone, I yank the curtains closed and slide an armchair in front of the door.

All night long, I don't sleep. I sit on the sofa with a knife in hand, keeping a vigil on the front door.

Twenty-Five

The sun rises. It's hard to see at first. The curtains are pulled, but I see it in the small break between the dark flax panels: a sliver of early morning sun. I leave my post, my body stiff and exhausted. If I nodded off on the sofa for fifteen minutes that was all; otherwise I didn't sleep. Instead I spent the night thinking about Ben and Caitlin, imagining them together, wondering if he or she found our old high school yearbooks on the built-in bookcase in the condo's living room, and if they looked through them together, snuggled in bed maybe, finding pictures of his and my high school life, for research, for reference. There is a picture in the yearbook of Mandy Cho, my doubles partner, and me, taken after we'd won a match, standing with our arms around each other, tired and sweaty but elated. I think back to the night we met for coffee, when Caitlin asked, *Do you still talk to anyone else from high school, besides Ben?* before asking specifically about Mandy. She and Ben must have seen the picture of Mandy and me in the yearbook.

I go to the window, pulling back on a curtain panel to look outside. The street is quiet, still half-asleep, but the sunlight is a comfort. I tell myself that bad things don't happen in daylight, but they do.

The last twenty-four hours prey on my mind. I turn away from the window, moving toward the kitchen to make coffee. On the way, my phone dings the arrival of a new text, and I jump, my heart quickening.

Can I see you tonight?

Ben. My pulse races. The text takes me back to last night, to sitting on the sofa beside him when I asked about his girlfriend's name and, at the time I thought the question was innocuous, just idle conversation if not something teasing, flirty. I was wrong.

Caitlin. I obsess over that one word. I overanalyze the tone of his voice, and what his eyes looked like as he said it, whether they were hostile or if he watched me, curious and knowing, waiting for my reaction.

I step into a pair of shoes and leave the

apartment for the basement, where I find my own copy of our senior year high school yearbook and bring it back up. On the sofa with the door locked, I flip through the pages, seeing Ben and me on the Homecoming court and then again at a football game. I leaf through the yearbook to the page devoted to the tennis team where, in the top right corner, Nat Cohen beams, holding a trophy, and it saddens me because, I know now that only a few years later, she would be dead. I turn the page and keep going. The inside covers of the yearbook are scribbled on by teachers and classmates, little slanted notes in various colored ink, like *You're a great friend* and *Keep in touch.* On the back cover is a note from Ben, an inside joke, one only he and I would get, which makes me think how I would have left a note in Ben's yearbook too, one which was probably something sappy with hearts. I wonder if he and Caitlin read it together and had a good laugh over it.

My phone dings again and I stiffen. I set the yearbook aside, reaching for the phone.

It's another text from Ben.

I'll cook dinner for us at the condo. Whatever you want.

Ben, Sienna and I used to live in a condo together in Lincoln Park. Now it belongs to him. When we got divorced and Sienna and I moved out, I mourned the condo almost as much as I mourned Ben. But now the idea of going there, of being alone with him scares me.

I don't reply. I put the phone down again and try to forget about it, to forget about Ben, but only minutes pass before the phone actually rings and I'm scared by his persistence. He won't give up.

I glance at the phone, feeling unwell, run down by stress and fatigue. It's not Ben after all. I answer the call, pressing the phone to my ear and ask, "Hello?"

It's someone from the hospital, from HR. They'd like me to come in and meet with them.

The early morning sun was a tease. No sooner did it come out than it disappeared behind thick, dense clouds that rolled quickly in. Outside the wind is tempestuous, the day just above thirty-two degrees so that instead of snow, I get pelted with sleet that comes down sideways and into my eyes. When I get to work, people stare at first — and then they go out of their way to look away, to avoid eye contact. By now everyone knows who I am and what I've done, how I killed a patient.

When I arrive at human resources, people wait inside a meeting room to speak with me, to go over it again, the details of what happened for a second and then a third time. Some faces I know but others I don't. They introduce themselves. It's HR, risk management, the nurse manager, more. I regret not listening to the charge nurse's advice. I should have gotten an attorney.

"Good morning, Meghan. Please have a seat," someone says. I pull out a padded chair and sink into it, but I can't get comfortable.

They go around the room and ask questions.

How long have you been a nurse?

How long had you been treating Ms. Beckett?

How did Mrs. Layley's insulin pen come to be in your pocket?

Is it common for you not to scan a patient's wristband before administering medication?

Can you describe your mental state at the time.

It's more of an interrogation than anything, and I realize quickly that what they're most worried about is their own liability. When they ask questions, I have to be careful that the details are the same as I told yesterday.

They explain what will happen next. They've already filed a report with the state board of nursing, who will review the report to decide if they have jurisdiction. The board will investigate. They will talk to my colleagues, to my superiors, to the Becketts — who may file civil charges all on their own if they so choose. It will take many months before the board decides if what I've done is actionable, if my nursing license will be suspended or revoked or if some other punishment will be handed down, though there may be none too. I may get off scot-free.

They put me on administrative leave pending the investigation.

I make my way slowly to the ICU to get my things out of my locker to leave. I don't know when I'll be back or if I'll ever be back. I'm not surprised this is happening. I knew there would be fallout, of course. Something was going to happen, but I haven't been fired. I'm not being escorted out of the building by security. Administrative leave isn't the worst thing that can happen. I'll still get paid. I'll still get benefits. The worst thing that could have happened is if the police came, if they were waiting for me when I walked into HR, if this became a criminal matter. As it is, even if I eventually get fired or have my license revoked, there are things I can still do like become a home health aide or I can switch careers altogether and become something else, become *someone* else.

I push open the door to the break room to gather my things to go home. There is a woman inside the room, a patient — completely out of place in the staff break room — standing with her back to me, with long dark brown hair that spills over the shoulders of a starchy, white hospital gown that ties at the back.

As she gazes back over a shoulder at me, her smile is sage. "You're going to pay," she says, and I recoil in shock, bumping into the break room door, taking in the hair and the eyes and the smile.

It's Caitlin. She's not dead after all. She's alive.

She turns her body completely around and when I take a fresh look at her, I see that it's not a hospital gown at all, but a long, slim white doctor's smock.

It's not Caitlin. Caitlin is dead.

"Pardon?" I ask, short of breath.

"I asked if I'm in your way," the woman, a physician, says kindly as I stare flustered and wide-eyed at her, trying hard to reconcile her face with the face of Caitlin Beckett.

My words are breathy as I say, "No. Not at all."

Her expression is kind. She smiles, thoughtful — she doesn't know who I am and what I've done — and then leaves and when she does, I drop down into a hard chair at the small, round table to catch my breath, before gathering my things to go.

I've just stepped out of the break room and am slipping my arms into my coat when I see two uniformed police officers down the hall. They stand over six feet tall and two hundred or two hundred and fifty pounds at the nurses' station with their backs to me so that I only see them from behind, just their broad shoulders and their husky frames. My legs stop suddenly dead so that someone crashes into me from behind by accident and I mumble an apology as I move to the wall, standing flush against it, hiding behind a pilaster, my heart in a flat spin.

The police are here. They know what I've done. They've come for me.

For a second, I can only watch, paralyzed, as they stand at the desk speaking to the charge nurse. One of the officer's hands is on the sidearm on his holster. I back slowly away and then, when I can, I turn, doubling back in the direction from which I came, moving toward the fire escape stairs at the other end of the hall.

I leave the building, wondering what I will tell Sienna when I get home.

TWENTY-SIX

I hear Sienna's voice as I come into the apartment later that morning, still on edge from seeing the police at the hospital, though I've tried to reassure myself that they could have been there for a dozen different reasons that had nothing to do with me, such as a belligerent patient or a criminal being admitted for care. I searched online while I walked, looking for any updates into the investigation of Caitlin's murder attempt and find a picture of Milo Finch in a newspaper article dated two days ago, saying how the police are asking for the public's help in finding him, which means that, as of forty-eight hours ago at least, they still think he did it, that he pushed her over the edge and she can't say otherwise. It comes as a relief, though my conscience hopes he's long gone or that he's found a good hiding spot. I don't want him to get caught, but if either he or I has to go to jail for it, I hope it's him.

Ben has texted for a third time and he tried to call. There is a message waiting for me on my voice mail, but I can't bring myself to listen to it. I walked home, flooded with emotion about the police, about Caitlin, about being put on administrative leave and about what I might find when I got home and if Ben would be standing in my living room when I came in.

He's not. At first glance, the apartment is empty except for Sienna, who is in her bedroom with the door closed, home from her sleepover with Gianna. I hear her and think she's on her phone, talking or on FaceTime with a friend because her voice is muffled and indistinct as I stand in the living room, just inside the door, shrugging off a wet winter coat. I can't hear what she says, but then she lets out a peal of laughter that slices through the air.

I'm about to call out to her to let her know I'm home, but then I hear Nico's voice from the other side of the closed bedroom door and I become stiff, clenching and seeing red, because Sienna knew I didn't want her having boys in the apartment when I wasn't home and she intentionally disobeyed me. Worse, they're in her bedroom with the door closed, which makes me wonder what they're doing in there.

I cross the room in three steps. Without thinking, I raise my hand and am about to knock on the door when something out of the corner of my eye catches my attention and I turn toward the kitchen, feeling my arm lower by instinct. Sienna's phone sits on the kitchen table, face up and illuminated, beside her overnight bag, calling for me because it's so unlike her to leave her phone out in the open like this, to not have that thing shackled to a hip.

But then again Nico is here, and he's stolen her attention, and she didn't expect me to come home and see it, because I told her I was running into work and she probably assumed that meant I'd be there all day.

I back away from the door. I drift toward the phone. When I get to it, Ben's name is on the screen. The incoming text is from him.

My heart beats faster. Ordinarily I wouldn't read Sienna's messages. But curiosity gets the better of me and my mind flashes again to last night, to him here in my living room with me, his eyes holding mine, his thumb grazing my neck.

I glance back to Sienna's door, where on the other side of it, she and Nico have gone quiet, their voices reduced to nothing, and I worry about what they're doing in there, but not more than I worry about the texts from Ben to Sienna.

I reach for the phone. I quickly enter her password to unlock it, which was another of my stipulations when she got her phone, that I always have access to it because, in essence, I pay the bill; it's *my* phone.

The message from Ben reads: Is your mom home or is she working today?

I close my eyes and shake my head. I don't know how it makes me feel, that he's texting Sienna to check up on me, that he's using Sienna to get to me. I'm about to set the phone back down. But then my eyes open and drift further up in the chain of messages.

Just above this latest text, I see Sienna's last words to Ben.

She's a liar.

They're caustic, blistering, and my first thought is to wonder who. Who is a liar?

And then I see my name.

In the text before, Ben says to Sienna: Mom said you had a headache, which was preceded by a series of incisive question marks from Sienna. ????

I breathe harder. They've caught me. *I* am the liar. Because in the text before that one, sent from Ben last night shortly after ten, he asks: How is your head?

Ben knows that I lied to him. He knows Sienna didn't have a headache and that she wasn't coming home last night.

That worries me. But it's not the worst thing, because what gets me more is the barbed, cutting tone of Sienna's words when she called me a liar. She's so angry, so bitter.

She's a liar.

My stomach tightens as I scroll further back to yesterday evening when Sienna texted Ben that I was being weird.
Weird how? he asked.

I don't know. She just is.

Are you home? Is she there with you? Did something happen?

No. I don't know. She just told me to go to Gianna's. She said I couldn't stay here.

I'm sure it's fine.

What if it's not?

Do you want me to check on her and make sure she's ok?

Yes.

Yes. There is a pain in my chest all of a sudden, a tightness spreading over it.

Ben wasn't lying then. Sienna was. She did ask him to come check up on me. All of a sudden, it calls the whole night into question. Was Ben's reason for being here not as malicious as I thought? Did he really come with good intentions?

Why would Sienna lie to me? Why would she call me a liar?

I don't have time to consider the possibilities when all of a sudden there is a strange sound coming from Sienna's room again and I look sharply up from the phone, sliding it into a pocket. I make my way to Sienna's door, rap once and then let myself in without waiting for permission, bracing myself for what I'll find, expecting to come in and see them making out on Sienna's trundle bed beneath its pink, puckered comforter, Nico's overzealous hand crudely up her shirt, pawing at her chest.

But that's not what's happening. Nico sits

439

at her little desk, looking far too big for the pink kids' desk chair that she's had since she was young. Her pencil cup has been knocked from the desktop, which was the sound I heard, the volley of dozens of pens and pencils spilling to the floor. Beside the desk, Sienna is on her hands and knees picking them up, her laugh a cackle. "You're such a fucking klutz," I overhear as I come unexpectedly in and Sienna flies to her feet.

"Mom," she says, flustered as Nico, at the desk, tries to cover whatever he was doing with his hands, so that all I can see of it is a swathe of red. "What are you doing here?"

"I live here."

"But aren't you supposed to be at work?"

"I just had to go in for a meeting today, but it's through. I thought we talked about not having boys in the apartment when I'm not home."

"You didn't say I couldn't."

"Yes, I did, Sienna."

"No," she says, "you didn't. You said you had to think about it."

I think back to the conversation and realize she is not wrong. That is what I said. "What are you two working on?" I ask. If not for Nico's quick attempt to hide it, I don't know that I would have noticed he was even writing something.

440

"It's nothing," she says.

"It's not nothing, Sienna. What is it?"

"Just something for school," she says, but it's too late because, at the same time, Nico's hands lift, revealing the item to me. It's a red envelope and, beside it, a torn piece of paper with the start of something written in Nico's all caps script: *I KNOW WHAT YO*

Nico holds a black pen in his hand. The envelope and the torn paper with its sawtooth edge take me back to that day in the hospital break room, when I pulled the red envelope out of my bag, the one I'd taken from the mailbox that morning, the one with my name on the front, but no postmark or return address. The one that said *BITCH*. At the time, I thought someone had broken into the building and into the mailbox to leave it, because how else would I have gotten it?

But what if it was as simple as that the person who put it there had a key?

My eyes go from the note to Sienna and back again.

"I think you should go, Nico," I breathe.

He nods, dropping the pen to the desktop, pushing back on the chair, rising. Nico says goodbye, though it's gutless, cowardly. He knows he's been caught though Sienna's response, on the other hand, is typical Sienna. As I move to the living room, she walks Nico into the hall to say goodbye and then lets herself back into the apartment, defiant as always. "That was so embarrassing," she mutters, angry with me. "You didn't have to kick him out."

"What was that note you two were writing?" I ask. *I KNOW WHAT YO*

Sienna just shrugs. "I told you already. It was nothing. Just something for school," she says, walking past me, like she's just going to go back into her bedroom and close the door.

"It's not nothing, Sienna. What was it going to say? Was it for me?" I ask, but Sienna just pulls a face, as if trying to refute it but unable to come up with the words to do so. It doesn't matter either way. Regardless of what she says or doesn't say, I know it was for me because the writing and the envelope match the first note, but now I wonder why she is so angry that she would lash out and call me a bitch.

"Did you text Dad last night and ask him to check on me?" I ask, letting the note go for now.

"Why do you keep asking me that?" she barks this time before narrowing her eyes and insisting, "I already told you no."

It's convincing. If I hadn't just seen evidence to the contrary, I would believe her, which makes me wonder how often Sienna lies and how many times I've fallen for her lies.

Her phone is still in my pocket. I slip my hand into it and produce the phone.

Sienna gasps. "You took my phone?" she asks, incredulous, reaching out to grab it from my hand as if I'm the one in the wrong.

"*My* phone, Sienna," I say, staying composed. "And no, I didn't take it. You left it on the kitchen table and I just happened to see an incoming text from Dad." I pause, as Sienna looks down at her phone to see the text and to ascertain what else I may have seen, the blood leaching from her face until she's milky white. "Why did you lie to me last night about texting Dad?" When she doesn't answer, I go on. "Why are you sending me these awful notes? Don't even try to lie to me Sienna. I know you left that last note in the mailbox, calling me a bitch." It's hard to get the word out. I choke on it and then, fighting tears, because I never thought my child would say something like that to me, I ask, "What have I done to you?"

Sienna knows she's been caught, except she doesn't break down. She doesn't cry or beg forgiveness. Instead, she lashes out, asserting, "I know what you did."

"What do you mean?" I ask slowly, feeling the bottom drop out. Sienna knows that I pushed Caitlin Beckett off a bridge, that I killed her with insulin?

"What do you mean, Sienna?" I ask again because she's said nothing. "What did I do?"

"She told me," she says.

"Who told you what?"

"Dad's girlfriend. Caitlin. She told me what you did. She told me Dad isn't my real dad," she says, and I feel the tables turn before she crumbles, breaking down as I reach for her, to fold her into my arms, the relief a thousandfold because she doesn't know all the terrible things I've done; she only knows one.

"Sienna," I murmur.

"Don't even try to deny it," she says, pushing me away so that I fall back. "You know it's true."

I steady myself. "When did she tell you this?"

"After Dad took me to see *Dear Evan Hansen.* She was here the next day when I got home. She told me everything."

My throat tightens. That's what Caitlin did then. After I opened up to her about

Sienna's real father, after I spilled my guts to her, telling her things I'd never told a soul, she had what she needed. She had something on me. I went to work the next day while she stayed alone in my apartment, going through my things, finding and stealing my rings, killing time until Sienna came home and she could tell her about that night at Guthrie's. I imagine Sienna coming home, expecting to see my friend and finding Caitlin instead. I think of how Caitlin would have said it, if she would have broken the news lightly or if she would have found joy in breaking Sienna's heart.

It was only two or three weeks later that I found that first note in the mailbox, *BITCH*, giving Sienna time to agonize over it, to conspire with Nico, to think of a way to get back at me.

"Why didn't you talk to me, Sienna? Why send these awful notes instead of coming to me and telling me the truth?"

"Just like you told me the truth?" she fires back, and she's right; the hypocrisy is glaring. I have no right to question her lack of honesty when I've been dishonest. Sienna is also sixteen and sending these anonymous notes was probably the only way she could think of to express her feelings and to confront me about her father.

There are hot, angry tears in Sienna's eyes all of a sudden. "I fucking hate you," she seethes. "I meant what I said in that note. You are a bitch. I wish you would have died down there in the basement. I wish you never would have gotten out."

The basement. My mind reels. I think of the night I was locked down in the basement and scared. At the time, it didn't feel like an accident. It felt intentional. Sienna was home. She was here, alone in the apartment. In fact, she's the one who sent me on a hunt for the baby pictures. My mind goes back and a picture forms, imagining Sienna slinking down after me, imagining her closing the door and moving the door wedge so that I was locked downstairs, and then coming back up, getting under the blanket with her laptop to do homework, not the least bit worried that I couldn't get out.

What happened? she had asked when I finally made it upstairs, shaken and upset. But she didn't need to ask what happened. She already knew.

I'm mad. I want to punish her. She can't get away with this. She can't swear at me and speak to me like this. It's not okay to send hate mail or lock someone in the basement. What if the neighbor hadn't come home when he did? Would she have left me there all night? Would she have pretended she fell asleep on the sofa and say she didn't realize I hadn't come home?

But what I've done is infinitely worse, and she's only lashing out in response. She's angry, understandably so. I got pregnant by another man. I let someone who is not her father raise her. I never told either of them. For all these years, I let them live a lie.

"Does your dad know?" I ask, staying composed, as if she didn't just call me a bitch or say she wished I was dead.

"Is that the only fucking thing you care about, Mom? If Dad knows?" she asks, and then she laughs, this cynical, mocking, droll laugh and says, "*Dad.* He isn't even my dad."

I want to hold her. I want to console her. I want to tell her how sorry I am, and I want to explain, to let her know how I grappled with whether to tell Ben when I found out she wasn't his, but ultimately made the decision that I thought was best for everyone.

But I know if I reach out again, she will only push me away.

"Did you tell him, Sienna? Did *she* tell him?"

"Why do you even care? Because he might stop paying child support?"

"No," I say. "I don't care about that. I just

need to know. Does he know?"

"He doesn't know. Okay, Mom? He doesn't fucking know. Because I didn't want to make him feel the way I do," she says then, and my heart breaks because I know inside, her own heart is broken. I step tentatively closer and set a hand on her arm, testing the waters, and then, when she doesn't pull back, I reach for her, wrapping my arms around her.

I feel relieved. The other night with Ben — it wasn't like I thought. He didn't come to hurt me. He came because, as he said, Sienna asked him to check up on me. He was telling the truth. He and Caitlin had broken up and I think now that what happened is that, in anger, jealousy and in spite, she took it on herself to get close to me and try and ruin my life, which she did by telling Sienna about her father. Ben didn't have anything to do with it. For all I know, he doesn't know she's dead.

"What happens now?" Sienna asks, her face wet and red. "Do I even get to see him anymore?"

"Of course you do, honey. He's still your dad," I try saying, but it falls on deaf ears as, all of a sudden, she says she hates me again before pulling away from me, turning, running to her room. The door slams with such ferocity that a picture on the other side falls, slamming to the earth, shattering, and I want to ask if everything is okay, if she is okay — to tell her to be careful of the broken glass — but I don't because I need to give her space, I need to leave her alone for now, I need to give her time to breathe.

In the moment, I don't think things can get any worse.

TWENTY-SEVEN

I get a text from Luke. Hey there, it reads. Just wanted to check in and see how you're holding up. The text is like one of those lifebuoys that lifeguards toss into the water to save someone who's drowning. I latch on to it, desperate to stay afloat.

Honestly? Not well. I'm a wreck, I say. I clutch my phone in my hands, dropping down onto the sofa, feeling tears well in my eyes, threatening to spill over.

You want to talk about it? he asks, and I do, but it's too much to type into a text. I wouldn't even know where to begin. I haven't seen Luke since what happened with Caitlin, and now there's so much more with Ben and Sienna.

As if he can read my mind, Luke texts again before I can respond, Let's meet for a drink, suggesting a bar between our apartments.

That's sweet. But I don't want to take you

away from Penelope, I say, remembering how upset she was the night Luke worked late, and how she thought he was cheating on her with another woman. I'll be fine. I just need some time for things to diffuse, I say, as if it's that simple, as if time can heal all wounds.

Penelope is pissed again. Giving me the silent treatment. I'm being selfish. I could use a drink and someone to talk to too, Luke says and I feel a wave of relief wash over me. It's not that I want Penelope to be mad at him. It's that there is nothing more I want in this moment than to talk to a friend, and so I say okay.

I rise from the sofa. I go to Sienna's door and gently knock. "Sienna," I say, leaning into it, knowing without testing the knob that it's locked.

"What?" she snarls.

I take a breath. "I need to run out for a few things," I say, feeling bad lying to her again. "I won't be gone long. Maybe an hour or hour and a half at the most." Sienna is quiet. "Would that be okay?" I ask, walking on eggshells. "I can stay home too. I don't have to do it tonight."

"Just go," she says, and at first I'm indecisive, but then I decide to go. Sienna needs time to be alone. She needs breathing room.

I don't want to suffocate her.

I change my clothes and run a brush through my hair. I try and do something with my makeup to look more put together, but it's not working and so I give up.

It's dark outside by the time I leave, the cold air against my face numbing. I'm thinking about myself and what I need — a drink and a friend — and what Sienna needs — time by herself without me breathing down her neck.

I'm not thinking about what's been happening to women in the city as I walk alone down the darkened city streets, leaving Sienna by herself in our apartment.

Luke is already at the bar when I arrive. He has a table for us. He waves me over as I walk in and I return the wave, picking my way through the crowded bar. When I reach him, I slip out of my coat before lowering myself into a chair. "Is this for me?" I ask, seeing a glass of white wine on the table.

"I thought I remembered that you liked chardonnay, but you don't have to drink it if you don't want. Feel free to order something else. You won't hurt my feelings."

"No," I say, reaching for it. "This is perfect. It's exactly what I wanted. Thank you." I press the glass to my lips and sip, eager for the anesthetizing effects of the wine.

"I've been worried about you," he says as I return the glass to the table, my hands wrapped around the stem.

"What are people saying at work?"

Luke was there at the hospital the day of the insulin overdose, though I don't remember seeing him again after we ran into each other in the hall before Caitlin died, when he suggested going on a double date with Penelope and her friend.

"You know how it goes. The usual, lots of exaggeration, white lies and half-truths." He pauses, and then says, "I wouldn't mind hearing it from you, if you're up to it."

"I'm sure everything they said was true. I did it. She's dead because of me."

"Listen," he says, his voice a balm when he speaks. He reaches his hand across the table to set it on mine, and it calms me. He leans in. "You show me one nurse who's never made a medical mistake in his or her career and I'll show you a liar." He takes his hand back, reaching for his own drink and sips. "How did it happen?" he asks, lowering the glass.

I hate lying to him, but being honest isn't an option, even with Luke. "I was taking shortcuts. I was moving too fast and wasn't

453

thinking. I didn't scan the barcode on her wrist."

"We've all done that before."

"I hadn't slept the night before, and I was beat. I wasn't in the right mind to be at work, but you know how it is, how hard it is to take time off. It's no excuse, I know. I fucked up. This is on me. We can't be making mistakes like that, not when lives are at stake. When she started coding, I knew what I'd done and that the consequences could be deadly. My heart stopped, Luke. I couldn't breathe. I don't think I've ever been so scared in my whole life. That was the worst part, that total paralysis. Now I keep thinking that if I hadn't panicked, if I had responded more quickly, we could have saved her."

"You did everything you could. You're a good nurse, Meghan. Don't ever doubt that."

"*Was*. I *was* a good nurse," I say. "I'm pretty sure my nursing days are through. The hospital put me on administrative leave. I'm not surprised. I don't blame them, but I think it's only a matter of time until I get fired. I've thought about resigning."

"And beat them to the punch?"

"Yeah. Why not? It's not that great of a

job anyway. The long hours, the pay."

He nods, though I'm being overly cavalier. I love the job. But I love my life, my freedom more.

"What did Sienna say?"

"I haven't told her. She's not speaking to me, but that's a story for another day. She's at home by herself right now, ruminating on how much she hates me, on how I've ruined her life."

I reach for my wine, taking a long sip. Luke is quiet for a minute, contemplative, reading my face, before he motions for the waitress to order me another drink because mine is nearly gone. "You want to tell me about it?" he asks as she leaves.

"No," I say swiftly, decisive. I'd love to get it off my chest, but I'm embarrassed for everyone to know my secret. What would Luke think of me if he knew what I did, how for over sixteen years I let Ben raise a child that wasn't his? "Enough about me. I'm being a total killjoy. Tell me about Penelope. It will make me feel better to know I'm not the only one whose life is falling apart."

Luke smiles, empathetic. "Same fight, different day. I can't say or do anything right. I just hope that things go back to normal when the baby comes."

He looks sad, tired, defeated. I feel sorry for him, but I also empathize with Penelope and where she's at with the pregnancy right now.

"I'm sure they will," I say, trying my best to be uplifting, though I'm not in the most encouraging mood. "Penelope is going through a hard time. The bed rest, the hormones, worrying if the baby will be okay. It must be overwhelming. And lonely."

My phone rings then. I just barely make out the sound of it from inside my bag and I reach a hand in, searching. I find the phone and pull it out, wondering if it's Sienna, hoping it is, hoping she wants me to come back home to talk, but the number on the caller ID is one I don't know, a local 773 number. For a second, my stomach flips as I think again about seeing the police at the hospital today and wonder if they're looking for me.

"Who is it?" Luke asks, and I turn my phone around so he can see it.

"I don't know. Not anyone I have in my contacts."

"Probably a telemarketer then. Just ignore it," he says lightly, reaching for his drink, and I do, setting the phone on the table as the waitress returns with my wine and I thank her, grateful. I probably don't need a

456

second glass of wine, and under normal circumstances I wouldn't have one, but today is an exception.

"Listen, I hate to do this," Luke says after a minute, "but I should go home and check on Penelope, and see if she's ready to talk." I nod. I don't want him to leave, but I know he needs to go patch things up with her. "Will you be okay?" he asks, finishing his drink.

"Yes. Go, please."

"Are you sure? It's just — what you said about her being lonely. It got to me. I feel guilty."

"Yes, of course I'm sure. You're a good man, Luke. You and Penelope are just going through a rough patch too. Everything will be better when the baby comes. I promise."

"What are you going to do?" he asks, his expression thoughtful. "Are you going to stay here awhile or are you heading home too?"

"I'm going to stay for a bit," I tell him. "I'll head home after I finish my drink."

I'm not in a rush to go home, and Sienna is probably happier without me.

"Okay," he says. "I might be back if Penelope tells me to fuck off."

I smirk. "I'll save your seat."

He takes one last sip of his beer and then

says, "I always knew I could count on you," with a wink. He leaves and I wrap my hands around my glass of wine, nursing it, grateful for the noise in the crowded bar. It's a nice distraction. I people watch, jealous of all the happy, laughing people, hanging out with friends. I lose track of time. Twenty or thirty minutes pass and then my phone rings again and I look, wondering if it's Sienna, but it's not. It's the same local number that called before, when Luke was here. I feel suddenly anxious, wondering who it is and what is so urgent they would call twice.

This time I answer the call, pressing the phone to my ear, bracing myself for who is on the other end of the line, expecting the voice for some reason to be bold, brusque, male, but it's not.

"Is this Meghan Michaels?" a woman asks, her voice reluctant.

"Yes, this is she."

"Meghan. Hi. It's Penelope Albrecht. Luke's wife. I'm sorry to just call like this, but I found your number in some of his things."

"Penelope?" I ask, feeling thrown. It's been years since I've spoken to her. We met only once, at Luke and her wedding, though even that was quick, a passing nice-to-meet-you.

"Have you seen him?" she asks, clearly upset, and I don't know what to say because I don't want to make her more upset than she already is. I don't want to get him in trouble. He did me a favor by coming to meet me tonight, but I think she will be angry if she knows he was with me.

But then I think of how very pregnant Penelope is, and I start to wonder if she's gone into labor or if there is something wrong with the baby.

"Yes," I say, being honest. "I just saw him, maybe twenty or thirty minutes ago. He's on his way home now. He should be there any minute," I say, wondering why Luke isn't home yet, but telling myself he might have stopped for ice cream or flowers on the way as a peace offering. "I'm sorry. Please don't be upset with him. It's my fault. I asked him to meet so we could talk about something that happened at work."

Penelope is quiet at first, and then she says, "I don't think so. I don't think he's coming home."

Her words take my breath away. "Is everything okay, Penelope?" I ask softly, worried, wondering if their fight was much worse than Luke suggested. "Are you and the baby okay? Is there anything I can do?"

She doesn't say. Instead she says, "The

police were just here, at our apartment," and I shift gears, I go into a flat spin because that means that after I saw them at the hospital, they came looking for me. They must have gone to my apartment before going to Luke's. It must have been sometime after I left to meet him. I think of Sienna home alone, of her answering the intercom and letting them in. What would they have said to her? What would she have told them?

"Are you there?" Penelope asks.

"Yes," I breathe. "I'm sorry. I'm here. What did they want? Did they say?"

"They wanted to talk to Luke."

I nod, feeling sick. Of course they did. The police want to talk to Luke, to ask him questions about me. It's part of their investigation and I wish in vain that I could talk to him before he gets home, to appeal to him not to lie — because Luke wasn't there in Caitlin's hospital room that day, he didn't see anything — but to defend me, to say Meghan would never intentionally hurt a patient, that it's simply not possible, that Meghan doesn't have it in her to hurt someone at all.

"They had a warrant for his arrest."

My throat goes dry. The color drains from my skin. "What?" I ask, completely caught off guard and trying to make sense of it. "I

460

don't understand. I don't —"

"His DNA, Meghan," she says, cutting in. "They found it under that last woman's fingernails. It was a match. I saw the scratch on his neck the other day, but he said he'd nicked it shaving and I believed him."

"What woman, Penelope? I don't understand. What are you saying?"

"All these women who have been being attacked, Meghan. It was Luke. Luke's the one who has been hurting them."

I start shaking. I lose my hold on my wineglass and it falls, toppling over, spilling onto my lap. I feel the cold moisture on the thigh of my jeans. This can't be right. She must be mistaken. Not Luke. Luke couldn't have hurt those women. It's impossible.

But then I think back to college, where I took a criminal justice class and learned about serial killers and sexual predators. I learned how they come across as relatively normal, meaning you wouldn't know it to look at them and that there probably isn't anything in their everyday life that suggests they're predators. Usually they have normal jobs, families, wives and kids, a mortgage, a 401k.

I think back to what Luke told me about his past, how he was raised by mostly absentee parents, an abusive father and how his own teenage years were marked by delinquency, a stint in juvie before supposedly turning his life around.

But what if he didn't? What if he just got better at hiding his crimes? What if, over time, he only became more violent?

The first time Penelope called, thirty minutes ago, Luke took a passing glance at the number on the display. Not two minutes after she called, he left.

"Meghan? Are you still there?"

"Yes."

"There's more, Meghan. That's why I'm calling you." She takes a deep breath. "After the police left, I searched through his things. There was a shoebox in our closet." Penelope speaks haltingly, having a hard time getting the words out. "It was just a shoebox in a stack of shoeboxes. I never thought there was anything off about it. But there were things inside, Meghan."

"What things?"

"Online newspaper articles he printed and kept, a heart-shaped locket —" she pauses, choking on the words "— a woman's thong."

"Mementos," I breathe, my hand rising to my mouth as my stomach roils at the thought of Luke walking away from someone's apartment with a pair of women's

462

underwear in his pocket — a souvenir, something to remember her by — leaving her alone and crying, scared for her life.

"Yes. There was a picture in the box too. Taken from outside a three flat, from across the street."

"A picture of who?"

"It was of you, Meghan." She takes a breath, loath to say, "And your daughter. He took it, I think, without you knowing."

The air leaves my lungs. "Can you text me a picture of it?"

She does. When I click on the photo to enlarge it, I find Sienna and me stepping out of our apartment sometime in the fall because the ground is dry, orange and brown leaves losing their grip on the trees, building on the sidewalk and street.

The picture isn't of both of us, not really, but it's of Sienna. It's zoomed in close on her face while I'm an afterthought in the corner, my body turned away from the lens, pulling the door closed, just enough of my face visible for Penelope to recognize me, but not much more.

I imagine Luke standing on the street opposite our apartment, hiding behind a parked car or one of the L's steel structural beams, taking pictures of Sienna without us knowing.

He was always so kind to ask about her, how she was doing, how school was going, if she had a boyfriend.

I never thought of it as anything more than him being thoughtful.

The blood drains from my face, remembering.

Sienna is home alone — which Luke knows because I just told him.

Twenty-Eight

I call Sienna first. She doesn't answer and so I call 911 as I push past people in the crowded bar to get out. I tell the dispatcher that Luke Albrecht, the man the police think is responsible for attacking those women in the city may be on the way to hurt my child. "The police have a warrant for his arrest. My daughter is home alone. She's not answering her phone. Please," I say, panting, winded as I make it outside, turn and race gracelessly down the street, "hurry."

"What is the address, ma'am?" she asks, and I tell her. "How old is your daughter?"

"Sixteen."

I run the whole way home, not bothering to stop for red lights, but dodging traffic instead, cars blaring their horns at me as I snake between moving vehicles, forcing them to step hard on their brakes. It's only a couple blocks from the bar home, and so I get there before the police do, tearing up the steps outside the building, taking them two at a time to the front door. I cast around in my bag for my keys, uttering profanities because I can't find them at first, but when I finally do, I unlock and pull open the door, and then I sprint inside, bumbling, tripping, falling once to my knees on the maroon carpeting, though I force myself up and keeping going.

When I get to the third floor, I come through the apartment door, clipping a shoulder on the way in. I run from room to room, screaming, "Sienna! Sienna!" praying to God that she'll appear like magic from her room, asking, *What?* when she sees me, put off by my urgency and the shrill, unmistakable panic in my voice.

She doesn't.

Sienna's bedroom light is on. I go in, bracing myself for what I'll find. Her laptop is on her bed, the comforter pulled back, a movie paused — as if time stood still the minute Luke arrived — and I picture her under the covers, watching a movie in bed when the front door buzzed. I see her getting out of bed, going to the intercom, looking out the bay window for the street, seeing Luke.

Her phone is on her bed, tucked partway beneath a pink throw. My heart stops and I reach for it, sliding it out, knowing that Sienna would never leave her phone behind, not on purpose, not if given the option. The only way is if someone forced her out of the apartment against her will. My hand goes to my mouth and my knees buckle beneath me so that I almost collapse, I almost fall to my knees, sobbing.

But I don't have time to go to pieces. I have to find Sienna, except that without her phone, I have no way of tracking her location. The city is huge. She could be practically anywhere and I don't have the advantage of Life360.

The police arrive and I let them into the apartment. Standing in the small living room, they ask questions. They want me to go over again what happened. They ask for pictures of Sienna and for what she was wearing, and by chance I remember what she had on hours ago when we were arguing — before she said *I fucking hate you* and *You are a bitch,* before slamming her bedroom door closed on me — though I wonder if she changed after I left, if she put on pajamas, which makes me wonder things like if Luke let her take her coat and shoes with her when she left or if, wherever she is, she is cold and barefoot. I can't stand to think about it, about Sienna in something like the plaid, flannel boxer shorts and the boxy, cropped T-shirt she usually sleeps in, braless, midriff showing, painfully cold on this dark and bitter January night.

An AMBER alert is issued not only because Sienna is missing but because the police think she is in grave danger.

"What happens now?" I ask them.

"We'll be looking for her and for Mr. Albrecht. But in the meantime, you need to stay here, in case your daughter comes home on her own," the officer says, and I say okay, nodding through tears, but even as I do, I know it's a lie. I won't stay here. I can't stay put while Sienna is out there somewhere and in trouble. She needs me.

When the police leave, I find Penelope's number in my call history and call her back.

"He has my daughter, Penelope. He took her."

"Oh my God. Meghan." Her voice seeps with guilt and with shame. She apologizes, as if it's her fault and maybe it is, maybe in some subconscious way she knew what he was doing. I think of all the times Luke said goodbye to me at the end of his shift. I picture him leaving work, stalking and then raping women before going home to Penelope.

I think of all that I know about this man,

all that I heard on the news. How he would hide out in the shadows, waiting for women to open the door and let themselves into their own homes, and then he'd come at them from behind, threatening their lives.

I double over, moaning, thinking of Sienna alone with him.

"Meghan, are you okay?" she asks, and then, when I don't respond because I can't respond, "Meghan?"

I force myself upright, getting it together for Sienna's sake. I wipe at my face with a shirtsleeve. "Can you think of anywhere he might have taken her, anywhere he might be?" I run over in my mind everything Luke has ever told me. I don't know him as well as I thought.

Penelope thinks. "He runs sometimes on the 606. Or he'll take the Lakefront Trail to Northerly Island," she says, thinking aloud, running through every place Luke has ever been. "He proposed to me in the Art Institute's South Garden." But that's not right, none of these are right, because they're outdoor and they're public places and Luke's methodology, his blueprint, is to attack women in private, in their own homes and in secluded parts of apartment buildings, except that he couldn't do anything to Sienna in ours because I would come home and find them.

"Can you think of anything else?" I ask. "Somewhere more isolated, off the grid?"

"I'm sorry, Meghan. I can't. I can't think," she says, and I tell her okay, but to keep trying and to call me if she comes up with something.

Not five minutes later, I receive a text from Luke, an address on Leavitt Street, and the words: Come alone. Tell no one. If you do, Sienna will pay for it.

I consider calling the police, but I'm too afraid of what Luke might do to Sienna, and so I don't. I just go, racing down Dakin Street for Sheridan, where I hail a cab, climbing in, leaned forward in my seat, giving the driver the address. I beg him to hurry. It takes an eternity for us to arrive.

The home on Leavitt is new construction. It's a teardown most likely, slotted between two existing single family homes with Tyvek house wrap still visible on the outside. There are no windows or doors, which means it's cold on the inside, winter seeping in, making me think of Sienna again, of her frozen to death and scared. The house is dark, and I don't think it's that Luke hasn't turned on any lights but that there is no electricity in the home.

I make my way into the backyard, slipping

down the narrow gangway between homes and into the yard, which is small and longer than it is wide.

There is no back door on the house either; there is almost nothing to stop the winter air from getting in except for some plastic construction sheeting. Carefully, I slip an arm inside, pulling the plastic back, just enough that I can get past, and then I enter the house. I'm disoriented from the darkness. I need time for my eyes to adjust. The moon is nearly full. Outside is a streetlight that gives off just enough light for me to vaguely see the inside of the house: the wooden studs, the vertical wooden beams, rough openings for windows and doors, all of it revealed to me in small increments as I drift forward, dragging myself across the subfloor, careful to avoid making noise. I want to know what I'm getting myself into. I want to take Luke by surprise. I hold my breath, cutting back on the amount of air I take in until my lungs burn.

It can't be more than forty degrees inside the house, the cold air numbing.

As I circle the first floor, slipping between wooden beams, holding on to them for support, I have the feeling of being watched. My back arches all on its own, the hairs on the nape of my neck rising to stand. I spin wildly around, expecting to see Luke some-where behind me, a silhouette standing further back, but he isn't; I'm alone, I think.

But then upstairs comes a subtle noise, the sound of someone softly crying.

I don't so much hear it as I feel it in my core, a mother's intuition.

I find the stairs. I start to climb them. There are no risers yet, only treads. There are no handrails either and, in the darkness, it's easy to lose balance because there is nothing to hold on to, nothing to steady me. My legs are weak, shaking, and the effort to go slowly, to be quiet, makes my thighs ache.

I reach the second floor, which is no dif-ferent than the first. I make my way from room to room, moving between beams.

"You made it," I hear, and I turn toward the voice to find Luke standing in some back room, separated from me by beams. "I knew you would come."

"You have my daughter. How could I not?" I ask.

Slowly my eyes adapt to see Sienna beside him. The moonlight shines in from behind, illuminating her so that I just barely see her on her knees on the hard subfloor, her breathing heavy, labored, scared. She shakes from fear and cold, not just the occasional shiver, but a whole body convulsion. Luke stands behind her, the puppet master holding a gun to her head while Sienna whimpers, quiet, restrained tears silently falling down her cheeks.

"Stop right there," Luke says as I go toward her. "Don't come any closer, Meghan."

"I'm sorry," Sienna cries, her voice infused with fear, and I want to run to her, but I stop because of the gun, because I worry if I don't, Luke won't hesitate to pull the trigger.

"Why, baby? You have nothing to be sorry for," I say to her, and then to Luke, "I will do anything. Please," I beg of him. "Take me. Just let Sienna go."

"I'm not going to jail, Meghan," Luke says, his voice controlled.

"What are we doing here, Luke? Why did you bring Sienna and me here? What is this place?"

He becomes suddenly sedate. His posture slackens and his shoulders round, though the gun remains pointed at Sienna's head. "I brought Penelope to see this house," he says, and I remember him telling me how he had done that, though I didn't know it was *this* house. But I remember him saying how he took her to look at homes once and how he wished he could buy a single family home for them before the baby was born, because their small one-bedroom apartment wouldn't do for a growing family.

"I wanted to provide for my family in the way that a father should. I've told you about my own dad, haven't I?"

"Yes," I say. Luke's father was no good, an abusive alcoholic who was only sometimes around, though it was better when he was gone. He would go on a bender, hit Luke and his mom and then take off, only to come back days or weeks later and do it again, a never-ending cycle of alcoholism and abuse.

"I didn't want to be like him. I wanted to do better, to *be* better."

"And you are," I say softly to appease him.

"Don't fucking lie to me, Meghan. I'm worse," he says, and it's true. What Luke has done is so much worse. I've lost track of the number of women he's hurt. "This house was supposed to be a fresh start, for us, for me. I brought Penelope here," he says. "We came inside and I showed it to her, I gave her the grand tour, and I told her that one day I was going to buy it for our family, that we were going to raise our children here, and do you know what she said?"

"No," I breathe, afraid to hear. "What?"

"She said I was fucking delusional if I thought I could ever afford this home."

I wince. Her words sting. "I'm sorry Luke. That wasn't right of her."

"Oh don't worry, she said she was sorry later. She said she shouldn't have said it like that, but that she had to be so blunt because sometimes I get these stupid ideas in my head and can't be talked out of them."

"This must be a million-dollar home, Luke," I say gently. "Not many people can afford it. That doesn't make you any less of a man. It doesn't make you a failure."

His head snaps up all of a sudden and his posture straightens. He readjusts his grip on the gun, asking, "Is that what you think, Meghan? That I'm a failure?"

"No," I say swiftly, briskly. "No, not at all. I would never think that. You're a good man, Luke. An incredible nurse. Think of all the patients you've taken care of over the years, of all the people you've saved."

"Don't patronize me. Don't fucking patronize me."

I don't try telling him I'm not because he can see through me.

I change tack. "What do you want from us? What do you want with Sienna?" I ask, letting my eyes go to her, wondering if he laid his hands on her, if he touched her. "Did he hurt you?" I ask her, but she shakes her head, tears running down her face.

"You and Sienna are going to help me find a way out of this," Luke says, and I understand. He took her as a hostage because he needs our help getting out of the city and getting away.

"Okay," I say, nodding. "We can do that. What do you need Luke? Money? A car? I can rent a car for you and give you as much money as you need to get away from here. I have money saved. I just need to get it out of the bank." I have the rest of my grandmother's inheritance, what wasn't already stolen from me.

Luke snickers. "How do you think you're just going to walk out of the bank with that kind of money?" he asks. I could. But I couldn't do it in a day and I couldn't do it tonight, not when the bank is already closed.

"The ATM then. Let me and Sienna go to the ATM and I'll take out as much as I can, as much as it lets us. We'll bring it back."

"Be honest with me, Meghan," he says, raising his voice, the barrel of the gun pressing harder against Sienna's head, who breaks down, pressing her eyes closed tight, waiting for the gun to go off. "What are the odds of you coming back if I let Sienna leave?"

"Then let Sienna go," I beg. "Keep me. Please. Let her go. I'll stay here while she goes and gets the money from the ATM. It should be enough to get you out of the state, if I rent you a car. The police are looking for you, Luke. I don't know that you can rent a car yourself. You need me. Let Sienna go get the money, and I will make arrangements for a car."

I want to ask him why, how he could do this, how he could hurt all those women.

I want to ask him if he really thinks he can get away with it. Wherever he goes, the police will be looking for him. If he shoots Sienna and me, it will be so much worse, murder in addition to rape.

"Is that okay, Luke?" I ask, pleading, desperate, when he says nothing. "If Sienna goes to get cash from the ATM and I stay here with you to make arrangements for a rental car, so you can leave?"

Luke hears something then. His head darts toward the stairs, listening, and then he turns back to face me, eyes narrowing. "Did you call the police, Meghan? Did you tell them where I am?"

My throat tightens.

"Answer me!" he screams in my silence, his voice resounding. Beside him, Sienna tries to lean forward, to fold herself into a ball, wrapping her arms around her knees, rocking. He doesn't like it. Sienna gives a short, sharp cry of pain as he snatches her by the hair, righting her so that she's on her knees again, whimpering. He holds on to her hair. Sienna is crying harder now, and it's desperate, heaving as the barrel digs further in and she braces herself to die.

"No," I say. "Honest to God, Luke, I did not call the police. I swear to you, on my life, on Sienna's life," I say, stepping forward by instinct but, as I do, Luke turns the gun toward me, and I stop short, and then he brings the gun around to Sienna again, which is so much worse. "You told me to come alone and I did. I'm not lying to you, Luke. I promise. I wouldn't lie to —"

There is no advanced warning before the sound of a loud, deafening blast slices through the night from behind, followed by another; a bright yellow flash of light temporarily brightens the room before it all goes black again, the flash as the bullet escapes Luke's gun. Luke falls back as Sienna falls forward, crashing face-first to the ground, and then there is blood, oceans of it on the subfloor, spreading.

I race toward Sienna. An officer appears from out of nowhere and steps in my way, and I pummel into him. He catches me, holding me. "Ma'am," he says. "You can't go in there." He won't let me past. I rain blows on his chest with my fists and I scream, an agonizing scream. My legs give, and I half fall, but the officer catches me. He rights me, he holds me up.

"Sienna! Sienna baby," I call out over the officer's shoulder. "I'm right here." I look the officer in the eye, gathering strength. "Let me see my daughter," I demand of him. "Let me go. Get your fucking hands off me. Is she okay? Is she alright?"

There is blood everywhere. On her clothes. Her skin. Her hair is red with it.

She lies on the floor unmoving, hung at an impossible angle with her arms bent beneath her and her hair fanned around her head, turning red, and I wonder if I deserve this, if this is the price I'll pay for killing Caitlin Beckett.

TWENTY-NINE

The EMTs come and take Sienna out to the ambulance on a stretcher. I trail behind, someone holding me by an elbow, helping guide me down the stairs and outside where it's begun to snow.

As a crowd gathers in the street, the EMTs load Sienna into the back of the ambulance, where the bright ceiling lights make the blood all the more evident. There is no end to the amount of blood on her and the paramedics quickly apply themselves to finding where the bullet went in and how to stop the bleeding.

I hang back, watching, as if in a nightmare. I don't even notice the cold. I don't know I'm shaking until someone wraps a blanket around my shoulders from behind. I don't see it happen. I don't feel it happen. I just know that all of a sudden the blanket is there, limp, barely hanging on and then it starts to fall, and someone comes and rights it. They anchor it to my hand, and I find myself vaguely clutching a fistful of wool as I go over it again and again in my mind: how the police crept into the house from behind and shot Luke before the gun in his own hand went off.

Luke is dead. He lies inside the house as police come and go from it, circling the area with crime scene tape. Lights and sirens fill the night, multiplying. Reporters come. There are video cameras, microphones, spotlights, though they're all in my peripheral vision because I can't tear my eyes away from Sienna in the back of the ambulance.

An EMT comes to me and I brace myself, knowing he will tell me that the hemorrhaging was too severe, that Sienna lost so much blood she couldn't be saved.

"She's okay," he says.

"What . . . I . . ." I stammer. "But the blood. There's so much."

"She isn't hurt, nothing life-threatening anyway. Some cuts and bruises, a busted up ankle. But the blood," he says. "It isn't hers."

We go to the hospital anyway. The EMTs want Sienna assessed by a doctor because, if nothing else, she has a bruised and swollen ankle from falling in the dark inside the house and will need X-rays to see if it's broken or sprained. She lies on a hospital bed in the emergency room, waiting for the doctor to come. I stand beside her, finding it hard to believe she's alive, and mostly, physically okay, though emotionally is another story.

Before we left for the hospital, a police officer told me that Penelope called the police. That after giving it some thought, she remembered the home, Luke's preoccupation with it, and thought it might be somewhere he would go to hide.

Now Sienna says, "He said something happened to you."

"Who did?"

"Luke," she says, the blood on her face and in her hair hard to look at, and I have to remind myself that it's not hers, it's Luke's. "He said that you were hurt, like really bad. He told me to come with him and that he'd take me to you." There are tears in her eyes as she says it. Of course she would have let Luke in when he came to the door. Sienna knows Luke. They've met a handful of times, but I talk about him all the time. If Luke came to our apartment door, if he buzzed up and said something bad had happened to me, Sienna wouldn't have hesitated to believe him. "I was so scared. I thought I'd lost you. I kept thinking about all those mean things I said and what if they were the last things I ever said to you?" Her face crumples and she sobs, shoulders heaving, having trouble getting the words out. "I don't hate you."

"I know, honey, I know," I say, pulling her into me, grateful when she doesn't resist but gives in, surrendering and sagging against me. "I was just as scared," I say, running a hand over her hair. "When I found out about Luke, about who he was and what he'd done, and then I realized you were with him." My voice catches. It's hard to get the words out, to think how close I came to losing her tonight. "I'm just so sorry, Sienna. About everything. About Luke. That I let a man like that into our lives. And about your dad."

Sienna pulls away to look me in the eye. She says, pleading, as if she's been thinking about this for a while and has decided, "Can we keep that just between you and me, Mom? Please? It will only hurt him if he knows. No good can come of it. It's not like I ever want to find my real dad, and if Dad knows, then it will be weird. Nothing will ever be the same again. What's that saying? Innocence is bliss?"

"Ignorance," I correct her gently, wondering if Sienna and I could really keep this secret from Ben, if Ben doesn't need to know that he's not her father. Sienna is right; no good can come of him knowing. It will only hurt him. He'll feel like he's lost a child, and then there will be past custody payments to pay back, and it will all be a big mess. Feelings will be hurt. Everyone will suffer in some way, all of us, but especially Ben.

"Do we have to tell him?" Sienna begs.

"Tell him what?" I hear from behind and I spin around as Ben slips through the curtain, a nurse with him, showing him where we are. He turns and thanks her, and I take him in, wondering how long Ben was standing on the other side of the curtain before he came in and how much of Sienna and my conversation he overheard.

I haven't seen Ben since that night in my apartment. I know now that it was going too far to think he was there to hurt me or worse. I know the truth now, that Sienna asked him to come and he came only out of concern for me. He came because he was worried about me, because he wanted to see if I was okay, and maybe, just maybe, because some small part of him still loves me.

I think what it would do to me if, however

impossible, I were to find out right now that Sienna wasn't mine. It would break me.

"The doctor," I breathe out, trying to keep my voice level. I swallow, biding time to think, feeling Sienna grip my hand from behind. "She was talking about the doctor. Sienna is worried about needing a tetanus shot. She asked if we need to tell the doctor about this scratch, and we do. There were exposed nails all over that house." I look back to Sienna and say, "You can't be taking any chances with tetanus," and she nods, an understanding, a secret pact, in our mutual gaze. We won't tell Ben about Sienna's real father. Not now. Not ever.

Ben steps past me to go to her, taking her into his arms. Tears prick my eyes as he says, "I'll be right here when they do it. I can hold your hand. It won't hurt at all," and I know that even if he isn't her biological father, he's her father and always will be.

Thirty minutes later, Ben and I sit in the waiting room alone as they take Sienna for X-rays of her ankle. "About the other night," Ben says shyly, and as I look him in the eye, there is something earnest in them, something hopeful and practically begging. I think of all the times he's called me since that night. All the texts and voice mails, asking me to come over, offering to make dinner. He genuinely thought we could get back together.

I think of that night in my apartment, how solicitous he was, how he held and consoled me when I was upset. I think of his hand slipping under the hem of my shirt, his body weight pressing me into the sofa, and the way I felt, wanting him.

But I think too of the way he reacted when Sienna texted, how he was put off, inconsiderate, how his temper flared, how he reacted like a child and how his own needs trumped hers.

Both of these men is Ben.

"I love you, Ben. I will always love you, but not in that way," I say, stopping the conversation short. "I don't know what got into me that night, but I'm sorry that I led you on."

He nods, reaching for my hand in a way that is familiar, comforting.

"Hey," he says, very pally, smiling humbly, hat in hand, "it was worth a try."

He wraps an arm around my shoulders and I lean into him, knowing that despite everything we've been through, despite our differences, we are family.

EPILOGUE

It's my first day back to work in almost a month.

It's February now. The days aren't any warmer or less gray, but the promise of spring on the horizon makes it easier to bear.

I follow my usual route to the hospital, feeling nostalgia mixed with anxiety and nerves, wondering how my coworkers will react now that I'm back.

On top of that, I worry about Sienna at home alone, getting ready in our empty apartment before she leaves for school. This is the first morning I haven't been at home to see her off, and it makes me sick to my stomach, though I reminded her at least a dozen times to text when she left the apartment and again when she got to school.

I don't even like the idea of her being twenty feet away in her bedroom anymore.

The first day she went back to school after

what happened with Luke, I wanted to go with her to make sure she got there safely. I knew it wasn't healthy to project my own fears onto her, but the world is a dangerous place, and despite the number of weeks that have passed, I still can't get over the image of her covered in someone else's blood or of Luke, standing behind her in the dark, empty house, holding a gun to her head.

I arrive at the hospital and head in, leery as I wait for the elevator to come, my stomach in knots. The state board of nursing went easy on me for what happened to Caitlin. It helped that I confessed, that I owned up to giving her someone else's insulin *by mistake and that I have almost twenty years' experience without a blot on my resume.* There have never been any other incidents like this at work. Now I'm under probation, I'm being monitored by the hospital and by the board, but I'm allowed to work. It doesn't always happen like this. I could just have easily lost my license, but the truth is that the more severe the punishment handed down, the less nurses will be willing to report their mistakes, which makes patients less safe. There will be more cover-ups and more lies, though I didn't, of course, give Caitlin someone's insulin by mistake, but no one knows that but me.

I enter the unit. Despite killing a patient, I'm not some curiosity like I thought I'd be. Instead, Luke is, and any fears I had at coming back are instantly soothed when people come rushing up to me, saying, "Oh God, Meghan. I heard what happened," and they're not talking about how I killed a patient, but how Luke kidnapped Sienna and how my daughter and I watched him get shot by the police and die.

"Are you okay?" Bridget asks in the break room and I nod and say yes, though I'm not, not yet, and I don't know that I will ever be entirely okay, but I'm trying. It gets easier every day.

Another nurse wraps her arms around me and says, "I missed you. I'm glad you're back."

"I can't believe it was Luke all along."

"What kind of person does something like that?"

It's a good day. I'm happy to be back. I leave, lighter and smiling, and then later that night, after I'm home, Ben comes for Sienna, who's in her room packing her bag for the weekend, and this time, he's patient with her. He doesn't get upset that he has to wait, but he stands instead in my living room, drinking a beer, asking about my day.

"I have something for you," he says, after

I've finished telling him about work.

"For me? You didn't have to do that," I say, thinking stupidly than Ben has bought something for me and feeling a spark of guilt that I don't have anything for him in return, but also worried that he didn't get the message about us not getting back together when I told him in the hospital, and still thinks it's possible. How many times, I wonder, will I have to tell him no?

He sets his beer on the coffee table. "Close your eyes and hold out your hand."

"Ben," I protest, feeling silly.

"Just do it. Please, before Sienna comes out," he says gently, and I do. My eyes sink slowly closed and I hold out a hand, palm facing up, feeling Ben's warm hand clutch me by the fingers, holding on a minute too long before he places whatever he has for me on the palm of my hand.

The thing is practically weightless. I almost don't know it's there until Ben softly says, "Okay. You can open your eyes."

I do. I open my eyes to find Ben watching me, a sparkle to his own eye, a smile playing on the edges of his lips. I smile back out of instinct, because his own smile is contagious.

But when I look down at the thing on my hand, my smile fades.

My missing engagement ring.

"Where did you . . . how did you . . . ?" I ask, fighting for words, never finding them.

"It was in my condo," he says. "I can't explain it. Maybe Sienna took it and left it by mistake? I don't know."

I look up. Our eyes meet and I try in vain to read his, wondering if he's telling the truth or if he knows more than he's letting on.

"Yeah maybe," I say but of course it didn't happen that way. Sienna didn't take the ring. Caitlin did. She took my rings from me that day she left, the day she told Sienna that she wasn't Ben's, but what happened after that is a mystery because, in theory, Ben and Caitlin had broken up by then. How did the ring come to be in his apartment if their relationship was through? Did she go back that same day to tell him the truth about me? Did she break into his condo to leave the ring?

Or was their relationship *not* through?

What if Ben only said it was to throw me off?

"I thought you'd want it back," he says.

"Yes, of course. I do. I didn't . . . I didn't even know it was gone. I thought it was in my jewelry box."

He shrugs. "Well," he says, "it's back

491

where it belongs, and that's all that matters."

He leans in to kiss me chastely on the cheek. He pulls back, holding my eye too long so that my breath catches, heat filling my face, before Sienna's bedroom door opens and she appears all of a sudden behind us.

"You ready?" Ben asks, releasing and looking past me, and she says she is.

As Ben turns to walk away from me, to leave the apartment with Sienna, I realize that I may never know how much he knows.

He might have something on me forever. I might not have gotten away with it after all.

ACKNOWLEDGMENTS

Thank you to my editor and agent, Erika Imranyi and Michelle Brower, for championing this book and being so enthusiastic about it from day one. Thank you to the entire Park Row Books, HarperCollins and Trellis Literary Management teams (including Randy Chan, Natalie Edwards, Rachel Haller, Amy Jones, Nicole Luongo, Ana Luxton, Allison Malecha, Margaret Marbury, Lindsey Reeder, Brianna Wodabek, copy editors, proofreaders, sales and marketing teams, and so many more) and to everyone who has a hand in bringing my books to readers, especially my publicists, Kathleen Carter, Emer Flounders and Justine Sha; my cover designer, Sean Kapitain; my film agents, Carolina Beltran and Hilary Zaitz Michael; and my dream entertainment attorney, Scott E. Schwimer.

Thanks to the booksellers, librarians, Bookstagrammers, Booktokers and to every single reader who has ever read one of my books and recommended it to a friend. Without you, none of this would be possible.

Thank you to Erica Gnadt, Janelle Kolosh, Marissa Lukas, Vicky Nelson and Nicki Worden, my friends and first readers, for the constant support, the honest critique and for finding just a few of my many typos. Thank you to Katie Aler, Karen Banas, Jola Gargano and Erica Gnadt, incredible nurses who let me pick their brains, who read drafts of the manuscript and offered expert knowledge and advice. I learned so much from you. Any medical mistakes in this book are mine.

Thank you to Addison Kyrychenko for the late-night brain-storming session, and to Pete, Addison and Aidan for the many boosts of confidence. Thanks to my parents, my sisters and their families, and to the Kyrychenko family for the encouragement and support. I couldn't do this without you.

ABOUT THE AUTHOR

Mary Kubica is a *New York Times* bestselling author of thrillers including *The Good Girl, The Other Mrs., Local Woman Missing,* and *Just the Nicest Couple.* Her books have been translated into more than thirty languages and have sold over two million copies worldwide. She's been described as "a helluva storyteller" (*Kirkus*) and "a writer of vice-like control" (*Chicago Tribune*), and her novels have been praised as "hypnotic" (*People*) and "thrilling and illuminating" (*Los Angeles Times*). She lives outside of Chicago with her husband and children.

3 1333 05408 3694

The employees of Thorndike Press hope you have enjoyed this Large Print book. All our Thorndike Large Print titles are designed for easy reading, and all our books are made to last. Other Thorndike Press Large Print books are available at your library, through selected bookstores, or directly from us.

For information about titles, please call:
(800) 223-1244

or visit our website at:
gale.com/thorndike